THE GALES OF ALEXANDRIA

EHAB ELGAMMAL

ESCAPE
EDITIONS

Published by Escape Editions

This is a work of fiction. All names, characters, places, and incidents are either products of the author's imagination or are used fictitiously. Any resemblance to actual persons, living or dead, events, or locales is purely coincidental.

Cover design by Adam Hay.

ISBN (Hardcover): 978-1-0691674-1-5
ISBN (Paperback): 978-1-0691674-4-6
ISBN (eBook): 978-1-0691674-0-8

To my mother . . . we miss you; it hasn't been easy.

*The gales carry memories and secrets
across Alexandria's streets and shores—
ancient and sweeping, a presence
as constant as the sea.
What remains—and what fades?*

EPILOGUE

ALEXANDRIA, EGYPT: 2014

THE LIBRARY OF OMAR
EL-MOHAMMEDI

APRIL 7, 2014 • 4:15 A.M.

OMAR EL-MOHAMMEDI HAD WAITED all evening to face the task. He'd thought to embark on the disquieting journey that lay before him in daylight, looking for the light's solace—but he discovered again that, for him, there was no solace anywhere. So, he'd waited for nightfall to hide his heartbreak, but when the sun had set and the big window of his library had darkened, he still could not begin. For a long time, he didn't even turn on the lamp. It was a moonless night; the blackness settled heavily over him and over his hundreds of books and desk with its scattered papers.

Omar was an old man now, in ways he had not been even a week ago. He breathed and was aware of his own breath, and how his lungs seemed to echo the creak of his leather desk chair as he shifted his weight, how every breath seemed heavier and more difficult than the last. *He breathed, time passed*—and he reflected that a life might be summed up in those two phrases.

At some point, his daughter, Houda, had opened the library door. He heard her whisper something to herself, but he did not know what she said. She entered the dark room uncertainly, stopping when her thigh made contact with the edge of Omar's desk. Then, having located herself, she leaned over and turned on Omar's reading light.

Squinting up at her, Omar knew she wanted to say something, to tell him not to sit here in the darkness, that he should go to bed, that he needed rest. Tomorrow would be monumental—the burial of his son, her brother, Nasser. But Houda respectfully held her tongue. No need to remind Baba of something so heart-wrenching. Instead, she set two small dishes on the desk in front of him—a plate of *ful medames*, a basket of unleavened bread. Still wearing the black of mourning, Houda seemed part of the darkness, and when she left him, Omar hardly noticed.

That had been hours ago, and now it was nearly dawn. He blinked, taking in his surroundings. *Did I sleep?* Who knew?

The pool of light Houda had left behind continued to illuminate the plates of food he had no intention of touching. The journal still beckoned; there was no avoiding it. Taking a deep breath, Omar raised his right hand toward the notebook and paused, noticing the trembling of his wizened fingers.

Look at you, old fool, he thought. *You've spent a lifetime reading the most magnificent books on Earth, and now you're frightened of a puny diary. What is this compared to the Qur'an, the Upanishads, the Bible, Das Kapital, the Iliad? Nothing, nothing at all.*

And yet his hands trembled.

An old man ought not to begin a journey all alone. For him, there ought to have been only one solitary journey, one that had begun a lifetime ago, the final one. But Omar El-Mohammedi understood that it was his fate, now, at the end of his life, to begin again. So, he breathed once more and took up the notebook. Even the first line tore at his heart:

I, Nasser El-Mohammedi, child of Omar El-Mohammedi and son of no one, was born in the Library of Alexandria.

Because I am the child of my father, I was born among books. Here in the city where the modern world was created, where the greatest library humanity had ever seen was built and then destroyed, I entered the universe as if from nowhere and took up my being, shelved between theology and history. Because I was born among books, I am the son of no one.

When I was a child, the Great Library of Alexandria was the study of Omar El-Mohammedi, and my playground was his mind. Between the gentle Islam of his own upbringing and the humanism of his profession, I kicked my football and wrestled with other boys. I thrived in the sunlight of his tolerance and his intelligence, and grew strong; among the other children, I excelled. But from the time I was very young, I understood the playground Omar had created for me was only half a world. I knew the universe was made not only out of light.

My mother, Fatimah, was a strong, kind presence, yet she had a dimension she kept hidden from my father. She was not, I think, conscious that she was hiding part of herself, nor did she consciously reveal this dimension to me, but I nonetheless glimpsed it as a boy. The intelligent daughter of good people with a rigid worldview and fixed expectations, she grew up, like many women everywhere in the world, with thwarted ambitions, bruised by the heavy hand of patriarchy. She nursed angers she had learned never to express, and passions about which Omar El-Mohammedi knew nothing.

I inherited that rage and that lust for transcendence. It led me into the darkness where I upended every pebble. Under one distant stone, I uncovered a long-buried secret that would topple my father's house of cards by bringing to light the nefarious lie behind my mother's death . . .

Omar blinked. He reread the sentence, his tired eyes instantly alert.

His mind began to quicken as he skimmed forward, flipping

pages at random, searching irascibly for the next part of this unnerving thread that had landed like a grenade on the desk of his study. Heart racing, Omar saw the numerals scribbled at the corner of each page—a cryptogram for which they needed to find the cipher. That's what the American had explained when he handed over the precious journal—*the truth will be hidden in code between the lines.* Omar noticed white space following many of the journal entries—blank areas that Nasser had left, then gone back to fill with further reflections—a method that Omar had taught him when he was a boy as a way to deepen his thinking. There were afterthought writings about the iconic Alexandrian gales, scribbles about Qur'anic interpretation, random reflections and memories. What was the pattern?

Omar slowed himself, mocking his own impatience. Nasser may have emerged from Fatimah's fiery womb, but he had Omar's blood and temperament too, which meant he'd weave his story like a labyrinth, with trapdoors and hidden hallways. That's why the American had said the journal must be read with care and deliberation—and yet urgency too. It was a conundrum. With a sigh, Omar released his haste and returned to where he had left off:

My parents were naïve—both of them. I am the child of their mutual, loving obliviousness. But I am the son of no one, save the city of my birth: Alexandria, a capital founded by a brilliant Macedonian tyrant who, longing to be Greek, conquered Greece and then came to Egypt to build the perfect city, which he left behind to become a god. I am Alexander's child, and like him I will not live long. I am Alexandria's child, and like her I will live forever. I am the child of every book in Alexander's great library, scattered to the wind and doomed to fire by conquerors and colonists. And every year, when the first gale comes, it washes the dates and douses in its mercy our smoldering past.

The library in which I was born was an echo of that history. I grew inside an echo. It was in the library of Omar El-Mohammedi that I honed Greek and English; I shaped the clashing sounds of their words against my tongue and read their shapes in books; I saw how alien to each other they are, how they murder each other and beget children on one another's silences. I am one of those children.

Thank abandoned tomes that were begotten and destroyed in that annihilated library—they are my ancestors, my forebears, my siblings, and my own offspring. The sunlight of my father's reason, the fire of my mother's rage, the obliviousness of both . . . fall into that darkness too.

I am the child of everything that ever happened in this city. But if I am the son of anything, I am the son of darkness. Where no eye can see.

Then light came—just the faintest of glows at first, a shimmer beginning to bloom in cracks between the shutters. Soon enough, a fiery ball would rise above the Sinai dunes to the east of the city, sweeping across the sand. Later, when the sun had traversed the sky, they'd be gathering at the cemetery. And then, after the mourners dispersed, Omar would be expected to return to the unnerving journal. It was too much. He felt as if the foundation of his life were under siege, a heavy bombardment laid upon him. The task at hand was excruciating. Why had he agreed to it?

It was the humanitarian in him—but at what price? Omar shuddered at what he might discover in the pages before him. The son he was about to bury, who'd shown such promise in his youth, now lurked only behind a tapestry of words, camouflaged and convoluted by design, to conceal what intelligence officials were convinced was a road map to unspeakable horror.

No one knew Nasser like the scholar who'd raised him. That's why they'd beseeched Omar to sift through the journal to find the thread that could avert countless deaths and posthumously acquit the boy who'd spent countless hours on his lap in this very room, soaking in the greatest of human achievement. But what if Nasser had ventured to a place that was beyond redemption?

My son, my son; my poor, misguided son.

THE MOURNERS

APRIL 7, 2014

IT WAS MIDAFTERNOON—THE least forgiving time of the day, even in springtime. A cruel sun poured down like molten lead on the mourners in El-Manara Cemetery, pressing on their arms and scalps, making everything too heavy. This close to the Corniche, the cry of seagulls haunted them, though they were too far away to smell the Mediterranean's heady musk.

Mostly what they smelled was dust. It rose from the ground at every step and coated their skin except where rivulets of perspiration traced it away. And they smelled their own shock and disbelief. How had they gotten here? How had it come to this?

Rising above the palm trees and the traffic bustling along Abu Qir, they could almost see the palatial façade of Alexandria University's Faculty of Engineering, where they'd all once been together, young and full of dreams. And now they were all here, fourteen years and a lifetime later. Nasser was dead.

They'd come into El-Manara through the old door, where a couple of police vans were parked. Odd. Looking right and left, they wended uncertain steps through the tumble of ancient tombstones. In their grief, they stumbled; in their love for one another, they reached out to steady one another's steps. The beggar women extending their hands to them looked as old as the stones. "A Qur'an verse for you," they said, or, "I'll look after the gravesite for you," plucking at their shirtsleeves, at their skirts, never asking for the money directly. The beggars surrounded the mourners with grim, almost compassionate looks, but it was clear what they really wanted.

Everything was too bright, too loud, too hot. With every breath, the mourners sucked in dust. At the center of the maze of tombstones, they converged around a solitary grave. The gravedigger was still at work with his shovel, his thin cotton shirt soaked and plastered to his back. At the side of the pit, four men held Nasser's body, which seemed, in its white linen shroud, too small somehow. Nasser was slim, yes, but six feet tall, with eyes like inky pools, a big smile, a laugh that wrapped you up in a hug. His reach had been wide on the football pitch, and at a party or in a café he would have drawn all the women's eyes. This neat, white-wrapped package could not be him.

Something was wrong—the mourners sensed it—something beyond the wrongness of being reunited among the tombs, of finally recovering their long-lost friend only to lay him in the ground. It was hard to concentrate here, hard to think. The women huddled together in their flowing black silks and linens, and the older women wailed aloud. The Prophet explicitly forbids such extravagant shows of grief, but as Nasser's father, Omar, had said a thousand times, there was more to Egypt than just Islam. This ancient crossroads had been weathered by age long before the Prophet was born. And the numb, mute pits that yawned in the mourners' hearts felt ancient and vast enough to swallow propriety and religion itself.

All of them, Nasser's one-time inner circle, were tempted to ululate and tear their hair. Instead, Nasser's sister, Houda, hunched into herself, silently quaking, oblivious to the tenderness with which her friend Dalia—feisty, independent, yet so gentle when it was needed—held her to her bosom. A part of Dalia would have liked to have walked with the men, the pallbearers, but that would simply have fanned the whispers. It didn't matter that she and Nasser had once been engaged. She should have moved on long ago, people gossiped, to start a family. Egypt had no tolerance for women in their thirties who remained unmarried. It was maddening to Dalia, a lawyer like her father before her, with passion, ideals, and ambition. Dalia and Nasser had shared a hope and vision for their motherland. Where were those dreams now?

Despite being unwed, Dalia wore two engagement rings, which she fingered nervously in moments like these: one ornate and ancient; the other more recent, more modest. Only two people knew the story behind the twin rings, and one of them was about to be lowered into his grave. Dalia stared at the pallbearers standing in silence in their dark trousers and white linen dress shirts rolled up to the elbows to mitigate the heat. Adham—living in America now, where he went by *Adam*—looked ready to collapse. Dust plumed up like smoke as the gravedigger completed his work, moving slowly in the heat. Adham gazed blankly at his former classmate Youssef, whose thoughtful face was crumpled and tearstained, a study in defeat, as they supported Nasser's shrouded thighs.

Nasser had been an engineer like some of his pallbearers—friends and classmates from the esteemed Faculty of Engineering, whose elegant campus was within walking distance from the somber gravesite that reunited them in grief. Their paths had diverged dramatically after those innocent college years—geographically, politically, philosophically. And soon enough, Adham and Youssef would be departing once again in cars and planes for that distant land, known as "the Great Satan" by the extreme elements that Nasser, ostensibly, had embraced. His father, who stood at Nasser's shoulders, still could not fathom it.

Omar's role as a pallbearer was more symbolic than substantive; the professor had limped, even with the help of a cane, for as long as any of them could remember, and longer still since he had returned from the October '73 War—Egypt's last battle with Israel before peace. His elegant features, the image of Nasser's at an age he would now never reach, were twisted in pain, and he sobbed like one who didn't even know that he was sobbing. At the other shoulder stood Nasser's brother-in-law, Tarek. In this, as in all things, Tarek's demeanor spoke more of duty than of passion. His eyes were grave, controlled, his other features guarded by his dark beard. Who could have predicted that sweet, playful little Houda would have married such a stern man, imprisoned briefly for his political affiliations.

And yet there was hardly room in the mourners' minds for such thoughts. There was hardly room even for their over-whelming sorrow; the scene was so loud and busy. Skinny dogs slinked around the tombs farther out, sniffing for scraps—of what? A beggar worked the edge of the knot of men, his hand outstretched. Finally, Adham had enough. "Get out of here," he snarled, lunging toward the beggar, while on the other side of the grave a man who had walked here with them from the mosque held a Qur'an open in his hands and intoned, "God is great, the Lord of Mercy, the Giver of Mercy. Praise belongs to God, Lord of the Worlds, Master of the Day of Judgment . . ."

Here and there between the stones that surrounded the mourners, they glimpsed people they did not know from the corners of their eyes, and not just the beggars who lived in this place but also people who did not belong to El-Manara. The white-uniformed local police seemed to be here—not officially, not standing at the grave, but swirling around the edges of their vision. More disturbing were the others who, dressed in sharp gray Western-style suits and mirrored sunglasses, did not look Egyptian at all. Were they surveilling the mourners or mourning with them? No one could tell. At least the knot of praying men in white galabeyas, their beards longer than Tarek's, stood near the grave, murmuring softly to themselves. Their presence felt both visible and invisible, as though they were part of the mourning yet apart from it. No one could imagine how these men had known Nasser—or if they had truly come for him at all—but no one asked.

"It is You we worship," continued the man with the Qur'an, "it is You we ask for help. Guide us to the straight path: the path of those You have blessed, those who incur no anger and who have not gone astray." And on everything the brutal sun pounded, pounded, pounded.

Dust rose from the path as the mourners left the grave where they had laid their friend, and the fine grit settled all around them. The crowded stones were crumbling under the weight of centuries, and walking among them, Dalia feared Egypt was likewise crumbling, from pharaonic splendor into something unrecognizable. Everything felt too old, even the noise and the heat. New buildings and compounds may have been sprouting like palms bending to the Mediterranean winds, but that day the mourners felt as weathered as the stones around them.

As they reached the parking lot, a disturbance snatched their attention. By the police car an altercation had broken out. A couple of bearded men were standing too close to the white-uniformed police. They were trading barbs, but no punches were thrown. This confrontation was another index of the wrongness of the day, but everyone was too weary, too drained by grief, to stay and witness.

"*Ya* Dalia!" Adham beckoned Dalia with a blast of his car horn, the signature *hee-haw* donkey bray of the old Peugeot that had belonged to his late father. No one knew why the family still kept it; Adham insisted it had "character." Dalia climbed into the back seat. Youssef, riding shotgun in front, felt as if he might be smothered by the oppressive heat. Having experienced several seasons in America with real winters and summer sea breezes, Youssef wondered for the thousandth time since returning to his homeland how he had endured the stifling summer air of Egypt.

Adham pulled onto Abu Qir. Soon they were out of sight of the cemetery and their beloved Faculty of Engineering. Dalia stared ahead, looking at nothing. Youssef had his window down all the way, desperate to feel the breeze which, while still hot, was better than nothing. He could smell the sea, at least, saltier and fishier here than anywhere else he'd been. New York Harbor and San Francisco Bay didn't even rate. Only Boston Harbor was close, but still not nearly as pungent as the Mediterranean shore of Alexandria. To Youssef, it smelled like home.

As if Adham could hear Youssef's thoughts and smell his nostalgia, he finally broke the silence: "How long has it been since you had a *sobia*?" At the name of the milky coconut drink, a summertime favorite of every Egyptian child, Youssef smiled despite himself. Looking at his companions, he could see that Dalia was beginning to smile too, her tearstained cheeks somehow regaining their customary cheerful plumpness.

"I'll bet you can't even get *kebda* on *fino* in California," she said, reaching to pinch Youssef's cheek in a parody of aunthood. His stomach rumbled audibly, as if on cue, and fourteen years dropped away like a dream as laughter shouldered its way into their day of tears. "What about it?" she asked, with a brightness that was only a little forced.

"Aren't they expecting us?" Youssef objected, thinking of the others gathering now at Omar's—but Adham waved a dismissive hand. "They won't notice if we're a little late," he said. "Besides, can you imagine Nasser denying you kebda and a sobia?"

"Heaven knows how he stayed so trim," Dalia concurred. "I never saw a man put away kebda sandwiches like our Nasser."

Sitting moments later at one of their favorite haunts in Alexandria's old city, they ate and drank with gusto—but silence descended again. The words of the *Surat al-Fatihah* echoed in Dalia's head: "Guide us to the path of those who incur no anger and who have not gone astray."

Ya Nasser, ya habibi, she thought sadly. And, for a brief moment, Dalia allowed herself to indulge in a mental fantasy—a parallel world in which Nasser was still with them, sitting across from her in the café, making everyone laugh as always. What they could have achieved together with his charm and charisma, entwined with her gumption and single-mindedness. She remembered the many times Nasser had made her furious too, the times her love for him was an anger threatening to choke her, and she wondered just how far he had strayed. Not so far, surely; a grave in El-Manara was a coveted privilege, one of the few remaining advantages afforded to a family that had once been rich and powerful. But burials still required paperwork, and to lay Nasser to rest here, Omar must have greased many a palm. If the authorities believed Nasser was a violent criminal or a terrorist, surely they would have refused. Something didn't quite add up. Dalia half-expected Nasser to show up suddenly for his curtain call.

Adham, sitting at the opposite corner, was pondering a similar line of thinking. *Terrorists' bodies aren't released to their families, are they?* he wondered. Given that Adham's own brother, Sharif, had likewise been imprisoned and subsequently disappeared, the matter felt deeply personal. Surely if they had died committing violence, there would have been only a phone call months later, or maybe nothing at all. The funeral today ought to have dispelled their worst fears about Nasser. Yet Adham couldn't help but ask himself: *How exactly did he die? Who brought his body home, and from where? And whom did he put in harm's way?*

Half a world away, in a sunny kitchen in Berkeley, California, Youssef's wife, Risa, tried to picture her husband in the city where he had grown up. Almost a decade of marriage and she'd never gone there—somehow the timing had never been right. And in the fourteen years she'd known Youssef, since he'd arrived from Egypt, he'd been back only a handful of times himself. Still, she'd seen pictures and home movies; Dalia had visited them in America; and she knew Adam, of course, who lived in the United States too. She tried to picture all of them together, mourning their friend. Somehow it was hard for her to imagine people so vital, so lively, in a place so ancient and remote.

Easier to picture was the light she'd seen come into their eyes, each of them, when they talked about Nasser. She'd heard stories about his brilliance at soccer ("football," they called it) and chess, his impressive projects in engineering school, the girls he mesmerized without meaning to. She'd seen his face in photographs, his eyes big and liquid above carved cheekbones, his lips full and purple. She'd heard the devotion in their voices even as they worried about him. She realized now that she, too, had been waiting all this time for Nasser to reappear, to knock on the door one day and surprise them. To fix everything by calling forth from Youssef the special peals of unguarded delight her husband seemed to save only for stories about Nasser and, once upon a time, for her.

It was complicated. There were secrets now—secrets with life-and-death stakes. Her marriage on the rocks, she'd been lying to her cousin Stephanie—colluding with Stephanie's husband, no less. "Not a word to anyone," Matt had whispered, his eyes like ice. "Not to Stephanie, not to Youssef."

It was killing Risa to keep a secret this important from her own husband. She had wanted to shout it from the rooftops— desperate for Youssef to know where she had been, what she had seen, and what only she knew about the cherished friend he had just buried.

Would she be expected to take this secret to her own grave?

It was too big. Nasser had saved her life.

DALIA

DALIA OPENED the scrapbook she'd kept faithfully all these years, dreading what she might rediscover. It had begun innocently enough—photographs from their college days gave rise to an unexpected smile on Dalia's troubled face. Seeing a snapshot of Nasser ready for squash, racket in his hand, confident grin, prepared to demolish his opponent, made Dalia feel suddenly like a schoolgirl. Who could resist him?

In more recent photos, Nasser seemed like a different person. His once-shining eyes appeared dull; his demeanor, subdued. The moment that had marked Nasser's turn was clear. It had begun at graduation with the appearance of the bearded stranger who'd dropped the bombshell about Nasser's mother. That was when the constant tick-tock of worry began. But were there earlier signs —things she should have noticed? Nasser's transformation had felt sudden, its intensity seeming to ignite a sleeping fire within the family and precipitating a radical change in his sister, Houda, too—though her evolution had been more gradual.

How did I not see it coming? Dalia pored through the old photos, searching for red flags, but all she found was sunshine, washing out all the details. It seemed they were laughing in every one. Maybe she had never worried at all until it was too late. *Was there anything I could have done?*

17

One iconic photo felt particularly revealing: against a vivid clump of palms and bougainvillea, Adham and Youssef were beaming as they held up their university diplomas. Adham was leaning forward and holding his toward the camera, his lips pursed and eyebrows twisted into a hammy caricature of seductiveness. Youssef stood tall, his expression calm and composed, a quiet counterpoint to Adham's exuberance. In the foreground, arms spread in a gesture of triumph, Nasser knee-slid into front and center, his eyes and smile wide. The sudden motion of his entrance blurred his figure a bit at the edges. It wasn't a pose; he'd really slid into the photo just as Dalia snapped the shutter. Nasser looked cool and graceful, like he'd planned it, but she wondered, *What was in his heart? Was Nasser afraid they'd take the photos without him?* Had he already begun to drift away from them then?

Surely the handsome man in this photo would never have left them to spout murderous perversions of scripture, to stash guns in some cave in Sinai or Iraq, to plot, to kill, to end up lying under a cemetery stone.

Then she turned to the fateful news clipping from when Nasser had been arrested in 2002. Dalia felt profound sadness as she relived the moment in the police station where Nasser had paced like a tiger, his pride and idealism trapped inside walls that could never contain his boundless energy.

"*Ahada*, ya Nasser," Dalia's lawyer father had told Nasser. *Cool it down.*

"Why?" he'd seethed. "My only crime is wanting to fight injustice."

Fight, he had—with bruises to show for it. Could she have prevented it? Maybe, but Dalia froze. Even a decade later, she could still feel the pangs of guilt, so palpable and consuming in the moment, and reawakened now by a scrap of newsprint. It was she, after all, who'd diverted Nasser from his dreams of launching a startup as a tech engineer with an Ivy League MBA. Instead, he'd joined Dalia's hyperlocal nonprofit, serving the poorest of the poor—and it had landed him in jail, where people thought the seeds of radicalization were planted in Nasser's mind. No one had dared to say it aloud or blame her—except Adham in a moment of rage.

The news report, with its haunting photograph—Nasser holed up in his cell—accompanied by the sensational caption—"Jailed son of esteemed Professor Omar El-Mohammedi"—hurt her on so many levels.

Like all of them, Dalia held Omar in high esteem, yet she'd received nothing but grief from her nouveau riche mother about Nasser's family. When Nasser went dark and disappeared, her family began lining up "more suitable suitors." And then came the talks about hymenoplasty that made Dalia want to crawl out of her skin. Dalia found herself flushed with rage at her mother's presumption and assumptions about her virginity, which happened to be intact. Nasser had been the consummate gentleman—unlike her petty, intolerant family. Yet Nasser was complicated.

It was one thing to be a charismatic rebel, another entirely to be a jihadist—if that was really what he'd become. Dalia wondered which Nasser would live on in her mind and memory. For now, it was the gentleman—the one she'd fallen in love with. He'd been the brightest of them all, the best. If Nasser had lost hope and lost his way, then what would the future hold for the rest of them?

Or was it they, after all, who'd left *him* behind?

Dalia closed her eyes, willing herself back to that time. *Is the past a country we can visit?* Sometimes she thought so.

MATT

APRIL 7, 2014

MATT COULDN'T SHAKE the image of that old envelope. It had been hidden deep in Omar's library, tucked away in a bottom drawer as if meant to be forgotten. During the search, when Omar was conveniently out, Matt and his team had been meticulous, knowing they had little time before Omar's return.

He remembered the crinkle of the yellowed paper in his hands when he pulled it out, "America" scrawled in bold Arabic across the front. Inside, a single 7.62 x 51mm NATO round—used, its casing dented and tarnished. A relic from decades past. Why had Omar kept it, and why hide it so carefully? It felt like a remnant of a grudge that hadn't quite died.

Matt had to suppress the urge to take it with him for analysis. But he knew better. He carefully placed it back in the envelope and returned it to its hiding spot. They couldn't afford to tip off Omar that they had been there, not yet.

Now, as he stared at his own reflection, the weight of the day's events pressed down on him. Matt gazed at his tired face in the mirror and decided not to shave. *Why bother?* For a moment, he thought of his father. His mother often reminded him of how much he resembled Ambrozy, especially now that he was the same age his father had been in those last photos before his untimely death—thirty-eight. The thought stirred something deep in him—a mix of pride and the shadow of unfulfilled conversations.

He'd changed so much, he hardly recognized himself. Staggering over to the bedroom, he collapsed on the cot in exhaustion. Even with his service revolver tucked under the pillow, Matt doubted he'd be able to sleep. This was a CIA safe house. But was it actually safe? How could he be sure he hadn't been seen? After observing the funeral from afar through binoculars, Matt had followed the playbook to a tee, doubling back twice through El-Manshia's old streets and the winding alleys of Zanket El-Setat market, changing clothes in the alley, and waiting until nightfall; and yet still there were risks. Danger lurked everywhere in this part of the world. That's why Matt had told Stephanie he was in London.

Matt had lied so many times to his wife at this point, he could hardly remember that initial pang of guilt the first time he'd done it. He could never have imagined as a West Point cadet that his personal moral code would be dispersed so easily into competing silos—patriotism, the greater good, family. They had once been in the same cauldron.

Matt didn't even grieve the loss anymore. He'd fully accepted the new paradigm. The potential of saving thousands of lives far outweighed his vow to be truthful to his wife, despite the fact that he'd stated it out loud in front of 240 people at their Arlington wedding. Matt's geographical whereabouts were on a need-to-know basis at this point, especially when leaked information could endanger his family. He never lied about the important stuff. He had never cheated on Stephanie. His love for her was as strong as ever. Family was everything to Matt—one of the reasons he'd gone out of his way to help Risa, Stephanie's cousin, who happened to have married a close friend of their person of interest. Nasser, too, appeared to have been driven by principles that were sacrosanct, such as loyalty to his closest friends, which was why he had saved Risa's life—an act of valor to which Matt could relate.

After his intensive language training following 9/11, Matt had picked up rudimentary Arabic, which allowed him to understand parts of Nasser's writing without relying on the official CIA translators. He'd combed through the journal so many times, Matt felt he knew Nasser—at the very least, he knew the workings of his mind. The line that had given him goosebumps was:

I graduated top of my electrical engineering class, with a geolocation project that earned the applause of everyone at my matriculation.

At the time, Matt had also been working on geolocation algorithms for his West Point engineering thesis. He'd started his project on a whim, a clever hack to give an advantage to the high school robotics team he volunteered to coach. Under Matt's direction, the boys installed echolocation towers in three corners of the room that their android could ping to orient itself during the competition. The opposing coach cried foul, but nothing in the rulebook prohibited external support equipment beyond the arena, as long as a signal wasn't being sent from outside to the robot. The algorithm Matt had created ran within the robot's own CPU, sending an outbound frequency pulse that reflected off the towers they'd installed, which provided echolocation data to help the robot navigate to victory.

While that technology would soon become ubiquitous on smartphones everywhere, it had been a novel idea in 2000—the focus of only a handful of engineers, including this pair of ambitious undergraduates, who, despite being worlds apart, appeared to have similar minds, both of them having also been raised by professors of history. And one of these professors was now the essential link to potentially cracking the biggest terrorist plot since 9/11.

It frustrated Matt that he couldn't decode the journal on his own—that he was reliant on an old man whose allegiance was surely split. A number of Matt's CIA colleagues had questions about Nasser's true motives—why would he bury the secret in rambling words that only his father could untangle? There was too much at stake for ambiguity. Would they find the answers before it was too late?

And now, this envelope with its hidden bullet—another secret in a family where secrecy seemed to be a legacy. Like his son, Omar was full of mysteries, and Matt couldn't shake the feeling that there was more to uncover, more that Omar was hiding, the truth just out of reach.

It was in God's hands. *Inshallah.* That's how they said it in Arabic.

Matt needed sleep. Without sleep he was worthless. He shut his eyes and prayed.

God help me. God help us all . . .

PART I

GHASIL EL-BALAH

Ghasil El-Balah ("Washing the Dates")
is the name given by locals to the first *nawwa*,
one of the seasonal gales that mark the fall and winter in
Alexandria—
delivering fierce winds and heavy rain, and swelling the
Mediterranean,
which brings the ancient port to a standstill.

Fishermen are the first to see the signs—red sunsets,
a surge in the western breeze, and panic among the seagulls.

Each gale is uniquely named, and Ghasil El-Balah,
with its cleansing rains that bathe the date palms,
signals with a gentle reminder:
Winter's approach whispers through the wind.

2000: ALEXANDRIA

THE DAY COULDN'T HAVE BEEN MORE perfect, cooler than anyone could have hoped for so late in May. The sun was high and warm, and so too were Dalia's spirits as she filled her lungs, gazing across the symphony of flowers and folding chairs sprawled everywhere on the Faculty of Engineering's expansive back lawn, where a thousand engineers would be graduating that day. Dalia spotted her soon-to-be sister-in-law, Houda, and zigzagged to take the seat next to her. Houda looked especially radiant in a green sundress that showed off her long, tapered arms.

"You're Nefertiti herself!" Dalia told her, referencing the ancient Egyptian queen celebrated for her beauty. Houda laughed with her mouth and cheeks as well as with her almond eyes, which laughed all the time. Houda was only eighteen, but already she towered over Dalia like everyone else did.

As the engineering graduates began pouring down the aisles toward the stage, Dalia craned her head to catch sight of the inseparable threesome she knew like brothers. Nasser was easy to spot —tall, handsome in his robe, distinguished as a judge, flanked by his closest friends: Youssef, serious and a little dreamy; and Adham, mugging and winking at Dalia as he passed their row. Or was he winking at Houda?

Dalia decided to braid and unbraid Houda's silky brown hair, rich as mahogany, during the speeches, which were interminable, of course. Afterward they milled around on the lawn, sipping the lemonade the university served, everyone beaming and congratulating one another.

There was an enormous amount of attention paid to this trio of strapping engineers and the shimmering potential that lay before them. Adham and Youssef were off to find fortune in America, and Nasser—well, he could do anything he set his mind to. It was a real gift, therefore, that he'd committed to join his fiancée in her nonprofit. But there was something slightly bittersweet about the moment for Dalia—no one had made quite such a fuss when *she* had graduated from law school.

She glanced at Omar, the proud father, still slender and handsome despite his salt-and-pepper hair, his limp, his cane. From the moment they met, he treated Dalia as an intellectual. "Our Dalia's going to save Alexandria," Omar declared. "First Alexandria, then the world. And I'd say she'll do it single-handedly, but she's recruited my Nasser to be her partner."

Dalia, like Omar, knew she could have done it on her own. She already had the support of her father, a well-connected and accomplished lawyer, and her brother, Seif, a soon-to-be military officer. But having Nasser as a partner certainly added excitement to the enterprise—and it made everyone suddenly interested. "Youssef mentioned something about the nonprofit you're forming with Nasser," said Youssef's mother, Alhaga Soad, fanning herself with a ceremony program. "What's it all about?"

"It's an idea we've been batting around for a while now," Dalia told her. "A human rights and education nonprofit. A lot of resources are there, and heaven knows the need is there, but it seems like the people most in need aren't connecting with the resources that would help them. We'll help set up the neediest families with public social benefits and private-sector donations. I'm particularly interested in helping families who are falling through the cracks due to run-ins with the law, so I'll be coordinating with police and public defenders to identify clients. Educational interventions can help us break generational cycles of poverty and crime."

"Admirable," commented Youssef's mother, though Dalia could see the reservations in her eyes. Still, she seemed intrigued. "Sounds like a grand mission for a young lawyer—a young woman, at that. But where does Nasser come in?"

"Well, a lot of places, really. Honestly, the idea came from a conversation he and I had. I don't think I could have kept him from joining this project! And, of course, his charisma helps— people love him, so he makes everything go more smoothly. But in terms of his expertise," she explained, "he's mostly going to deal with data. A lot of the work a lawyer does is keeping vast amounts of information organized and on hand, and the more legal services you hope to provide, the bigger that data pool gets—not to mention all the social services we'll also connect clients with. To really do this right, we'll need to build software that can help us stay on top of which issues are relevant to what types of defendants, as well as what solutions are available. A good information structure will help me provide better service to our clients and keep me from getting overwhelmed and burned out. I saw a lot of that at the public defender's office during my summer internships."

"Enter a software engineer," Alhaga Soad murmured, and Dalia, seeing she was starting to feel impressed, felt her heart swell.

"Enter two," Nasser announced joyously, striding up with his arm around Youssef's shoulders. He took Mrs. Almasry's hand and kissed it. "Your two favorites, right?" he added with a wink at everyone in general. It would have been smarmy if anyone else had done it, but there was something so sincere, so winning about Nasser that you couldn't help but love his attention. "What are we talking about?" he asked with a grin.

"Dalia was telling me about your nonprofit," Mrs. Almasry said. "Very exciting."

"The idea was all Dalia's," Nasser insisted. "I think this could help a lot of people, here in Alexandria and eventually all around the country. My part honestly will just be helping her to get things set up. After all the software kinks are worked out, I'll go to America for my MBA. And when I come back, I'll be ready to bring Egypt into the twenty-first century." He said it with such unflinching self-assuredness.

Nasser had committed to the nonprofit for only the first couple of years. Then he would be on to other things. His family and friends all expected greatness from Nasser, and he'd never let them down. He dreamed big, though those dreams often changed from week to week. The Almasrys were more hung up on why an engineer would want an MBA; this was an idea Nasser had explained more than once. As the tech sector heated up in the global marketplace, Egypt would need people who understood both the science and the business sides in order to stay competitive. Besides, Nasser had a plan to create software that would streamline and guide novices through the process of starting a small company. He envisioned low startup cost and low-overhead businesses springing up all over Alexandria, these new entrepreneurs energized with the pride of ownership and employing the formerly destitute. He wanted opportunities for young Egyptians to flourish here the way young people did in the United States, so maybe his scheme made sense. Omar had raised him with a passion for Egypt, a passion that burned in him like a star. While America was seductive for so many young men, Nasser always intended to come back.

"I hope you'll be careful," said Youssef's father, Mr. Almasry, advising Dalia and Nasser, as Youssef put his free arm around his mother. Mother and son made a comical contrast—she was slight and birdlike, while Youssef was the image of his lantern-jawed father. Though Youssef was only of average height, his muscular build and perpetual five o'clock shadow somehow made him appear bigger. He was like Dalia's brother, Seif, in that way.

"Advocating for the poor is noble work, but it can put you at odds with powerful people," Mr. Almasry continued, his eyebrows as usual drawn together in thought.

"This is what I keep telling her," Seif agreed from behind Dalia. With the noise of the crowd, she hadn't heard him approach, and she jumped a little as her younger brother put his hands on her shoulders, showing up late as always. Dalia hadn't expected any of her family members to show up—certainly not her judgmental mother. So, she was glad to see Seif, whom she'd adored growing up, though he'd gotten more serious since attending military academy.

"Siding with criminals is a dangerous business," he said now. "I keep telling her Alexandria needs good prosecutors! There's plenty of charity work she can do without making herself a radical."

Dalia wasn't going to take the bait, though. Not in front of everyone. She and Seif had been having this argument all spring, and they'd had a hundred versions of it before, too. He wanted to protect her—it was what brothers did. And no one could accuse him of hard-heartedness. The poverty in this city hurt him as much as anyone. But there were so many poor, and alms helped them only for a day. Dalia wanted to create real structural change. She wanted to empower people to climb out of poverty, or at least give them a means of not sinking further in. Seif thought she was a silly, dreamy-eyed girl, but Dalia understood the dangers. It was just that, back then as now, she believed that leaving things unchanged was even more dangerous. So, she just squeezed his hands where they rested on her shoulders. "Always looking after me," she murmured, twirling away from his grasp, then pecking his cheek. "Seif is the best brother in all of Alexandria." She'd learned, frustrating as it was, that sometimes with her brother, a light and girlish touch was the sharpest weapon to keep him from standing between her and her goals. Dalia gave cheery nods around the circle and scurried along.

Houda was close by, in the shade of a date palm, trying to stifle her giggles as a cohort gathered around Adham. His knees knocked and his eyes bulged in mock terror as he held out his shaking arms. Houda reached her arm out toward Dalia, sisterlike, whispering, "Adham's doing Ismael Yassine!" He was good, Adham—those old black-and-white slapstick comedies, the stuff of their parents' childhoods, came right to life as he pantomimed them. Soon Dalia was giggling too.

Before long, Youssef joined them. "You have your camera, Dalia?" he asked. "My mother wants plenty of pictures." So, she snapped some shots against a mass of magenta blossoms—Youssef alone, Youssef and Adham, Adham with Houda . . .

Then Dalia said, "Just the graduates. The engineers, I mean," and that's when she got the picture that would become iconic: Nasser, surprising them all by knee-sliding like a triumphant footballer into center stage to seize the spotlight, although his image would be forever fuzzy, which itself spoke volumes—Nasser could never be pinned down. Yet the telling blur of Nasser's image would only become ominous in hindsight. At the time, they were so young and carefree.

Then came Nasser's broody question as the jubilant event wound down and families began to disperse. "Will we all be together like this anymore?" he asked pensively. "Just having fun?" He paused, then added, "They always say that commencement is the beginning of what's next. But don't you guys feel like this is just the end of something? Everyone's moving on."

It was at this moment that the bearded stranger appeared, seemingly out of nowhere. Dalia spotted him through the flocks of graduates circling their proud families, smiling, laughing, and celebrating. This man's face, on the other hand, betrayed little emotion. He stood, unmoving, staring directly at Nasser from across the lawn. The intensity of his fixed gaze seemed to beckon without words, compelling Nasser to lock eyes with him.

"Who is that?" Dalia asked Nasser.

"No idea." He began weaving his way through the folding chairs to approach the man. Dalia followed, watching closely as the men squared off.

"*Salam*, Nasser," began the stranger. No smile.

"You know me?"

"Oh, yes."

Nasser noticed the accent, so distinct and unmistakable—clearly an Upper Egyptian.

"I am your Great Uncle Ragab El-Saidi," the man explained. "It's high time you pay your respects, finally, at the true grave of your mother."

Nasser narrowed his eyes. "I was there last week."

"Omar's little decoy in El-Manara?" The man smirked. "That grave is empty. Your mother lies with her people in El-Karia."

Nasser had never heard of it; Ragab sensed his confusion. "South of Asyut, north of Sohag."

Dalia's mind was reeling. *Is it true? His mother—buried in Upper Egypt?* She'd visited El-Manara personally to pay her respects at Fatimah's grave. Nasser had taken Dalia there when he'd proposed to her two years prior, introducing his fiancée to his mother as if she were still alive. That's when Nasser had presented Dalia with the first ring—the smaller one.

Dalia, struggling to make sense of what they were being told, turned to the strange man and asked, "Who are you again?"

Ragab ignored Dalia, gazing only at Nasser and instructing, "Look for the El-Saidi family grave in El-Karia." And then he was gone.

Nasser stood there, motionless, for several moments before turning numbly to Dalia and saying, "I need some time."

He walked off, leaving Dalia to fend for herself in the swarm of graduates who were parading and singing in jubilation.

She felt alone, alienated.

Later that evening, their families took them out for an elaborate dinner with dishes of hummus and olives, platters of succulent grilled shrimp, saffron-yellow *sayadeya* rice, and crispy *besaria*. From their table, they enjoyed a gorgeous view across the Eastern Harbor to the medieval Citadel of Qaitbay, its upper ramparts glowing, spotlit from below. It spoke to the city's antiquity that the fifteenth-century fortress was less famous than the structure that stood on that spot before it—Pharos, the Lighthouse of Alexandria, one of the Seven Wonders of the Ancient World.

Omar held forth, as he tended to in settings like this, recounting how the Ottomans had overrun those golden ramparts in the early sixteenth century. Pivoting to Napoleon, the professor described the emperor's arrival in 1798, when he had famously declared, "Whoever is master of Egypt is master of India." For the El-Mohammedi family, there was an even deeper truth, which Omar delighted in sharing with those gathered at the table: *Alexandria is the pearl of the Mediterranean, and the Mediterranean is the center of the world.*

But more interesting for Dalia than Omar's stories, which she'd heard countless times, was the expression on Nasser's brooding face. Was he even listening to his father? Nasser rose from the table without words and walked away.

Tick-tock. The worries began. They still hadn't been able to find a moment to talk about the bearded stranger and his alarming allegation.

After dinner, the parents went home. The friends weren't done celebrating yet, so they went to Stanley Beach, crowded as always and festive. Spring was sufficiently advanced that the sun was setting late, and they strolled on the promenade, ice creams in hands, then descended the steps and warmed their toes in the sand while that great radiance slipped beneath the horizon. Workers were taking in the big striped beach umbrellas for the night. Dalia took the opportunity to pull her fiancé aside.

"What a day with that crazy man," she opened.

"What if he's not crazy?" replied Nasser.

"It makes no sense." Dalia found her pulse quickening. "That would mean the professor lied—" She stopped herself, regretting that she'd even raised that possibility.

"My mother was from Upper Egypt," Nasser said softly. "That much I know."

He looked at her, took a breath, and declared, "I'm going there."

Before Dalia could react, Adham and Youssef ran up to drag Nasser into a game of "keep-away" with a football, a proposition he apparently could not resist. *Or is it a welcome distraction?* Dalia watched how quickly Nasser seemed to morph back into his fun-loving persona, competitive yet carefree, master of his universe. It was the first time she thought, *It's a façade.*

Then Houda ran up to link arms with Dalia and walked with her along the surf, waves lapping at their ankles. The day faded; stars emerged. The city lights of Alexandria made a crown to rival the twinkling in the sky. Somewhere nearby a radio was playing, but they were a bit too far away to catch more than a note here and there. Houda ran ahead, the wind changed direction, and Dalia recognized the tune—Mohamed Mounir's *"El-Leila Ya Samra."*

The distant music slid her into a recollection—the day she and Nasser had met as first-year undergraduates on a bus trip to Cairo. Mounir's song had come on the radio, and everyone was singing along—everyone except Nasser, who watched in silence, scanning the bus until he locked eyes with Dalia and listened to her sweet mezzo-soprano voice. She was embarrassed at first by his unwavering attention—then she embraced it by singing directly to him. Later, Nasser told Dalia that she reminded him of Samra, the girl from the song whose complexion was kissed by the Mediterranean sun.

Dalia sighed, wishing she could live forever in that memory. She was so wrapped up in their moment, she didn't notice until the song was over that Houda, farther down the beach, was calling in alarm across the dark waves.

"Nasser, come on," urged Houda. "It's too dark to swim!"

She scooped up his shoes and wallet from the beach, then called again.

"Nasser! I can barely see you. Come on, let's go home."

But Nasser stayed out among the waves, swimming beneath the stars for a long, long time before he emerged wet and alone.

2000: WEST POINT

On the Tuesday night before graduation, Matt and his buddies stayed at the Firstie Club until it closed. He hadn't even started packing. He'd already shipped his trunk of gear to Fort Leonard Wood, to be sure it would be waiting and ready to go when he hit the ground for BOLC, the leadership training that would turn him into a commissioned officer. What he hadn't gathered together were his personal things, which wasn't a big deal—he didn't have much to pack. But his mother and stepfather had warned him they would be there early on Wednesday morning, and *early* meant something different to Iowans than it meant to East Coasters, even if they were West Point cadets. Wednesday through Saturday would be jam-packed with barbecues, parades, and graduation itself. Saturday morning before the ceremony, the barracks had to be spick-and-span, as if Matt had never lived there, and Saturday night, he'd be on a flight to Missouri.

It was not like Matt to leave things to the last minute. He liked the feeling of having things buttoned up. Unfinished tasks cluttered the mind, and Matt had never liked clutter. Back in Mason City, most days he used to finish his homework before he even went home from school. He didn't want to be worried about biology or civics while he was at baseball practice or church or a Scout meeting. At baseball, he just wanted to think about the ball;

at Scouts, he just wanted to earn the next merit badge; and church, he wanted it to be just about him and God. That was what getting things done gave you: focus. Finish tasks promptly, and you got rewarded with the luxury of thinking about one thing at a time.

He was more than ready to graduate. He knew every inch of this post and had seen just about all of it that he needed to in this lifetime. He'd worked hard, learned a lot, and made some amazing friends, but his feet were getting itchy again. Those feet had been restless ever since middle school, when life finally started to regain some rhythm after his father's sudden death, which marked the first turning point in his childhood. The loss left a void he couldn't quite name, and he often turned to books and stories as a way to escape and make sense of the world. That was when his mom, the school librarian, brought home a box of discarded books for the summer.

That box marked the second turning point in Matt's young life. BB (Before the Box), he'd read DC Comics and the occasional Choose Your Own Adventure book. AB (After the Box), he discovered real American literature and began pining to see the world, as much of it as possible.

The third turning point came when life felt, in many ways, normal again—when Matt's mother, Cecilia, married Tomas Drabek, a former work acquaintance of her late husband. Cecilia, a devout Catholic, had leaned heavily on the church during those hard days of grief, navigating life as a single mother with a ten-year-old son. The church guided her toward Tomas, who brought his own steadiness to their home and was a good stepfather—calm and quiet, even if he was the opposite of Matt's charismatic father, Ambrozy. While the void left by his father's death was never fully filled, it became a quieter one from then on. As time passed, his father's memory began to fade no matter how hard Matt tried to hold on to it.

Matt's pivot toward learning was inevitable, perhaps, given his late father's position as a history professor at Waldorf, an evangelical college in neighboring Forrest City. His mother, however, was wise enough not to push—just offer the box of books and see what happens. Matt devoured them. In particular, a short story collection by Ernest Hemingway and Herman Melville's *Typee* shaped his thinking and his future. He still carried them everywhere he went. Besides his clothes, those two crumbling volumes were the main things he'd need to pack up that night.

What did they teach his twelve-year-old self? First: sentences could be beautiful—and not just the ideas in them, not simply the stories they told, but the sentences themselves, which could be compact and smooth, perfect to run the tongue over as a river stone is perfect under the thumb. Second: the real world, the one people really lived in, was full of exotic lands and unimaginable wonders. It was wilder and more romantic than anything George Lucas or Rudyard Kipling could dream up. Third: enlisting in the armed services afforded you the opportunity to visit those amazing foreign places and have adventures there.

So, now, at last, it was all going to start. First, he'd spend a few picturesque months at BOLC in the Ozarks—and since he'd never been to Missouri, it, too, would be something new. And then, instead of reading about foreign countries in novels or international relations textbooks, he would be going there for real. With his training in electronic engineering, he'd be responsible for mobile communications and making sure the flow of American data through foreign networks was secure. On weekend passes wherever he was sent, he'd be eating food he'd never dreamed existed or letting a pack of local kids give him impromptu soccer lessons so he could learn what he really wanted from them: their language. He'd be rowing tribal princesses around midnight lakes or running with the bulls. And he'd be showing America's best face to the world.

His class standing was strong. He figured, *I'll get one of my top three choices and be sent to the Congo, to the Balkans, to the Gulf.* But some kind of nostalgic whim or self-defeating hubris had made him include Rock Island Arsenal on his list of choices; some gremlin in him had prodded him to flirt with the Midwest. And when Post Night came and he learned where he was heading—

after exotic Missouri—to a Mississippi River town in Illinois, not four hours away from his Mason City hometown, he was crestfallen.

His mother, of course, would be ecstatic. "I know the wall is down," she'd ruminate. "I know the wars are over, I know we're at peace. But I would have worried anyway." She'd go on and on. "So, let your mom be happy, for a little while anyway, to have you back nearby."

Matt would make the best of this assignment and then never look back.

"Earth to Paderewski!" somebody shouted in his ear, and his consciousness snapped back to the Firstie Club, back to the here and now. Next to him stood Kyle Primeaux, a lanky olive-skinned cadet from Southern Louisiana, holding out a brown paper bag, the kind you'd pack your lunch in. "Goat fund," he drawled. "Be generous—Sherman's gonna need it."

Primeaux shook the bag, and Matt could hear the soft rustle of bills inside it. He fished out his wallet and chucked in a five. Poor Jim Sherman—sly as a fox and strong as a lion, but no good in the classroom. Graduating last in the class had gotten him posted someplace in South Dakota. But as Matt watched Primeaux finish working the room with that bag of money, he figured being the goat couldn't be all bad. Matt was headed to Nowheresville, Middle America, too, and no one had given *him* a sackful of cash as a consolation prize.

At the same time, Matt knew there were guys who would've killed for the Rock Island posting. Aircraft weapons subsystems, tank components, simulators—it was an engineer's dream. The work would be important and exciting, there was no doubt. Matt would make things, really *cool* things, that would save American lives and defend democracy everywhere. He'd have a hand in designing that stuff, in making it work better and smarter. That was surely what he had been thinking of when he put Rock Island on his post list, and that was probably why he'd matched. It was a place where everything Matt had learned about information assurance, and all his side projects on robotics and communications as well, would be put to the test. He would get to show them what his mind was truly made of. He would get to build the weapons of the future.

The Firstie Club staff unplugged the jukebox for the night and put on the godawful Wagner opera CD they always used to get the cadets to clear out at closing time. Jamal put his arm around Matt's neck—half hug, half headlock—and they headed back to barracks. Jamal had been Matt's roommate since they were plebes, the only one who knew Matt wasn't thrilled to be headed to Illinois. They hadn't had some big heart-to-heart about it, but he knew.

A few days later, they were all in Michie Stadium. Matt's suitcase was already in the trunk of his stepfather's car when he threw his cadet cap in the air and marched off the field. He wondered which of the kids he'd seen around the field's edges would take his cap home. These were all kids who lived at the base—people tended not to know it, but the military academy sat on an actual army base, home to real military families. So, who would have Matt's cap? The serious-faced blond boy with the missing front tooth? The Asian American girl who kept trying to suppress her giggles? The pudgy little redhead a few years shy of the growth spurt that would take him past six feet? Matt pictured all of them here in ten or fifteen years, throwing their own caps to the generation after them, and he felt a lump rise in his throat.

Inside his mortarboard, he had taped a five-dollar bill. On one side, in his own handwriting, he had carefully written two sentences from his father's note—a final memory his mother had saved for him until he was about to enter West Point: *Duty means doing the right thing, no matter what. And patriotism means that America sets an example for the world to follow.* On the other side of the bill, he had written his own mantra—words that had always guided him and kept him focused, even in the face of challenges: *Take it step by step. One thing at a time.*

The full note, carefully folded, stayed in his pocket, written in Ambrozy's careful hand. Cecilia had always believed those words could guide Matt through the challenges ahead:

Duty means doing the right thing, no matter what. Sometimes it's hard, sometimes it's boring, sometimes you don't feel like it. But stick with it. Do your chores, go to practice, do your homework. Duty is what makes you strong. Honor means sticking up for the little guy, taking care of old people and kids, treating people right even if they'll never know. Honor is what makes you one of the good guys. And patriotism means that America sets an example for the world to follow. Our country is the home of the brave and the free. Never forget how lucky you are to be an American.

He used to ask his mom if his father had left anything else, hoping for more of Ambrozy's words or insights, but there was nothing more. The only other keepsake was an unpublished paper his father had written on the clash between American patriotism, values, and actions abroad, drawn from Ambrozy's short but formative tour in Vietnam. Matt didn't fully understand its practical significance, but standing here today, about to begin his own service, he felt its emotional weight and the legacy it carried. His father's passion for history had always been there, shaping everything. But even with the note, the paper, and the stories his mother told, Matt couldn't shake the regret of never having truly known his father.

Jamal's commissioning ceremony was after that, and then Matt's. It was strange and thrilling to take off his grays and put on starched dress greens for the first time. Matt's senior-thesis advisor issued his oath of office. And when his mom pinned the gold butterbar to his collar, there were tears in both of their eyes.

After that, Matt's folks took him for one last dinner at Francesco's and then put him on that plane to Missouri. It all finally hit him. He was an officer in the US Army. It was real.

His country, he thought, had given him a world-class education, and now it was going to give him the world. Okay, the world starting with Rock Island, Illinois. But Illinois, Matt told himself, was America's heart. What better place to begin his service? He had to remember to take his father's advice—a man who had passed long ago but whose values still lived on in the note now safely tucked in his pocket. Duty and honor: it all made sense. Rock Island was where his adventure would begin. After that, he'd see the world and serve his country. His father's words might guide him, but Matt had his own mantra to hold onto: take it step by step. One thing at a time.

2000: ALEXANDRIA

HOUDA'S EYES blinked open in excitement as the predawn light began to filter through the shutters of her bedroom. It was rare for her to wake up this early, in time for the *adhan al-Fajr*—the call to the first prayers—but Houda's heart was aflutter. Today was the day—the last chance she had to give Adham a clear message of how she felt before he left for America.

It had been unspoken until now. Furtive glances between them, shared laughter, shared smiles. Did Adham know the secrets of her heart? And what about him—did he feel the same? *He must!* Their eyes had spoken it a thousand times. There were obstacles, however.

Houda was the younger sister of his best friend—not entirely off limits, but a situation that would require some finesse and blessings from Nasser and Baba, which raised a bigger issue. The El-Mohammedis were revered and respected, with a family history going back centuries, unlike the Mekawys, who were shopkeepers in financial trouble. Adham, with his engineering diploma and scholarship to continue his studies abroad, was doing his part to improve the family fortunes. That would require some time, however. He was in no position at the moment—without an apartment of his own, nor solvency for the *mahr* gift required of a groom—to court Houda in any kind of formal way. But none of this mattered to Houda. She was patient; she would wait. She just needed to make this clear to Adham, somehow, when she saw him at the farewell get-together later that afternoon. She had made him a parting gift—a special mixtape of Abdel Halim Hafez and Amr Diab love songs—for which she now reached in the dresser drawer near her bed, then held it close to her heart.

"This is for you, ya Adham." She rehearsed the moment in her mind. "So that you'll think of me when you hear these songs in America."

Houda felt immediately foolish, knowing she would never be able to say those words. She was far too shy and self-conscious to make a bold move like that.

If only I was daring like Dalia, she thought, returning the mixtape sadly to her drawer.

Perhaps she'd sufficiently done her part already—made it clear with looks and laughs that she was available to Adham. It was up to the man, after all, to make the first move. Houda had had her share of suitors and had turned down the attentions of kind men, good men—but men who couldn't hold a candle to Adham Mekawy. Yet Adham had been hesitant regarding Houda—*why?* There was a class and status disparity between their families, but this wouldn't have presented an issue for a progressive and humble man like her father. Houda believed that Adham's hesitation boiled down to the shame he felt surrounding his older brother, who was serving prison time for—as much as they tried to avoid this word—*terrorism*. It was a stigma that Adham did not want to bring upon the house of Omar El-Mohammedi.

That's the real reason he's hesitating, thought Houda, who sighed, gazing up at the fan on her ceiling. *Are those cobwebs in the corner?* It was time to get up and begin her chores, which included preparing breakfast for Baba—even though he always told her not to—and a thorough dusting of the shelves and artwork, which seemed a daily battle during these windy days.

Houda's mother had died when she was very young, so it was

up to Houda to keep the household up and running, a role that gave her great pleasure and satisfaction. She loved making things nice for her father and older brother, who'd become almost like a surrogate parent to Houda in the absence of their mother, Fatimah.

Houda glanced at the photo that sat in a silver frame on her desk of her elegant mother, with her kind eyes and noble features. Houda tried to bring her to life in her imagination, but it was fragmentary. She knew Fatimah had been pious from the stories told to her by her father. She knew her favorite recipes from the recipe book she had left behind. But Houda had never had that maternal attention every daughter needed. All she had were Baba and Nasser—Houda had learned how to deal with life from them. And that was why Houda was more than happy to keep Nasser's room tidy and manage the household laundry. Nasser said it was not her job to wash his clothes, so he pitched in from time to time; she insisted, nonetheless.

But it was a constant challenge to keep up a home this old—especially financially. One might think owning an apartment building in Kafr Abdu would have been enough to make a family rich all by itself, but the truth was the rents they brought in barely covered the building's maintenance, and Baba's university salary was modest at best. A place this old was charming, true, with its balconies, cool marble floors, and gracefully arched windows. But even though the tenants were a skilled and friendly bunch who often pitched in, a big old place cost a lot to keep up. Their family fortune had dwindled to nearly nothing after the wave of nationalizations in the 1950s and 1960s. The army officers running the country had wanted equality, and, in the process, the El-Mohammedis had lost all they had except this building. Baba never spoke about that, but they had plenty of conversations about the state of Egypt, particularly around the issue of religion.

"Never listen," Baba had told her a thousand times, "to those who would have you believe a virtuous Muslim woman must be meek." Lest she be bullied or fall victim to those who sold scripture for their own ends, Omar patiently taught Houda the Qur'an and Hadith. He rejected strict dogma, understanding the importance of navigating Islam thoughtfully. He wanted her to be armed with the knowledge to stand against the weight of expectations. He explained the *ayat* about women's roles and always emphasized that wearing the *hijab* was Houda's choice, but that she must understand first: faith, interpretation, and context. Of his many lessons regarding strong Muslim women, Khadijah was the one he most favored.

"The first wife of the Prophet was a fierce and hardworking businesswoman," he would say. "Nothing could stop her from prospering. This strong woman was the Prophet's best beloved, so never let anyone use religion to intimidate you, my daughter."

Just as Baba's guiding words were swirling inside her head, a sound from the outer world pulled Houda from her ruminations —the call from the mosque for *salat al-Fajr* prayers.

Houda finalized her *wudu*, then pulled the prayer rug sitting on top of the chair and unfurled it toward the window on the eastern wall, which faced Mecca. She stood in silence for a moment, raised her palms, and chanted, "*Allahu Akbar.*"

She bowed, dropped to her knees, and bent her forehead to the rug.

"*Subhaana Rabbi Al-A'laa.*" *Glory be to my Lord, the Most High.* Houda lost herself in the solemn prayer sequence as it continued, step by step, in the prescribed rhythm—a tradition across ages and geography that went back to the time of the Prophet. Houda felt at peace and deeply connected to her heritage when she did her prayers—more important, she felt connected to her mother, who'd been devout.

What a peaceful feeling!

After concluding her worship, Houda promised herself, for the thousandth time, to be more regular with her prayers. She'd been skipping them recently. *Why miss out on something so beautiful and beneficial?*

～

"Good morning, ya Houda," said Omar as his daughter entered the study with a tray of tea. "What are your plans for the day?"

"I'm going to school, then meeting Nasser and his gang around 6:30 p.m.," responded Houda, who was enrolled in classes at business school, though her heart was not really in her studies. She did it more to please her brother and father, who taught in the same university compound.

"Are you teaching today?" she asked. "Want to head there together?"

"No classes today," he said. "But I'm going in that direction to drop the dagger for cleaning." He pointed to the impressive box on his desk containing a silver dagger, which was a precious family heirloom.

Houda decided to have some fun with it. She seized the weapon suddenly and lifted it in the air like a sword, declaring with fervor, "And our troops, under Mohammed Ali Pasha in 1815, stormed the Arabian Peninsula, crushing the malignant armies of fundamentalism." Then, with a theatrical flourish of the dagger, dropping her voice to sound like her father, she said, "Two hundred years—and Islam is still fighting this serpent at its breast."

Omar laughed. "Ya Mishkala, good one!" He'd called her by her nickname, *Mishkala*, meaning "Miss Trouble," which was ironic, of course—compliant Houda was the opposite of trouble.

"Be careful with that weapon, ya Mishkala. And please return it to its box." The dagger was part of their family history of fighting the invading Wahhabis in the early 1800s. Other ancestors had fought against the French and British invaders. And then there was the bullet—the one he kept hidden away and had shown only to her and Nasser. It was something she could never joke about; her heart wouldn't allow it.

"You can tease me all you want." Omar turned suddenly serious. "But we are still fighting colonial legacy and fundamentalist doctrines that don't belong in Egypt."

Omar was pensive for a moment as Houda poured his tea. "Did you begin the Nawal El Saadawi book I asked you to read?"

"Not yet," said Houda, turning toward the door. "But I promise I will."

He called after her, "I know you just—"

"I promise," she said quickly as she exited her father's study.

Returning to her room, she was grateful not to have been Omar El-Mohammedi's firstborn son. From the moment her brother could read, Nasser had been indoctrinated with Baba's lessons—on history, politics, philosophy. Omar was determined to impart to him the wisdom of the ages. Houda got her share of it too—but more focused on the role of women in modern society and Islam. Offering up the writings of Nawal El Saadawi —who'd published a feminist magazine in 1981 called *Confrontation*, which landed her in jail—the professor had left a copy of her most controversial book, *The Hidden Face of Eve: Women in the Arab World*, on the side table adjacent to his daughter's bed. But Houda hadn't touched it. As much as she appreciated what Baba was trying to do, there were times when Houda felt a deep yearning to know what her mother would have thought—what she might have said to her daughter.

Why were you taken from us, Mother?

The Grand Café, with its comfortable outdoor seating, great food, and plentiful *shisha*, was a favorite among Nasser and his friends—a nice spot where the heady musk from the sea mingled with the scent of flavored tobacco. While their go-to place for gatherings like this would often be Smouha private club, Adham was not a member, so Nasser had decided that they should meet at the café instead. Houda had made sure to arrive early and was hoping that Adham might get there before the others too. She'd brought the mixtape in her purse and was praying for the courage to present it to him.

As she took a seat at their usual table, a waiter swooped in to take her order. "Just water for now," she answered with a nervous smile. Then she turned, and her heart skipped a beat. There was Adham, waltzing through the door with a big wave, hamming it up like a circus clown, pretending to trip and fall, then snapping up in mock indignation. She cracked up. She loved how he made her laugh all the time. That's what she wanted—a lifetime of laughter.

His eyes were smiling at Houda as he approached the table—and hers were smiling back. They'd exchanged so much meaning this way throughout the years, without a single word. It went back to the very first time they'd met, when she, at age fifteen, was visiting Nasser one day at the university, and he invited her to join him for a casual dinner with some friends, which included Dalia, Youssef, and a new acquaintance, Adham, who sat across from Houda. He was four years older but immediately caught Houda's attention. When they locked eyes for a brief instant, Houda felt a jolt of electricity coursing through her. *Did he feel it too?* A complete stranger, and yet what a connection!

She stole glances at Adham between bites and laughter. More than once, she found him gazing back, then looking away suddenly, self-conscious at having been caught. She, too, would look away shyly in these moments, with a sudden quickening of her heart. One time Adham smiled at her, and Houda smiled back briefly—but then she hid her face in her napkin, worried that she might be blushing.

Who was this guy? What could he feel for a girl of her age?

Houda was thrilled when Adham became a regular part of her brother's gang. There was genuine camaraderie between Nasser and Adham, which Houda saw and appreciated. But it was also no accident that Adham became part of the group. He had made sure of it, for that lightning bolt had struck him too. Adham wanted to get to know this extraordinary girl. So, he began to pay visits to Nasser's home, ostensibly to meet and interact with his learned father, but invariably—she made sure of it—Houda would be around as well. And then there were outings, gatherings like this one, where Nasser would allow Houda to tag along. In time, they had gotten to know one another. And here they were, three years later, across another table. This time they were alone.

Houda stood quickly to greet him. *If only we could hug*, she thought. But Houda knew her interaction with Adham would be restricted to a handshake—yet she used both her hands to take his. And lingered.

"Ya Adham." She smiled. "You look well."

He grinned. "You too, ya Mishkala," he teased, using Professor El-Mohammedi's nickname for Houda.

She rolled her eyes and smirked as Adham took a seat across from her. "Did you order?"

"Not yet," said Houda. "I wanted to wait for the others." But in truth, she really hoped everyone else would be delayed so she could have a moment alone with Adham.

Alas, it was not to be.

"Ya Adham, Houda!" came the booming voice of Youssef, who had his sister, Iman, in tow.

Houda hid her disappointment and welcomed them.

"Where's your never-on-time brother?" he asked.

As if his ears had been burning, in walked Nasser, hand in hand with his beloved Dalia. The engineers greeted each other with big grins and slaps on the back. They ordered chai and sandwiches, then got down to discussing the elephant at the table— the "Alexandria Four" (three engineers, one lawyer) would soon be cut in two, when Youssef and Adham left for America the following day.

Dalia, a natural litigator, was never shy about asking a direct question. "So, Adham, what are your plans after you finish your studies in the US? I know Youssef is thinking of staying and gaining some work experience. Will you be staying or coming home?"

It was the question Houda had been dying to ask but couldn't muster the courage to. Adham hesitated for a moment, avoiding Houda's gaze, then he looked directly at Dalia and said, "It depends, honestly, on what opportunities present themselves."

Houda was crushed. She knew that Adham's family was

depending on him to make something happen in America—that he represented their hopes and dreams—but it still hurt.

What about her dreams?

Adham tried to make a joke out of it by ribbing Nasser, who was sitting next to him. "Maybe when Nasser comes to America for his MBA, we can open a business together and become millionaires!" Everyone laughed, except Houda. Losing her mother was hard enough. She had no intention of losing Nasser too.

She looked squarely at her brother and said, "If and when you go to America for your MBA, you will be returning on the first flight after your final exam."

Nasser stared at his little sister in understanding and with an unspoken communication—*I'm not leaving you.* Then, in classic Nasser fashion, he turned the moment into a joke by standing erect and saluting her like a soldier. "*Tamam ya fandem!*" *Yes, sir!*

"Aren't you going to back me up?" Houda turned to Dalia. "Future sister-in-law?"

Dalia smiled, sipping her tea. Everyone expected the litigator to issue a fiery endorsement of Houda's ultimatum, but Dalia simply said, looking at Houda and not Nasser, "Your brother knows very well that there is nowhere on earth he can go where I won't be able find him and enforce our contract."

As Youssef and Iman cracked up, Houda skillfully used their laughter as an opportunity to face Adham with similar authority that belied her eighteen years. "You too, ya Adham. We expect you to return home. We'll miss you." She didn't quite have the confidence to use *I* instead of *we*, which was the feeling in her heart. But at least the sentiment had been spoken.

Houda saw Nasser observing the looks between her and Adham.

Does he know? Is he on my side?

"No one knows what the future holds," Nasser said in a moment of seriousness. "It's in the hands of Allah."

Houda sighed. He was right, of course. How could any of them know the path their lives would take?

More food arrived, along with strong coffee, and the friends traded stories until long after sundown. Then it was time to go home. Houda looked into Adham's eyes for a long beat as she said farewell to him.

But she forgot, despite everything, to give him the mixtape.

2000: MANHATTAN

THE HEAVINESS that invaded Adham's lungs in New York that December left him feeling more than a little homesick for Alexandria's balmy breezes and mild winters. He could swear that here, in arctic New York, he was developing asthma. This morning, even as he lunged for the ringing phone, heavy frozen air poured into his lungs as if directly from the Hudson River.

"Adham! I caught you at home, finally!" The voice was so crystal clear, Youssef could have been in the next room. There was none of the echo or static Adham got on his calling-card calls home or to Nasser. It was hard to believe that Youssef was three thousand miles away in California.

"How's New York?" he asked. "You taking the city by storm?"

"Making out like Michael Corleone," Adham wheezed. His skin was still stinging from the cold, even after the elevator ride up and running and diving for the phone. He'd known when he heard it from the hallway that it was going to be for him. His Taiwanese roommate Kuo's family only called in the middle of the night, while his Nigerian roommate Olawale's people never called at all.

"That's my boy," Youssef said, apparently not worried that his friend's lungs were turning into ice blocks. They laughed. Adham missed his classmate.

"Don't worry, I'm *El-Nemer El-Aswad*—Egyptian Rocky making good in the West," Adham said. They both loved that classic movie starring Ahmed Zaki—it was adored, for that matter, by any Egyptian with expatriate dreams. Adham struck a triumphant pose—well, a parody of one, anyway—that he knew Youssef couldn't see, but somehow Youssef's chuckle let him know he was imagining it anyway. Anyone who'd known Adham as long as Youssef had understood all his movie references, Egyptian and American alike. If they didn't, he'd sit them down in front of the VCR until they did.

"How's Berkeley?" Adham continued.

"Oh my god, man," Youssef groaned. "I don't know if I'm going to make it through Ramadan, much less through the whole winter. It's way more work than I expected, and that's hard to get through when we're fasting. Plus, they keep saying it's no colder here than winters back home, but I have a hard time believing it. It feels colder. I think it's the damp."

Happy as Adham was to hear from his friend, he thought he might have to hang up on him. "What are you talking about, crazy person? You're in *California*. I woke up this morning with my backside frozen to the radiator."

"California's not what you think, man," Youssef insisted. "Back in August when I got here, sure. Everything was the color of wheat, and there was not a cloud in the sky. But the last few weeks? It's not windy like Alexandria, but it drizzles *all the time*. And when it's not drizzling, there's this mist that creeps in off the bay. The damp just gets inside your bones. I'm telling you, it's not like anything we've ever felt at home."

Changing the subject to keep things cheerful, Adham asked, "So, what's going on with that girl? Is she still returning your calls?"

Just after landing in Berkeley, Youssef had met a real live California girl. Pictures Adham had seen suggested her hometown was built in a Spanish architectural style that seemed familiar enough. Still, the scent of patchouli and fantasies of blond women practicing yoga under giant cedars clung around the word

California, giving it a special incoherence, even within the general strangeness Adham associated with America.

Youssef had insisted that this girl was very down-to-earth, though, bright and easy to talk with. "Somehow she makes me think of Dalia," he'd confided, which was about the highest praise any of their university friends knew for a smart and independent woman. Youssef and a California girl made sense. He'd always been liberal, adventurous. He didn't dream of a classic Egyptian girl like Houda the way Adham did. "Being from California doesn't mean what you think it means," he had told Adham more than once.

Now, as Adham asked about her, there was a pause on the line. He could practically hear Youssef blushing. "She *is* still talking to you, isn't she? So, things are moving along then. Youssef, you sly fox! And here I am just trying to get American girls to pronounce my name correctly. They all want to call me *Adam*. Like Adam and Eve, you know? But you! You've captured the heart of an American girl. Tell me everything."

"Well, she's . . ." Youssef trailed off, inarticulate in a way Adham had never known him to be. But then he found his voice. "She's not like any girl I've ever known. She's so sure of herself. She's always stopping and thinking things over, and then when she speaks, she has such confidence. She's always thinking about the political and moral consequences of . . . well, of every little thing. Of a phrase, of a picture. She has such a way of viewing the world. Everything is active, everything is political, and she has such hope that everything can be *better*."

"Whoa, Youssef," Adham teased. "Are you dating Mother Teresa?"

He laughed proudly. "She's no nun, I can assure you. But she is a bit younger than us," he admitted. "She's only a junior! And, well . . ." He went silent.

"Youssef?" Adham prompted.

"You see, there's—there's something I should tell you about her." His voice grew soft.

He sounded nervous. A nervousness Adham understood.

That was how he'd felt around Houda, from the moment her classic kohl-rimmed eyes smiled into his. So, he wasn't entirely joking when he half-teased his friend at Berkeley, half-guessed, "She's fifteen years old? What? Youssef, you've got me scared here." He didn't like the heavy tone that had crept into Youssef's voice.

"She's . . . she's Jewish," Youssef whispered.

There was a pause—one which Youssef had expected. Adham's values were more conservative.

Then Adham jumped back in with, "This is America, Youssef. Have your fun—"

"It's not about having fun," Youssef interrupted. "I like her."

"She's not how you think she is," Youssef continued, his voice somehow defiant. "She's not a Zionist. She's majoring in Peace Studies and Conflict Resolution—she hates how Israel treats the Palestinians. And Adham, you'll never believe it! Her grand-mother was an *Iskandrania*! Right to the end of her life, she loved her *Misr* homeland."

Calling Alexandria and Egypt by their Arabic names made the words feel all the dearer, both closer and more mythic, to its far-flung children.

"So, she's a good Jew, and together you will solve the Middle East conflict," Adham said jokingly.

"As you know, Adham," Youssef took a serious tone, "the history of Jews in Egypt goes back to biblical times, their popula-tion rising and falling like the tides as despots and colonists expelled or welcomed them—everyone claiming Alexandria as their city. The establishment of Israel as a Jewish state is what caused tension for Egyptian Jews who'd been members of our society for centuries."

"You sound like Professor El-Mohammedi." Adham laughed, though his doubts lingered. "So, she has Iskandrania blood, but . . . you know Jews, Youssef. They have the world in their pockets—"

"I'm telling you, Adham, she's not like anyone we've ever met. She's tender and tough all at once . . . and you've got to see her.

She's blond. Small, but leggy. And her hair is cut *short*! I would never have believed I could fall for a woman with such hair. She's like—I don't know—like a creature from another world. Like an elf!"

"Youssef, you're worrying me," Adham said, but he was back to teasing. "An elf? It'll be boys next. Toy-making boys from the North Pole," he added, thinking of the bizarre, over-the-top displays that had been sprouting up in department stores all over New York in the past couple of weeks. "What will your mother say?"

"I assure you, my friend, Risa is all woman," Youssef shot back, mock-dignified. "And if you could see the little skirts she wears on the tennis court, you would never question it again." He held his serious silence for another moment, and then they started giggling like a couple of schoolboys.

Yet the moment Adham ended the call, he found himself in a pensive mood, his mind a storm of thoughts. How quickly things were evolving. While his current relationship with Youssef was strong, Adham wouldn't even have been friends with him were it not for Nasser acting as a bridge. Youssef, raised in the Gulf, came from oil money; Adham, from a line of middle-class shopkeepers and factory foremen. It must have surprised Youssef that Adham had somehow managed to find a way to study abroad. He would never have been able to pull it off, in fact, had it not been for Nasser's coaching and encouragement to apply for grants and scholarships. Creating opportunities for all Egyptians was a big part of the El-Mohammedi family's values, as Adham had learned during his many visits to their home.

Omar, with his long historical view and precious family treasures, seemed so different from Adham's father, who'd come in the sixties from a Nile Basin farming town to Alexandria University, which was public and easily affordable. Unlike Omar, Adham's dad never talked about the past, only about the future. When Adham was a kid, his father was middle management in a state-owned cotton-spinning company. They didn't have a summer vacation apartment on the north coast or anything extravagant, but as long as they were what his father called "prudent," they were comfortable enough in their rented place.

Adham's father kept promising that one day he'd get that big promotion, and they'd buy their own place in Roshdy. As far as Adham could see, Roshdy wasn't all that different from Moharram Bey—once a preeminent neighborhood for the affluent—but changing neighborhoods would make it feel like they were moving up. By the time Adham got to university, though, the cotton industry had been privatized, his dad had been downsized into a miserly early retirement, and Adham knew they'd buy their own apartment right around the time the Egyptian football team won the World Cup—which was to say, only in his wildest dreams.

Privatization had been supposed to modernize Egypt, intensify production, and kick-start the economy, but instead factories began shutting down and then getting torn down. Adham's father couldn't bear to look at the condominiums that had taken the place of his spinning plant. His eyes would get weepy when he talked about how harshly the workers who'd protested the closing had been dealt with. Even as a young boy, Adham had surmised that improving "the economy" was not meant for them, and certainly not for everyday workers, but for people who already had money and connections to buy factories and gut them. So, maybe it made sense that Nasser kept saying that when *he* came to America, it would not be for engineering, but for an MBA—as part of a new generation of young professionals in Egypt, eager to join the global economy and, in doing so, revitalize their country's economy.

∽

Later, after the sun had set and Adham had broken his Ramadan daytime fast, he let Olawale talk him into going to a gathering in Astoria. It was the first time he'd made it over to Queens, and as they walked from the Astoria Boulevard subway stop over to the party on 25th Avenue, Adham couldn't believe all the Arabic he saw in shop windows and overheard on the busy street. He heard Egyptian accents everywhere, some that could have been from Moharram Bey. It was exciting and fascinating—this neighborhood was so distinctly New York and yet so full of pleasantly rearranged familiar elements enticingly mixed with foreign ones. The cafés from which the smell of shisha wafted, the small Egyptian restaurant he spotted—they were all full, their windows steamy with heat and giving off a sense of gracious welcome and modest prosperity. It was much more inviting than the cramped little Arabic place near Columbia where he'd been getting his shisha fixes. He made a mental note to come back here to explore as soon as he possibly could.

The party turned out to be a crowded but relaxed and chatty gathering of friends and neighbors. Olawale's friend shared this apartment with two other Nigerians and a friend from Morocco. In one corner, a group of drummers jammed, teasing and cheering one another on. Nearer the kitchen area, people handed around cookies, meat pies, and fruit skewers. Someone pressed a hot paper cup into Adham's hand—it turned out to be strong coffee, spicy and syrupy sweet. He drank gratefully, still shivering a little from the cold outside.

Olawale introduced Adham to a couple of people, then joined a group of men drawing on an apple-scented shisha that was set up on a low table by the window. Adham found himself in conversation with a woman named Esther. She was older than most of this crowd, fortyish but still pretty, with coal-black skin, enormous eyes, and a ready, musical laugh. A vibrant yellow silk scarf wrapped her hair modestly and seemed to bring sunlight into the room.

"You haven't been in New York long," she observed in a lilting accent that Adham recognized as similar to Olawale's.

"How can you tell?" he asked her.

"The way you were shivering when you came in," she said. "You're not used to the cold yet. But you haven't even seen a real New York winter. Just wait until February." She laughed her lovely laugh as Adham groaned.

"Where are you from?" she asked—the perfect conversation starter for a pair of outsiders.

They swapped stories about growing up, Adham in Alexandria and Esther in Kano, a big inland city in the tropical steppes of Nigeria. She was telling him about a troublesome, stray urban goat when a pair of carefully manicured hands covered her eyes, and an alto voice from behind her demanded, "Guess who?" Esther turned around and, amid mutual joyous squeals, embraced a tiny Latina woman bedecked in a great deal of gold jewelry. Esther turned back to Adham and said, "This is my neighbor Carmen." Carmen, in turn, introduced her cousin Valería.

Carmen had brought a tin of treats from her father's taqueria around the corner, and she and Esther bustled off to put them out on the table, leaving Adham with Valería, who was quite beautiful, almost distractingly so—Adham was unaccustomed to being in such close proximity to a woman like this. They stood awkwardly for a moment, and then each said, in unison, "So—"

They both smiled. That broke the ice, and before Adham knew it, Valería was telling him stories about her family's shoe store in Secaucus, where she used to work weekends and summers as a child, and now full time. She made the long hours and outrageous customer demands sound hilarious; soon he found himself matching her one for one with stories from his dad's supermarket —such as the time Baba had Adham stuff the backs of the shelves with empty boxes when they were low on inventory so it would appear that they were fully stocked. As she laughed, her long, thick hair shook, silken waves against her deep-caramel skin.

Adham was shocked by the way she made him feel. *What about Houda?* he thought. It had been more than three months since he'd seen Nasser's little sister—Adham's balmy memories of sweet Houda and warm breezes along the Corniche were being challenged by the harsh loneliness of a New York winter. Houda suddenly seemed like a girl in the face of Valería, who was all woman and, in her stilettos, almost as tall as Adham. He was intrigued by her.

They found a spot at the end of a sofa to sit together, and

Valería told him, "You know, when I was a little girl, before we left Ixtepec, my papa tried to open a supermarket. He couldn't make it work, though. Every time my sisters and I complained about the shoe store, we'd get the speech about how we didn't know how good we had it in New Jersey." She rolled her big dark eyes exaggeratedly, miming her teenaged response to her dad's lectures. She leaned toward him, her face serious, and said quietly, "But you know what? I think Papa was right. We go back to Mexico every few years. I've seen how my cousins live, the ones who stayed. Things are better than they used to be, but it's still slow, even desperate at times. We really do have more here."

She leaned back into the sofa, thoughtful for a moment. Then that lively spark animated her eyes again, and she asked, "But what about you? You're not in the supermarket business here, are you?"

"No, no," Adham demurred, "I came here to study. I'm in a graduate program at Columbia. Engineering."

"Oh," she said, an awed hush coming into her voice. "You must be smart. Graduate school. I couldn't wait to be done with classes and tests!" She laughed, and Adham blushed a little.

"I don't know about that," he admitted. "I like engineering, but sometimes I think if I were really smart, I'd be looking for a way to stay in America permanently, not just on a student visa. Like you said, people can really do well for themselves here." To keep things light, he added, "And the shoes they sell in this country." He kissed his fingertips and turned an enraptured face to the ceiling. "Just exquisite!"

She laughed again. He decided he really liked her laugh. "You're funny," she said and then added, as if reading his thoughts, "I like you. I'll bet you *will* find a way to make it in New York, Adam."

There it was again. He swatted away his exasperation with these Americans who couldn't seem to get it right. *Adham*. What was so difficult about that? It was getting late, and Adham could see that Olawale was heading for the coat closet. This was his moment: he wanted to see Valería again, and he couldn't risk it by correcting her pronunciation of his name.

Adam, he thought. It wasn't so bad. If you wanted to get by in America, you had to play along a little. He could be "Adam." So, he tried out a line he was pretty sure he'd heard in an American movie, "I hope that means you'll let me take you to dinner and a movie next weekend."

～

Given the frigid air, Adham and Olawale decided to splurge and ride back to Manhattan in a taxi—mercifully warm with a smell of sweet oranges and new leather. Still buzzing from the party, hand closed around the slip of paper in his jacket pocket on which Valería had jotted down her telephone number, Adham settled gratefully back against the seat—the first time he'd been in a car since coming to New York. It was nice. He missed the drives along the Corniche at night with his buddies, the comfort and semiprivacy of an automobile in a big city full of pedestrians.

He thought of Houda, then stopped himself. Houda was an ocean away in Alexandria, and Valería was here. *It's just a date*, he told himself. But in truth, Adham couldn't wait to see her again. There was something about Valería. She had self-assurance, spice. And they had laughed as if they'd known each other their whole lives.

From their vantage point as the cab crossed the Triborough Bridge, Manhattan looked huge, crystalline, and beautiful. New York wasn't *so* much bigger than Alexandria, but Adham was becoming enamored of its variety, its abundance. Where in Alexandria could he have gone to a party and met one woman from Nigeria and another from Oaxaca? Where in his home city could he see a Bangladeshi restaurant next door to a Panamanian bakery? Everything here felt new, global, and charged with opportunity.

2000: EL-KARIA, UPPER EGYPT

DALIA FELT the familiar squeeze she loved so much of Nasser's hand. But when she turned to him, he did not meet her gaze. Nasser was staring ahead at the bumpy road in silence, which seemed to deepen what he was saying by taking her hand: *I need you. Do not leave my side.*

For Nasser—destroyer in squash, chess, and all things cerebral —this was big. Never having seen him so vulnerable, Dalia felt her eyes well up in compassion. She wanted to reach out and pull Nasser close. Not now, of course. That would come soon enough. In this moment, Nasser simply needed a trusted friend, a role that Dalia felt honored to play. She squeezed his hand in return, and it said, *I'm with you.*

But in truth, Dalia felt jittery, suspicious. Ever since their graduation encounter with the bearded man—Nasser's Great Uncle Ragab—her mind had been haunted with the thought: *Could it be true? Could Omar have lied for all these years to his own children?* She was having trouble believing that honorable Omar would have lied for all these years about something as sacred as the passing of his wife. It would buttress her mother's disdain for the professor, along with her judgment about their engagement. Dalia had lied to her family about what she was doing that day. She'd said they were driving to Cairo to apply for a grant for their nonprofit. But upon arriving in Cairo, they had parked at the train station and boarded a Luxor-bound train, disembarking at Asyut where they'd hired this *mashrue*, a small microbus, to serve as their taxi for the whole day. While these vehicles were often shared by up to twelve passengers, Dalia and Nasser were alone as they approached El-Karia—a town that seemed frozen in time, like a 1950s movie version of an Egyptian village. The car lurched along the pockmarked village road, weaving around stray dogs and a couple of camels. Dalia adjusted her headscarf to ensure her attire was sufficiently modest—this was not the time to make a statement about women's rights. Every woman here was well covered in a traditional headcover—a hijab or even a *niqab*, the black head-to-ankle dress with slits only for the eyes.

While Dalia was feeling uneasy, Nasser had an entirely different read of the situation. He'd always suspected there was more to his mother's story, wondering, for example, why they'd never visited her in the hospital if she had really been that ill. All Nasser remembered at age ten was traveling in the car during a violent sandstorm that raged around the city, then returning to their apartment that spring evening when his father told them the tragic news. Nasser sensed that Ragab was like a special messenger, handing him the keys to a secret portal of a history that his father didn't dare to touch. And, despite his outward bravado, Nasser had a highly sensitive aspect at his core. He was nervous, therefore, about what he might discover, which was the reason Dalia had insisted on joining him.

"Here, ya *pasha*," said the driver, pulling up to a gate and pointing. "El-Karia Cemetery."

Nasser told him to wait, and then he climbed outside with Dalia right behind him. The first thing that struck them was the sun blazing across the desert sands, powerful even in winter. Closer to the equator and farther from the sea, it was often twenty degrees warmer here than in Alexandria with its coastal breezes. Nasser gazed up at the line of palm trees that ran along one side of the graveyard, marking the edge of the town. Beyond those trees was nothing but sand.

The cemetery was small, so it would not take long to survey the graves. *Is this a terrible idea?* Dalia continued to wonder.

"I found it!" Nasser shouted, two rows ahead. Dalia ran to join him. Nasser used his fingers to brush away the sand, revealing the words: "*La Elah Ela Allah.*" *There is only one God.* And below that: "Tomb of El-Saidi."

The names of the men in the family were listed first, then below came the women. Nasser spotted the name *Fatimah El-Saidi.* He took a long, deep breath and stared. *Could it be?*

"They went through hell," came a scratchy voice from behind them. Nasser and Dalia turned to behold a very old woman standing by a nearby tombstone. "That family was tested by God."

"You knew them?" Dalia asked.

"Everyone knew them."

"Are they still here?" Nasser asked. "Where's the El-Saidi home?"

"*Baat Al-Imam,*" the woman said—*the imam's house.* She pointed with her cane toward a modest structure adjacent to the village mosque.

Minutes later, Nasser and Dalia approached the entrance and knocked on the dark-red door. No response. Wind whistled across the desert. Nasser knocked again; the door swung open.

"I thought you would never come." It was Ragab, unsmiling as always. He regarded Dalia enigmatically, then made a gesture of welcome. "Come. This is your family home—where your mother was raised."

Nasser entered, his eyes darting everywhere. The house was shuttered to keep it cool, and details eluded him in the darkness. Ragab invited them to sit on a pair of ottomans in the parlor, calling into the kitchen for refreshments, which came out on a tray held by a pretty girl who was careful not to make eye contact with the guests and who then left in a hurry.

A daughter? Dalia wondered, glancing at Ragab as the elder poured mint tea into silver-rimmed cups. *Or had her family forced her to marry this man?*

As Nasser's eyes adjusted to darkness, he was able to take in his surroundings. He glanced at a black-and-white photograph on the wall of an older man with soft features, a big mustache, and piercing eyes—not unlike Nasser himself. Dalia, following his gaze, noticed the resemblance. There was a plaque below the picture, which read, "*Elshikh Atef, Imam Almasjid.*"

"Your grandfather," explained Ragab. "Man of God." He distributed the tea. "A good man, my brother. We ran a shop together. He studied in Al-Azhar—the renowned Islamic university—and married at twenty. Latifa was fifteen. They had your mother two years later." Dalia noticed the absence of photographs of the women.

"There were no more children," Ragab continued. "He never remarried to have his sons, decided instead to devote himself entirely to God. He was the imam of our mosque."

"Tell me about my mother." Nasser looked his great-uncle in the eyes.

"Smart, even smarter than a boy." Ragab felt Dalia staring at him but kept his gaze fixed upon Nasser. "She memorized the entire Qur'an by the age of ten. My brother indulged her intellect and allowed her to be educated." Ragab sighed. "I told him nothing good would come of this, but he wouldn't listen. The school was twenty kilometers away. Fatimah even wanted to go to college." Ragab gave a wry smile. "That's where the family drew the line. Her marriage was arranged for the week after high school graduation. But on the morning of the ceremony, her bed was empty. She had run away."

"The shame, the disgrace." Ragab shook his head. "Our family was never the same."

He took a breath. "We searched everywhere—Asyut, Sohag, even Cairo. No one guessed she had made it all the way to Alexandria. My brother, his heart broken, retired from the mosque. His only child was dead to him. Then, many years later, we heard from the police. They'd found the birth certificate in her pocket and delivered the body. In pieces. It was awful."

Nasser and Dalia exchanged a startled glance. *In pieces?*

"When the train derailed, the bodies were scattered every-where, mangled, unrecognizable . . ."

"My mother died of a heart attack," Nasser interrupted abruptly.

"Yes, that was Omar's story." Ragab gave him a look of sympathy. "No one dared to doubt the professor." Nasser's face appeared ashen. "You're a man. It's time you know the truth, don't you think?"

THE LIBRARY OF OMAR
EL-MOHAMMEDI

APRIL 7, 2014 • 6:20 PM

NEVER BELIEVE. Question. Reflect. Open your eyes. Use discernment.

Those were the dictums that esteemed scholar Omar El-Mohammedi took such care to impart to each of his students. It had begun at home—with his own son. Now, all the mourners had departed, and Omar returned to reading Nasser's journal, where he was being asked to taste his own medicine—to proceed with healthy skepticism, even some doubt—as he sifted through this jungle of words, not knowing precisely what he was searching for. A clue. But what exactly? And these appalling stakes—were they really true?

"Thousands could die," the American had said. "Even hundreds of thousands."

Who can I trust? Omar breathed heavily.

Still defeated from the deep melancholy of the afternoon's funeral, his hands trembled slightly as he turned the pages. The writing was poetic yet precise, each word measured. Then there was the white-space diary structure that Nasser had learned as a boy, leaving room to come back after time passed to add further reflections.

"Reactivity can hijack our intellect," Omar had patiently taught his impetuous son. "Give yourself time and space for rumination. See what some distance can do, then add your new insight."

"Ghasil El-Balah,." Nasser had added the name of Alexandria's first gale to the white space of the page that Omar was reading. Then he'd gone on to describe it thematically: "After the long summer of my youth, storm clouds came and eclipsed the sun, signaling the arrival of winter."

It was perfunctory, not nearly as lyrical as the journal entries themselves, which indicated perhaps that there was a message in these gales. But what? Was this hasty addendum related to the journal entry on that page? Omar had no way of knowing. He hadn't yet cracked the cipher. Painful as it was, Omar had no choice but to read—line by line—the scathing words of his departed son.

November 7, 2000

Blinded eyes see what they're shown,
the master's secrets remain unknown.

When I was a boy, my father would take us to ride the *hantour*. I remember thinking, *Those poor horses with their blinders*. They see only what their masters want them to see: the road ahead and nothing else. Yet this is how it is with all of us. There are masters everywhere, some hidden, some overt, who manipulate how they wish us to interact with the world around us.

My father was one of these masters. How hard he tried to make us see the world through his eyes. I resisted the blinders he tried to impose upon me, for they were made of lectures, speeches, idealism, and lies. The fabrications about our past were the most insidious, for they were spun like fairy tales. How many times was I forced to endure his polemic of the glorious and noble patrilineal ancestral line, which was patriots and Pashawat, fighting the colonizers and fundamentalists, with artifacts to prove it; or the myth of an orphaned mother, taken in by kindhearted strangers, then taken away from us far too soon because of the sudden capitulation of her own ailing heart? Her heartbreak was real, but it stemmed from the narrow vision of his secular tyranny. In the light of this new day, the blinders are gone. I am my own master, and what I see is a travesty.

Omar paused, overwhelmed with a flood of memories. He thought back to one of the last times when they had had fun together as a family. The sound of squawking seagulls that filled the briny breeze blowing along the Corniche were overpowered suddenly by a little girl's shriek, "Nasser! Nasser, where are you going?"

It was little Houda, age five, calling out to her nine-year-old brother who'd wriggled free from his mother's grasp in the hantour—the horse carriage—as it bounced along the Corniche seaside road. The year was 1985, the first week of September. With the "Ghasil El-Balah" gale nearly upon them, they'd decided to sneak in an outdoor excursion before the punishing winds of winter would arrive and force them to shutter the windows. It had been Fatimah, to the delight of the children, who'd proposed the idea of a hantour ride. And here was Nasser, being Nasser.

While Houda sat happily ensconced in Omar's lap, restless Nasser had something else in mind. He lurched free from Fatimah and clambered forward past the alarmed hantour driver. "Nasser!" Fatimah shouted in mounting concern. She looked lovely in her headscarf despite the worry in her eyes. Before anyone could stop him, the boy had leapt onto the horse's rump.

"Nasser!" Omar called out suddenly. "Come back here at once."

He wouldn't listen. The determined boy sat astride the horse like an Arabic knight and methodically shimmied forward. The driver pulled the reins to stop his horse. He leapt off the cart and hurried ahead to pull the boy down to safety, but not before Nasser had achieved his objective—having navigated forward and holding the poor beast by its mane, he'd ripped off its blinders.

"Let him see!" shouted young Nasser. "He needs to see!"

Omar's mouth curled up in amusement as the hantour driver attempted to negotiate with the headstrong boy.

"It's the passing cars," explained the driver. "They frighten him."

"He must be allowed to see," insisted Nasser.

Houda giggled at the antics of her beloved brother as Omar and Fatimah exchanged a glance. Nasser had a will of his own. There was no stopping it.

And that thought brought Omar back to the present, where all that remained of his willful son was the searing journal that sat open on his desk. Tears welled up in the old man's eyes.

He missed his boy; he missed his wife.

Why did I drive her away?

PART II

EL-MAKNESA

El-Maknesa ("the Broom Gale")
lashes with violent winds
that sweep the sea with such force that the Mediterranean
erupts into chaos.

If there was any doubt before, it is gone:
the dark winds of winter are here.

2001: KAFR EL-DAWWAR

If only she'd been able to crawl into his head—to know just when and how his world had begun to unravel. The change had been gradual at first. On the six-hour train and car ride from Asyut back to Alexandria last year, Nasser had hardly said a word; he'd gazed broodingly at the passing Nile, where fishing boats appeared as ancient as the land itself. The encounter with his great-uncle had been deeply unnerving. Dalia herself had been troubled by the incident, which put into question the integrity of Omar El-Mohammedi, her beloved mentor and friend.

Dalia's lawyer instincts told her to question, investigate, and come to her own conclusions. In the weeks that followed, Dalia pored through newspaper archives and police records. She quickly confirmed that there had indeed been a major rail accident on the southbound Luxor line in 1986—the year of Fatimah's death. Train 63 Kably had derailed from the faulty tracks north of Asyut, leaving seventy-two dead and over three hundred injured. While train accidents were not uncommon in Egypt, this one was one of the biggest transportation disasters on record. The deceased were not named, however, meaning there was no written proof that Nasser's mother had been on that train. Nonetheless, Dalia observed Nasser's growing agitation in the days and weeks that followed.

Even more disturbing was the information Dalia uncovered about Nasser's Great-Uncle Ragab. Apparently, he had spent a decade behind bars as one of the Islamist conspirators behind the assassination of former Egyptian president Anwar Sadat, who'd become divisive in the Muslim world for making peace with Israel, among other things. In Dalia's eyes, Ragab's association with militant extremists disqualified him entirely as a credible source of information. "You can't possibly believe the word of a terrorist over your own father's," she'd pleaded with Nasser, who was becoming increasingly obstinate. It had led, in fact, to their first explosive fight.

Seeing how desperate Nasser was to learn the truth about his mother, Dalia apologized and offered to help. She, like Nasser, knew surprisingly little about Fatimah's upbringing, beyond the fact that she'd been adopted as a child. Despite Omar's progressive views on the role of women in society, conversations about El-Mohammedi family lore nearly always focused on the paternal lineage. One day, during Omar's afternoon nap and after Houda had left the apartment to run errands, they went digging through some old documents hidden in the closet of the professor's study. One box contained letters to Fatimah, written by a woman named Zahra, whom Nasser knew to be one of his mother's closest friends—though, strangely, he'd never met her. When they went to visit the return address on the envelopes, they discovered that Zahra and her family were long gone. A neighbor seemed to think the family had moved to Kafr El-Dawwar, a modest industrial hub about thirty kilometers east of Alexandria. He recited a phone number that Nasser scrawled on a scrap of paper.

When Dalia came to pick him up the following morning, she had hardly slept. By the looks of it, neither had Nasser. "Did you call her?" she asked.

"Of course," he snapped. Dalia read the signal. Nasser did not want to engage in conversation. He gazed at the countryside as they crossed Abees on the old highway and finally spoke. "My father loved Kafr El-Dawwar—he took us here as kids."

Dalia had a sudden flash. "There's a story about it from your family's history."

Nasser smirked. "The Battle of Kafr El-Dawwar in 1882, where Ismail, my father's great-uncle, died. He was an artillery officer in the Urabi Army, defending Egypt after the British invasion of Alexandria. Glorious history, isn't it? My father never misses a chance to remind me of how his family resisted British colonization."

Dalia nodded. "Yeah, I remember the professor showing us a letter that Ismail had sent to his wife before he died—one of your family artifacts. What an incredible history you have."

"History, always *his*-story," Nasser said, his tone sharp, the bitterness unmistakable. "Never *her*-story."

When they arrived at Zahra's modest apartment, she was genuinely happy to see them and gave Nasser a big hug. "*Ahlan, Ibn El-Ghalia*," she said, again and again—*welcome, son of the precious one.*

When Dalia went to hug Zahra, she could see the tears in her eyes. This woman had been like a sister to Fatimah. The lavish breakfast she'd prepared for them could easily have fed a family of twelve—*feteer meshaltet, asal aswad*, cheese, eggs, and more.

"Eat, eat," she insisted. And they did, though neither had any appetite.

Then, after answering Zahra's string of questions about himself and his sister, Nasser set down his tea and looked her in the eyes. "We went to Upper Egypt recently to meet a man named Ragab who claimed to be my great-uncle . . ."

Zahra appeared shaken. Nasser continued softly, "Is it true? My mother is buried there?"

Zahra took a breath and nodded. "I visit her grave every year."

"I knew this day would come," she continued. "The last time I saw your father, I told him that he had to tell you . . ."

"So, it's all true?" Nasser went pale. "My mother died in a train accident! It was never a heart attack?"

"Heartbreak, maybe. Omar tried so hard to shield you children from all of this." Zahra let out a deep sigh. "After Houda was born, Fatimah felt a strong need to reconnect with her actual mother; she wanted to make peace with her dad for the shame she was sure he felt."

Zahra smiled. "Your mom was stubborn. *Saidia*, a true Upper Egyptian."

"Your parents were arguing more and more," Zahra continued. "One night, she called to say she was leaving to visit El-Karia. She asked me to wait a day, then reach out to Omar to help with you and your sister. Then I heard the news about Train 63 . . ."

Zahra trailed off and started crying. Dalia consoled her. It was several minutes before she could speak again. "Your father is a good man, ya Nasser," she said. "He created the grave in El-Manara so she'd feel closer to you."

Seeing the bitterness on Nasser's face, she stood suddenly and crossed the room to fetch something from a jewelry box on her dresser. Returning to Nasser, she handed him an ornate and ancient ring.

"This belonged to your mother," she said solemnly. "Now it is yours."

Nasser stared at the ring in confusion. Surely this had come from the El-Mohammedi side.

"Her engagement ring from Omar," Zahra explained. "She gave it to me for safekeeping when they were fighting."

Outside, as they got into the car to leave, Nasser looked away from Dalia, trying to hide his rising emotions. He covered his face in his palms and began to heave. It was the one and only time Dalia saw him weep. She held him close, consoling him.

Suddenly, Nasser wiped away his tears. He turned to Dalia

and handed her the ring. "Take this," he said. "You're the only one I trust."

Dalia was touched. She held the precious ring reverently in her palms for a moment, then met Nasser's eyes. Dalia sensed that of everything Nasser had learned about Fatimah's secret past, the hardest part involved Omar. His father had lied to him for longer than he could remember.

2001: ROCK ISLAND

"You guys are knocking this out of the park," Matt gushed, and he really meant it. He loved working with kids, especially ones like these—smart, passionate, and obsessed with robotics, just like Matt had been in high school. Even with his grueling course load at West Point, Matt had still managed to find time to volunteer at a local robotics club. He was happy to be following suit here on Rock Island.

Upping the ante this time, Matt introduced his team to the geolocation algorithm he'd been tinkering with as a cadet, which could be a game-changer in robotics arenas. Beyond the cameras and "whisker" touch probes that every android used to navigate unfamiliar terrain, Matt had the inspiration to introduce towers on the periphery of the arena, which would provide reference data their robot could mine for triangulation, enhancing its ability to navigate obstacles.

Matt was amazed at his team's ability to debug the code and make it run seamlessly. Every time he challenged them, the kids rose to the occasion and wanted more.

"Mr. Matt?" Vinnie Gutierrez waved his hands from the back of the room, where he was fine-tuning the team's latest prototype. "When are we gonna get into public-key cryptography?"

"Hold your horses, kiddo." Matt laughed. "One step at a time."

Matt loved working with kids and couldn't wait to be a dad, which now, all of a sudden, seemed like an imminent possibility. He was amazed at how quickly it had all happened. Matt had never imagined he'd meet the love of his life so soon, at his very first post, no less, especially a woman as amazing as Stephanie Bradford.

It was the hand of God—of that Matt was certain. Who else would have whispered the idea in his head of requesting Rock Island as one of his choices? Who else could have guided the assignment officer to pick this match? And what had prompted both Matt and Stephanie to attend the "Blue Jeans & Bling" fundraiser last spring for CASA, a local organization that supported foster children? It was their love of kids, no doubt, but it was also something else—and that something else had also pulled cosmic marionette strings to arrange for them to be seated at the same table.

Their chemistry had been instant. She was his type—athletic, ambitious, sassy, and smart enough to impress the top professors in her MBA program. Stephanie was equally impressed with this strapping young West Point grad clearly destined for great things —with his degree in electronic engineering and his vision of using technology to make the world a safer place. The conversation flowed effortlessly, and by the time they hit the dance floor, well, that was when Cupid pulled out his quiver. Matt, a seasoned jitterbug, led Stephanie with confidence and grace, swirling her in for a sudden kiss, perfectly timed to coincide with the final down-beat of the song. From that moment, they became inseparable.

When Stephanie introduced Matt to her impressive *Mayflower* family of bankers, lawyers, and politicians, her Uncle Pete took her aside and whispered, "This one's a keeper."

Stephanie nodded vigorously.

"Does he have political aspirations?" he inquired.

"Not yet." She smiled. "But he's ambitious—like me."

"Good," said Uncle Pete. "I could see a guy like that in the Oval Office."

Stephanie blinked. That meant a lot coming from her uncle, who just happened to be a United States Senator. Republican, of course.

~

The full-court press began three months later at their wedding, which took place at Quarters One, a sprawling Italianate villa that had once served as the residence for the commanding officer of the Rock Island Arsenal. With its fifty-plus rooms and some twenty-two thousand feet of floor space, Quarters One ranked among the largest federal residences in the United States—second only to the White House. While parts of the building were available for private events, especially for members of the military, all it took was one phone call from Uncle Pete to secure the entire estate for his beloved niece—waiving the fee, no less, even though the Bradfords could certainly afford it. They even got the grand lawn, with its spectacular views of the Mississippi River, which was where they'd set up the seating and outdoor altar.

Matt looked impressive in his army formals and spit-shined shoes; Stephanie was stunning in her Vera Wang dress. The wedding photographers couldn't get enough of them, and they'd also invited press, naturally, having secured top billing above the fold in the wedding section of Sunday's *Tribune*, courtesy again of Uncle Pete. All of this was a bit head-spinning for Matt and his family, who were accustomed to a more low-key way of doing things.

Still, Cecilia Drabek was beside herself, handkerchief at the ready for the tears of joy that kept flowing and flowing. Matt was her only child—a son who had lost his father far too young. Her second husband, Thomas Drabek, was a gentle and supportive man, but he could never replace what had been taken from Matt. And yet, Matt had grown into the kind of man she always believed he could be.

She leaned close, her voice trembling with emotion as she whispered in his ear, "Ambrozy would have been proud of you. You deserve every success."

Matt felt the weight of her words settle into him, grounding him. But more than anyone, it was his mother who had shaped him. She had been the one constant in his life, steadfast through every twist and turn.

In his first act of chivalry, Matt was willing to set aside his Catholicism to have their wedding officiated by a Methodist minister who happened to be a cousin of Stephanie's dad;

but to purify himself before God, Matt had slipped off earlier that Sunday to receive Holy Communion at St. Mary's. He made sure to tell his mother—he wanted her to know he hadn't forgotten their church. And even though Matt would've been content with a "best friends and immediate family" wedding, he conceded to the large guest list that Stephanie favored. She had a huge heart, and it gave Matt great joy to see her so happy. For him, shaking two hundred hands on the receiving line was a little surreal, but he accepted it with grace as another act of chivalry.

Stephanie wanted everyone she knew to be there when she walked down the aisle—her sorority sisters, the high school swim team she'd captained, and even her kindergarten teacher, Mrs. Staples, whom she still adored. The biggest hug of all went to her cousin Risa, from whom Stephanie was inseparable. Their mothers, Sarah and Sophie, were twins—so identical that no one could tell them apart. They'd even swapped identities a few times in school to prank their teachers. So, it had come as a shock to everyone when Stephanie's mother, Sarah, converted from Judaism and became a Methodist to marry her dad.

"*Mazel tov!*" exclaimed Risa, holding Stephanie's hands.

"Thank you, cuz." The bride beamed. She'd heard that Risa had a new mystery man in her life, and she couldn't wait to meet him during the New York trip the cousins had planned for the end of summer. "I'm aiming at *you* when I toss the bouquet," Stephanie threatened with a smile. Though she was eager to continue gossiping with Risa, her mother soon swooped in to whisk her away for the next phase of the carefully orchestrated evening.

When Stephanie and Matt took their places at the table, the pressure escalated. No sooner had Stephanie made a comment about their adorable flower girl than Mrs. Bradford came in with, "You're not going to make us wait too long to have one of your own, are you, Steph?"

"Not so fast," Mr. Bradford interrupted. "First she gives me one or two years at the bank." He had proudly built Arsenal Savings & Loan from the ground up—every pencil and every paper clip—sometimes referring to it as his first child. Stephanie was excited to follow in her father's footsteps, but she also wanted to forge her own path.

Next, it was Matt's turn to be interrogated when Uncle Pete pointed his fork at him with a smile and asked, "Tell me, Matt, what are you working on over at the arsenal?"

"Keeping our boys supplied with ordnance, Senator," Matt replied. "The usual stuff. We're also doing a lot of encryption work, finding new ways to communicate without the enemy listening in, and a whole new generation of surveillance technology that I'm not at liberty to discuss."

"I'm assuming you mean the new UAVs," said Pete, who chaired the Senate Intelligence Committee. "We had a briefing on the Hill."

"I can't confirm or deny that, sir," Matt demurred.

"Good boy." The senator grinned. "You know, I was thinking, Matt, that we oughta get you over to DC."

Matt winced slightly, trying hard not to show it. He knew that Uncle Pete had parlayed a stint in the military into a successful run for elected office—and that the Bradfords expected Matt to follow suit. But Matt, like Stephanie, cherished his independence. He wanted to make his own way without help from family. He certainly didn't want to be a pawn in someone else's chess game. Plus, while Matt considered himself a Republican and had voted for Bush, the Bradfords were unabashedly right wing and talked openly about it. In his family, politics was a private matter, to be wrestled over in each person's conscience. With the Bradfords, party dogma was shared as easily as English peas.

"I could make some calls," continued Pete, "probably get you a staff position with the joint chiefs. That'd put you into the White House. We'd have to get you a security clearance, of course, but that shouldn't be a problem. In fact, you might want to consider joining 'the Company.'"

Matt knew, of course, what he meant—an insider's moniker for the CIA. It was the first idea from Senator Pete that held a certain appeal—espionage had been a fantasy of Matt's since his boyhood when he'd devoured books by John le Carré and Ian Fleming.

"We'd have secrets, you and me." The senator winked. "Even from her." He pointed to Stephanie, and that's when Matt realized that for the Bradford clan, whose roots traced back to the *Mayflower*, country came before family.

Matt caught Stephanie's eye. *Could I really do that?*

2001: MANHATTAN

No one in her family knew she'd been seeing a Muslim man for almost nine months. While Joe Bradford had married across faiths when he'd wedded Risa's Aunt Sarah, Methodist and Jew seemed less of a leap, somehow, than Jew and Muslim.

What am I so afraid of? Risa wondered.

Her own grandmother had grown up in Alexandria, so dating an Egyptian wasn't such a stretch, was it? But it felt different—weightier, even. Risa's Nana had resided in Egypt at a time when Jews were welcome there, decades before the formation of the state of Israel. But those were different times.

Don't overthink this; you're allowed to be exactly where you are.

This was what Risa loved most about her yoga practice—it met you where you were. Her kundalini teacher had said that in class once, and it made so much sense. Yoga didn't displace your religion or belief system; it simply became an overlay or addendum to who you were. That was why it had spread from its roots in India to countries across the world—because it worked for millions—including Risa: a foolproof way to calm her nervous system. And this was the perfect moment to put her yoga practice to the test.

As the plane taxied for takeoff, Risa turned off her cell phone, closed her eyes, and began the ancient yet timeless technique of alternate nostril breathing: inhaling through the left while pinching the right with the thumb, then releasing through the right while pinching the left with the ring finger. Youssef watched her in amusement from the window seat. *Whatever works.*

They were traveling together for the first time, visiting New York—Risa would be meeting Youssef's Egyptian friend, who lived in Queens, and Youssef would meet Risa's cousin Stephanie, who'd agreed to meet them in Manhattan where Youssef had been asked to give a keynote at a conference on cybersecurity. When he'd asked Risa to tag along, she accepted on the spot, excited to be traveling with Youssef and have the opportunity to meet one of the friends from home she'd heard so much about—the one who'd recently Americanized his name to *Adam.* Youssef talked about him less than he did about Dalia and Nasser, but Risa heard plenty of stories all the same. She wanted to get them all straight.

"So, your friend Adam," Risa asked, "he's getting his master's at Columbia?"

"Yes, in civil engineering," Youssef confirmed, "though it sounds like he might drop it to start a business. He's more of an entrepreneur. Not a nerd, like me." He grinned with this little piece of self-deprecation; Risa laughed and took his hand. This square-jawed, dark, and handsome man, with his dreamy eyes and cosmopolitan accent, couldn't have been further from her image of a nerd.

"Adham's here on a student visa," Youssef continued. "But he's trying to figure out a way to extend it, make some money, and send it home to help his family. They've been really squeezed by the government's privatization policies."

"Wait." She stopped him. "I thought your friend's family lost their money during the *nationalizations.* Or was that someone else?"

"You mean Nasser." Youssef's eyebrows drew together. "His family once owned huge stretches of land and gins to process cotton. But it was all seized by the government when the free officers rebelled in the 1950s and decided to redistribute wealth. The

El-Mohammedis were left only with the apartment building where Nasser still lives."

Risa nodded. "He's the one you're closest to?"

A smile spread across Youssef's face. "Nasser is one of those people who comes along in your life, and you know the moment you meet them that they'll be a part of you all the way until the end." His eyes softened in memory, then focused on Risa's face. "Like you," he said, stroking her hair the way she liked so much.

"Tell me more." She smiled.

"We'd spend hours at Kahwaht Sidi Gabr, our favorite café by the sea, Nasser and me," Youssef went on. "We'd argue endlessly about Egypt's future and the role of Islam in politics. I love history, but Nasser *is* history . . . history come to life. Knowing him is like knowing a character in a book. Every name, every date, every dusty old battle I mentioned, Nasser would infuse with resonance and meaning. He could fill in all the nuances, implications, context—all the stuff you don't get in school. His family has *been* there, you know? His home is littered with historical relics that are personal to his family. There's this old rifle hanging over the mantle, for example, that belonged to a distant uncle who fought in Palestine during the Nakba War of 1948—"

"You mean the War of Independence?" she interrupted. "When Israel successfully defended its sovereignty?"

"Yes, that's the same one." Youssef sighed, knowing where this was going.

"And what does *nakba* mean?" she asked, feigning innocence.

"You know what it means." He rolled his eyes—it meant "catastrophe."

"I guess we see it a little differently," Risa teased.

"The perfect place to apply your conflict-resolution skills." He smirked.

"Piece of cake!" Risa laughed, thinking about the many case studies she'd read in her coursework on the tension in the Middle East, which went back to biblical times. Youssef explained that Omar was an expert on every skirmish, and he'd bring them to life in a living history by pulling down a rifle from a wall or sitting astride a saddle that stood on a pedestal in one corner or pulling a prized dagger from his desk.

"To hear Omar talk about these wars . . ." Youssef gazed out of the window for a moment before turning back to Risa. "You'll get to meet him one day," he said, looking deeply into her eyes in that way that always made her heart flutter. "A truly extraordinary man."

Like you are, she thought but dared not say—at least, not yet.

"Are they devout—Nasser's family?" she asked. "Are they conservative?"

"No, Professor El-Mohammedi is very much opposed to extremism. I guess you could say he's spiritual, religious, and liberal all at the same time," Youssef explained. "Of all our gang, Adham is probably the most conservative. He definitely has the most conventional taste in women. He wants what we call a *bint al balad*. Literally, that means 'a daughter of our country,' but what we mean by it is closer to 'a true daughter of Egyptian culture.'"

Risa stared at him, her curiosity most certainly piqued. "Describe her," she commanded. "This mythic 'daughter of Egypt.'"

Youssef sighed, knowing that coming from an ardent feminist like Risa, this was surely some kind of test. Figuring that honesty would be best in this situation, Youssef launched in without apology, "A bint al balad is a girl who breathes and bleeds Egyptian culture, who can manage a crisis as effortlessly as a household. She is a hostess of the first order. But she's fierce too. She drives a hard bargain and doesn't take foolishness from anyone."

Risa couldn't wrap her mind around the concept of the bint al balad. In some ways, she sounded like an idealized American homemaker, concerned with domesticity and decorum, but then what to make of her shrewd business sense and fierceness? Weren't "idealized" Muslim women supposed to be submissive, docile, veiled? Clearly, Risa's stereotypes needed some updating, prompting her to quietly wonder what else she might not understand.

"Is that what you want," she asked him pointedly, "a bint al balad?"

"I want you," he responded with alacrity that surprised him even more than her.

⁓

When they deplaned at JFK, Risa recognized the guy from Youssef's photos jumping up and down, waving gleefully when he caught sight of them. A tall, dark beauty clutched his arm and waved too. Risa raised an eyebrow, and so did Youssef, who thought to himself, *This must be the girl he's been talking about.*

The captivating Latina elbowed Adam. "Are you going to introduce me?"

"This is Valería," said Adam slightly sheepishly.

Youssef gave his friend a look. *You sly dog.*

They grabbed each other in a bear hug. Even though they were the same height, Adam had a good thirty pounds on Youssef. He was built like a wrestler; everything about him was broad: his shoulders, his forehead, his smile. Risa was surprised by the deep indigo color of his wide-set eyes. Valería took Risa warmly by the arm and led them all to the baggage claim while the boys drifted off to one side. While Risa watched the carousel for their bags, she half-eavesdropped on Youssef and Adam's conversation. They were speaking Arabic, but from Youssef's inflection, she knew he was asking questions, and Risa was pretty sure she heard the words *Valería* and *bint al balad*.

Adam replied in English, "Well, she's *like* a bint al balad," he said, "only from Mexico. Full of fire. Really, I'm amazed how much their culture is like ours. Besides, who doesn't want a girl who looks like Valería?"

Risa hoped Youssef didn't. With her cropped cut and petite build, Risa felt small and sexless next to Valería's impressive curves and long, luxuriant hair.

As they made their way back to Manhattan in Valería's dark-green Taurus, Adam turned around with a CD in his hand.

"Guess who's got the brand-new Mohamed Mounir? I'll bet you haven't heard it yet, have you?"

"'*Fi Eshg El-Banat*,'" Youssef exclaimed, citing the Mounir song that translated to "for the love of girls." He clapped his hands like a teenybopper fan. He'd played some Mounir for Risa —it was nice, though different from her Radiohead and Liz Phair collections. Adam inserted the CD and cranked it up. As the opening drums poured out, Valería laughed. "I'm practically singing along with it already. It's pretty catchy. You guys really love this Mounir, don't you?"

"The king is the king," Adam pronounced.

Risa couldn't help but laugh at that. "Okay," she said. "I'm all for celebrating cultural differences, but you've gotta understand something. There's only one king, and that's Elvis Presley."

"I keep trying to tell him this!" Valería exclaimed, but Adam and Youssef shouted them down. Apparently, "Jailhouse Rock" meant nothing to Egyptians.

Later that evening, after Youssef and Risa had put their bags down and emerged into the city, strolling down Fifth Avenue, he asked casually, "You've seen *Sleepless in Seattle*?"

"Of course!" Risa's lightning-quick mind knew exactly where this was going. She'd been mesmerized at age fourteen by the dreamy, romantic meeting between Meg Ryan and Tom Hanks atop the Empire State Building—and so had Youssef, age fifteen, at the Cinema Metro in Alexandria, which was why he had secretly planned a visit to the cheesiest and yet most requisite destination for all new couples visiting the Big Apple.

"Two tickets to the observation deck." He fished them out of his pocket with a grin. Risa was enchanted.

Riding up in silence in the elevator, she felt that flutter again —their hands were not clasped, but their shoulders brushed as they stood close. The gentle hum of the elevator filled the silence with a comforting tension, each touch a testament to their growing closeness. Risa knew that even though his eyes were looking straight ahead, all his attention was on her. She loved how slowly Youssef had moved with her, how modest he was. Their courtship had taught her to appreciate the thrill of the subtle. Youssef's hand on hers was more intimate than any of the more carnal attentions she'd received from others before they'd met. Their romance had begun slowly, and he had courted her traditionally for the longest time.

At the top, looking out over the lights of the city, Risa marveled at the view from the tallest perch in Manhattan. "Second tallest," Youssef corrected her. Little did they know how violently that was about to change, how the whole world was about to change.

~

Their hotel was conveniently located just four blocks away from the NYU building where Youssef's conference was taking place—he wouldn't need to be up any earlier than eight to make it to the first panel at nine o'clock. Risa would enjoy the rare opportunity to sleep in. They'd meet for lunch, and she would come and hear his paper at the early-afternoon panel. Things would wrap up at about four, they'd have dinner with Adam and Valería, and then they'd dash to their late-night flight.

That Tuesday, though, wouldn't go according to plan.

On his way to the conference, Youssef stopped by a cute mom-and-pop place for a paper, coffee, and bagel to go. By eight-thirty or so, he was tucked into a comfy chair in the corner of the conference lobby, polishing off the last of his breakfast and getting ready to shake hands and exchange business cards with other young software engineers. He scanned the headlines: Gary Condit was embroiled in another sex scandal; Jay-Z and Mariah Carey had released new albums.

Folding his paper neatly and leaving it on a side table for whoever else might enjoy it, Youssef stood up and walked over to the trash can with his bagel wrapper and coffee cup. A red-haired man in a bow tie was throwing out his coffee cup; his conference badge identified him as *Steve Someone* from MIT. They shook hands, and Youssef asked him about his project.

Then, time began to warp.

As Steve from MIT introduced Youssef to a colleague, he heard a sound like distant thunder and cast a confused eye toward the big window nearby that looked south across Washington Square Park and a big patch of perfect blue sky. Youssef noticed that Steve had heard it as well. Steve's friend did not react, however—too absorbed in describing an idea he was working on to counter DDoS attacks. This type of malicious hacking was becoming increasingly common lately, he told them, bringing down some major websites, and it was a challenge that many in the field wanted to work on. Youssef was nearly able to forget about the odd blue-sky thunder to focus on these ideas. Nearly, but not quite. Youssef asked him about his mathematical analysis of backscatter, but that strange thunder was still in his mind when even Steve's friend stopped talking and cocked his head to listen.

Sirens began sounding from all around—first one or two, then a few, but now far more than what seemed normal, even for New York City. They looked at one another, and then back to the window. Several fire trucks and police cars raced by, all heading south. But it was what Youssef saw far off in the distance that he would remember until his grave—the image that would come to him, unbidden, whenever someone asked, *Where were you when . . .?*

A column of black smoke rising into the blue at the southern tip of Manhattan.

The hearty conversational buzz in the lobby died down as dozens of engineering grad students stood looking from one another to the window for a long moment, and then, from down the hall, they heard a woman's voice: "Oh, god. *Oh my god!*"

Another long moment went by, and then a professorial-looking fellow with a grizzled beard came running down the hall toward them. He motioned with his arms. "Come in here, all of you! Come into the office. Something terrible is happening! You've got to see this."

Youssef didn't even notice what office they all crammed into. All he knew was that they were packed together tightly as a man hoisted a little TV set onto the top of a filing cabinet so that everyone could see. Crowded as they were, no one spoke; still, Youssef didn't register the newscasters' words so much as the confusion in their voices. The image playing across the television screen was alarming: thick charcoal-colored smoke billowed out of one tower of the World Trade Center, which had a gnarled, sickening gash ripped through its midsection.

"Some sort of explosion," the newscaster's voice said. "There is one report, as of yet unconfirmed, that a plane has hit the World Trade Center." *A plane? How could that be?* Youssef watched in speechless shock as the first shot of the Twin Towers was replaced by one from a different closer angle that showed fire and smoke raging within the hideous laceration. The steel girders striping the building's face were splintered like matchsticks.

The image on the screen flickered. The first moment of an advertisement played, then was cut off; the screen reverted to the first image of the two towers, one drowning the other in its smoke. "A small plane, maybe a private plane," one eyewitness told the newscaster. "It sounded more like a missile," described another.

"How could an accident like this happen?" someone in the room asked. "Don't we have air traffic controllers?"

Murmurs erupted all over the room from the engineers, their analytical minds trying to make sense of something that defied reason. It was amazing, in retrospect, that for sixteen minutes, no one left the small office to find a larger television or some other source of information. Like moths to a flame, they were all riveted by the image sequence unfolding and repeating on the small monitor propped up on the file cabinet while they vigorously debated its significance.

Then a sudden shushing as a female newscaster gasped, "Jesus, no!" What Youssef saw next made no sense. In the lower left-hand corner of the screen, a billowing orange explosion bloomed on the *second* tower. His mind could only process so much violence as real. This new explosion went beyond his limit; he was overtaken by the sensation of watching a video game or a sci-fi movie. "Oh no, *no!*" the newscaster exclaimed again. "A second plane has just crashed into the other tower!"

The broadcasters worked to control their voices, but as they replayed the unreal footage of the second explosion, their newsroom colleagues began to shout and gasp. "It banked sharply and hit directly, perhaps deliberately," the newscaster told viewers.

Another interrupted, "This seems to be on purpose."

Youssef's heart sank in realization. *A terrorist attack!* That was the only explanation that made any sense. And it probably meant that Arabs were involved. *God help us.*

He remembered all those nights sitting with his family and watching the 9 p.m. news on television as yet another Islamist terrorist attack was reported, claiming more lives and flooding all Egyptians with anger—over a thousand in 1993's gruesome daylight ambushes alone. He felt sick to his stomach. *Has this evil arrived in America, raised to an entirely new and more horrific level?*

Suddenly nauseated, Youssef elbowed his way out of the crowded office and ran. He managed to make it to a trash bin in the lobby before he lost his breakfast. Shaking, he leaned on the bin with both hands, waiting to be sure that the nausea had passed. He looked back over to the big south-facing window. To the south and east, the smoke was now unmistakable. Against the sky, so much bluer in real life than on TV, it made a big, ugly smudge.

He found a water fountain and took a long drink, then looked down at his watch: 9:15. Except for his footsteps, the newscast's muffled echoes, and the wail of sirens outside, the hallways were deadly silent. As far as Youssef could tell, he was the only one who had left the office where the horrific images were playing out across the little TV screen. No one had even bothered to unlock the auditorium where the morning conference panels were supposed to be held.

Youssef cast a glance back toward the crowded university office, then thought of Risa. *She can't be alone when she finds out about this!* Youssef sprinted for the exit.

Outside, the sidewalks were weirdly empty; the few people he saw made frantic dashes toward subway stations or doorways. The acrid stench of fire and smoke hung faintly in the air; southbound sirens still screamed, but otherwise, traffic was light. The brilliant green of Washington Square Park, the perfect blueness of the autumn sky, felt surreal, out of place. Like the other scattered pedestrians, Youssef raced toward the hotel as if through a blizzard.

Even though he was panting, his heart pounding like a drum, Youssef entered their hotel room as quietly as he could, guiding the door to close softly. Sprawled against the sheets, a pillow clutched to her chest and sunlight spilling down her cheek, Risa was sleeping the sleep of the innocent. As Youssef watched, Risa's brow furrowed, and her mouth moved as if speaking. Then a smile played across her lips. It broke his heart to wake her from that dream.

Youssef sat on the edge of the bed, put his hand on her shoulder, and leaned down toward her. "Risa," he whispered. "Risa, wake up." She stirred a little, mumbled something, clutched her pillow tighter. "Risa," he said quietly. "There's been an explosion at the World Trade Center."

Risa stirred and sat up. She squinted at him, her forehead furrowed, and she said in a hoarse, confused voice, "The World Trade Center?" She rubbed her eyes and straightened her pajama top. "What time is it?" she asked. "Why aren't you at your conference?"

"Risa," he said gently, "there was an explosion, two explosions, this morning. It appears that two planes flew into the Twin Towers. It seems like—" He stopped. He didn't want to say too much, didn't want to upset her more than he had to. "Nobody really knows what's going on yet," he backpedaled. "But it seems like it might be some sort of an attack."

Her eyes grew wide. "An attack? I don't understand. Are we safe here?"

That question hadn't even occurred to Youssef until this moment. Were they safe? He couldn't imagine anyone flying a plane into a small hotel in the East Village, but then again, sixty minutes ago he wouldn't have been able to imagine anyone flying a plane into the World Trade Center either.

"I think so," he told her. "I don't really know. This all happened pretty much just now. We should turn the news on."

Youssef stood up, went to the TV on the nightstand at the foot of the bed, fiddled with the remote, and found CNN. In the lower-right-hand corner of the screen, the time was 9:54.

" . . . what appears to be a premeditated attack on the World Trade Center in New York City," the announcer was saying. Risa's eyes widened in horror. Having become like colossal chimneys, the fire rocketing up through the buildings had grown so intense that people trapped on the top floors were leaping out of shattered windows to free themselves from the raging inferno, plummeting one hundred stories to certain death.

Risa gasped. These were the images from disaster movies, not real life. It was unfathomable. "Those poor souls!" Risa said, her voice cracking. Cross-legged on the bed, rocking slightly, she pulled the covers up around herself as if they would protect her. Youssef sat down next to her, and they watched together. Theories flew back and forth among the talking heads on the news: A Palestinian group. Disaffected former Soviets. Domestic terrorism. A criminal mastermind named bin Laden.

"We should be helping," Youssef suggested. "All those people in those buildings. We should go there. We should help."

"What would we do?" asked Risa, her face puffy and pink.

For the second time since he'd walked into the room, Youssef had no idea. "First aid?" he wondered aloud, but even as he said it, he knew how ridiculous that was. They would probably only be in the way. Still, he hated the horrible helpless feeling that had seized him—history was happening, people were suffering and dying two miles from where they were sitting, and they couldn't think of a single useful thing to do.

Risa's hand slipped out from under the covers and took Youssef's. It was a small gesture, but it felt for a moment as if a great weight had lifted from his chest. They were together, and

Risa loved him, and somehow everything would be okay. And forever after, for the rest of his life, Youssef would be grateful to Risa for taking his hand at just that moment. Because on the television screen, where CNN was covering the towers live, one of them was starting to quake. A cloud of dust and smoke roiled up to its height from below. And then, faster than he could have imagined, yet so slowly that he thought the horrible moment would never be over, the south tower sank into that cloud and was gone.

Youssef's heart stopped as Risa squeezed his hand so hard that it hurt, while her other hand clamped over her mouth, fingertips whitening from the pressure. From outside the window, Youssef could hear the rumbling, low but distinct. It reminded him of the quieter thundering sound that had been his first clue this morning that something was wrong.

They sat frozen together, saying nothing, for what could have been seconds or hours. Over and over on the screen, the building crumbled and vanished. Newscasters said words, but nothing made any sense.

Then Risa announced, "I've got to call my mom." She leaned over to her handbag and pulled out her little black Nokia. Eight months ago, when Youssef had gotten his cell phone, Risa had laughed at him. "Only doctors and drug dealers need cell phones," she'd teased. But in Alexandria, lots of people had mobiles. Many people in the Third World had leapfrogged the promised landline infrastructure that would never arrive, getting mobiles as their first telephones. And now, everybody they knew in Berkeley had a cell phone too.

Risa dialed, and the uniquely irritating American message intoned via the robotic operator voice: "Your call cannot be completed as dialed—all circuits are busy." They exchanged a look of concern. She pressed the *END* button, then tried her mother again, with the same result.

"Stephanie!" Risa suddenly remembered her cousin they'd planned to meet later that evening; she tried calling her to no avail.

"I should try my family," Youssef said, pulling his phone out of the messenger bag into which he'd stuffed his paper, wallet, and business cards the night before. He sat on the bed and took several deep breaths to compose himself before dialing his parents' number. He didn't know what he had expected—all the circuits were busy for him too. Almost reflexively he tried Nasser and then Adam. He couldn't get through to any of them.

In the interim, Risa had washed up and put on jeans and a yellow T-shirt. She sat down beside him and tried phoning her mom from the hotel's landline, but that didn't work either. "We can email our families from the hotel's business center," Youssef pointed out. "If the phones aren't working, that might be the quickest way to let them know we're all right."

"We should try to eat," Youssef added, thinking of what the dislocation of the day ahead would bring. He wondered what food they would find out there but then reminded himself that this *was* New York City. The world could be ending, but they'd still be able to find a bagel somewhere.

"Is this what it feels like?" she asked.

"What *what* feels like?" Youssef asked.

"Living in other places," she said. "Like . . . Bosnia. Or Palestine. Not being safe. The people you love not being safe. Americans are so used to feeling safe. Is this what it feels like? For everyone else?"

Before Youssef could answer, he was cut off by a furious banging at the door. Both of them froze. The news was still on, and they hadn't said anything about attacks on people in their homes or hotels, but . . . the banging continued.

Youssef looked around for a weapon, panic sharpening his instincts as irrational fears flooded his mind. The only candidate was a nearby glass ashtray, which he grabbed and held up like a hammer before cautiously opening the door.

It was Adam with coffee and pastries. Youssef and Risa exhaled.

"Oh my god, man," Youssef said gratefully, taking the coffee tray and setting it on the TV stand, then hugging Adam. "Thank god it's you!"

"Are you okay?" Risa asked him. "What are things like out there?"

"Eerie. Quiet. Everybody's confused; nobody knows what's happening. I tried calling you, but of course the circuits are all jammed. And then I was trying to decide what to do, whether I should go downtown and find a way to help or just go home. But subways, cabs—all the bridges and tunnels are open going out but closed coming back in, so if I leave the island, that's it. I figured I should come check on you guys, take you back to the house. I don't know what the airports are like, if anything's going to go out tonight, but—" Adam stopped midsentence, his eyes suddenly fixed on the TV.

Youssef turned around; Risa, too, was staring at the screen, her face blank and numb. On the screen was what looked like a desert dust storm. The North Tower of the World Trade Center had collapsed too.

The room seemed darker. Youssef looked toward the window. No longer perfect and autumnally clear, now the air outside seemed hazy. Looking back at Adam, Youssef noticed that a fine dust clung to his hair and jacket, as if he'd been at a construction site. "How close were you?" he asked him.

Adam followed Youssef's eyes and noticed for the first time the dust clinging to his jacket. "Not close," he shuddered, trying to brush it off, but it was everywhere, even on his hands. "The air's just full of this crap. Lots of businesses are closed, but a bakery down the block was open. They were giving out free coffee, and tons of people were in there watching the news."

"They don't want to be alone," Risa said softly, her numb face still glued to the TV.

"We need to help them," Adam said. "We can't just stand by, doing nothing . . ."

Youssef jumped in. "What if we handed out bottles of water? To, you know, people walking out of all that. The air's awful; people must be thirsty."

Adam nodded vigorously. Having a plan—any plan—seemed to make the situation slightly less awful. "There's a Morton

Williams a little south of Washington Square Park," he said. "I'd be amazed if they weren't open. We could get a bunch of bottled waters there."

Risa jumped up, suddenly galvanized too. "Let's empty out our suitcases," she suggested. Smart—they were on rollers.

~

Out on the street, all three of them were quickly coated in a thin layer of grime. The air smelled of burning plastic and metal, sickly and sharp in their throats. The streets were even emptier than they'd been when Youssef had left the conference to find Risa. The supermarket's aisles, too, were strangely deserted, but at the checkout line, the salesclerk was warm and concerned.

"Are you guys all right?" she asked. "You didn't have anyone down there, did you?"

Risa shook her head.

"Marie—on register two this morning . . ." She shook her head sadly. "Her husband works downtown. She was worried sick. I told her to go on home. That's where he'll be heading, I said. Thank god my kids are all in Crown Heights." A tear rolled down her cheek.

Risa reached out to touch the woman's shoulder. "You did a kind thing for Marie," she said. "I'm sure her husband is fine." They loaded up the bags and suitcases with all the water they could carry, then headed south.

Block by block, the air got sharper, dustier, harder to breathe, and soon they started to pass dazed people in dusty businesswear heading north. They offered each one a water bottle.

Some accepted gratefully, stopping to talk; others just accepted the water passively; a few walked on by as if not seeing or hearing. A woman was missing a shoe. A man wearing a yarmulke seemed to be mumbling to himself, his face bruised and scraped.

"Do you need help?" Adam asked. "Can we get you to a hospital?"

The man waved him off. "I'm fine." Then he went back to his mumbling, which Youssef recognized as Hebrew.

"He's reciting the mourner's kaddish," Risa explained grimly. Risa's mood fluctuated as variably as the passersby—sometimes she was her usual kind, perceptive self, and other times she seemed absorbed by some private worry.

God, Stephanie! Where are you? She scanned the faces on the streets.

Farther south still, volunteers were wrapping people's shoulders with blankets. The better-equipped groups had hotel or hospital blankets, but several people appeared to be giving out their own personal household linens. Nurses performed first aid and triage at makeshift stations, and elsewhere groups of people served free coffee and sandwiches. The smoky air rang with sirens and car alarms, and every few minutes, an ambulance or fire truck raced by. Occasionally they would pass a knot of people clustered around a radio or small television, and they would stop to see if there was any news, but it seemed like there was nothing but confusion.

Every now and then, someone panicky and tearstained would stop them to ask if they had seen a husband or wife or dad or friend. One or two had pictures, the rest just descriptions. They weren't able to reunite anyone, but at least they gave people water.

Finally, in an area where the smoke and dust hung thick as fog, they encountered barricades and police who forced them to turn around. They gave out the last of the water, then looked at each other with blank expressions. *What now?*

Ever-practical Adam said, "Manhattan's a mess. Let's check you guys out of your hotel, and then I'll take you back to my apartment." It seemed like a reasonable plan.

They wandered, shell-shocked, back to their hotel. The doorman was long gone. Youssef held the door for Risa, who entered the lobby, saw someone, and began to weep.

It was Stephanie, looking like a ghost. The cousins rushed to embrace each other in tears. Stephanie was convulsing. Risa had never seen her sob so hard.

2001: ALEXANDRIA

Afternoon sunlight was streaming in, along with a pleasant breeze, through the big window that overlooked the kitchen garden, a luxury Houda appreciated more with each passing year—it made her understand just how crowded and barren city life could be for most. Her family still owned this building, so they got to live in the beautiful ground-floor apartment with its serene garden where one could sip tea under the palms and poincianas. It made Houda so grateful. Puttering earlier among the greens, Houda had seen that her *molokhia* patch needed trimming. *Molokhia with chicken,* she thought, *that's what we'll have today.*

The football match wouldn't be starting until later that evening, but Nasser and Omar had invited Dalia to come for a late lunch and then to hang out until the game. Houda, in her usual upbeat mood, was busy preparing the house to receive guests. This felt like a get-together of her "bigger" family—Dalia loved to be around Omar, and she felt like a sister to Houda ever since she and her brother had gotten engaged.

Nasser had been moody and withdrawn of late. Even though it had been his idea, he did not seem to share Omar's enthusiasm about the satellite dish they'd recently installed, allowing more access to European football matches. Tonight, they'd be tuning in to the big game between Real Madrid and AS Roma, and she knew that Zidane, Nasser's favorite player, would be playing. Houda loved the fact that they had a nice family room where guests could come and watch the game together. She imagined herself living in a home like this one day—happily married with adorable children. In fact, she might actually spend the rest of her life right here in this very apartment. Depending on what happened with Nasser and the upstairs tenants, who'd been talking about moving to Cairo, maybe her brother would move right above her. That was the life she wanted. Despite all the lectures from her Baba about maintaining her independence, despite women like Dalia who dreamed of changing the world, Houda was perfectly content imagining herself as a bint al balad.

What's wrong with that? What's so bad about modesty and traditional values?

Houda remembered how uncomfortable she had felt last summer when she'd gone to a private beach west of Alexandria with her friend Heba. The girls there were trying so hard to imitate Western girls by being sexy with boys, hitting on them in every way. It all felt fake to her, and Houda was sure this was not the life she wanted. She liked simplicity and ritual—like putting water to boil on the stove and chopping up some fresh mint for the tea she planned to serve.

Outside through the window, she could hear doves cooing in the branches. Houda reached up to the shelf above the stove for the family recipe book. Earlier in the day, she'd prepared her mother's ful for breakfast with olive oil, lemon, and cumin—a recipe she knew by heart. The molokhia was more complicated, and that's why Houda wanted to consult the book. She'd already poached the chicken with onion; now she was straining the broth and adding molokhia leaves when Nasser entered, asking, "Is the food ready?"

"You're welcome." She smiled at his lack of manners, which prompted him to soften.

"How are you, Houda? Can I help with anything?" He dove a finger into the *salatet zabadee* yogurt dip for a quick taste, but

Houda swatted his hand away with her spoon. "Save it for our guest!"

Omar made a deliberate cough from the doorway; Houda understood the hint, asking her brother, "Aren't you waiting for something?"

Nasser looked a little puzzled. "No, not really. Is there something I should be waiting for?"

"This." Omar was holding a large official-looking envelope whose mailing label said, "Graduate Management Admission Council."

"They came!" Nasser cried, snatching the envelope.

"Yesterday," Baba confirmed.

Nasser opened it purposefully. He was silent for a moment, serious, reading, and then he said, "It is fine." Nasser laid the papers with his test scores back down on the table, and Houda leaned over his shoulder to see.

"Seven-fifty composite!" she read. "Ninety-eighth percentile worldwide! That's phenomenal, Nasser!" She put her arms around him and kissed his cheek, adding saucily, "With a score like that, we'll definitely be rid of you." She stuck out her tongue and gave him a big smile before quietly turning away to brew the tea. Houda was thrilled for her brother but also inwardly devastated. *Will he really be leaving us to go to Harvard for an MBA?*

But Nasser wasn't as enthusiastic as Houda thought he would be. He didn't even acknowledge what she had just said as he picked up a piece of bread and chewed on it. Nasser hadn't been himself for a while, and whenever she asked him or Dalia how they were, they seemed to always say the same thing: "Probably tired of all the work we're putting into the nonprofit."

But Houda knew more. She felt it, and her father felt it as well when he asked her, "Have you noticed anything going on with Nasser? He is just not himself."

∾

Everything was ready and laid out on the side table by the time Dalia arrived. After greeting the professor, Dalia gave Houda a long hug, the way an older sister would, then she turned to give Nasser a quick peck on the cheek.

Nasser quickly moved away from them to grab the new TV remote. That was the moment when everything shifted for four people in Alexandria—as it had for people everywhere.

Nasser blinked in confusion at first, then his expression turned to consternation. Dalia's jaw dropped as she tried to comprehend the horrifying footage from Manhattan. Omar approached with his cane. The entire group was stunned into silence as they watched one plane, then another, hitting the two tallest buildings in that tallest of American cities. At 4:37 p.m. local time, a third plane crashed into the Pentagon. When the first tower fell at 4:58, the only sound they made was the collective intake of breath. Omar tried flipping among stations, but which channel they watched didn't seem to make much difference. All just played the live footage, and no one seemed to know what it meant.

When Houda couldn't stand the horrible images any longer, she went to the kitchen to brew more tea. The afternoon was hot, though not as hot as it had been a month ago; outside, bougainvillea made a cheerful riot of the quiet, shady street. The destruction they'd been watching was far, far away, after all. A world away. Here, it was just another sunny afternoon. Nothing had changed, right?

But Houda was Omar El-Mohammedi's child. She knew too much history not to know that everything was connected, and Manhattan was closer to Alexandria than it appeared on any map. Heartstrings brought all cities close. *Allah*, she prayed, *be with Adham in New York today.*

The water boiled, and Houda strained it over loose black tea and fresh mint leaves, then added sugar to each cup. *This is a time to be kind and nurturing despite how I'm feeling inside*, thought Houda as she carried the fragrant tray back into the family room, where the television cast its blue glow over the faces of her family.

Nasser, Dalia, and her father had been sitting there for an hour or more, still looking stunned. They accepted their teacups with shocked passivity.

Houda thought how much more innocent they had all been earlier that afternoon, when she, Nasser, and Baba had gathered in the kitchen and rejoiced over the results of his test. *Was that really just three hours ago?*

Everyone sat ashen-faced in the sullen television light.

Finally, Dalia spoke. "Isn't Youssef in New York this week visiting Adham?"

"Adham and Youssef," Nasser echoed. "That's right. Youssef emailed me to say that he was going to New York for a conference." He pulled out his phone and dialed Youssef's number, then Adham's, but couldn't get through to either of them. Houda watched Nasser dial, his handsome features twisted with worry, and she thought about how she would have felt if her brother, too, had been in New York today. Maybe Nasser would now reconsider his plans to go so far away from his family. He kept dialing without success. Even if Nasser could have reached Adham and Youssef, what help could he have offered them?

It was horrible to watch the destruction of the towers, to imagine the pain and death of so many. But when the speculation began about reasons and culprits, it became much worse.

"Middle Eastern men admitted to the US on tourist visas," CNN reported. "An act of Islamic terrorism," another network confirmed.

"Will the United States go to war?" Houda asked.

"War against whom?" said Dalia. "No nation makes its attack using stolen planes. This isn't war; it's crime. There will be an investigation, trials . . ."

"You don't think any of these hijackers were Egyptian, do you?" Houda had a sick feeling in her stomach.

"Egypt has had friendly relations with the US ever since the Camp David Peace Accords," Dalia reassured her quickly. Omar was strangely mute.

"That doesn't mean there won't be consequences," countered

Nasser. "Are you hearing the commentary? All these reporters are jumping to conclusions about 'Muslims,' 'Islamic terrorists.'"

"Are Youssef and Adham safe?" Houda asked quietly.

There was silence. No one could know for sure. But Adham lived in Queens. She had looked to see where that was on a map, and Houda knew it lay across the river from Manhattan. So, it was unlikely that Adham would have been close enough to the towers to be hurt in the actual attack. But what about mob thinking? What about prejudices when emotions were beginning to run so high? Despite how much Youssef and Adham appreciated the United States, would they simply be seen as Middle Eastern men, Arabic-speaking Muslims? Would they be beaten? Rounded up as suspects?

Nasser tried to dial them again, with no success. Houda felt nauseated. *If only Mother were still with us.*

"You are Fatimah all over again," Baba had told Houda throughout her childhood. "A beautiful soul; tender but never weak." He would remind her that she came from a long line of fighters: against the French and British invaders; against religious extremists, from Wahhabis to Zionists. But when Houda thought of her legacy, she didn't feel much like a fighter; she just felt exhausted.

What Houda loved most was to make people happy. She loved their smiles when she served them tea and sweet *basbousa* or homemade lamb *fateer*. University aside, the truth was that all she wanted was to be a good girl and someday a good mother, the happy wife of a kind and playful man with blue Circassian eyes . . . like *Adham*.

Houda looked over at Baba, brooding in his armchair. So far, he had said nothing. Now, though, he leaned forward and cleared his throat. Everyone fell silent; they had been waiting for him to speak, to offer the wisdom and weight of a historical perspective. *Please, Baba, make everything better*, Houda thought. His words could be so soothing. But when he began, Houda could hear sadness beneath the calm of his voice, and rage boiling too.

"This *is* a war," he said, "and not just a war on America. This is the war we Muslims have been fighting amongst ourselves for centuries. Men like the ones who attacked New York today blame America, blame the West for our failures." His voice shook a little. "They blame the West for their support of dictators, and for the inhumane treatment of Palestinians by Israelis, and for the suffering it causes—"

Omar broke off to collect himself. "You know, I believe such men have lost their way, strayed from the true path. It all starts with a good cause, with the good fight, and all end up with the blood of the innocent. America has made its missteps, and they have blood on their hands as well. But *this*, to do *this*—"

His eyes searched one corner of the ceiling, then another. It was strange for Houda to see her wise Baba groping for words. Finally, he said, "This is a sad, tragic day. They may have done their violence in faraway America, but those who interpret Islam to justify mass murder are at war with *us*. With us, here, in this room, and with decent and peaceful Muslims all over the globe. They have been at war with us for a very long time."

Omar paused, his gaze growing distant for a moment. "I have been on the receiving end of American bullets, and I carry the scars they've left behind. Scars that are not just flesh and blood, but shadows that deepen the darkness within and around us." A tear slid down his cheek.

Then his voice grew firmer, and he looked each of them in the eye, one by one. "Although all of us pray that it will be otherwise, I fear your concerns may not be misplaced. As a great Japanese admiral said after the Pearl Harbor bombing, 'I fear all we have done is to awaken a sleeping giant and fill him with a terrible resolve.'" Baba paused for a moment, then opened his hands as if addressing the heavens. "What we must hope for now is that the giant's resolve will be matched with the wisdom of power and not the power of vengeance."

2001: ARLINGTON

MATT COULD NOT FATHOM the magnitude of what had unfolded in mere hours. He'd woken up at 5:58 a.m.—two minutes before his alarm—using an internal timekeeping sense he'd developed in high school. He began his day, as always, with a prayer of thanks for all the blessings in his life, starting with Stephanie, his amazing wife, and the support of their loving families who'd helped them to make an offer on their first home. After considering the best options in the DC environs, Matt and Stephanie had settled on a town house in Alexandria, Virginia, a quaint, historic borough on the Potomac River just south of the capital. The inspection had proceeded without a hitch; they were on the verge of closing escrow.

Matt also felt gratitude for his health and self-care routine, which included five circuits of push-ups, crunches, and squats, along with curls and skull-crushers using twenty-five-pound dumbbells. With Stephanie out of town on business, he'd even had the luxury of taking a quick sauna while reading his latest inspirational leadership book, *Straight from the Gut*, by Jack Welch, who'd joined General Electric as a junior chemical engineer in 1960 at a salary of $10,500, then risen to become its youngest CEO just two decades later. After his motivational reading, Matt had taken the time for twenty minutes of journaling, which capped a picture-perfect morning in preparation for a 9 a.m. meeting, about which he was excited.

Though he'd chafed at first against the relentless prodding by Uncle Pete to join the CIA, Matt was grateful finally to have succumbed to the senator, who knew the ins and outs of Washington like no one else. They'd placed Matt on a top-secret decryption task force, responsible for cross-referencing intel across agencies in this new age of digital information-gathering. Matt's 9 a.m. meeting this morning was to meet his military intelligence counterparts at the Pentagon to set up a sharing protocol.

At 8:30 a.m., as Matt emerged from the Metro station with two CIA colleagues, he'd gazed up at the Pentagon in awe. It was his first visit, and he couldn't help marveling at the world's largest office building—over six million square feet of floor space, with five sides, five stories, and five rings, accommodating some thirty thousand people on any given day. Their meeting was to be in a subterranean office in the G ring. Like all visitors, they'd proceeded to the southeast entrance, where they went through security and signed in. A military attaché was waiting to escort them to the meeting room. By 8:45 a.m., Matt had pulled out his laptop to begin his 9 a.m. presentation. That's when everything went haywire.

The first reports trickled in from New York. Monitors lit up with images of the impact on the North Tower. Matt was horrified—*this can't be accidental!*

Then he remembered—Stephanie! She was in New York.

He tried desperately, for seventeen minutes straight, to reach her. But all circuits were busy. No one, not even an intelligence analyst at the Pentagon, could get through to Manhattan.

When United Flight 175 hit the second tower at 9:03 a.m., the slim possibility of this being an accident evaporated entirely. It was unquestionably an act of war. And here was Matt at the US Department of Defense headquarters—exactly where the response to such a threat would be coordinated. Matt felt the adrenaline surge as all his senses suddenly went on high alert—this was exactly what he'd trained for at West Point. But he was having trouble maintaining his focus, his mind haunted with worry about Stephanie. *Is she safe? Please, God, let her be with Risa.*

He couldn't bear the thought of her being alone—and afraid.

To steady his nerves, Matt began reciting alternately a Hail Mary and the Lord's Prayer over and over in his mind.

Thy Will be done . . .
Pray for us sinners . . .
Deliver us from evil . . .
Mother of God . . .

Matt's meeting was postponed, of course; he and his team were summoned back to Langley. But no one could have predicted what was about to happen next.

Just as they were crossing the southwest plaza toward the Metro station, Matt saw something that would haunt him for the rest of his life as a recurring nightmare. At 9:36 a.m., as Matt spotted an American Airlines Boeing 757 gliding in from the west, his heart stopped in sudden horror. There was something terribly wrong. The plane was coming in way too low—and nowhere near an airfield.

Oh, shit!

There was nothing anyone could do to stop the plane, which, one minute later, struck the southwest façade of the Pentagon, ripping a gaping hole in the once-solid structure. Bricks, glass, mortar, and assorted shrapnel rocketed in every direction at deadly speed. Even fifty yards from the building, the debris rained upon Matt, cutting his arms, leaving him bruised and bleeding. It felt like Armageddon.

In the weeks that followed, they would learn that this incident, the first attack on the American capital since the War of 1812, had taken 190 lives all told—65 people on the plane and 125 inside the Pentagon. The experience changed Matt forever. Emotions swirled like storm clouds in his consciousness—outrage, indignation, a desire for blood. The soldier in him was disgusted by this unprovoked mass murder. He wanted vengeance.

He'd cooled down somewhat back at Langley, where he was surrounded by data screens and fellow analysts, whose somber expressions told a story of horror and incredulity at how easy it had been to kill so many Americans without firing a single shot. Knowing that Stephanie was safely back at their Arlington home, Matt buckled down like his colleagues and got to work.

In one briefing after another, the world's greatest superpower tried to calibrate its response. Matt came to realize it had not been an intelligence failure—it had been a failure of *imagination*. The CIA had been tracking the hijackers; they knew they'd enrolled at various flying schools across the country. What no one had predicted was that they would weaponize planes.

"Oil money, Egyptian intellectuals. It always means trouble," commented a colleague.

The Egyptian ringleader, Mohammed Atta, had been well educated, from a good family.

While his fellow analysts were regarding Atta with utter contempt and vitriol, Matt found himself feeling something surprising—admiration. Talk about courage and commitment. In his willingness to die to bring down "the Great Satan," the Egyptian must have felt like David standing up to Goliath. Matt knew that he needed to step up too. Everyone needed to step up. But it was a tall order. Even if American intelligence could find the people responsible for the attack—they'd certainly gone into hiding—how exactly would they respond? Would retaliation bring another asymmetrical counterstrike? Would it escalate, endangering more American lives?

As the briefings and brainstorm sessions continued, Matt found himself mentally writing code. He was thinking of combining his geolocation method with a cluster algorithm. Though the hijackers had used disposable "burner" phones, they could still be traced and tracked. The NSA's supercomputers could easily sort billions of data points to detect patterns. Matt ran the simulation through his mind:

Recently arrived in the United States, clustering in shared locations.
Cell phones at flight schools, newly activated and talking to each other.
These devices move to airports nationwide on the same morning.
A final contact between those phones before they all shut down.

There was no way to claim that surveillance like this could have prevented 9/11, but it was better than nothing. The algorithm could cross-reference the NSA database of sensitive targets —sports arenas, train stations, nuclear power plants—detecting cluster movements and communication patterns. When Matt pitched the idea to his superior, the answer was immediate: "Get it up and running as quickly as you can."

THE LIBRARY OF OMAR
EL-MOHAMMEDI

APRIL 7, 2014 • 9:06 P.M.

October 11, 2001

An eye for an eye, a nose for a nose,
an ear for an ear, a tooth for a tooth . . .

These are the words from *Surat al-Maidah*, verse 45. My
Baba, Omar El-Mohammedi, had me examine them from
his precious hand-scripted copy of the Holy Qur'an,
which he'd placed with great reverence on the oak desk of
his book-filled study. I was only eight at the time, and my
legs still dangled from the swiveling desk chair. After I
dutifully read the verse, Baba explained the context—
ordained to the Children of Israel as part of ancient law.
He produced his translations of the Bible and the Jewish
Torah. He showed me how the admonishment was fundamental to the three great Abrahamic religions.

"How do you feel about this principle?" Baba asked
me the open-ended question, his style of teaching at the
university: questions first, then the lesson. I paused under

his intense scrutiny, which seemed to reflect the gaze of generations, of tribes and warring factions going back to the dawn of time. Swallowing under the pressure, I finally spoke four carefully chosen words I remembered from Gandhi, "When does it end?"

Baba nodded enigmatically, pleased that I had reached that conclusion on my own accord. With quiet pride, he slid a paper across the desk, the weight of his life's work reflected in his eyes. The title, written in bold English letters, read: "If We Cannot Carve Space for Change, Tradition's Roots Will Stand Unshaken and Fight Fiercely." Beneath the title, in neat, understated print, was his name: *Omar El-Mohammedi*.

He watched me closely, then asked, "So, what do we do?"

I paused, unsure, but before I could find my voice, he continued, "We carve the space for change, Nasser. But we do not do so with swords or anger. We fight with the quiet strength of peace. This is how we stand against those who wield violence. We must fight, not just to resist their fear, but to shield the hearts and minds of those who suffer—so that we do not let the darkness claim them."

Baba paused, his expression softening but his voice steady. "This idea—this principle—runs deeper than you think. It's been with us long before Gandhi, woven into our culture and human history. All my work has been about finding answers from our ancestors. The strongest answers, Nasser, always come from within. Our culture, our history offer us many answers, and we must choose which path we follow—and make sure we are not following the rotten parts of the traditions."

He leaned forward, his gaze sharpening again. "Al-Ghazali and Ibn Rushd debated many things, but both believed in the power of restraint. Al-Ghazali, one of our most esteemed conservative Islamic philosophers, taught that personal revenge is the worst kind. 'To seek vengeance for oneself,' he wrote, 'is to bring injustice upon your own soul.' He called for restraint and forgiveness, knowing that revenge only feeds the fire."

Baba's tone shifted. "Ibn Rushd, also known as Averroes—a renowned Andalusian philosopher and jurist who championed rationalism and was one of my heroes—believed justice should be guided by reason, not emotion. 'True justice,' he said, 'is about balance, not vengeance.' We will learn more about them, Nasser, as you grow, but for now, know this: both understood that retaliation only deepens the wounds."

Baba leaned back again, his voice quiet but firm. "The sword may win a battle, Nasser." He paused, letting the words settle. "But it will never win the war for the soul."

But now, I can barely stand to think of that little compliant boy, so desperate for his father's approval. Back then, I nodded along, trying to believe in everything Baba said, in the world he wanted me to see. Years later, I learned something different. The ideas in his books—noble, idealistic—never fit the world I saw outside his study. He was always looking at the world through the same narrow lens, one where peace and reason would triumph. He never understood what I came to know: that power doesn't care for ideals. Power only listens to strength, and the world we live in is full of Goliaths wielding that strength, spinning lies that sound like truth.

And the Davids? They never win. Not in the real world.

That's why I've cast aside my father's work now. He wrote of carving space for change as if it could be achieved with words alone, never grasping that true change is seized by those who dare to carve it with force. There was a time, I'll admit, when I wanted to believe him, when a small part of me thought his ideals might be right. But the world—cruel and unyielding—taught me differently, over and over, until even that hope was ground to dust.

I've had to become someone different. That's why retaliation can't be equal. It has to be asymmetrical—it has to hit harder than they expect, because if it doesn't, you'll always lose.

OMAR WINCED. *Forgiveness is what I taught him.* He double-checked the date of the entry—written one month after 9/11, though, like many parts of this diary, it could have been amended years later. Omar shook his head sadly, eyes lingering on the words, a knot tightening in his chest. Had he failed Nasser? Had his teachings, meant to guide and protect, crumbled in the face of a world too harsh for ideals? He wondered if the seeds of wisdom he had planted were trampled beneath the weight of cruelty before they ever had a chance to grow.

He wondered, for a fleeting moment, if his own ideals had been too rigid, too naïve. But no, he had to believe in them. Without those beliefs, what was left?

A sudden beeping startled the elder, who trembled, disoriented in the darkened study, then fumbled to open his desk drawer and attend to the source of the beeping—an encrypted phone.

"Anything to report?" It was Matt, the American who'd clandestinely delivered the journal to Omar, along with this secure communication device.

"Not yet," Omar sighed.

"Where are you?"

"October 2001," he reported.

"Keep going. Time is of the essence."

After the line went dead, Omar felt paralyzed. He still couldn't quite fathom the situation. The world's foremost super-power—with all its resources, intelligence experts, data analysts, supercomputers—was depending on an old Egyptian professor to prevent a catastrophe that they feared could dwarf the death toll of 9/11. Omar gazed at the numbers scrawled after the fact in the four corners of each page—some of them arithmetic numerals, some geometric hieroglyphs from ancient times. Was there a pattern?

"It's code," Matt had explained. But he hadn't needed to describe the fundamentals of cipher cryptography to Omar—a practice dating back to the Gutenberg revolution, the dawn of printed books. The oldest and most foolproof way of delivering a coded message was to write a series of numerals to specify a word. The first number would indicate the page of a book you were referencing, followed by the paragraph and sentence number, along with the word number within that sentence. The parties would secretly need to agree on this code-cracking volume in advance, of course, which was not the case here. Nasser had apparently buried its identity somewhere in his writings. Matt had a hunch about where they'd find this book—it had come to him from rereading the very first entry of the journal where Nasser had written:

I am the child of every book in Alexander's great library, scattered to the wind and doomed to fire by conquerors and colonists . . .

And then:

The library in which I was born was an echo of that history. I grew inside an echo. It was in the library of Omar El-Mohammedi that I honed Greek and English . . .

That was when Matt had had his epiphany. Omar's library was where Nasser had "decoded" Greek and English, with their unfamiliar alphabets that must have seemed like gibberish to a young Egyptian boy. Excitedly, he had called Professor El-Mohammedi on the secure cell phone.

"I have a feeling he picked a volume from your library as the cipher," said Matt, which was why Omar and Omar alone was now the key to unlocking the journal's secrets.

But which book? The old man gazed at his shelves. There were countless books.

The world's top cryptographers, along with the most esteemed Arabic scholars, had been stymied. The mystery came down to a book that only Omar would know. Perhaps that was Nasser's parting gift, or his demand—making certain that his father would be forced to read every word of his writings.

Omar cleaned his spectacles. Steadying himself with a sip of tea, he returned once again to the journal. On the following page, he noticed the white space with some added text describing one of Alexandria's storied storms:

El-Maknesa—"the Broom Gale"—arrived in the fall of 2001, when an Egyptian underdog had the temerity to fly into the tower of power, sweeping the planet from its arrogant slumber. Two of the four from Alexandria were at Ground Zero—my plans to join them disintegrated.

Omar remembered the moment vividly—the sudden interruption of the televised football match and the disturbing images of Armageddon as Nasser's dreams to join his classmates in America to pursue his MBA were shattered in an instant. Nasser, Adham, and Youssef had been the original "Three Musketeers" at the university—then Dalia had come along as D'Artagnan, their fourth. It must have been so hard for Nasser, who'd been longing to study abroad since boyhood.

But the winter of my life was already underway . . . it had come when I discovered my father's complicity in my mother's death. By pushing her away from us and onto the train where she perished, his hands will be forever awash in blood, his tongue forked in a lifelong lie . . .

Omar shuddered and braced himself for what was coming—a gale of scorn, sweeping away all his efforts and best intentions in the challenge of raising Nasser as a single father. As he read his son's fiery condemnation, Omar's tears swirled with regrets that could never be erased.

PART III

QASIM

Qasim
visits Alexandria in the first week of December,
one of the most dangerous gales,
bringing southwesterly winds and severe storms.

This gale takes its name from a boy—the son of a seasoned
fisherman,
who, despite his many years and experience at sea,
lost his beloved son to the merciless waters.

2002: ALEXANDRIA

THE MAN who answered the door when Dalia and Nasser knocked was around forty, lean and muscular, his plain, honest face still discolored here and there by the traces of nearly healed bruises. He moved somewhat stiffly, as if in pain.

"Hassan Mansour?" Nasser asked. The man nodded and invited them in, escorting Nasser and Dalia to a sitting room at the rear of the apartment, where his wife stood surrounded by furniture that was ancient yet immaculately clean. She gestured for them to sit. As they exchanged pleasantries, a girl of about twelve came in and served tea. "This is our Hannan," the wife declared proudly.

"Such pretty eyes you have, Hannan." Dalia smiled to the girl, who beamed.

"Walid is probably playing football around the corner," Hassan added quickly, making sure to mention their son, the eldest. "He should be home before long."

As if on cue, a strapping, sweaty teenager burst through the front door, carrying an old football. Nasser smiled—that was *him*, ten years ago.

"What's your favorite position, Walid?" Nasser asked. The boy hesitated, taking in the strangers, aware of the class difference. He glanced at his father. *Should I speak?*

Hassan nodded, so the boy said, "Midfielder."

Nasser clapped his hands in agreement. "Me too! Good boy. Everyone always wants to be striker, but midfield gives you more options for a sneak attack. I'll bet you score a lot."

Walid was smiling now, fully engaged. Nasser exchanged a quick glance with Dalia—*mission accomplished*. The best way to gain the trust of anyone was to praise their kids. "May God bless them for you," Dalia said, turning to the mother. "So beautiful and bright."

There was a specific advantage to knowing a couple's oldest son's name, which would allow an Arabic speaker to address the parents using polite honorifics. Now that they knew that Hassan Mansour's son was named Walid, they could do Hassan the courtesy of calling him *Abu Walid*, meaning "Walid's father"; his wife would be *Umm Walid*. These little courtesies went a long way toward putting skittish clients at ease.

"Abu Walid," Dalia ventured to the man of the house, "my colleague Nasser and I were disturbed to hear about your recent troubles. We want to help. Can you tell us what happened?"

"Well," he said, clearing his throat and looking down at the arm of the couch, upset and ashamed, although he knew why they had come. They'd heard his story at the coffee shop from their regular *kahwahgi*. They'd been told he was a plumber who'd been wronged by the system, which was the mission of their nonprofit: to bring justice to those who couldn't make their voices heard. But it had been hard to get him to agree to meet—such was the stigma of having been arrested, even without cause. His shame only made Dalia angrier on his behalf; he had been the victim of gross injustice. *Why should he be ashamed?*

"Speak to us, Abu Walid," she pressed. "You can trust us. We've been successful in working with many people who have been stepped on by the system."

Very often Dalia's clients did not understand that her relentless pursuit of justice on their behalf was her way of showing them how deeply their troubles touched her heart. They needed Dalia to be soft and kindly, as you might expect from a woman—

though often this ended up being the role of Nasser, the consummate statesman. Dalia's nature was fierce, sometimes ferocious, but she did her best to give them what they needed.

"Please start at the beginning, and tell us everything that happened," she requested in her softest, most supportive voice, drawing a pen and legal pad from her bag.

Abu Walid took a deep breath and shifted his gaze. When he finally spoke, his voice was steady yet distant. "It was very late on a Tuesday night," he began. "I'd just finished snaking a drain in Sidi Beshr, and I was worn out, more than ready to come home. But a friend of mine who lives over in Fleming owed me a bit of money, and he had told me that if I came by, he'd have it for me. Fleming's out of my way, but I needed the cash, so I flagged down a microbus that was headed that way. As soon as I was on the bus and the door shut behind me, I realized I was looking at a policeman.

"'*Ahlan beek*,' he said, welcoming me as if the microbus were his, and then he asked for my ID. 'Why?' I asked him. 'What did I do wrong?' I had done nothing wrong, you see. Why should he ask me for my ID? But he smacked me on the head and yelled, 'Don't talk back to the pasha.' That's when I knew that I was in for it.

"So, I gave him my ID. 'Hassan.' He smiled as if we were friends. 'Where are you from?' 'El-Mandara,' I told him, but he said, 'It says Montaza here.' Which is true, it does. 'I live right on the edge between them,' I explained. Then he wanted to know what I did for a living, and why I was on a microbus that wasn't headed *to* El-Mandara. He asked for my friend's name, the one I was going to see. 'Rashid Mustafa,' I answered. Perhaps that name meant something to him because he said, 'Okay, well, you're going to join me for a chat down at the police station.' He handcuffed me and everything, and he hauled me down to the station.

"So, we got to the police station, and he took me over to another policeman at a desk and said to him, 'This is the guy.' Meaning me, I was the guy. I don't know what guy I was supposed to be. But this second policeman stood up from his desk, walked right up to me, and slapped me in the face. I was shocked; who expects something like that? And both policemen started yelling at me. 'Why did you rob the apartment? What did you do with the jewelry? Who helped you? Where's the money?' It was humiliating. I didn't rob any apartment; I had no idea what they were talking about. I pleaded with them. 'I didn't rob anything,' I tried to say, but it's hard to talk when you're being slapped. I knew I hadn't done anything wrong, but I felt guilty at the same time. I think it was because of how they kept hitting me on the back of the neck. It made me feel so low."

"That's horrible," Dalia murmured. Umm Walid laid her hand protectively on her husband's shoulder, a simple gesture that warmed Dalia's heart and gave him the courage to continue.

"There was worse to come," Abu Walid went on. "They took me into a cell and left me there for a few hours. It's hard to say for how long, exactly. There weren't any windows or clocks. When they came back, I was sure they would tell me they'd made a mistake, but no. They kept harassing me and insisting I was a thief.

"Then they told me that they were going to bring me before the public prosecutor to charge me for my crime. They put a black cloth over my head and marched me up and down a series of hallways and staircases. When they took the bag off, I was standing in a small room in front of a desk with a man behind it. 'Please,' I said to this man. 'Help me, ya pasha.'" Abu Walid had addressed the man with a term of utmost respect. "'I haven't committed any crime. Please help me.' Then, before I could say anything else, the policemen put the bag back over my head and led me back to my cell. Many hours later, they came back. 'We're going to the public prosecutor for real this time,' one of them said. 'Can we trust you to behave?' And again, they marched me back.

"When they took the bag off my head this time, a different man sat behind the desk. I decided to wait until he addressed me before I spoke. He said my name, then read out the charges against me and asked me what I had to say about them. 'Ya pasha,

I am innocent,' I insisted. 'I was arrested on my way home from work, but they made a mistake. I am a poor man, working hard to provide for my family. Please, for my children's sake, let me go.' And then down over my head came the black bag again, and again the walk back to the cell. It went on and on, all night. They were trying to exhaust me. They didn't care whether I was innocent. They needed to charge someone so they could close the case.

"Every time I was brought to be sentenced, I could never be sure whether the man I was talking to was the real public prosecutor or not, because surely they would never take me before the real prosecutor if they thought I might speak out against them. So, the next time they took me to a room with a man behind a desk, I said as little as possible. I still denied any involvement in the crime, but I said nothing about the police mistreating me. This man must have been the real public prosecutor, because after he read the charges and I said as little as possible, only that I was innocent, he said there wasn't enough evidence to hold me, and he let me go."

He took a deep breath and looked at them—first Nasser, then Dalia, then back to Nasser.

"Abu Walid, Umm Walid," Nasser said to the couple with strength in his voice, "Don't worry. We will get justice for you."

"What do you mean?" Umm Walid asked, her face pale and drawn, her eyes wide. "What justice can we have? People have heard about what happened, and they are afraid to be associated with us. We count on his plumbing work to feed our family. All we want is to find him work."

"We can help with that," Dalia assured her, "but I would also strongly advise you to let us file a formal complaint on your behalf. I—"

She cut Dalia off. "We are poor people, ya *binti*," she said, referring to Dalia kindly as her daughter. "We can't stand up to the police, to the government. These things happen, you hear about them. But—praise be to God—life goes on. We were lucky; my husband was returned to us, and we are healing. We just want to keep quiet and earn a living."

"Of course, we won't do anything you don't want," Dalia responded, trying to suppress her disappointment. "But I urge you to let us seek justice for your husband's mistreatment. Holding the police accountable for their misdeeds is good for all Egyptians."

"It will take some courage," Nasser added. "You've been through a terrible ordeal. But Dalia is an excellent lawyer who's won dozens of cases. She'll file your complaint. And I'll be right here too."

Nasser noticed their lingering hesitancy. He spoke softly. "This police officer, the man who harassed you—his name is Abbas Abbas, right?"

Abu Walid didn't answer with words; he simply nodded. Nasser continued, "It's not the first complaint against him. Abbas Abbas is already under scrutiny. We, ourselves, filed three petitions on behalf of clients—and there has been no retaliation against them. Once your complaint is filed with the court, you will have protection. Nothing will happen to you or your family, I assure you."

"Assure us? *How?*" Umm Walid jumped in, her brows furrowed with worry. "The entire system is corrupt!"

"Not everyone is corrupt, Umm Walid," said Dalia with a steady voice. "Abbas Abbas is a known scoundrel. That's why we must bring him to justice. But we can't do it without citizens like you stepping up bravely to offer their testimony." She extended the clipboard in her hand toward Abu Walid. "Will you sign your statement?"

He looked over at his wife, who hesitated for a moment, then gave him the slightest nod. Nasser and Dalia glanced at each other in triumph.

∾

The fourth complaint seemed to make the difference. Dalia succeeded in scheduling a hearing date when Abbas Abbas would be compelled to appear before a magistrate. She and Nasser decided, therefore, to pay the Mansours another visit and give them the good news in person.

Nasser had purchased a brand-new football for Walid. From the look in the boy's eyes when he saw it, one would have thought it was a brand-new car. They kicked it around for a few minutes outside, then Nasser followed Dalia as she entered the apartment, carrying a celebratory lunch. Umm Walid was delighted, calling to her daughter and husband to join them around the small kitchen table where they devoured their *kebab wa kofta*.

Then the apartment's front door began to shudder under a hail of fists. "Police! Open up!" The Mansours froze in shock, as did Nasser. Dalia took charge, standing to open the door just a crack and demanding, "Do you have a warrant?"

The police officer at the door was large and impossibly strong. Both Nasser and Dalia recognized him from photographs—it was the man they were after, Abbas Abbas. Even though Dalia braced the door against her foot, he had no trouble pushing it open, thrusting her roughly out of his way, and striding into the apartment's front hallway. There, he encountered Nasser, who made himself as large as possible to block the officer's further progress. "How dare you push her aside like that!" Nasser yelled, seizing the officer's arm.

Abbas punched Nasser in the face with his free hand, a blow so violent it sent him to the floor with bleeding lips. Nasser's animal instincts kicked in. Before he could think, he lurched upward with a sudden uppercut to Abbas's nose. There was a sickening crack, followed by a waterfall of blood.

Four policemen who'd followed Abbas into the apartment converged around Nasser. Two grabbed Nasser, one on each arm, while he wriggled and bucked, trying to get free. He shoved and elbowed, landing at least one solid blow; his voice came louder and wilder as his anger mounted. "You're not going to get away with this!"

Abbas, relishing the upper hand, worked Nasser's restrained body with both fists like a heavy bag, blow after blow, cracking ribs and leaving him limp. Two of the policemen threw a net over

Nasser's head and shoulders; the other two cornered Abu Walid and did the same to him. They began herding the two men out toward their waiting police van as Umm Walid wailed, seeing the terrified expressions on the faces of her beloved children who'd witnessed the atrocity. Walid, flushed with adrenaline, seemed ready to fight.

"I'm a lawyer! I know who to call. You won't get away with this!" Dalia shouted. One of the policemen glanced over at young Walid, making fists with his hands. Dalia quickly realized the situation could get even worse. She restrained the boy, pulling him back into the apartment as the police escorted Nasser and Abu Walid into their waiting van. The doors slammed; the vehicle screeched off into the night. All that remained was dust and indignation.

Tempering her own anger and fear, Dalia consoled the family as best she could, but for her, the greatest consolation had always been action. "Now is the time for me to get to work," she told Umm Walid. "Don't worry. I'll have them back before you know it."

She grabbed Nasser's car keys, which, thankfully, he had set on the kitchen table when they first sat down. "I'll call you as soon as I know anything," she promised.

Dalia used the drive back to her small office in El-Manshia as a chance to clear her head. Her pulse began to normalize, her hands stopped shaking, and she used her analytical mind to deconstruct the surreal events that had just transpired. Could it really have been a coincidence that the police had just happened to raid Abu Walid's home at the same moment when she and Nasser had come? Dalia began to have a disquieting feeling in her gut.

Parking the Honda, she dashed into the building and took the stairs up to the office two at a time. Cramped as it was, the office was her haven, full of comforting resources and plans. But what she saw when she came out of the stairwell into their hallway made her feel dizzy.

The office's door was leaning out into the hallway at a wild angle, its top hinge broken.

Steeling herself, Dalia went in. The place had been ransacked; papers were everywhere, emptied-out boxes thrown into piles in the corners. The computers were missing from both Nasser's desk and hers. File drawers hung open and empty, their contents either scattered or stolen.

She collapsed into the chair at her trashed desk, then searched the wreckage at her feet to find the office telephone. The chair wobbled a little under her. She set the phone on the desk, hung up the receiver, then lifted it again. She couldn't remember ever feeling so relieved to hear a dial tone in her life. She punched in the numbers she knew by heart, reminding herself to breathe, counting the seconds until she could put this all into the hands of a lawyer more experienced than she was. She listened as it rang once, twice, and then he picked up. "Baba?"

"*Mahkamah!*" bellowed the bailiff. Everyone rose from the courtroom's hard wooden benches as the judge, a large bald man in a long black robe and bright-green sash, took his seat and pounded his gavel. He glanced, stifling a yawn, at the day's docket —another unruly stack of cases.

Dalia tried to read him—a typical autocrat, not likely to be lenient. She glanced at the side walls of the large hall, where two dozen prisoners were crammed into a series of wire mesh cages, most of them staring hopefully at the man who would soon decide their fate. But not Nasser; his eyes were averted. *Had he been mistreated?*

Dalia shuddered at the thought. Surely they wouldn't abuse a software engineer, a respectable nonprofit founder, a university graduate who'd grown up in Kafr Abdu? It was a strange, sick feeling to see him there, behind bars and metal mesh, crowded shoulder to shoulder with criminals. Dalia wondered how many of the others were as blameless of any crime as Nasser was. Where was Abu Walid? Probably still waiting for his court date—like so many others. The guilt twisted in her gut, a quiet, relentless ache.

His wife had made it clear—she wanted nothing more to do with Dalia or her promises.

She looked from one face to the next, wondering whether each man's family and friends had been as devastated by his incarceration and had worked as tirelessly toward his release. But always her gaze drifted back to Nasser himself. He was thin, haggard, badly shaven; his eyes looked bigger than ever, glassy and fevered. He refused to make eye contact with anyone, not with Omar or Houda, and not with Dalia or her father, who'd graciously agreed to represent him. Seif, her brother, was also present, and Dalia was glad to have his support.

But just as she began to feel hopeful, Dalia noticed a figure in the courtroom that made her sick—it was Abbas Abbas, smirking at her from the witness area, where he was preparing to testify against Nasser and, presumably, other defendants. Dalia wanted to shout out loud that *he* was the criminal—it was Abbas who should be behind bars.

Next to Dalia, Houda prayed silently, her lips moving. On the other side of her, Omar stared ahead as listlessly as Nasser. Dalia had been in court with clients dozens of times, but today her belly was filled with butterflies as if it were her first time. Taking in the courtroom's elaborate wrought-iron balustrade, Dalia remembered the first time she and Nasser had sat in this room. On that day two years ago, their briefcases bursting with papers and their hearts with optimistic idealism, they were going to argue for the release of a young mother falsely accused of adultery. If someone had told Dalia then that she would be here now, waiting and praying for Nasser's release, she would have laughed.

Houda reached and patted her father's shoulder; he caught her hand in his and squeezed it. Dalia's telephone vibrated. Youssef. She silenced it, then texted him that they were in court at that very moment. Moments earlier, Adham had tried to reach her. Under any other circumstance, she would have taken a few minutes to craft a deliberate and elaborate response. This time, Dalia typed three words: *Pray for us.*

When Nasser's case number finally came up, the bailiff went

to his cage, unlocked the padlock, and escorted him to the judge's bench, where he was joined by Dalia's father, who pleaded eloquently for clemency. The judge appeared unconvinced. Banging his gavel, he said, "Charged with attacking a police officer and running a nonprofit without the proper filings, I hereby find Nasser El-Mohammedi guilty of both crimes—with the sentence of two years in prison."

Houda burst into tears. Dalia audibly gasped. Mixed with her incredulity was that same gnawing guilt. It had been *her* who'd founded the nonprofit, yet she hadn't been charged—not that there was any crime; everything was in order. All their paperwork had been filed correctly; Dalia had been meticulous about following the law to the letter. This ruling was a mockery.

Adding to the injustice, Dalia saw Abbas Abbas grinning at her, while pointing mockingly at Nasser. She felt her blood boil. Dalia had no idea how she managed to cross the crowded courtroom with such alacrity, but she found herself suddenly standing before the corrupt officer and shouting, "Ya *zabela*, you garbage of a human being!"

Abbas frowned, raising his burly hand to slap Dalia, when Seif swooped in to intervene. "You know who we are? You know who I am?" Though Seif wasn't in uniform, policemen like Abbas knew that he was a military officer on a rising trajectory—someone not to be messed with. So, Abbas backed off as Seif escorted his shaking sister toward the exit in tears. The thought that kept swirling through her head was, *It is all my fault.*

2003: BERKELEY

NEVER HAD she felt more isolated. It was confusing. It made no sense.

Here she was, holding hands with the Egyptian engineer who'd swept her off her feet, surrounded by thousands of fellow activists, all marching for peace, and yet Risa felt like she was entirely alone. It was the nature of the times—a nation more divided than ever before.

In the wake of 9/11, the country had briefly come together with support and sympathy from all corners of the Earth. How quickly that had crumbled. Less than two years later, America was now split into two opposing camps—each entrenched and utterly convinced of its position. One side believed war was folly, particularly this war, given that Iraq had nothing whatsoever to do with the 9/11 attacks; the other side felt Islam was evil, and that an overwhelming show of force was needed to keep America safe from extremists. This divide had become vividly apparent to Risa one month earlier, when she'd attended a dinner party hosted by her cousin Stephanie in Alexandria, Virginia. Knowing it would be a right-leaning crowd, Risa had wisely decided to leave Youssef at home, a decision she did not regret.

Stephanie's husband, Matt, was in town, and he'd invited his West Point classmate Kyle Primeaux, who now worked at the

Pentagon and had very strong opinions about Muslims. Stephanie had cooked gumbo with homemade croutons, but all the spoons were set down suddenly as the group gathered around the new plasma screen Matt had recently installed above the hearth to watch a scheduled prime-time speech by the president.

The initial images were confusing—the broadcast seemed to be originating from out at sea. The dozen guests watched curiously as a fighter jet came plummeting from the cloud cover for an arrested landing on an aircraft carrier. As the Lockheed S-3 Viking taxied to its parking berth and folded its wings, Kyle noticed its designation: *Navy One.*

"Holy shit." He glanced at Matt. "Is this what I think it is?"

Sure enough, the cockpit opened to reveal President George W. Bush, waving, all smiles in his green aviator jumpsuit. Every seaman on the ship stood ramrod straight, proudly saluting their commander-in-chief as he strode nonchalantly toward the bridge, where a giant banner read, "Mission Accomplished." That's when Risa's heart sank. This was no press conference; it was a staged propaganda event, which seemed to be working brilliantly.

"Fuck yeah!" Kyle hooted.

President Bush, having swiftly changed into a black suit and red tie, addressed the American public, declaring, "Major combat operations in Iraq have ended. In the battle of Iraq, the United States and our allies have prevailed."

What a joke. Risa rolled her eyes in derision.

For Risa, the so-called "war on terror" was the biggest disaster in American history—one that would cost hundreds of thousands of lives and trillions of dollars, while also eroding the most sacrosanct constitutional rights in the name of "homeland security." That was why, a month later, antiwar activists now gathered for this protest march. Many of the faces surrounding Risa were her classmates and professors in the Peace Studies and Conflict Resolution program.

"Stop this war!" they shouted in unison, marching through Sather Gate with its iconic ironwork to storm onto the UC Berkeley campus. Holding Risa's hand, Youssef felt both nervous and exhilarated. On one hand, it was thrilling to be in a country where such demonstrations were not only permitted, but this right to protest and even criticize the government had been written into its very constitution. Yet, with distrust of the system deeply embedded in the DNA of those who didn't enjoy that right, Youssef found himself glancing around in concern, half-expecting the gathering to be shut down by soldiers and tanks. There would certainly be undercover FBI officers at a gathering like this. Youssef noticed an aging hippie with mirrored sunglasses, a Woodstock-era denim jacket, and a rudimentary placard that said, "Down with Bush!"

Is that a wig? Youssef wondered. He imagined a buzz cut underneath. *Is there a lipstick camera hidden in the top button of his jean jacket?*

"Are you okay?" Risa asked, noticing Youssef lost in his thoughts.

He squeezed her hand and smiled. "Great!" he responded, which was partially true.

They marched past the Cesar Chavez Student Center and Bancroft Library, then along the Campanile Esplanade at the heart of campus, where they stopped to hear the speakers. Imogene Sanchez, founder of the Berkeley Indigenous Coalition, an organization that Risa supported, took the podium to address the crowd underneath the iconic bell tower.

"What'd we learn from Watergate?" she bellowed into her megaphone. "Follow the money!"

"You tell 'em, sister!" Risa shouted.

"Who's getting rich off this war?" she asked the crowd. "It ain't rocket science. When America sends soldiers to the Mideast, it always comes down to one three-letter word. Say it!"

"*Oil!*" the protestors shouted in unison.

"That's right, people," continued Imogene. "Have you heard of a company called Halliburton that was awarded no-bid contracts worth billions? It's *our* money, people—it's taxpayer money. Guess who used to be the CEO of Halliburton? I'll give you a hint: his first name is Dick."

"Cheney!" The crowd was lapping it up.

"Yep. That's him. The puppet master—the guy who's working those marionette strings." Imogene was on fire. "He started pulling those strings as secretary of defense under Papa Bush. Guess who got one of the biggest contracts to clean up Kuwait after the First Gulf War?"

"Halliburton!" responded the protestors.

"It ain't rocket science, people," Imogene continued.

Risa nodded and whistled. But Youssef suddenly felt his heart race, pumping cortisol and adrenaline throughout his body. Breaking into a cold sweat, Youssef realized he was experiencing PTSD. The mention of Kuwait was rocketing him back to a traumatic memory from his childhood.

"*Yalla, yalla!*" Youssef's father shouted on that terrifying night in 1990. No one in the family had slept. All night, Baba had kept going outside, then coming back drenched with sweat. He wouldn't let any of the rest of them go out—not Youssef; not his big sister, Iman; not even his wife. But now, with sunrise still an hour off, he told them, "There's no time. We have to go *now*." He shouted frantically for everyone to get in the car.

Young Youssef dashed into his room and stuffed his duffel bag with his favorite jeans and T-shirts; the latest action novel about Ragol El-Mostaheel, *The Man of the Impossible*, which his friend Marwan had loaned him; a football autographed by Ahmed El-Kass. As an afterthought, he added his toothbrush. Youssef was in the living room trying to wrangle their new Nintendo into his pack when his father appeared over him and said, "No, Youssef! Only the essentials."

"This *is* essential," Youssef insisted. Then they heard a gunshot, clear in the night. After a heartbeat of silence, there was another. Suddenly, Youssef understood what his father meant. He dropped the game console and went instead for the framed school photos of his sister and himself that sat atop the television. He grabbed his parents' wedding album from the sideboard too and dashed to the door.

The heat outside was like a wall. Youssef held his breath as he ran from the cool of the air-conditioned house to the family's Chevy Caprice, which had seemed deliciously roomy when they'd bought it. Now, as he shoved first his duffel bag and then himself into the roasting back seat where his sister waited with her two bags and her body pillow, it seemed impossibly cramped. He buckled himself in as his mother started passing in bags and plastic containers full of food.

Another round of shots pierced the predawn stillness as Youssef's father cranked the car and they sped out through the sleeping neighborhood. They kept to the back roads, away from lights and soldiers and shouting, driving in silence, muscles tensed as if for a fight. As the sun's first light broke over the horizon, Youssef could see abandoned cars along the sides of the road. A tire lay on the sand, burning. Everything seemed unreal.

"The night has ended," Youssef's mother, Soad, sang, a tremor in her voice. "And the sun has risen, and the bird sang, *saw saw.*"

"Mama, we're not babies," Youssef started to protest, but before he could finish, his sister joined in. When Youssef was little, his mother had sung this song to distract him when he skinned his knee or woke up from a nightmare. Now his mother's and sister's voices strengthened one another.

Finishing the song, they fell silent once again, which quickly became too foreboding. Baba turned on the car stereo; from the cassette deck, Mohamed Mounir's newest, "Ya *Iskandaria,*" blared from the speakers. Youssef and his sister both idolized Mounir. Baba caught the boy's eyes in the rearview mirror. "It's a good omen," he said, giving his son a smile—the track that happened to be cued up was Mounir's love song to Alexandria. "Inshallah we will cross over into Saudi Arabia soon, and then we will be fine all the way home."

Home . . . to Iskandaria. It felt strange. They went to Iskandaria—Alexandria—for most of their holidays; it was where Youssef's grandparents and cousins lived. But most of his childhood had been spent in Abu Dhabi, Doha, and now in Kuwait City, where Baba worked as a petroleum engineer. Was Alexandria, was Egypt, really home?

Youssef thought back to earlier that night, when he'd stopped pretending to be asleep. He had been lying in bed, the sheet pulled up over his head, but his ears wide open to catch every scrap of his parents' tense conversation. The house was small, its surfaces stone for coolness, so voices carried through it.

"Can't we wait and see?" his mother asked.

"Saddam has a million soldiers," his father reflected, "and now that the long war with Iran is over, they have no jobs. Their lives are a mess. They left their wives to go to Iran, they left their educations unfinished, they left behind any prospect of decent civilian work. And now they're here. What do you think will happen?"

His mother's reply was too quiet to make out, but his father went on more loudly. "He ruined his country. I don't care what the Americans, Saudis, or Kuwaitis promised him; I don't care if they used him; and I don't care if he let himself get played. All I know is that a strongman with an army is always dangerous."

"But do we have to cross at Khafji?" Soad asked. "It takes us so far out of our way, and we don't know that road."

"It's got to be Khafji," his father insisted. "It's the only official crossing point from Kuwait into Saudi Arabia, and it takes us directly away from Iraq. If we leave tonight, we may be able to avoid Saddam's troops altogether. Listen, Soad. This is a confusing time. Arabs invading Arabs! Sunnis killing Sunnis! These are not Shia from Iran. There's only one thing we can trust: oil. Oil is a line even Saddam can't cross. The Saudis have the biggest oil reserves in the region, which means America will not allow this madman to invade them. Oil and Israel: those are the two things America will protect at all costs, so that's where we'll be safe. We can slip away to Saudi Arabia tonight, but I swear to you, Soad, if I had to go to Israel to keep my family safe, then so help me, I would do it."

Hours after this fraught argument, the packed-to-the-roof

Caprice sat in a line of other packed-to-the-roof cars, most of them nice ones like theirs, all of them headed south along the coast to Khafji. The road curved slightly, so Youssef could see all the cars between his family and the border checkpoint, where uniformed guards were reviewing documents and waving cars through one at a time, stopping to search some. To pass the time, he counted the cars ahead of them in line: fifty-one. Then he looked more closely to see if he recognized anyone in any of the cars. It would have been fun to see his friend Marwan here, in the middle of this crazy adventure.

When it was finally their turn at the crossing, his father had the family's passports and an envelope full of cash ready, but the guard made him open the trunk anyway. Youssef turned around in his seat to watch the soldier's inspection. He reached into the trunk and pulled out the Super Nintendo. *Baba brought it after all!* Youssef thought excitedly. *What made him change his mind?*

The guard held up the game console. "This is a nice device," he remarked.

"I brought it as a gift for you," his father lied. For a moment, Youssef was furious with him for giving away his game, but then, reflected in the rearview mirror, he saw his father's eyes. They were full of fear. Youssef hated that fear. He hated how afraid all of them had been all night, and he especially hated seeing his strong, smart father afraid. He hated that smug guard who grinned as he waved the Caprice through, the Super Nintendo tucked under his arm.

On the outskirts of Khafji, Baba pulled the car over to let everyone stretch their legs. He stayed with the car, poring over maps he had spread out across the trunk. The rest of the family took a walk along the roadside, enjoying the space to move and the relief of having avoided a danger they still couldn't quite imagine. Even the harsh morning sunshine seemed cheerful after the night's turbulence. Iman had pointed out a small oasis in the distance when a passing car slowed almost to a halt and rolled down its window.

"Ya *hurma*!" a man shouted from the passenger window.

Youssef's mother looked over at him, confused, but it was clear he wasn't talking to her. "Woman!" he shouted again.

Finally, Iman turned around. She was fifteen, but she looked older, tall and pretty. Her flowered walking shorts covered her legs nearly to the knee but revealed her strong, slim calves. "What are you doing, woman?" the man yelled. "Go cover yourself! You should be ashamed!" He hissed like a cat. Iman stood paralyzed for a moment, then bolted for the Caprice like a deer.

His father ran over to the man in the car. "Sorry, sorry," he said. "My daughter is young. She doesn't know better. I'm so sorry." Apparently satisfied, the man rolled up his window, and the car sped away.

"I forgot what they're like around here," Baba mumbled to himself. "I love the Saudis, but some of them are just too much." He shook his head.

Iman huddled in the back seat, her eyes tear-filled and her face flushed with shame. Ummi was rummaging through the trunk for a suitable skirt. It seemed cruel to make a person wear a long skirt in this heat, but ten-year-old Youssef guessed it beat having strangers yell at you. He wondered why that man had been so angry at his sister. Youssef stared silently as his mother quickly handed the skirt to Iman, who wiggled into it; then Soad wiped away Iman's tears, braided her hair, and tied it under a scarf. "Just for the trip," Mother promised.

She got back into the front seat, and soon they were on their way again. And with each landmark they passed that showed them getting closer to Alexandria, Youssef's father muttered under his breath, "*Alhamdulillah.*" *Thanks be to God.*

2003: EL-HADRA PRISON, ALEXANDRIA

Sharif Mekawy watched along with the other prisoners as Nasser was led in handcuffs through the iron gates. Nasser had been transferred here after serving six months in a temporary prison—and his arrival caused quite a stir. All newbies received heavy scrutiny, especially when they hailed from prominent families. Sharif, who knew of the El-Mohammedis through his younger brother, Adham, was excited by the prospect of getting to know Nasser, of whom he'd heard so much. But having Nasser here as a fellow prisoner was also a painful reminder to Sharif of the *real* reason he was behind bars. It was not for "terrorist activities." That was simply the cover story his family had adopted to save face.

Since his youth, Sharif had felt urges and love for boys, not girls. He knew that acting upon those desires would have brought irreparable shame to his father, a deeply conservative man who never missed a prayer. And Sharif would never have explored these feelings had it not been for that boy in high school, Adel, who'd touched his hand like he understood Sharif even before he understood himself. When they'd jumped the fence to go to the movies, Sharif had felt electrified, especially after they'd kissed in the darkness of the theater. But Sharif had also felt deep shame about the incident, ignoring Adel for a month afterward. He'd been careful to avoid eye contact at all costs, to keep those forbidden feelings from growing. But Adel cornered him one day with an alluring proposition.

"My father is away on business," he whispered. "We can take his car. I'll bring you somewhere we can be free."

Sharif felt his heart flutter, along with a wave of apprehension and guilt. *Should I go?* His mind was in turmoil throughout evening prayers and dinner with his family, when his father kept peppering him with questions about school. Mr. Mekawy expected great things from his eldest son, which worried Sharif even further. *Does he know?*

Finally, his father turned his attention to teenage Adham. "Engineering," Mr. Mekawy declared definitively. "That's what you will study." Adham nodded, appearing to smile inwardly. Sharif knew his brother loved to dismantle the radio and other household items and put them back together to see how they worked. He felt jealous. *Adham gets to pursue his dream—and me?* Sharif had always felt like an outcast. He decided in that moment to honor his own heart.

That night, he sneaked out through the window to meet Adel, who was waiting with a big grin in the alley, having "borrowed" the family car. Sharif climbed nervously into the passenger seat and asked, "Where are we going?"

"You'll see," Adel replied with a confidence belying his age. As Adel floored the gas pedal and started singing along to the radio, Sharif felt his pulse quickening. They arrived at an old abandoned building at the outskirts of the city. Heart pounding, Sharif followed him inside.

It was a shady place of seemingly deserted apartments. Sharif saw the shadows of men hugging one another through half-open doors. Adel took his hand and led him into a room with an old mattress. But just as Sharif began allowing himself to relax, his world turned upside down. The sound of whistles and shouting assaulted his ears as a half dozen policemen barged into the building with flashlights. It was a raid!

The humiliation Sharif felt in the holding cell of the police station became even worse when his father arrived and could hardly look at him. Mr. Mekawy learned the police had received a tip-off about a terrorist safe house that happened to be adjacent to the building where they found Sharif, which they'd raided as an afterthought. He heard some of the junior policemen snickering and pointing. "Gays, ya . . ." That was the moment Mr. Mekawy made a decision that would forever change the life of his eldest son.

Turning to the officer in charge, he said, "My son is not gay. He was in the wrong house. He's an extremist. Extremely intolerant with dangerous views . . ."

"You are saying—" the charge officer began.

"Yes," Mr. Mekawy pounced. "My son is a terrorist."

Glaring pointedly at Sharif, who looked mortified behind the iron bars of the holding cell, Mr. Mekawy declared, "He will admit to his crimes. He will sign the confession."

And that was that. Barely having kissed a boy, Sharif was charged with terrorist activities and sentenced to ten years in prison. None of the family members were present for the verdict. Sharif was as alone as ever.

He'd changed dramatically in the eight years since that fateful moment—by embracing Islam. It, in fact, had saved him.

Now, the life he'd left behind was back to haunt him—no avoiding it. Crossing the rowdy yard, where prisoners were smoking, arguing, and playing *tawla* with scavenged bottle caps, Sharif smoothed back his hair and found Nasser alone in a corner, writing in a journal. Sharif stood there for a moment, then cleared his throat. "*Ezzayak*, ya Nasser, I am Sharif Mekawy, brother of Adham."

Nasser looked up. His glazed eyes brightened as he took in Sharif's trim but muscular frame. The family resemblance was certainly there. "How did you know . . . ?"

"When the new pasha arrived," Sharif jumped in, "I asked around and recognized the name."

He hesitated for a moment. "Did Adham ever speak of me?"

"Yes."

Sharif nodded and changed the subject. "Okay, I never miss a prayer. You should join us. Best way to survive in here."

~

Prisoners wailed beseechingly through the bars of their windows, shouting down to their loved ones who'd formed a line along the wall outside the metal gate. Houda looked up anxiously. *Where is Nasser?*

"You won't find him up there," declared Dalia, who was dressed conservatively, her head covered, like Houda's. "The guards will have already brought Nasser down to the visiting area."

But that proved to be untrue. When Dalia and Houda entered the large, noisy hall—divided in the middle by a metal screen partition that separated prisoners from their visitors— Nasser was nowhere to be found. They waited and waited. He never came.

Twice, Dalia asked the guards to look for him, bribing them with a pack of cigarettes, which they grabbed greedily before shrugging uselessly. "No one can force them to come."

Dalia frowned in suspicion. She shuddered, trying to dismiss the mental picture that was beginning to form in her mind of what could happen to prisoners behind closed doors—and Dalia was hit by another wave of guilt.

"Let's go." She grabbed Houda's hand as the whistle signaled the end of the visiting hour.

The following week, to their great dismay, it happened again. Omar was with them this time, struggling a bit with his cane, as they waited in vain for the full hour—too long for an old man to be on his feet. Omar's legs ached, but not as much as the pain in his heart. *What has become of my boy?*

Dalia wrote letters, as did Houda. There was no response. Dalia's father intervened, calling the prison warden to demand an assurance that Nasser had been receiving their numerous messages. His confirmation made matters even worse—something was not adding up.

Why is Nasser shunning us?

They insisted on a face-to-face meeting with the warden and crowded into his cramped office, where an oscillating fan buzzed dust back and forth across the desk, fluttering stacks of neglected paperwork. Nasser had been sent for; the wait felt like an eternity.

When Nasser finally showed up in the doorway, flanked by guards, they all looked at him hopefully—Omar, Houda, Dalia, her father—but Nasser frowned. He looked different, a beard now concealing the strong line of his jaw. "Why have you all come?" he asked.

"We're here to see you!" Houda leapt up from her chair to hug him. Dalia did likewise, but Nasser gently pushed her back. "I am releasing you of all commitments." He looked Dalia in the eyes. "We are no longer engaged."

Dalia was stunned. The others watched in shock as Nasser turned his back on them.

"I'd like to return to my cell, please," he told the guards.

"Ya Nasser . . ." Omar tried to stand.

"Now!" Nasser instructed the guards, who marched him into the hall, leaving his family in bewildered silence.

Sharif had been elated when the religion study leader asked him to invite Nasser to join their group several months prior. These meetings were like a tonic—a way for their consciousness to transcend their confinement. Nasser appeared to embrace it fully and seemed to appreciate the value of daily prayers. It was the only time Sharif observed Nasser being truly calm, and it had happened almost instantly—the very first time he joined them.

"Pay attention, be quiet, listen carefully," Sharif had instructed Nasser on that day. "This is the man who saved my life, freed me from the prison of desires, and showed me a way forward."

They entered the corner cell, where six men sat on the floor before a diminutive yet dignified-looking man. Nasser recognized him.

"That's the El-Sheikh who—"

"Shhh!" Sharif silenced him. "He doesn't like to be called *Sheikh*. In here, we call him *El-Muealim*." *The Teacher*.

As a boy, Nasser had seen this distinguished face in the newspaper. It was Roken, the well-known intellectual, author, and educator-turned-fundamentalist who'd been arrested decades earlier for his involvement in the assassination of Anwar Sadat.

Roken's eyes were closed as they took their places; they remained in silence for some time. When he finally opened his eyes, the Teacher was looking directly at Nasser.

"*As-salamu alaykum*," he said warmly. "Ahlan, Ibn Omar."

Nasser was surprised to hear the Teacher say his father's name. "There were moments when our paths intertwined," Roken continued, "and in those times, we came to understand one another in ways few could. We had our differences, of course, but our encounters left an impression on both of us. We read history differently, very differently. I'm assuming you share your father's ideas, ya Nasser?"

Sharif noticed the slight tension in Nasser's posture, a small crack in his usual composure. "I am my own man," he responded.

Roken nodded. "Good answer."

Over the following weeks, Sharif and Nasser spent every afternoon with the Teacher. They would pray *Asr* in the courtyard, then head indoors for a lesson. Sharif had heard from Adham that Nasser had a powerful mind, yet he was still impressed by the breadth of his knowledge. Nasser always had a provocative comment, which would elicit a nod or smile from the Teacher, who invariably shot back a question. Nasser's responses were often electrifying.

"Omar taught you well," the Teacher would conclude.

One day, the Teacher started his talk with the following: "We live in a *jahiliyyah* society, a community of ignorance and barbarism." He looked at his students with fire in his eyes. "This ignorant society that surrounds us, that put us all in jail—this society is not a Muslim society. We cannot regard its citizens as Muslims. Their government ID cards may say they are Muslims, but they are not, let me assure you, my brothers."

"And these educated liberal fools—oh, how they love their grand ideas, writing papers about change." He chuckled darkly. "Yes, 'change,' they say, but what they do not understand is that change can only be carved by force, born from the strength of Islam and the weight of our centuries of tradition. Tradition's roots will stand unshaken and fight fiercely—more than they can ever comprehend." His eyes grew darker, sharper, the intensity cutting through the room like a blade. Then, as if the moment had passed, he relaxed again and added, "The West's values have always been for the Western people. They will never give us the same justice; they only care about their own. Islam doesn't bend to Western lies. Its roots run deeper than anything they can imagine."

He leaned forward slightly, his voice rising again. "So, for those who write these papers, I say, *yes*, and, *yes*—tradition, and Islam, will stand, and we will fight and fight and fight. The real fight is on the battlefield and in the hearts of true believers." His gaze locked on Nasser, his eyes narrowing as if to drive the point deeper.

"This elite ruling class has betrayed us, betrayed Islam, and many are nothing but shells for the West. Since these infidels are only Muslim in name, we are allowed to fight and even to kill them."

Sharif's heart raced, his mind reeling from the intensity of the words. He glanced quickly at Nasser.

Nasser was totally focused, yet his expression betrayed nothing.

At the conclusion of the lesson, the Teacher signaled for Sharif and Nasser to stay behind. Once the room was clear, he leaned closer and said, "You two are needed to help restore our society to its greatness." He focused his gaze on Nasser and continued, "True Islam is nonnegotiable; it is true because it is constant. We can't change who we are because of the time or some passing ideas. We don't need anyone telling us how to think. We know who we are—we are the unyielding roots of a centuries-old tree, bound by Allah's words and the Prophet's message. No storm of Western lies can uproot us; no blade of time can sever our legacy. We do not bend. We do not break. And we are not going away."

Sharif could feel the tension building in the room, more than in any other lecture he'd attended in his years with the Teacher. This one was different—more powerful, more electrifying. He felt the urge to rise, ready to fight. But just as quickly, the feeling subsided as he glanced around. His eyes landed on Nasser. What was Nasser thinking? Sharif noticed the way Nasser's eyes flickered, as if deep in thought. Was he feeling the same fire, or was something else stirring beneath the surface?

El-Muealim leaned in, his voice dropping to a near whisper. "Tell me, does Omar still keep the bullet?"

Nasser's eyes narrowed in surprise. "How do you—"

Roken raised a hand to silence him. "There are things you will learn in time, ya Nasser. Your father and I fought for a cause we both believed in, though our paths diverged. When the moment is right, you will understand."

A pall of melancholy fell over the Teacher's followers in the prison, mixed strangely with joy. Their leader, having finished serving his sentence, was finally being released—which filled them with both hope and sadness. How would they survive without him?

As he packed his belongings to leave, Roken summoned Sharif and Nasser to his cell for one final talk. "America has come to our lands, and they have no idea what's about to happen," Roken said with deep conviction. "Our *jihad* is calling us from Iraq. We have them where we can fight them. The American infidels will cower when they witness our resolve."

Nasser nodded in agreement as Roken continued, this time in a whisper that barely carried above the distant clatter of cell doors, "Your time is coming soon. I need you both to join me. We will fight with our minds, our hearts, and our bodies."

"You are the future, my son." He gave Nasser a long embrace. "Our people need you. Islam needs you, and perhaps that bullet your father keeps will find its answer in your hands."

2003: NEW YORK

"ANSWER THE GODDAMN QUESTION," barked the officer. "I want to know the last time you heard from him!"

Adam was seated on a plastic chair under fluorescent lighting in a closet-sized interrogation room. This was his mandatory interview with the Immigration and Naturalization Service. Despite being married to a US citizen, he'd been forced to register as a *foreign national*, which everyone knew to be code for "foreign Muslim."

While it made him furious, Adam knew he had to keep his cool. This officer was clearly trying to intimidate him. He wanted blood. Adam had to assume they knew about Sharif—in prison ostensibly on terrorism charges, which would certainly raise alarms.

"When's the last time he contacted you?" the officer growled.

To get a sense of how America saw things—and to buy himself some time—Adam asked innocently, "Who are you talking about?"

The immigration officer looked at Adam as if seeing him for the first time, his gray eyes widening; his eyebrows, two dense sand-colored caterpillars crawling up his forehead. "Osama bin Laden, of course," he said. "Who else?"

It took Adam a moment to register what the officer was

saying. *Osama bin Laden?* Adam felt all his muscles relax at once —it was all he could do to suppress a wild laugh of relief and bewilderment. The officer may as well have asked, *When did you last speak with Mussolini or Jack the Ripper?* Adam felt a smile growing across his face against his will. "Osama bin Laden?" he echoed, letting his voice express his disbelief. "What do I have to do with that maniac?"

Was the officer messing with Adam? Was he joking? Was he just trying to trick Adam into revealing too much about some harmless infraction he didn't even remember committing?

"I'm sure you know I'm not connected with him in any way whatsoever."

The officer opened the file, apparently perusing it for the first time. He was silent, reading for a long minute, then another. His sand-colored mustache twitched. "Okay," he said at length, looking up and into Adam's face. "Wait here. I'll be back."

So, again, Adam waited. He sat there for forty-five minutes before the officer ducked back in for their next thirty-second conversation, then an hour and a half for the one after that. When it was all said and done, Adam had spent the entire day at the immigration office, with Valería, now pregnant with their child, sweating it out in the waiting room. At least she'd had pamphlets to read—"Citizenship and You" and "Importing a Vehicle to the United States"—while Adam had had nothing to help pass the time between officers poking their heads in and asking, "How often have you been to Al-Quds Mosque? When was the last time you were at Masjid Dar Al-Dawah?" Before it was over, Adam had started to wonder if his mother had paid Homeland Security to make him feel guilty about how seldom he'd been to mosque recently.

Just when he'd thought he'd go crazy—or at least break down in tears and demand a sandwich—the sandy-haired officer returned. "You're just about done here, Mr. Mekawy. Just sign here and here, and you're free to go."

As Adam stood up to leave, the officer handed him his card and added, "If you hear anything, just call us." Again, it was all

Adam could do not to laugh in his round, red face. He understood that after 9/11, an Egyptian engineer in New York might make people feel suspicious, but, come on, they *must* have known more about Adam than that.

The night before, Adam had called Youssef to commiserate. Youssef wasn't nearly as anxious about his own upcoming interview. Adam didn't understand how he could take a thing like this in his stride.

"Really, Adham," Youssef chided, perhaps the only person in America who didn't call him *Adam*. "We've seen governments behave strangely before. Egypt's been under emergency law since Ramses was on the throne!" His exaggeration made Adam laugh and relax a little. "Risa agrees with you, though," Youssef went on. "'These are not American values,' she says. 'Once we start down this road, who knows where it will lead?'"

"They're going to respect you," Youssef continued. "Tell them how much you love it here—that you came from nothing and built a business against incredible odds."

Youssef was proud of his classmate. In the third semester of his master's program, Adam had begun to have second thoughts about an engineering career. New York was so full of opportunities, and Adam knew he'd be able to send his family money sooner, and more of it, if he started his own business. So, with a pair of interest-free loans from Youssef's and Dalia's families, Adam had gone to an auction and boldly purchased two barely used Cadillac Escalades that had been repossessed. He'd gotten the idea of starting a limousine service from riding around New York in taxis whose drivers were often from the Middle East and North Africa, like Adam. "How long have you driven a cab?" he often asked them in Arabic. "What do you like best about it?"

Most of them said they enjoyed the social aspect of interacting with people from all walks of life, along with the chance to explore the far corners of a city as diverse as New York. One driver told Adam about an unforgettable ride he had had rushing a pregnant couple to the hospital. When the mother became fully dilated in the back of the cab, the panicked dad dialed 911. In the ten minutes it took for EMTs to arrive on the scene, the father ended up delivering his own baby on the back seat. Adam's eyes widened, glancing down at a strip of duct tape that had been used to patch a gash in the worn-out leatherette. He winced at the thought of Valería having to deliver their baby in such conditions. But he loved the idea of a car service that could be part of people's special occasions, like weddings, graduations, and birthdays. It was Valería, with her savvy business sense, who'd suggested limousines, an idea that quickly took off for them, allowing Adam to add a third vehicle—this one, a stretch limo—to their expanding fleet, driven by former taxi drivers whom he'd befriended.

It tickled Youssef that a Muslim and Latina were on their way to achieving the American dream. That was why he remained convinced that Adham wouldn't have any trouble in his interview with the INS. "Be grateful, and you'll be fine," he coached, which proved to be good advice.

～

The following day, Adam was back to his usual routine—happily cocooned in the safety and optimism of his favorite shisha bar on Steinway, which was packed with a boisterous throng of Middle Eastern men playing backgammon and arguing about World Cup standings. Adam sipped his tea, soaking in the warm atmosphere created by the room's potted palms and arched windows. He took a bite of ful; it didn't touch Houda's, but it was enough to remind him of home. Inhaling a lungful of tropical fruit–flavored smoke and closing his eyes, Adam allowed himself to relax.

Then Adam's cell phone's buzz jolted him out of his reverie. "*Mi amor*," Valería gasped on the other end, "it's time." Adam's heart leapt; he tossed a fifty-dollar bill on the table and was out the door, tobacco, tea, and baklava abandoned.

Minutes later, he'd picked up Valería in their new stretch limo and was shouting out the window at pedestrians to move their butts out of the intersections. A group of women in quilted parkas and scarves dawdling across Northern Boulevard cursed at him, but Adam was oblivious, concentrating fully on getting his wife to the hospital. The roads were slick and treacherous, the way they got in the early spring when the temperature kept wavering up and down past the freeze–thaw point. "You good?" he asked his wife through the limousine partition, which he'd slid all the way down. She had wanted to be in the back, where there was plenty of room to spread out. "Keep talking to me, baby. How are you doing?"

"I'm okay," Valería panted. "Just get me there, okay, habibi?"

"Be a good boy, Gibrail," Adam sang out. "Don't come just yet."

Valería had refused to find out the baby's sex, but Adam had been certain for months that it would be a son. They had spent the first seven months of the pregnancy arguing about names, settling quickly on a girl's name Adam was sure they wouldn't need. But she still wasn't entirely at peace with his determination to call their son by the Arabic version of *Gabriel*, which they'd chosen for its importance to both Islam and Roman Catholicism. Adam was resigned to raising a son the world would call *Gabe*; he just wanted him to know that he would always be *Gibrail* to his father.

It was just one of the million cultural issues they had to work out. Valería wasn't a practicing Catholic, not really. Of course, she'd been confirmed and knew her catechism and crossed herself when she was reminded of mortality. But to her family's great chagrin, she only went to Mass on Christmas Eve and Easter Sunday. In recent years, Adam had gone with her. It gave him the same sense of community, of ritual, of connection through the centuries as the prayers and services he'd grown up with in Alexandria.

While American culture was full of images and stories to help a child understand Catholic culture—prayer candles, *milagros*, churches in every city—Valería insisted Catholics were a minority in America, and Adam could see that it was true, but not in the same way Muslims were. He worried that if he didn't raise Gibrail as a Muslim and give him a community to belong to, the only story America would tell him about his Baba's people was that they were backward, woman-hating, camel-riding terrorists. That Adam couldn't allow. It had nearly broken them, but eventually Valería agreed that Gibrail would be raised in the peaceful tradition of true Islam.

Adam wondered how many struggles lay ahead for this innocent soul about to enter the world. Were Mexico, Egypt, and America simply too many cultures to juggle? But when Adam glanced in the rearview mirror, he felt a surge of gratitude for Valería. Her sharp instincts and hard work had been the backbone of their success. After years of helping out in her family's shoe store, she had developed something like a sixth sense for when to take risks and when to play it safe, when to cut costs and when to invest, how to handle employees, how to keep good records—so many of the issues that Adam's father had struggled with in his business. She knew New York and New Yorkers, too, and seemed to have endless energy and patience. Adam called her the consigliere of his limousine empire, and she pretended to be annoyed. It was one of their little routines. And when he caught a glimpse of her dark eyes shining from beneath the silken curtain of her hair, he realized how lucky a man he was—she was the loveliest woman he'd ever seen.

They arrived at the hospital just as Valería was coming out of a contraction—perfect timing. She took a deep breath and said, "I'm fine to walk, habibi. Why don't you drop me off at the admissions door and go park the car?"

"Leave your bag," Adam told her. "I'll bring it. But take a cup of ice with you!" She stuck her head through the partition, they kissed, and then she got out. Even hauling that massive pregnant belly, she managed to stride with confidence and grace toward the hospital's big glass doors. Adam pulled away, parked the car, and fished out his phone as he opened the trunk to get Valería's things. Hurrying back toward admissions, he dialed her mother's number.

"Your grandson is coming!" Adam exulted. "Yes, we're just

arriving at the hospital now." Then he dialed Youssef. "We're at the hospital, man! It's crazy! I can't believe it!"

"Not a moment too soon," Youssef joked. "Tell the kid we've been waiting for him to get here and make that green card marriage of yours legitimate."

Adam laughed. The truth was he felt a little bad about how conveniently things had worked out. The stars had aligned. Valería, the woman of his dreams, just happened to be a US citizen.

But dating had been confusing—their first kiss, for example. Back home in Alexandria, Adam wasn't supposed to kiss a woman who wasn't his wife. Of course, many guys did that and more. However, it was just not the way nice boys were taught to do things—it was *haram*, forbidden. In New York, it was a more complicated game. Some Egyptians here fooled around with Americans, adding notches on their belt to prove their manhood so long as they married someone within their community—or, if no suitable match was found, they would bring someone over from back home. Others saw getting a girl to convert as the ultimate romance—they'd become the Prophet *and* Omar Sharif, all in one package. Adam had tried to talk to Youssef about it, but it was useless. Youssef himself had drifted so far away from any notion of *halal* and haram in his relationship to Risa.

So, Adam had to figure it out on his own. He felt like Valería had been giving him "that look" for a while—she wanted him to take things to the next level. One night, when they were watching a movie at Adam's place and Olawale and Kuo were out, he went for it.

Adam looked deep into her eyes and leaned in. She melted against him. He had never imagined that lips could be so soft, so sweet. It was intoxicating, and looking back, he guessed he got carried away. He kissed her again and again, held her tight against him, let his hands roam. And as quickly as their idyll had begun, it was over. She slapped him once across the face, hard, and was out the door without another word.

Adam spent the night torturing himself, praying for guidance, meditating on halal and haram. His face was tender in an area shaped like her hand. He was afraid she'd never speak to him again. But when Adam called her the next day, she agreed to meet him for coffee.

"I'm saving myself for the man I'll marry," she explained to him. "I didn't kiss you until I was sure I loved you. I'm trusting you not to cross the line again—not unless we have a wedding night."

No surprise then. Valería and Adam got married at the courthouse in Jersey City, he
stopped going to school, and now they had a sunny apartment in Woodside with access to a cozy back garden shaded by an apple tree. Would he have married her if he'd gotten his green card already? *Of course*, he told himself. *What would life be without my Valería?* He didn't let himself think of Houda, his impossible infatuation back in Iskandaria.

"Hey," Adam teased Youssef now, "some people like to move at a snail's pace." He wondered if Youssef would recognize the irony in his saying that Youssef and Risa were moving slowly. "But some of us know a good thing when we've got one."

"Well," Youssef laughed, "we snails are thrilled that there will be three of you at our wedding. Go have your baby, brother!"

Adam hung up and dashed toward the admissions door. He bolted over to Valería, who was sitting calmly in a chair in the reception area, a clipboard tucked between her belly and her long, elegant thighs. They kissed again in nervous excitement. Adam sat down next to her, their overnight bag between them—her bag, really, but she'd graciously allowed him to pack his toothbrush in it.

"I hope he comes soon." Adam glanced at the vending machine with a smirk. "I'm getting hungry, and I don't want to welcome my son into the world with Funyun breath."

It was all so surreal. Growing up, Adam had daydreamed about owning a successful business; marrying a gorgeous, passionate woman; and even welcoming the birth of a son. What he'd never imagined was that these things would happen in a country where he could also eat ersatz onion rings that he bought from a vending machine. Gibrail's birth, he was coming to understand, would anchor Adam in this country as nothing else had—not his marriage, not his green card, not his business. America would forever be the country of his son's birth, and as much as Adam loved this country, part of him was heartbroken.

Adam had been born in a land of ancient wonders, and no matter what he did, those wonders would never belong to his son in the same way that they belonged to him. No matter how much Arabic Adam spoke to him at home, Gibrail wouldn't thrill to every new Mounir CD; he would never break the Ramadan daytime fast with family and neighbors, gather at the mosque for *Tarawih* prayers, then run out with all his friends to play night football. To him, a football would be oblong and brown, not a sphere of black-and-white pentagrams. But it also occurred to Adam that even if his son had been born at El-Shatby Hospital like Adam, every father is a foreigner to his son.

Valería pulled out her phone. "Let's call your parents," she suggested. Adam let her do the honors. His parents had been over the moon ever since Adam and Valería first told them about the baby. Adam was their oldest child, and Gibrail would be their first grandchild. One would have thought they were the first grandparents in the history of the world. They'd never mentioned visiting New York before, but now it was all they could talk about. Ultimately, they'd decided that they shouldn't plan to come for the birth itself, in case the baby came early or late, and they were disappointed. But they would come and stay for three weeks later in the spring. Valería couldn't wait to meet them and kept making ambitious itineraries for all the things they *must* see when they came to New York, until finally Adam reminded her that she would be in no condition to play tour guide. Plus, as far as they were concerned, their *grandson* would be the only celebrity, event, and landmark on the North American continent they truly cared about.

As they made their way to the delivery floor, the nurse came to get Valería ready; Adam would be called in to the labor room shortly. After drumming his fingers restlessly against the armrest for a minute or two, Adam unzipped the overnight bag to check its contents, making sure they were organized and that they hadn't forgotten anything. Everything was there. They'd even remembered to pack the tiny, adorable matching socks and hat that Dalia had knitted for the baby.

Then a giant flock of balloons in every imaginable shade of the rainbow nosed its way through the waiting-room door. Behind the balloons came Mr. and Mrs. Cabrera, Valería's parents —her mother's arms were laden with pink and orange roses, his with large Rubbermaid containers in which Adam's nose anticipated Oaxaca-style *tamales*, *tres leches* cake, *tejate*, and who knew what other delicacies. Next came Valería's three younger sisters, hauling various parcels and packages, some of them gift-wrapped. Their cousin Claudia brought up the procession's rear with a large insulated beverage dispenser. "*Agua de sandia*," she explained. "My mother had twelve babies, and she swore by it."

Adam remembered how nervous the Cabreras had been about his marriage to Valería and how reserved they were with him at first. Unlike Valería, they were still observant Roman Catholics, with prayers and candles and attendance at Mass at least twice a week. Mrs. Cabrera wore a Virgin of Guadalupe medal around her neck and kissed it frequently. They made it clear that a Muslim son-in-law had never been part of their plans.

But none of that reserve was in evidence today. As soon as Mrs. Cabrera spotted Adam, she threw her arms around him. Then she presented him with the bouquet of balloons; he now saw that their ribbons were tied to the handle of a beautiful silver baby rattle. Setting the food on a chair, Mr. Cabrera shook Adam's hand, then pulled him in close and kissed both his cheeks.

The nurse appeared and ushered all of them into the room where Valería lay, resplendent, if somewhat sweaty, in a blue-and-white patterned hospital gown. Tears of joy shone on her cheeks as her mother and sisters kissed her. Suddenly, everyone was talking at once, just like his family back in Alexandria did. Claudia was serving everyone tamales and agua de sandia. One of Valería's sisters was rubbing her shoulders while another lit a candle to St. Gerard and popped a Mounir CD Adam had given her into a portable CD player, which made him smile. Then Mrs. Cabrera took Adam's hands, and they twirled around the room. She held Adam close to her and laughed, and he knew that it didn't matter how many thousands of miles away Egypt was. To the sounds of Mounir, and Juanes, and even Mariah Carey, they danced and danced until his son was ready to dance into this world.

2004: ALEXANDRIA

THE LONG BEARD—THAT was the first thing Dalia noticed as Nasser emerged, newly freed and squinting into the sunlight. It flowed freely now like a flag.

Houda ran across the street to greet her brother, throwing her arms around him as tears streamed down her face. His response was stiff, uncomfortable; his demeanor, subdued—it had clearly been many months since he'd experienced this type of contact. Still, Houda refused to let go. Dalia, watching from the waiting car, felt herself choke up upon seeing the fierceness of Houda's sisterly embrace—a moving testament to how much they all had missed their beloved Nasser.

When Houda finally released her brother, she immediately led Nasser to the waiting car, where Dalia stood with Omar, who reached out, trembling, for his son. In his father's arms, Nasser looked strangely small, as if he were a child again. He said nothing. Knowing there was little chance that Nasser would accept another hug, Dalia tried to squeeze his hand, but he pulled it away, not even meeting her eyes. Then, as if Nasser were the one with an injured leg, Omar helped him to the back seat of Dalia's car. They all piled in, and Dalia nosed into traffic to drive them home.

As Dalia navigated the narrow streets of Kafr Abdu, her eyes kept drifting toward the rearview mirror, where she could see Nasser's face. Omar was speaking to him steadily in a soft voice; she couldn't hear the words but caught the inflection of a question here and there. Nasser, his gaze on his knees, answered in monosyllables. "I'm tired," she heard him say at one point. "I just want to get home." His face was lax, slack; his lips chapped; his eyes ringed in shadows. He badly needed a haircut.

When Dalia pulled into the poinciana-shaded parking space, Houda leapt out and led Nasser inside by the hand. Dalia walked with Omar. "My boy." Omar's voice cracked with pain. "He's so weak and thin."

"You know Houda's cooking," Dalia said cheerfully. "She'll have him strong again in no time." She hoped she sounded more certain than she felt.

They followed brother and sister into the front room with its blue-and-white tiles and its potted palms. Not quite taking it in, Nasser stood passively, his face a cipher.

"Please excuse me," Nasser muttered to all of them, or perhaps to none of them. He was looking at no one in particular. At first Dalia thought he was apologizing for his bad behavior, but then he turned to her for the first time and said, "You shouldn't have come. As I said before, I release you from all obligations. We are no longer engaged."

Houda, as stunned as Dalia, shouted, "Nasser!" But he turned away from them with the gait of a man dragging iron ankle chains and shuffled quietly toward his bedroom.

Hours later, after Omar had retired too, Houda poured Dalia a cup of tea in the kitchen. They both needed to deconstruct what they'd witnessed in Nasser, who appeared to be an entirely different person. But there was surprisingly little to say. Incarceration had changed him dramatically—of that there was no question.

But who could ever know exactly what had transpired behind those prison walls?

Houda felt numb as she waited for the elevator—such an unfamiliar feeling. Normally, the smallest things could so easily fill her with delight: birdsong, a sudden breeze, the smell of the sea. None of these stimuli were present in the CIB Bank office building, but still, she'd just emerged from an interview for her first proper job, a prospect that might have filled Houda with happy jitters. Instead, her heart felt like stone.

Then there was Adham, who'd just returned to Alexandria, which normally would have been a reason to rejoice. Even while she'd accepted that Adham had found love elsewhere, Houda still loved to see him and laugh at his jokes—but not under these circumstances. Adham had flown back strictly to see Nasser, as perhaps the only person who could still talk sense into him.

The elevator arrived. Houda stepped in, not even bothering to check whether the car was going up or down. *What did it matter? Everything goes down in the end, right?*

Her phone lit up with an incoming text from Dalia: "How did it go?" In the wake of her sorrow and confusion following Nasser's arrest, Dalia had paused the nonprofit and taken a job as an associate at a law firm, which happened to represent CIB Bank. Despite Nasser cutting ties with her, Dalia had remained loyal to Omar and Houda, whom she loved like a sister. It had been Dalia who'd helped Houda land the appointment.

Houda replied with an "OK," hoping it would end the conversation, but also realizing her uncharacteristic terseness might trigger concern in Dalia. The truth was Houda had no idea how her meeting had gone. "Inshallah we will be in touch very soon," the CIB Bank interviewer had said rather generically.

But Dalia's endorsement would certainly help. That was the way things worked in Egypt; it was all about who you knew, meaning Houda would probably be offered the job as an intern and be forced suddenly to work long hours away from Omar and Nasser—a prospect that terrified her. Houda was wired to tend gardens and nourish her loved ones with tasty food, not to be trapped behind a screen in some gray cubicle. More than ever, her family needed her at home.

Exiting the lobby through its revolving door, she made a beeline to Kafr Abdu. Although salty wind wrapped around her with the song of seagulls, Houda's expression remained taut—that is, until she passed the Corona Confectionery & Chocolate Shop.

Houda stopped. Staring at the mouthwatering delicacies in the window display, Houda found herself launched back into childhood. How many times had she and Nasser been taken into that store for sweets? It was, in fact, the only tangible recollection she had of being with their mother, other than the memories she'd reconstructed by looking at photographs. Houda decided to poke her head inside and was instantly intoxicated by the heady smells of sugary treats. Her eyes were drawn magnetically to the shelf of Bimbo biscuits that Nasser used to love so much as a boy.

Normalcy—that's what we need, thought Houda, reaching for a box of Bimbos. *We could watch a movie. I'll make chai.*

Nasser loved to dip Bimbo biscuits in his tea. *Maybe it will remind him of Mother.*

Houda knocked on Nasser's bedroom door, but there was no response. She hesitated, knocked again. Nothing. *He's in there; I know he is.* She opened the door.

Nasser was sitting in his armchair, reading a book, which he put down upon seeing her enter. "Hey, what's going on?" she asked cheerfully.

"Nothing," he responded curtly, glancing down at the skirt she was wearing. Houda held up her box of Bimbos. "Look what I have!"

"Thanks, I don't feel like it."

"Okay," she said, hiding her disappointment. "What are you reading?"

"A book."

"*Really?* A book! No kidding?" She was hoping a little sarcasm might elicit a smile from him, but his expression remained flat. "What about a movie tonight? The professor is bringing dinner."

"I don't want to waste my time with a movie."

"You can choose what we watch. You can be the dictator." She was trying to be funny—anything to elicit a modicum of reaction. But Nasser remained robotically calm.

"I don't watch TV or movies, ya Houda. It's a waste of our time and our mind."

She caught him glancing again at her skirt, which barely covered her knees. "Do you think our mother would approve of how you live, how we live?" he said.

Houda almost gasped. "The way I live . . . our mother?" she stuttered.

"Yes, our mother. Your mother." His voice remained eerily placid. "She's not simply some instructions in the cookbook she left for you. Our mother was a devout Muslim who would have wanted you to pay attention to what's important to Allah—and to His will for us."

"Our mother?" She was still trying to get over her shock at this line of conversation, so unlike any discussion she'd ever had with him or anyone else in the house.

Nasser continued, almost paternally, "You're not a young girl anymore; you need to understand what's important in this world. Pay attention to what you wear, how you behave, and—"

"Nasser, are you joking? You're really telling me that Mother would have had a problem with my skirt?" His silent, unflinching gaze served as confirmation. Houda was beginning to get riled up. "How would you know that? And since when—"

"I know because I know the true story of our mother and her family."

"What story? What are you talking about?" Houda frowned, unsure of what to expect.

"Everything you know is a lie. Your father lied to us. She was pure, and God showed her the way, but your father couldn't take it; your father wanted her to be something else, and he didn't even tell us the truth about how she died. Mom died in a train crash when she was going to visit her family back in Asyut."

"I don't understand!"

"Let me tell you what you need to understand," Nasser continued. "You need to understand that your mother wouldn't have been proud of the way you live, the way you dress."

"My mother—" Houda's head was spinning.

Nasser stood up abruptly and walked past her toward the door. "I have to go."

Houda grabbed his arm. "Wait, Nasser!"

Nasser pulled away gently and left the room. Houda followed him into the vestibule just as Nasser muttered, "As-salamu alaykum." And he was gone.

Houda wasn't sure how much time had passed—only that there were tears in her eyes and bitterness in her heart when Omar walked in through the front door with a bag of groceries. She quickly dried her tears and went to embrace him, but Omar could sense that something was amiss. "What's wrong, ya Mishkala?"

"Nothing, just a very long day," she deflected. But Houda was dying to pepper him with questions about the bombshell from Nasser about their mother and her death. *Could it be true?*

"Let's talk about it," Omar persisted. "What happened?"

"*Wallahy*, I swear—it's nothing."

"You know you can tell me anything, don't you?"

"It's okay, ya professor." She smiled. "I'm good."

He smiled back. "I brought *tageen bamia* for dinner. I know you and Nasser love it. Go and tell him we can eat. I'm hungry."

"Nasser left," she said. "He had to go."

"Oh," said Omar. "I had hoped we would have dinner together."

Houda knew he was disappointed, as she was. As much as she wanted to find out more about what Nasser had said, she bit her tongue. *There will be a better moment*, she thought. Her job right now was to cheer her father up.

"What? So, I'm not good enough to be your dinner companion?" she joked. "Come on, professor. We'll have the best dinner, just me and you. You change, I'll heat the bread."

Omar laughed. "Okay, ya Houda."

This was the new normal: Nasser home, but very far away.

∼

Alhamdulillah—it's unoccupied!

Adam found their regular table from the old days, tucked in a corner of Kahwaht Sidi Gabr. The air was thick and heady with shisha smoke. He ordered *tafaaha*—apple-flavored tobacco shisha —while he waited for his old friend, who was late as usual. But there was nothing usual about what happened next.

When Nasser finally arrived, he scanned the environment as if taking in an unfamiliar place, which seemed strange since he'd been here countless times. Adam studied him from afar for a moment before standing to greet him. He'd been forewarned that Nasser had changed, which was true. Nasser's angular face was set and stern, half-shrouded by the new beard, his gray shirt stiffly ironed and tucked into his severe black trousers as if they were meeting to discuss business, not to catch up as old friends. But Adam saw nothing in Nasser's appearance that seemed *zombielike*, the word Dalia had used. Nasser's keen intellect was still very much in evidence, albeit with a robotic kind of impeccability—like a quantum-level AI android assessing enemy territory.

Enemy territory? Adam couldn't believe he'd had that thought. This used to be a second home to them. Letting all his reservations go, Adam stood and approached Nasser, opening his arms, allowing the joy of seeing his old friend to spread across his face.

"*Wahashtene*, ya Nasser." Adam grinned. *I missed you, Nasser, my lost brother.* He gave

him a friendly punch in the upper arm, American style, and channeled his best Detective John McClane. "Welcome to the party, pal."

If Nasser recognized the *Die Hard* reference, he gave no sign.

"You want some chai?" Adam signaled the waiter. "You won't be sorry you came out of your cave when I show you these pictures," he promised. "Cutest kid in the West or the East, I swear. Personality! He was born with his own opinions. I think he could give you a pointer or two in the debate department. And he doesn't even talk yet." He handed Nasser an envelope of snapshots.

"Ya Adham—" Nasser allowed the hint of a smile to spread across his face as he flipped deliberately through the photographs. "But no," he corrected himself. "It's Mr. Adam now, isn't it?" His eyes brightened. "Mr. Adam, the American family man."

Something in Nasser's look seemed to peer into Adam's mind —to know just what he was thinking. In the old days, Adam had accused Nasser more than once of reading his thoughts. The familiarity of the feeling delighted Adam. "You know me better than anyone," he chuckled. "Ya man, life just isn't the same when we're so far apart."

Adam felt the irony of what he'd just said. Even with this proximity, there remained a chasm between them. His friend flipped through snapshots of people who meant the world to Adam; but to Nasser, they were total strangers.

Adam tried to keep it light, nonetheless. "I swear I was going to stalk you at your house and make you look at these. I'm glad you finally agreed to come out to our old stomping grounds."

How could Nasser resist these pictures? Here was Gibrail nestled against Valéria's chest on the day he was born; Adam dipping Gibrail's toes into the waves at the Jersey Shore; a plump and grinning Gibrail in a cable-knit sweater sitting up all on his own in front of an autumnal display of gourds and Indian corn.

"He really is something, ya Nasser." Adam beamed. "I'll be back soon with him and Valéria. I want you to meet them."

"Inshallah," Nasser breathed. "I'm happy to see you doing well."

"And how are you, how's life treating you?" Adam rushed in, then felt the blood rising to his face. *Was that too quick?* He wanted desperately, as everyone did, to hear about what Nasser was thinking, about what he'd experienced in prison and during the time since his release. But Adam also knew it couldn't be broached so lightly. He felt clumsy and foolish and, above all, guilty.

While his best friend had been suffering here, he'd been far away. Adam hadn't been here for him. Worse—while Nasser had suffered, Adam's business had grown. His son had been born and had thrived. Adam was happy.

"I'm sorry," Adam said after a moment. "Sorry I wasn't here for you. I wish I could have been."

Around them, the room buzzed with other men's conversations over their games of chess and backgammon, their shishas, their endless cups of coffee. All of Alexandria seemed to teem with joyous life, while Nasser sat there without expression.

"Talk to me, Nasser," Adam pleaded softly, leaning toward him. He started to reach for Nasser's hand, but checked himself, then wondered why he'd stopped. The situation had made the simplest gestures of humanity feel complicated and fraught. Silence screamed from Nasser's face.

"I can't imagine how hard it was in there for you." Adam did his best to keep the one-sided conversation afloat. "*Anta akhoia,*" he added. *You are my brother.* "You mean the world to me. Let me be here for you, Nasser. Let's talk it out. You don't have to carry all this weight alone."

Nasser stared at him. "What about *akhoik*?" He had asked about Adam's blood brother. "Who carried *his* weight?"

Adam was momentarily speechless. "You know, you know the whole story, why—"

"Go home," Nasser interrupted, his voice cold and stern. "Go back to America, ya Adham."

Nasser stood abruptly to leave. Adam rushed after him. "Sit with me, Nasser. I'm sorry! I didn't mean to upset you. Nasser, I'm sorry!" He urgently wanted to learn what Nasser knew about Sharif. *Did they meet in jail?*

But Nasser was done talking. He turned to Adam one last time before exiting. Of all the changing glimmers in Nasser's eyes, this last one scared Adam the most. His rage gone, along with his feverish intensity, Nasser's eyes were as dull and blank as stones.

Crossing the Corniche, Adam was so lost in his thoughts, he didn't see the old forest-green Lada until he almost collided with it. The driver rolled down his window and cursed him, but Adam didn't have the bandwidth to respond—especially now that his cell phone was buzzing.

Adam flipped it open. "What happened? Did he talk to you?" Dalia had a manic pitch to her voice.

"Slow down," Adam said.

"Where are you?" she persisted. "Come over. I'll meet you downstairs."

Minutes later, Adam entered the apartment building with its upscale marble lobby, where Dalia rushed to intercept him, not having seen him in three years. But she didn't spend even a moment catching up. Her mind was focused only on Nasser.

"What did he say?" she fired breathlessly. "Tell me!"

"Not much," Adam sighed.

"Come on," she insisted. "You must have learned *something*."

"We couldn't get into anything. It was short . . ."

Dalia narrowed her eyes. "I can't believe it!"

"Cool down, Dalia." Adam was trying hard not to get worked up.

"Don't tell me to cool down," she spat. "You were supposed to help. You're useless!"

"I am not the one who got him into this," Adam shot back. "It was you!"

Dalia looked at him in shock. "You're blaming me?"

"Are you that naïve? He wanted tech. It was your nonprofit that got him into trouble!"

Dalia was speechless. He'd said out loud something everyone knew but no one dared to say. Maybe she'd been lying to herself, but there was no denying it—Dalia had roped Nasser into *her* dream and away from his.

Adam was just getting started. "Look at you, safe in your little palace. With all your family connections, you still couldn't help him?"

Dalia, her face beet-red, shoved Adam suddenly in the chest. "Get away from me!"

Adam immediately regretted having lost his cool. The anger was simply a mask for what he was really feeling—guilt and helplessness. And it was not simply about Nasser. Adam's turmoil went back to his boyhood with Sharif, who'd been mocked and bullied throughout their youth.

Why didn't I stand up for him?

"Leave!" Dalia shouted. "Get out of my sight!"

He departed quickly, shaking, as Dalia ran toward her elevator in tears.

2005: ALEXANDRIA

THAT NIGHT OMAR waited for his son in the front room—the elegant but uncomfortable parlor where no one ever sat. He knew that in that room he couldn't miss Nasser when he came in, so there he waited. Silver moonlight poured in through the room's arched windows, casting magic on everything it touched and throwing the deep shadows of the furniture and the big potted palms on the floor.

Lately Nasser had taken to sitting in this room, with its hard, high-backed wooden chairs, antique and beautiful and cruel to old bones like Omar's. He kept half-expecting Nasser to appear from one of the inky corners.

Omar had wrapped himself in a light blanket against the chilly night. In a few short weeks it would be spring, and the city would be redolent of jasmine blossoms, but in the meantime, he was still layering on sweaters and drinking his tea extra hot. As a boy, he'd railed against Alexandria's crowded, sweaty, sun-drenched summers, but now he spent the winter pining for them.

Time, he reflected, *does strange things to us all*. Just look at what it had done to Nasser. A family album lay open across his knees, Nasser's chubby, grubby face radiating joy and trust from the pages. How could this adventurous little sprite have grown to be the stern and silent figure who now haunted Omar's apartment? Where had he gone wrong? Houda still lived the same way, still sat with her father in the evenings, still talked with him over the delicious meals she prepared. But even she seemed to be hardening somehow, growing more distant. Omar wished for the millionth time that Fatimah had lived.

Nasser, Omar's brilliant boy, his heart's delight, had become a disapproving stranger. Worse, Omar feared he was becoming an ideologue of the most dangerous kind. After all the history Omar had taught him, he had been certain Nasser would understand that peace, amity, and progress were the roads that led people to greatness, no matter the era. Omar had given him all the tools he needed to understand the world, to navigate its dangers, and to foster its delights. Or so he'd thought.

Since coming out of jail, Nasser had begun frequenting the purist mosque, and yet Omar had held his tongue. *Let him get to know them for himself,* he'd thought. Omar had taught him about the importance of context, the dangers of literalism. How many times had they sat up through the night, debating the hard questions?

The boy has a skeptical mind. Soon enough, he will discover the errors of their ways. Religion can foster social good as well as danger. We studied all the religions; surely he will find the wisest path.

But instead, Nasser had drifted further from his family, spending more and more time with his new fundamentalist friends. Just like them, Nasser was angry. The crisis had disrupted everything within him. *Intelligence becomes dangerous when it is yoked to rigidity.* The time had come; Omar had to confront his son. He only prayed it wasn't too late.

Quiet footsteps outside roused him from his meditations. Nasser unlocked the door with a light touch and took off his shoes before he stepped inside, moving silently so as not to disturb anyone's sleep. He still kept his habitual consideration for others, at least. The moonlight gleamed on his glossy beard. He'd been growing it for several months now, but Omar couldn't get used to it. It hid his son's handsome face and gave him an ancient, unyielding aspect. This bearded man belonged not on the football pitch or at a software startup but in the desert, somewhere far, far away from the civilization of which Omar had tried so hard to make him proud.

When he saw his father, Nasser froze with a sharp intake of breath, then he pulled himself up to his full height before the chair.

"As-salamu alaykum, *walidi*," Nasser said quietly.

"*Wa alaykum as-salam*," Omar responded, then said a silent prayer that peace truly would stay with the two of them tonight. "Nasser, my son. I need to talk with you."

"It's late," Nasser observed, which was true enough. In the silver moonlight, Omar could see the deep shadows under Nasser's eyes, even as he looked away from his father toward the back of the apartment where his bed awaited. "I'm tired now. Another time."

"Now is the time," Omar insisted. They were speaking quietly, but Nasser could sense the command in his father's voice. His eyes returned sharply to search out Omar's.

"Fine," he consented, pulling up another of the front room's tall, ancient wooden chairs. "What is it that you want to talk about, Father?"

"I have to ask, what's going on with you?" Omar poured out. "You're drifting away from us. Away from the people who love you. Where are you going? How have we wronged you? How can we persuade you to come back to us?"

Where he sat in the tall chair with his back to the window, Nasser's face was almost entirely lost in shadow; only now and then could Omar see points of moonlight glinting from his eyes.

"I'm following God's words, walidi. I'm letting go of this world and its materialism. Is that what you mean by 'drifting away'?"

"You've made me proud so many times, my son," Omar told him. "And there's nothing wrong with seeking God or following a strong moral system. Yet I worry."

Omar leaned toward him, hoping to see his face more clearly, to know that he was paying attention. But Nasser was lost in shadow, sitting very still.

"We've spoken before of those who talk about Allah, who talk about virtue, but whose purposes are otherwise. I've raised you to understand religion and its part in society. I've encouraged you to look at the Qur'an and the *Sunnah* with a critical eye. I've done my best to teach you to live with love and purpose. I don't want to see you fall under the influence of cynics who twist religion away from those ends."

Nasser snorted. "I *am* living for a purpose, *now*," he announced, loudly enough that it startled Omar. He leaned forward into the light, his eyes filled with fury.

Omar was frightened—frightened of his beautiful son. It took him a moment to catch his breath, to recover himself. He breathed deeply and kept his voice soft and mild.

"I know that you have struggled. The world has not always been fair to you. But Nasser, anger is not the way to deal with—"

Nasser cut his father off with a snarl. "I *am* angry!" He had quieted his voice, but it was compressed now, straining to contain its intensity. "I'm angry at a corrupt system with dictators everywhere, even in the so-called democracies. I'm angry at the Americans, I'm angry for the people of Iraq who had nothing to do with anything. And I'm angry for the suffering of the Palestinians, who endure their own struggles daily—"

Omar tried to calm Nasser. "I understand, my son, but—"

Nasser stopped his father midsentence. "Most of all, I'm angry on behalf of my mother! I know the truth. I went to El-Karia. Her blood is on your hands . . ."

Omar was shocked. "My son . . ." But Nasser's eyes looked murderous.

"No one had a hand in it," Omar faltered. "It was an accident . . ."

"Ah," Nasser sneered, "so much for the myth of a sudden heart attack. So much for that pathetic decoy grave in El-Manara . . ."

"Yes, I lied." Omar's heart was racing. "You were young. I tried to protect you."

Nasser mocked, "Like a 'benevolent' tyrant?"

"You don't know the whole story."

"I know enough. You thought your in-laws were backward— ensnared by the chains of their pious stagnation. That's why you excluded them from our lives."

"It was Fatimah's choice. She ran away from them!"

"Then she ran back. She realized your secular world was just as intolerant. My mother wanted to follow her heart and practice her faith. You practically forced her onto that train!"

Nasser's vitriol was palpable. "You're worse than the dictators and the crusaders. We know those enemies, and we can fight them. But people like you are the sickness within. You want us to negotiate the words of Allah, make them hollow, pick and choose what works for you, or, even worse, leave Allah and his Prophet behind entirely so we can 'progress.'"

Nasser's tone seethed with contempt. "You are the most dangerous of all because you know some history and can twist words to manipulate the truth. And yet you're entirely ignorant of the most fundamental facts. You don't even know my mother's cause of death, do you?"

"Cause . . . ?" Omar echoed. "You mean, the accident—"

"She was decapitated by a flying sheet of window glass—her skull rolled down the embankment like a football."

Omar blinked in horror. Nasser shook his head in disdain. Abruptly, he stood; Omar tried to reach for him, but Nasser pushed his hand away and said, "Let me tell you: the glorious past belongs to Islam. And the most glorious days lie ahead of us still. Not the glory of failed morality of people like you, but the glory of God's Word revealed in Islamic values. It is time for the *Ummah* to stand up against our oppressors; not only against our local dictators and people like you, but also against their puppet master, America. They claim to be God's city on a hill, but they're so far up the slope they've lost sight of the people below. They can't hear our voices anymore. But now they will hear from me."

Omar's mind raced. *Hear from me? What could he be planning?* Omar's heart was beating so wildly that it threatened to bruise his ribs. He stood up too. "Nasser, please—"

"My father," Nasser said, his voice raw with anger and fatigue, "I won't forgive you for my mother, but my fight is not here with you." Quick as a cat, he departed.

Omar felt tears flood his eyes. Nasser was gone, and the front door was standing open to the dark and chill. Regrets from this altercation would linger for eternity.

It was the last time Omar saw his son.

THE LIBRARY OF OMAR
EL-MOHAMMEDI

APRIL 7, 2014 • 11:22 P.M.

February 14, 2005

Eyes in front, born to hunt.
Eyes on side, born to hide.

Tribal wars were settled with a single death. Each tribe sent its champion, and the matter was settled in minutes, fighting with fists at close quarters, looking each other in the eye. This was key for a battle with honor. You had to see, respect, even love your opponent before striking the blow that ended him.

"Progress" in the so-called "art of war" caused abomination. First came the sword, next the spear, the arrow, the cannon, the missile . . . and soon tyrants who pressed buttons in their ivory towers were continents away from those they vanquished.

OMAR REMEMBERED his lessons to Nasser on Sun Tzu's work, but these words were Nasser's, not his. He sighed, and his eyes traveled to the side entry, a faint annotation in Nasser's familiar hand. The words stood stark against the white space that Nasser had used to add his entry, dated October 2007.

Then these mass murderers had the temerity to hold conventions to codify their principles of warfare, stating that all aggression must arise from *military necessity,* with *distinction* (between soldiers and civilians), *proportionality, humanity,* and *honor*—hypocritical rules they established but broke at every turn, from Denshawai to Nisour Square.

Omar knew the references. He'd taught Nasser as a boy about the 1906 Denshawai Incident, a deadly altercation between British Army officers and local Egyptian villagers. One century later, and many times in between, it happened again when employees of Blackwater, private mercenaries contracted by the US government to provide security services in Iraq, killed seventeen civilians in Nisour Square, provoking an outcry that resonated across borders and beliefs.

The Teacher said the Great Satan will pay a price for violations of our Ummah, for the deaths of our brothers and sisters, for its attacks on Islam and the words of the Prophet, peace be upon him.

Aljihad is our duty, he reminded us. The ramblings of pacifists like my father are impotent in the face of Allah's commandments. That's why, according to my Teacher, Roken, we can and must use any means necessary to retaliate . . .

Omar stopped and stared at the page. *Roken?* That was the person who had mesmerized his son?

The name conjured up memories, not just from academic halls but also from a battle long ago. They had known each other in the most desperate of circumstances. Roken had appeared out of nowhere, a ghostly figure moving through the chaos. His actions had saved many lives that night. Omar remembered the searing pain in his leg, a bullet that had nearly taken him down. It was Roken who had seen it happen.

The bullet, now resting in his drawer, had been hidden away for years. Slowly, Omar reached for the drawer, pulling out the envelope. The weight of it in his hand felt like he was holding a shard of the past. He placed it on the desk, leaving it there in the open, a silent marker of the history they shared.

They had crossed paths again in the realm of academia, at one of those Ivy League universities in Cambridge, Massachusetts. Omar was there to present his paper, "If We Cannot Carve Space for Change, Tradition's Roots Will Stand Unshaken and Fight Fiercely," and he was surprised to see Roken in the audience. Given how extreme Roken had become, Omar hadn't expected him to get a voice in such a forum. It was hard to believe that this had been before Roken was brought to justice when his link to killing Sadat was found.

The symposium on civil disobedience highlighted just how sharply their ideologies had diverged. Roken, increasingly outspoken in his extremism, bristled at the sight of female academics indulging in Western customs and sipping champagne with ease.

"This is a decaying society," he muttered with disdain.

The next day, his rhetoric sharpened. When a panelist mentioned Gandhi, Roken interjected, his tone cold and absolute. "Even Gandhi admitted violence could be an option in extreme situations—such as self-defense and protecting the most vulnerable." He cast a gaze over the audience. "When a superpower attacks innocent Muslims, nonviolence becomes useless; the Afghani people have the right to kill the godless invaders."

Roken had a way of saying what people wanted to hear, with just enough edge to keep them listening. He was playing the West's game, but Omar could see the layers beneath—the deep-seated anger and the sense of betrayal that fueled his words. Omar watched with a mix of disbelief and concern as the audience reacted favorably, with some members of an influential foundation taking notice. The director of the foundation invited Roken to speak at one of their events the following week. After the event, unbeknownst to Omar, Roken met with the CIA, discussing how they might use him in their grand strategy—proxy wars against the Russians, or perhaps direct involvement in Afghanistan, Meanwhile, Omar boarded a plane back to Egypt, frustration mounting after his paper was rejected by the journal he had aspired to publish in.

As Roken's views became increasingly radical, Omar saw less and less of him. It was disquieting to think this extremist had swayed his son. But the full story of their intertwined pasts—the battle and what followed—was not for now to think of. He needed to keep looking.

Returning to Nasser's journal, Omar's eyes drifted toward the white space, where he noticed the gale reference written as an addendum.

My father has lost me to the waters like Qasim . . . He knows nothing of who I am now. I am become Death, the destroyer of worlds . . .

Omar swallowed in sudden terror. He lunged to grab the encrypted phone. The American picked up immediately. "You have something?"

"The Gita reference!" Omar responded breathlessly.

"Oppenheimer," said Matt.

Both were familiar with the statement by physicist Robert Oppenheimer following the first successful test detonation of a nuclear weapon on July 16, 1945. As a mushroom cloud rose above the Nevada desert, Oppenheimer, an American Jew, stunned by the colossal power that had been suddenly and irrevocably unleashed, quoted an ancient Hindu scripture, the Bhagavad Gita, where the deity Lord Vishnu says, "I am become Death, the destroyer of worlds."

"They have a nuclear weapon?" Omar was in shock.

"Dirty bomb, we think," Matt clarified, meaning using a conventional explosion to spread radioactive material, with the potential to kill tens of thousands—some immediately, some after years of suffering. The mayhem would be indiscriminate, across borders, religions, classes, ages.

Omar felt as though he'd collapse under the weight of the responsibility before him.

Had Nasser come around, like Matt was insisting, by burying a clue in his journal to prevent the unspeakable calamity? Or had he remained under the Svengali spell of Roken, playing them all for fools?

God Almighty, Omar thought as he turned the page with a racing heart . . .

PART IV

EL-FAYDA EL-KABIRA

El-Fayda El-Kabira (the "Big Flood")
surges in January.
The sea overflows, streets become rivers.

Everything stops.
everyone surrenders
in the face of Nature,
the all-powerful.

2006: BAGHDAD

IT HADN'T RAINED in six months. The parched ground, cracked open in jagged fissures, radiated heat like a convection oven in ripples that blurred vision. Matt couldn't remember the last time he'd experienced sustained triple-digit temperatures like this—even on his trips to the ops center in Arizona. He was hydrating religiously and still felt a near-constant headache. The canopy was practically useless. Despite the tent's flaps being tied open in the vain hope of a cross breeze, the blazing Iraqi sun turned it into a kiln, especially late in the afternoon.

"Listen up," the commanding officer said, striding to the podium. Soldiers waiting to be briefed stood up quickly and saluted. "At ease, gentlemen," said the CO, and the men took their seats. A sergeant distributed printouts to everyone in the room, and Matt felt that slight quickening of his pulse that he always felt on the eve of an operation. Tomorrow, of course, there'd be the adrenaline.

"Operation Makan is set for tomorrow morning, 0600 hours. Targets are two Al-Qaeda operatives. It's all there in your briefing packets. Questions?"

"Are these the guys who killed those Blackwater contractors, sir?" somebody asked from the rear.

The CO's eyes tracked to the side for a moment, and then he

answered, "Affirmative, soldier. We are awaiting intel to confirm the location. Be ready, men. That's all." He strode out again into the blinding sunshine, and the assembled soldiers scattered to their various tasks.

How many times had Matt been in briefings like this one? He'd spent the summer supporting Operation Arrowhead Ripper, both stateside and here in the field. Intel had been excellent and critical—between what they collected and their new ability to geolocate insurgents and cut them off from their sources of support, the surge was working beautifully.

But something was different this time. Matt's electronics team had retrieved the intel for this mission partly from Al-Qaeda's internal network, known as Obelisk, and partly from a series of text messages a source had provided. If the meeting location was included in any of those electronic communications, though, it was encoded so ingeniously the engineers couldn't quite see it. Not yet, anyway. The enemy, realizing that US surveillance was near total, had gotten cannier. Matt's team would normally have planted a few fake messages to draw out the information they needed, but the timeframe on this mission was too tight. And this furnacelike heat was cooking Matt's brains.

Matt headed gratefully toward the air-conditioned comms center to wait for word from an informant who was out collecting location intel the old-fashioned way. The comms center here at Camp Taji was a real building, unlike the one at Camp Victory— basically a modified shipping container. The sun heated those cans up like furnaces, made worse by the heat output of the computer equipment, so much so that even the grid of window-unit ACs that pumped cold air in at one end of the container was hopeless at keeping the center comfortable. But Camp Taji's cinder block comms center was nice and frosty. In the summer months, that just about made up for the occasional attacks the camp had to fend off.

They had been experiencing a deadly Sunni insurgent attack nearly every other day, even with Zarqawi out of the picture, which was why they'd deployed Matt and an intel team to set up a complicated NSA Real-Time Regional Gateway in the middle of the action—to expedite the processing of intelligence and mitigate casualties where possible. The system was incredibly sophisticated, analyzing every call, every text message, every email, every drone video, every piece of intel from hacked insurgents' computers or informants' tips. Hardware and code had to be perfect, but getting shot at didn't exactly promote anyone's best engineering frame of mind.

And yet this was what Matt had trained for. His decryption team was made up of some of the most talented computer and communications hackers in the world, using cutting-edge American technology—systems he'd studied at West Point and later tested hands-on at Rock Island. Matt was grateful for his army education. The new talent the unit brought forth was invaluable: a wave of brilliant kids recruited from the private sector. But army discipline, and the incredible cooperation the unit was getting from the NSA, still made real army personnel more reliable than the jittery net cowboys the private outfits like Blackwater were bringing over.

As if someone were reading Matt's mind, he overheard a couple of enlisted men grumbling, "Goddamn mercenaries pay way more than Uncle Sam, and it's like the Keystone Cops. Bunch of grandstanding, patriotic hotshots running into battle all half-cocked. And now we have to go in and clean up their mess. Does that seem right to you?"

"Bunch of assholes," agreed his buddy, a lanky Black soldier who reminded Matt of his West Point classmate, Jamal. "Blackwater's some kind of private army doin' the White House's dirty work, doin' shit the American people never agreed to. Just this month they—"

"Watch that kind of talk," interrupted a sergeant, barrel-chested and pock-faced. "Those mercenaries protect *Americans*. The Blackwater guys are just doing their jobs. Don't forget, the real assholes are the ones blowing us up. Those towelheads fucked with Americans, and now they're gonna pay." Their chatter faded into the general background buzz of the camp as they walked away, and soon they were out of sight.

The truth was Matt understood the complaints. It boggled his mind that America, the greatest military power on Earth, was paying private mercenaries for protection. Iraq was awash in these guys—it was like the whole enterprise of war was being privatized. Matt could see the advantages in terms of efficiency and competition, but the legal gray area these killers-for-hire skirted worried him. They did what they wanted with total impunity. No Iraqi court could prosecute them.

Halfway to the comms building, Matt checked his watch—almost 5 p.m. He'd soon be slammed for the rest of the evening studying the briefing; if he was going to catch Stephanie before she left for work, he should call her now—8 a.m. in Illinois. He turned off toward the MWR building and its semiprivate phone booths, hoping he wasn't already too late.

She picked up right away, thrilled to hear from him. "How are things going, hon?"

"Five by five," Matt reported. "Wish it were cooler, though."

"I'll bet," she acknowledged. "Drew went to the zoo yesterday with his class. I guess they saw scorpions. He wants to know if there are scorpions where you are."

Matt laughed. "Tell him I'll send him pictures of some Arizona scorpions that'll knock his socks off."

"He'd like that." Stephanie laughed. And Matt felt guilty. He hated the fact that he still had to lie to his wife about where they were sending him. How could he, when together they'd built so much so quickly? Matt and Stephanie had already started their own family with two wonderful children, Drew and Claire. Stephanie, ever the multitasker, had also begun supporting her father at the bank, balancing family life and work with a quiet determination that Matt deeply admired.

Matt was now unofficially "on loan" to a special counterintelligence field unit of the CIA, which had been tracking him since he'd become one of the decryption rock stars at West Point, and the intel community had their own set of stringent nondisclosure rules. *It's for her own safety*, was the line he told himself, *and the kids too.* And that had some truth to it. "Loose lips sink ships." The stakes of the intel war were so high, God forbid he should be compromised by someone getting to his family. So, Matt played the game, which meant calling home like everything was rosy.

"How's your hedge fund doing?" Matt asked. Stephanie had been sweating a lot over the small portfolio of securities her dad had finally allowed her to invest in as an experiment at the bank.

"Could be better," she understated. "It's puzzling—all my research from the last five years, even the last eighteen months, shows record profits. But right when Daddy gives me the go-ahead, everything plateaus. It's driving me crazy. If it doesn't start looking lively soon, I'll have to kill it."

"I know you'll find a way, sweetheart," Matt said, meaning it. "Kiss the kids for me."

"Have a good day, baby." Stephanie's voice turned soft. "I love you."

Coming out of the phone cubby, Matt practically walked into a CIA analyst on his team. "There's a situation developing," he informed Matt. "We got a text from the informant."

Twenty minutes later, Matt's decryption unit was piling out of jeeps along a broad, dusty stretch of boulevard lined by blocky modern apartment buildings. The street was wide enough to have once accommodated four lanes of traffic and a palm-lined median, but now the asphalt was so pitted and buckled that the jeeps bounced along it like toys. Today, most of the other traffic was on foot. People bustled past, going about their daily business, one of them driving a herd of goats. A few of them paused to gaze at the Americans curiously.

The address they'd received was a three-story apartment block built of the same desert-colored stone as everything else. A few cracked tiles around the entrance suggested that it might once have been a nice place to live, pretty, a home someone loved. But now it had the dusty, desolate air so much of Baghdad seemed to share. A small advance team, weapons at the ready, went in first to secure the building. Matt waited on the sidewalk, tense and silent.

Once the racket of the advance team's footsteps had receded into the building, Matt became aware of a voice coming from somewhere high in the building. A muffled Arabic monologue drifted down to them, dampened and garbled by the building's stones.

After a moment, the advance team shouted down an all clear, then the team leader yelled, "Hey, Matt, come up here. What do you make of this?"

The building's shady interior was painted a swimming-pool aqua that at least gave an illusion of coolness, even though the air inside was stuffy. Matt made his way up the stairs. On the third floor, the interior walls had been knocked down to form one big room, empty except for an irregular circle of folding metal chairs surrounding a beat-up old boom box that sat on the floor. It was from this that the Arabic monologue droned on and on, taking on a tinny, echoing quality from the room's space and hard surfaces. On the seat of one of the metal chairs lay a cell phone.

"I don't like it," Matt said. "Let's get the bomb squad up here. Now. Move!" He noticed one additional detail before motioning for the advance team to fall back: a sticker affixed to the boom box. It was the Eye of Providence, an eye within a triangle surrounded by a halo. It took Matt back to his youth. Matt had had a sticker just like it as a boy that he'd stuck on his skateboard.

But there was no time to linger. The team hustled down the stairs with Matt in the rear. They emerged into the blinding sunshine, where Matt started giving orders. The bomb squad lifted their bot out of the back of a jeep. On treads like a tiny tank equipped with cameras, a mic, and jointed, grasping arms, the bot reminded Matt of the robot he'd worked on with his encryption and robotics team back in Rock Island.

"Bot is moving," the squad reported, then kept everyone at bay as they navigated it via radio controller up the apartment building's steep stairs to explore the bizarre cell phone and boom box setup.

While waiting for the all clear, Matt's analytical mind started decoding what he knew of the puzzle thus far. A tip-off from an informant had led them to this spot that was clearly staged to send a message, which could be hidden in any one of a number of clues: the audio recording, the cell phone. Then there was that sticker affixed to the boom box—relatively recently, it seemed, because the boom box was covered in dirt and grime and the sticker had appeared to be clean. *Is that meant to be some kind of message?*

Matt let the gears turn in his brain. The Eye of Providence had roots in Renaissance Christian art, symbolizing God's watchful eye over humanity. Later, it was embraced by Freemasonry in the eighteenth century and eventually became a prominent symbol on the Great Seal of the United States, representing divine guidance over the new nation. It was famously depicted atop a pyramid—an ancient symbol of strength—on the back of the dollar bill. What did it mean in this context? What was it trying to say here?

"All clear," reported the bomb squad, summoning Matt back to the scene at hand. He led his boys through the dust back to the apartment building and up the stairs. The advance team had been looking for hidden attackers, the bomb squad for explosives. Matt's team was looking for messages, clues, any form of intel. They went over the building's first two floors inch by inch and came up empty: abandoned apartments, broken furniture, forlorn kitchen appliances. The weird stage set on the top floor was all there was, apparently. While the bot crouched under a chair like a timid dog, waiting for the bomb squad to carry it back down to their jeep, Matt's guys bagged the cell phone, a recent model but cheap, readily available anywhere in Baghdad. Matt put on a pair of latex gloves to grab the boom box and noticed a sheet of notebook paper that had been placed underneath it.

To Matt's surprise, the short message was written in English, in small but nice, even elegant, handwriting. A few team members turned toward Matt questioningly, so he read aloud: "When you go out to war against your enemies and see horses and chariots and an army larger than your own, you shall not be afraid of them, for the Lord your God is with you, who brought you up out of the land of Egypt."

Matt recognized the passage right away from his Sunday school days—Deuteronomy 20:1. His mind raced to another passage in Deuteronomy—the one that Muslim scholars considered to be a prophecy of the coming of Mohammed. That wasn't something he'd learned in Sunday school; it was only after 9/11, when he began reading more about Islam and the region in preparation for the war, that he came across this interpretation: *I will raise up a Prophet from among their countrymen like you, and I will put my words in his mouth* . . .

Matt was beginning to feel like he knew this guy; he couldn't help the feeling that the messages were meant personally for him. The Eye of Providence, for example.

How to decode this?

When they got back into the merciful AC of the comms building, Matt's team got to work analyzing the cell phone, which had been reset to factory specs, so it was blank. There was nothing on it. *Then why did he leave it?* Matt loved puzzles like this. They did a full scan of the phone to see if there had been any hardware modification. Negative.

Matt hit the floor and did thirty push-ups to get his blood flowing—something he liked to do when he was stuck. When he reexamined the phone after his mini-workout and a silent prayer to God, something came to him like an epiphany. Check for unsent messages.

There it was—sitting in the outbox of the phone—a series of numbers:

14-5 14-1 7-1 1-4 11-1 11-2 11-3 2-1 2-2 2-3 5-1 5-2 5-2

Matt felt goose bumps. This was basic Ottendorf cryptography. The cipher had to be that passage from Deuteronomy, with the number pairs pointing to the word and letter within the passage. The message began with word 14, which was *chariots*, and letter 5, which was *I*. Matt grabbed a pad and continued.

14-1, that was *C*.

7-1 was *A*.

1-4 was *N*.

Within thirty seconds, Matt had decoded the message, which read:

I CAN SEE YOU TOO

Direct communication from a terrorist—it gave Matt chills. But the feeling quickly turned to resolve. If this was a game, he was more than ready to play—and win. He would catch this guy.

2006: ALEXANDRIA

THE STORM PELTED the windows again and again. It was hard for Houda to get any work done with this weather. She was seated at her small desk in the shared secretarial office at Salema Shipping Co., Ltd., a job she'd started six months earlier after working at the bank internship. She'd really enjoyed the bank work. This position was far more mundane. Still, it kept her out of the house, which had become almost unbearable since the day Nasser had left and never come back. For months, they'd searched for Nasser to no avail. *Had he been arrested again?* Who knew? They'd pulled every string for answers. Houda finally came to a disquieting conclusion: the reason they could not find Nasser was because her brother did not want to be found.

That was why it was so important for Houda to stay busy—or else the heartbreak might sweep her away like the storm that was flooding the streets. Alexandria was smack in the middle of *Nawet El-Fayda El-Kabira*, the "Big Flood," which churned big waves and stormy weather and pelted endlessly at her office window, making it impossible to concentrate. But whenever Houda stopped working, her mind went to her lost brother. It brought tears to her eyes.

"Anesa Houda," came a voice. She turned to the muscular young man who'd interrupted her thoughts: Bassem, the general manager and son of the company owner. He smiled at Houda and said, "Can you file these invoices, please?"

"Of course!" Houda replied. Bassem smiled again and turned to walk to his office.

Gigi, the girl who worked at the desk across from Houda, made one of her funny faces, holding up her hands to cover her mouth in "pretend" shyness. Houda raised a finger, signaling, *Shh! Stop it.* But Gigi giggled and covered her entire face with those long, painted nails of hers that Houda found so distracting.

Gigi loved to remind Houda that Bassem had a crush on her. Bassem seemed to stop at Houda's desk way more often than he needed to, trying to chitchat and make small talk. "What a catch!" Gigi sneaked over and whispered in Houda's ear, reminding her again of how desirable Bassem was to many girls. "Good-looking, nice family, and above all financially secure. And he's modern, not *Si-Elsayed*—you know, the kind of man who thinks he owns his wife and family." Then Gigi whispered one of her inappropriate comments with a hand gesture that made Houda's face flush red. Houda looked around quickly to see if any of the other girls in the shared office had noticed. Gigi was a master of these hand gestures, the Iskandrani way—she was something, this girl, no shame about anything. Houda darted off to file the invoices, getting away from the teasing and scrutiny of her coworkers.

In reality, Bassem was a decent guy and very respectable, handsome enough. But the color of his eyes reminded Houda too much of Adham's, although they didn't carry the same warmth. While Bassem tried to be funny, his laughter felt rehearsed, lacking the effortless charm that Adham always had. Adham could draw out her deepest laugh, one that came from a place she hadn't felt since he had left. No one could replace him, and the emptiness left in his absence seemed to widen with each passing day.

She wondered how life would have turned out if Adham had stayed here and spent time with Nasser after he was released from jail. Could he have been the difference that might have kept

Nasser among them? Houda wanted to shout across the ocean, "Adham, I need you!"

Your brother was jailed for terrorism. You're the only one who could understand!

Could she develop feelings for Bassem now? Was it worth exploring? And if she gave him the right signals, would he make an official move? Maybe not.

Houda wondered how much Bassem knew about her family. People were surely whispering things about her brother's arrest and disappearance, as well as the untimely death of her mother, now shrouded in a veil of deceit. In all these months, Houda still hadn't mustered the courage to confront her father about these secrets. Scandals like this could be a problem for a family like Bassem's.

Returning to her desk, she stared at the rain pounding relentlessly against the windowpanes. Houda felt her world getting smaller.

"Want a ride home?" Gigi was at her side again. Her fiancé was downstairs with his car.

"I still have work to do," Houda lied. She knew riding with them would be nonstop gossip, and she just wasn't in the mood. "A friend is coming to get me."

"Dalia?" Gigi was always prying.

"Yes." Another lie.

Houda waited for Gigi to leave, then went to fetch her purse and umbrella. Downstairs, the rain was coming down in buckets. Strong winds washed sweeps of water into the building entrance where Houda huddled, hoping to flag a taxi. But they were all taken, this being Thursday night, the beginning of the weekend.

～

The storm raged all night, infecting Houda's dreams. She woke up tired.

Dutifully, she prepared breakfast for her father. They ate

without talking. It was happening more and more. *Should I ask him now?* Houda wondered. *Is this the right moment?*

As always, Houda bit her tongue, torn between her desire to know the truth about her mother and her aversion to putting her father on the spot—calling him a liar would only add to his gnawing guilt and shame about Nasser.

So, forks clinked against the flatware. Tea was sipped in silence. Then the professor retreated into his study, while Houda got busy with her chores.

Keeping busy, that was the key. Even though there was not much to do—dust was not much of a factor during these rains. Still, she puttered around, she tidied up. An hour went by, maybe two. The sun finally burst through the clouds.

Then her father emerged into the hallway. "I'm going to leave soon for *Jummah*."

Houda looked at the wall clock. "A little early, no?" The small mosque that Omar liked to attend was only three minutes away.

"I'm going to Nasser's mosque," Omar explained. "That's where I wish to pray."

Houda nodded. Since her brother's disappearance, she'd accompanied her father several times on the long trek to the more conservative mosque that Nasser had started frequenting after his release from prison. They'd searched for him repeatedly and asked around to no avail.

What is the point of going back?

"Isn't that a little far, ya Baba?"

"The sun has finally come out," he said softly. "I love Alexandria after the rain. I feel like walking a little."

Houda, feeling a wave of compassion for her father, gazed at him tenderly and said, "I have no plans today; let me join you."

It was a rarity for them to go to prayers together. The mosque that Omar attended for Friday prayers was very small, with no women's section, unlike Nasser's mosque, which had a big separate hall for wives and daughters.

"*Mashy*, ya Mishkala, get ready quickly," Omar said. "We don't want to be late!"

The asphalt still glistened as they set off for the mosque. Her father was happy to have Houda at his side. They didn't mention Nasser, not once. But that's all they were thinking about.

As they approached the large mosque, their eyes swept in every direction, like the gusts of the gale—searching for a ghost that wasn't there.

～

The Jummah prayer came to its conclusion, and Houda was about to leave when she heard a whisper in her ear. "Your brother is a hero."

Startled, Houda turned to see who was saying such things. She found herself bathed in the warm glow of a pair of large, friendly hazel eyes, mottled brown when they faced Houda full-on, strikingly green when they shifted away. The rest of her face and body was entirely hidden by a flowing black niqab, and still Houda could have found her in a crowd of ten thousand, her eyes were that unique. They were ringed by lashes so thick and long they needed no mascara, and topped by a pair of trim, expressive brows. Her name, Houda would later learn, was Shahinaz.

"We've all heard of Nasser's bravery in fighting the crusaders." She smiled.

There was a group of other women behind her, all of them covered head-to-toe in black niqabs with windows only for their eyes, which appeared to be smiling, like Shahinaz's. For a moment, Houda was at a loss. Putting put both hands on Shahinaz's arm, she gasped, "What do you know about Nasser?"

Those unforgettable eyes darted about, sunbeams from the clerestory windows above picking out their rich mica flecks. "Shhh," she cautioned, "lower your voice, Sister Houda. We don't want to attract attention." Her eyes flickered back and forth once more, and she leaned in toward Houda to murmur, "The walls have ears."

Another niqab-draped woman put her hand on Shahinaz's

shoulder. "We have to go," she whispered. "My brother is waiting to drive us home."

Shahinaz looked up at the other woman, who took a step toward the door. Shahinaz turned back to Houda with a warning. "Please keep this conversation to yourself. Don't tell anyone. Let's meet here again tomorrow after *Maghrib*. We'll talk then."

Shahinaz took the hand of her friend, who said to Houda, "As-salamu alaykum, sister," and then they were gone. Houda found herself alone with a thousand questions and a wildly beating heart.

Strolling home with Omar, she didn't say a word. She needed more information before sharing any of this with her father. Holding this secret in her heart gave Houda an unexpected feeling. It felt powerful.

Later in her bedroom, Houda began her nightly prayer for Nasser. Lately, she'd been reciting it in the morning too. In fact, she'd found herself saying it at all hours of the day. Each time her thoughts turned his way, she prayed: *Ya Allah, you heard Younis in the darkness and returned him from within the whale. Ya Allah, you saved Moses from the Pharaoh and ransomed Ishmael. Ya Allah, you showed mercy for Adam. O God the beneficent, God the merciful, return Nasser to us. Forgive him and show him the way. O God the beneficent, O God the merciful, O beneficent and merciful . . .*

There was no sleeping.

~

The following day, Houda left an hour before Maghrib to allow herself ample time. She tried to dally, taking in buildings and gardens along the way, but still found herself in front of the women's door of the mosque with half an hour to spare. Houda adjusted her headscarf nervously. She did not wear the hijab, but she had been covering her hair when she came here to pray. Most of the women who prayed here wore the full niqab, tenting the entire body in black, save for a narrow slit for the eyes.

Houda entered the hall and found herself in the familiar, dim, filtered light. A few women were already here, smoothing out their prayer mats on the worn green carpet, chatting in low murmurs. She decided to read the *Surat Ya Sin* to calm her nerves. Houda knew it by heart, but she drew out her Qur'an anyway.

"*Ya sin*," she murmured, "by the wise Qur'an, indeed you, ya Mohammed, are from among the messengers on a straight path . . ." Houda quickly realized that even though her lips were reciting, her mind was racing, and her eyes had strayed from the Qur'an's pages to survey the congregation growing around her in the women's gallery.

Is Shahinaz here yet? Even after meeting her just once, Houda knew she would recognize her hazel eyes anywhere. But she could be in front, concealed by her niqab, her back to Houda.

The tinny *Allahu Akbar* of the adhan came from the loud-speakers mounted in the minaret far above. Everyone stood to begin the prayer, but even then Houda's eyes kept sliding to the door. "*Hayya ala salah! Hayya ala falah!*" came the muezzin's flattened, processed voice—*come to prayer, come to success*. Finally, she saw Shahinaz come through the door. Their eyes met; Shahinaz came toward Houda.

"No time to talk now," she murmured as she took a place next to her. The prayer began, and Houda did her best to concentrate on the words as they recited the prayer, but it was hard. Houda's eyes kept sliding toward Shahinaz, her mind pawing at the question, *What does she know?*

Finally, the prayer was over, and they sat on the soft carpet in the corner. Houda whispered, "Sister Shahinaz, please, please tell me. Where is Nasser? How is he, what is he doing? He is my only brother, my best friend, and I'm afraid that . . . I'm afraid—" Houda choked back a sob.

Shahinaz took Houda's hand. "I can see the sadness in you, Sister Houda, and it touches my heart," she said softly. "I don't know much," she admitted. "I only heard about Brother Nasser once, just in passing, when someone told me who you were. They said he is a hero in our jihad against the infidels—the American invaders."

"Who said this?" Houda was shocked.

"I can't tell you, Sister Houda," Shahinaz whispered. "It would put us both in danger."

Houda stared at her in a conflict of emotions. *Nasser—a jihadist? Where? Afghanistan? Iraq?*

The prospect of her brother in war zone made her feel sick to her stomach.

On the other hand, here was someone—like her, like Dalia, like all of them—who saw Nasser as a hero, which made Houda feel like she wasn't alone.

As the weeks passed by, Shahinaz and Houda saw one another with increasing frequency at the mosque's Islamic lessons, in which Houda had taken an interest. They never discussed Nasser again, but they talked about everything else. Sometimes Houda would visit Shahinaz's apartment and chat with her parents and younger sisters.

The first time Shahinaz came to Houda's house, Baba did a double take—his daughter had never brought home a friend who wore the niqab before. Omar welcomed her with his usual warmth and kindness, of course, and even after Shahinaz left, he said nothing about her niqab—but Houda knew that Omar El-Mohammedi wouldn't hold his tongue forever.

One morning at the mosque, Shahinaz spent the *Duhar* service buzzing with barely contained excitement. Houda could see it in her eyes and in her every gesture, even swathed in dark fabric as she was. Houda could hardly wait until the prayers were done to ask what had happened, but before she could even open her mouth, Shahinaz burst out, "Sister Houda, you *have* to come over this afternoon! You'll never believe it. You remember Zeinab? My next-door neighbor?" Houda had met her once or twice. "She has invited us to a private lesson with the Sheikh!" The Sheikh was a well-known TV host with a talk show about the Islamic way of life. Houda could see a thrill run through every muscle in Shahinaz's body, and she squeezed her hands so tightly that Houda thought they might crack.

Houda accepted. Curiosity flooded her. *What will the Sheikh speak about? And how did Shahinaz's neighbor get him to come?* Houda knew the neighbor's family was relatively affluent; they also probably knew many influential people as well. Even with that, Houda had heard it was nearly impossible to get an audience with the Sheikh even in Cairo, let alone inducing him to make the two-hundred-kilometer journey north to Alexandria. He must be visiting here anyway.

The afternoon took forever to arrive; Houda was at Shahinaz's an hour early. When the time finally came, Zeinab embraced them at the door and showed them into her family's salon area. The apartment was enormous—probably two or three apartments originally, now combined into one spacious place that was the latest word in interior design and pleasantly perfumed with a faint *bakhoor* incense.

In the cool salon, another ten or eleven women sat on comfortable chairs, divans, and ottomans. Everyone was chatting; some were drinking tea. About half wore the niqab and half the hijab; only one other woman's head was only casually covered, like Houda's. Shahinaz was just introducing her to a couple of acquaintances when the doorbell's clear tones resounded and someone cried out, "He's here! *The Sheikh!*" Houda noticed a couple of girls adjusting their scarves, tucking away stray wisps of hair, as all of them stood up.

The Sheikh gave a polite knock on the open door's frame, then entered. Houda had expected a showboating television personality, but everything in the Sheikh's body language spoke of humility. "As-salamu alaykum, my sisters," he said in a soft voice, his gaze lowered, not looking at anyone in particular.

"Wa alaykum as-salam," they chorused in response. Zeinab showed the Sheikh to a seat, and everyone sat down again as he began to speak. Next to Houda, Shahinaz leaned forward to listen more intently. Houda felt like a bit of an outsider. It wasn't her first *dars*—lesson—but the Sheikh's style was different from that of others. He was charming, his speech never forceful, his voice low and reverent. For fifteen minutes, he described his vision of a good Muslim life in the busy, confusing modern world. Then someone spoke up.

"My brother," she inquired, "what is your opinion of the niqab?" From the angle at which she was sitting, Houda couldn't see whether the woman who had spoken wore the niqab or not. But the daughter of Professor Omar El-Mohammedi was familiar with the perennial battle of the hijab and the niqab, the requisite covering of the head or face—lots of people, her own baba included, disputed their necessity. The Sheikh paused for a long moment; he seemed to be whispering something to himself. Houda wondered whether he was praying.

From such a modest, almost deferential man, the force of his words when they came out surprised her: "My sisters, the hijab is obligatory in Islam, and the niqab is recommended."

A little buzz went through the room; Shahinaz and Zeinab's pious friends were pleased to hear the Sheikh's opinions echoing their own. He continued with a Qur'an verse they all knew well: "Ya Prophet! Tell thy wives and daughters, and the believing women, that they should cast their outer garments over their persons when abroad: that is most convenient, that they should be known as believers and not molested. And Allah is oft-forgiving, most merciful."

Even before the Sheikh started to explain his position, Houda's father's oft-repeated words rang in her ear. How many times had he told her to understand the *context* of this verse? Opinions differed, the professor would say, about the meaning of *jalabib*, or "outer garment." Her father's approach was always guided by intellect, not by the faith that seemed to flow so naturally from the people around her. It was as if he stood outside, observing with curiosity rather than devotion, and that colored his judgment.

The Sheikh began to weave in a theme about the protection

of Muslim women from hypocrites, perverts, and mischief-makers. "Look around you, my sisters," he counseled softly, "to the lost men in the streets. They can't control themselves. Look at the collapse of ethics in our society. In today's age, the temptation of women can be too much for some men. It builds on them day in and day out. Sisters, how do you want to treat yourselves and others? You must be above all that. Above all, you must play your role to protect Ummah, the nation of believers."

In the days after the Sheikh's dars, Houda found herself paying more attention to her prayers. She went with Shahinaz to more lessons and found herself paying better attention there too. She was surprised at the peace that stole over her in those moments, peace that had eluded her for so long. When Houda was focused on the prayers and lessons, Nasser intruded less and less upon her thoughts. At first, she felt guilty about thinking of her brother less, but then she began to wonder whether he haunted Houda less as she began to live the life he had wanted for her.

That was when she first began to picture herself in the niqab. As summer cooled toward Alexandria's long and lovely autumn, she thought and prayed about it often. Was she swayed by the arguments the Sheikh had made in his lesson? She didn't think so —for the first time in her life, she felt like she was making a decision for herself alone. Houda wanted the niqab, she realized, because she was finding peace and solace in her faith, in true Islam.

Houda didn't take Shahinaz shopping with her; she wanted to do this entirely on her own. And as she fingered the cotton, silk, and cashmere veils at the shops in El-Manshia, she realized her heart felt this was the right thing to do. Her life had been so empty, so devoid of interests, but this called out to her. As the daughter of Omar El-Mohammedi, she certainly knew it might not be obligatory or even recommended. But Houda could think of no argument that said wearing the niqab was wrong. There was nothing against it in any strand of Islam.

Houda decided she should tell Baba about her decision before she began to wear the niqab. Her love and respect for him demanded it.

She prepared herself for a lecture from him: *This has nothing to do with Islam*, he would say. He would cite the Qur'an, stressing how moderate its views on gender were, how men were admonished to lower their gaze and not place the entire responsibility for their desire on women. He would go on about how this tribal and backward cultural practice, foreign to Egypt's traditions and its liberal movements, had been pushed on Egyptians in their time of weakness. He would remind Houda, as he often did, of the generation of women that had led the way for unveiling and emancipation. Did Houda want the progress they had made to be lost? He would say all these things and more, and Houda would show respect by listening.

On the evening she chose to tell him, they were sitting, as they often did, at the cleared-away dinner table, making conversation, which thankfully seemed to be finally reemerging in their lifeless home. Houda waited for a natural pause. Then she looked him in the eye and said simply, "Walidi, I have come to a decision. I'm going to wear the niqab. I've been thinking about this for a while, and I've made my choice carefully and freely."

Her father stared at her, for once at a loss for words. His gaze pinned her for what seemed like an eternity. Then he blinked, stood up, and kissed her forehead. "Houda," he pronounced, "I've taught you as much as I can. You are an adult with free will." Putting a hand on her shoulder, he smiled at her kindly. Before retiring to his bedroom, Omar paused to add the kindest words of all, "Your mother would be proud of you."

Houda was left at the table, pondering far into the night.

2006: NORTHERN CALIFORNIA

RAIN WAS TO BE EXPECTED. It was the Bay Area, after all, where morning fog and showers came on a whim and crashed all occasions—weddings were certainly fair game, especially in winter.

Risa had been fixated on having a New Year's Eve wedding ever since high school, after seeing *When Harry Met Sally*, a movie she insisted they watch together, convinced Youssef would love it as much as she did. And she was right. By now, he knew how much she adored these romantic comedies, and the sappy ending had them both in tears, clinching the idea of New Year's Eve as their date. Marin was likewise special to them as the place of their first kiss, which had happened during a drive through Muir Woods on their way to Stinson Beach.

Winding through the soaring redwoods, Youssef had been floored; he'd never experienced a biome like this, with trees far taller than the highest palms in Egypt. They'd stopped the car at a turnout to gaze up at the magnificence—trunks soaring so high they got lost in the low clouds. Youssef was in awe. Risa watched him, her heart full of love. Youssef was like a little boy, his eyes wide with wonder. When he turned to her, he whispered one word, "Wow." Risa nodded. They gazed at each other without speaking for a moment—and that's when it happened. They shared a kiss that seemed to echo with the promise of something lasting. Even now, she could still almost feel that first brush of his lips, a memory that warmed her whenever she thought of it.

That day, under the redwoods, a gentle drizzle turned into a steady rain, and he instinctively reached for her hand. They shared a knowing smile, savoring the shared moment as they walked back to the car together, the rain a soft rhythm around them. Risa remembered thinking, *I'm going to marry this guy.* It felt absurd at the time to have that feeling about someone so foreign to her— an Egyptian Muslim she'd only just met. But here they were now, still feeling the warmth of that kiss, just days from tying the knot. And the forecast: scattered showers.

They say it's good luck, thought Risa optimistically.

The weather was the least of her worries. More concerning to Risa were the brooding tensions and skirmishes stemming from travel logistics, missing luggage, cultural and time zone differences, jet lag, and the myriad complications of an ambitious destination wedding attempting to unite the major Abrahamic religions—a cohort of American Jews, scattered Christians, and a clan of Egyptian Muslims—most of them meeting for the first time.

"Every wedding has at least one good fight." Risa's sister, Suzanna, tried to normalize the inevitable. But no one could have predicted the breaking news bombshell that came out of nowhere and shrouded everything in a pall of uncertainty.

The weekend began innocently enough—a boisterous Friday welcome dinner, pungent Middle Eastern spices mingling with ocean salt and the smell of cedar that paneled the rustic dining hall of the lodge where everyone was staying. When laughter faded under the weight of jet lag, the Egyptians retired to their cabins. Risa and Youssef had been booked, for propriety and decorum, into their own separate rooms, to which they dutifully retired. Risa didn't mind; she respected the tradition and spent the night gossiping with her sister.

On Saturday morning, she sneaked into Youssef's cabin to see his face, which was pensive, staring through the window at the coastal fog. "You're thinking about Nasser." She read his mind.

He nodded, shrugged. Risa pulled him close for a hug. After Nasser's release from prison two years ago, they'd hoped for a minute that he might have made the trek to California. Youssef had even harbored fantasies of Nasser being his best man, an honor now bestowed upon Adam, who was more than happy to step in. But Risa knew that, for Youssef, no one could really replace Nasser, the de facto leader of the "Alexandria Four." She also knew, through her association with the Bradford clan, that friendship and family ties were often tainted by status and money. Even though they'd sent an invitation to Stephanie's Uncle Pete, it was no surprise that he'd sent his "regrets." The senator would not be attending their nuptials; neither would Nasser, who had been missing for months—no one knew where. Risa knew how devastating this was for Youssef.

She started to say something, when a knock on the cabin's door provided a welcome shift in mood. Outside stood her mom, Sophie, and Youssef's mother, Soad, their arms entwined. Her mother must have made some joke just before Risa opened the door, because she was snorting a little and looking smug, while Youssef's mother's head was thrown back, her body shaking with a deep belly laugh. Standing behind them, Youssef's sister, Iman, was laughing too, having translated and explained the joke for her mother, who had limited English.

Risa knew her family was doing everything in their power to make the Egyptians feel comfortable, but Risa wondered what her left-wing Jewish mom was really thinking as she stood arm-in-arm with Soad in her cheery flowered hijab. If Sophie was anything other than utterly happy, she didn't show it.

"You two shouldn't be together!" she admonished half-mockingly. "It's bad luck for a bride to see her groom before the ceremony."

"Our wedding is tomorrow," Risa pointed out.

"Still time to call it off." Youssef made a terrible joke, which had all the women scowling.

"Please forgive my rude brother," Iman said to Risa, taking her soon-to-be sister-in-law's hand. It was a sweet gesture that Risa appreciated. "I need you to cover your eyes." Iman moved Risa's hand gently to her face as she used her free hand to slip Youssef a small leather box containing the wedding ring that had once belonged to their grandmother.

The clouds parted throughout the morning, and by noon, dazzling sunrays lit up the rolling glades with patches of emerald brilliance. They split off into subgroups—a serene walk on the beach, a bucolic hike in the hills.

That evening, at the rehearsal dinner, was when the sparks flew—though they began innocently enough. Risa sat happily at the main table, loving that they were all gathering here: Adam and Valería, clustered with Youssef's parents, while Suzanna, Iman, and Sophie took turns playing with Adam and Valería's son, Gabe. Risa mentally invoked an image of her dad, an activist like her, who had struggled with alcoholism and was gone from the world far too soon. Risa glanced at Youssef. *He's going to make a great dad*, she thought.

Wine was flowing, and even some of the Egyptians, largely secular, were partaking, though not quite as much as the Americans, like Risa's distant cousin David.

"Congratulations, Joe," he said, putting his arm a little drunkenly around Youssef, who tried not to show how that Westernized version of his name annoyed him.

"You don't mind me calling you *Joe*, do you?" David persisted. "The name *Youssef* makes me think of Cat Stevens, whom I used to love so much as a kid, and then it all got so complicated when he changed his name to *Yusuf*."

"Who is this 'Cats Tevens' that became 'Yusuf'?" asked Adam curiously.

"You don't know Cat Stevens?" David was flabbergasted. "The amazing superstar singer who became a Muslim—it must have been major news where your family is!"

In fact, it hadn't been that big a deal in Egypt, particularly for the middle class. Even someone like Adam, who'd been exposed to Western culture through his love of cinema, was not familiar with him. "Have his songs been used in a movie?" Adam asked.

Valería racked her brain, then she exclaimed, "*Remember the Titans*! That song you couldn't get out of your head: 'Now I've been smiling lately . . .'" she began the tune in her beautiful soprano voice.

"I love that song!" Adam nodded. "What's it called?"

"Oh, boy, you guys really don't know 'Peace Train'?" David rolled his eyes.

"Do you know Iolanda Gigliotti?" Adam retorted.

"Who?" David squinted.

"Dalida?" Adam kept firing.

"Can I buy a vowel?" David shrugged.

"Oh boy," Adam teased. "You're really out of touch."

Risa glanced at Stephanie, who was attending solo like David. Matt was away as always—god only knew where. They shared a smile, amused by this innocent sparring between the camps.

"Iolanda Gigliotti changed her name to *Dalida*," Adam lectured David. "A famous world-class singer, she performed in eleven languages. Probably sold more records than your Yusuf guy. But really—we're happy he became a Muslim. That makes us, what, 1.3 billion plus one, I guess."

Everyone laughed.

"Whatever." David tried to save face by turning back to Youssef and saying, "I'm still calling him *Joe*."

Then a shriek came from the hall. Sophie came darting in, looking as white as a sheet. "They just hanged Saddam!"

Risa and Youssef looked at each other in horror as everyone rushed into the hallway where CNN was playing on a wall-mounted monitor—Saddam Hussein had indeed been executed for his war crimes. The timing of his execution had not been announced in advance by the Iraqi Special Tribunal, which had handed down the death penalty two months prior. They'd decided, for security reasons, to keep the fulfillment of Saddam's sentence deliberately under the radar and report it only after the fact. So, here it was—crashing the rehearsal dinner of their interfaith wedding weekend.

Thank god it didn't happen tomorrow, thought Risa, trying to grasp for a silver lining.

A different thought ran through the mind of Youssef and many of the other Egyptians. This was Eid al-Adha, the "Feast of Sacrifice," one of the main holidays of Islam, celebrated over four days according to the Islamic lunar calendar. Eid al-Adha, which had begun at sunset that day, honored Ibrahim's willingness to sacrifice his son Ismail as an act of obedience to God. Ibrahim, or Abraham, was the patriarch and prophet of Jews, Christians, and Muslims alike. For observant Muslims, celebrating this holiday involved slaughtering an animal and sharing its meat in three equal parts—for family, for relatives and friends, and for poor people. Even though they were nonobservant and did not partake in the sacrifices, the Almasry clan still appreciated it as an auspicious day for the wedding. Youssef was baffled as to why the Americans had chosen it as an appropriate time to execute Saddam.

This spells trouble, he thought, glancing at his relatives to gauge their reactions.

Risa was scanning faces too. Most people were subdued; some, like her tipsy cousin David, however, appeared celebratory, raising his almost-empty glass and declaring smugly, "The bastard got what he deserved—that's what happens when you mess with Americans!"

Here we go again, Risa thought as she sighed. Then David made matters decidedly worse by looking around at the Egyptians and saying, "No offense to you all."

Just as Risa was about to react, Youssef stepped protectively between her and David, squaring his shoulders and facing him man to man.

"Listen, brother," he said with astonishing poise, "you have this all wrong."

Risa watched her soon-to-be husband with a surge of pride. She could tell that Youssef was seething inside but containing it with striking dignity. "The Muslim world is complicated and very diverse—just like America," he explained. "You can't reduce us to a single point of view."

Adam nodded, impressed, like Risa, by Youssef's quiet power —he seemed to be channeling Omar. "Saddam is a ruthless tyrant who committed genocide against his own people," Youssef continued. "My family was almost killed by his aggression in the region. We were in Kuwait at the time. Egypt doesn't even share a border with Iraq; we are hardly fans of Saddam Hussein."

"I'm sorry," David mustered, feeling like an idiot.

"Apology accepted," said Youssef, extending his hand, which David shook clumsily.

Youssef's parents, brimming with pride, watched their son put an arm instinctively around his wife-to-be, as all eyes turned back to the news broadcast. Risa wondered if others were thinking what she was thinking. *Does this really make us safer? Will there be retaliation?*

She could tell that her cousin Stephanie looked unnerved too. Stephanie had recently confided in Risa that she suspected Matt was lying to her about his whereabouts. A few weeks earlier, she'd stumbled upon a pack of Cleopatra cigarettes in Matt's carry-on bag—certainly *not* available in Arizona, where he had claimed to have been traveling. Even while she'd suspected for some time that "military attaché" was code for "spy," Stephanie couldn't bear to think of Matt operating clandestinely in a war zone.

On the rare nights that they shared a bed, Matt would often wake up suddenly in a cold sweat, shaking off a nightmare. "What's going on, Matt?" she'd ask as gently as she could.

"The less you know, the better," he'd say, catching his breath. "Trust me."

Both Risa and Stephanie knew that Saddam being dead did not make the Middle East any safer. If anything, this kind of power vacuum made things even more volatile. The unexpected news flash had deflated their festivities—there would be no dancing that night. After watching the CNN feed for a few more minutes, the guests, whether jet-lagged or local, dispersed to their cabins.

Rain came again during the night.

By morning, any residue of Saddam had been washed away.

2007: ALEXANDRIA

DALIA FELT fidgety and out of place in the black wave of niqabs that swept across the women's section of the big mosque. She wasn't even wearing a proper hijab; she'd covered her hair respectfully but felt defiant nonetheless—the opposite of how she usually felt at ceremonies like this. Even for someone relatively liberal like Dalia, there was something sacred about weddings—though she'd never seen a couple getting married at a mosque before. All the weddings she'd attended had been at five-star hotels, where girls would jump on stage to join the singer and men would invariably flirt with the belly dancer. And the moment the couple became officially betrothed always brought tears to Dalia's eyes.

So, why am I feeling numb?

This was Houda—she was practically family, though covered in the niqab, she may as well have been a stranger. Tarek, the groom, was certainly a stranger; this was the first time Dalia had set eyes on him. Apparently, Houda had only recently met Tarek herself.

Why had Houda kept him hidden from everyone?

Courtship and the engagement process were normally communal affairs, with both families getting involved. None of this had happened. Dalia had no idea how Houda and her soon-to-be husband had even met. All Dalia knew about Tarek was that he seemed rather stern-looking, a bit stiff—clearly quite religious and conservative. It all felt so wrong. Dalia was now as worried for Houda as she was for Nasser.

"*Zawagtok Ibnaty,*" Omar repeated after the *alma'athoun*, the imam wedding officiant—*marry my daughter, the virgin, the mature, and the sensible.* Dalia couldn't quite hear them from her place in the back of the room, yet she was very familiar with these words, as was every Muslim in Egypt. Dalia had even imagined her own father uttering those very words for her wedding. That would have been to Nasser—the one everyone missed but dared not speak of. His absence was felt as a constant, like ancient history that lingered just beneath the surface, always present in its silence.

This was the biggest loss of all. Here they were, gathered in the very mosque that had drawn in first Nasser, then his innocent sister. In spite of Omar's teachings on tolerance—or perhaps because of it—both his children had rebelled. And where was the piper who had led the way? Haunting the room like a ghost from a time long forgotten.

After the couple had gone off to sign the marriage papers, Dalia tried to see things from Houda's perspective. Tarek was an educated man. A pharmacist who owned his own pharmacy, he could provide a very comfortable life for Houda. With some luck, he could even expand his pharmacy and create a chain. *Why do I have so much judgment?* She felt guilty.

Dalia tried to find Houda, but all she saw were niqabs. *Where are those eyes I love so much?* Dalia tried to remember the last time she'd looked directly into Houda's eyes. It had been months; Houda had been avoiding her, just like Nasser had before he disappeared. But Dalia had not given up on them. Again and again, she tried to make time for the El-Mohammedis—a visit to Omar, a call every other day or so—but the conversations were always short. Polite, brief, and not ultimately satisfying. Dalia was determined this time to look Houda in the eyes and convey her best wishes. *Where is she?*

Only a couple of the women had engaged her in small talk. One, with distinctive hazel eyes that shined through the small slit in her otherwise covered body, introduced herself as Houda's best friend. Dalia was shocked. Who was this new "best friend" whom Dalia had never even met? Had she and Houda grown that far apart? Dalia glanced around to survey the other women in attendance—strangers, all of them. She couldn't find even a single friend from Houda's school days. Dalia glanced over at Omar, seated with the men on the other side of the hall, doing his best to smile. Her heart went out to him.

The celebrations continued for another hour or so, but the opportunity never came for Dalia to have one-on-one time with Houda, who was constantly surrounded by her new friends in their niqabs. Finally, just as Houda was about to leave for her new home with her new husband, Dalia forced her way through the crowd to hug and congratulate the girl who'd always felt like a little sister to her. Dalia gazed at the bride and said, "*Mabrouk, ya Houda.*"

Houda nodded sweetly and said, "*Rabana ya barek fiki*"— *may God bless you.*

Then Dalia found herself unexpectedly in tears. "You are like a sister to me." Dalia tried to compose herself. "And you have never been a mishkala." Yet, no matter how hard she tried, the tears kept flowing.

"I know, ya Dalia."

"I wish you all the happiness and—"

Houda looked at her and interrupted softly, "I am happy, ya Dalia. I'm really happy."

Dalia stared at those eyes that peeked out through the small window of the niqab. *Is it possible?* Was Houda really happy in this new role she'd taken on so abruptly?

"I know, I know. Forgive me," said Dalia, loath to cast a pall on the wedding. "These are tears of joy."

"Time to go, ya Houda," came a voice from another niqab—the hazel-eyed girl.

"One moment, Shahinaz," said Houda, turning back to Dalia for a last hug. "I know, ya Dalia. I know." Then the niqabs swarmed around her and swept her out.

Dalia made sure there was no sign of her tears as she entered the car where Omar was waiting to be driven home. The ride began in silence, which soon became unbearable. Dalia forced herself to fill the void with congratulatory talk to lighten the mood. She talked in glowing terms about Tarek's family, even though she'd barely met them, doing her best to assure Omar that Houda was in good hands. She knew that he was about to return to an empty home, with no one to look after him anymore. The professor tried to keep a brave face and his dignity, replying to each of Dalia's well wishes with "inshallah."

When they arrived at Omar's house, she sprang out to open the passenger door and gave the professor a long and loving hug. Then Omar turned with his cane and limped quietly into the apartment. As Dalia watched him disappear, her eyes once again flooded with tears.

Nasser . . . Nasser—where are you?

Dalia was in a mood the following day at brunch with her mother at Smouha private club. She'd wanted to cancel, but her mother wouldn't have it. Dalia was still furious at her parents for skipping the wedding.

"How was it?" her mother asked without much enthusiasm.

"Good," Dalia replied tersely.

"Good," her mother parroted. "Then perhaps it's time to remove that ring—*rings*," she corrected herself, still confused as to why her headstrong daughter insisted on wearing two engagement rings—a symbolic gesture she'd adopted after Nasser's disappearance. Dalia knew that Omar had noticed the rings at least once, though he hadn't commented on them. *Why not?* she wondered.

Out of modesty, perhaps—Omar was sensitive enough to know that people processed heartbreak in their own way; they might not appreciate others' opinions. This boundary did not exist for Dalia's domineering mother.

"You are no longer engaged. Time to move on from *those people*."

"*Those people?*" Dalia practically spat out, covering her precious rings with her right hand. "That's what you call Omar El-Mohammedi and his family?"

Her mother shrugged nonchalantly. "This professor, he's not even worth three cents—and his crazy son, who is he? God only knows."

Dalia could not contain her fury. "Three-cent professor? Crazy son! That's what you call the man I love, my fiancé, the brilliant engineer, my business partner?"

"Your fiancé? Brilliant? Then why did he throw it all away? Where is he hiding?"

Dalia exploded, "This three-cent professor is like my father. He's my teacher, as he is to so many. Professor El-Mohammedi is—"

"He's not your father, that's for sure," her mother interrupted with venom. "He will never be your father—and thank God for that! It's time you started thinking about your family, your brother's future, and our standing in society. You can't be associated with people like this."

Dalia and her mother locked gazes, like two fighters circling and sizing each other up. Then her mother changed tactics. Speaking very softly, she said, "My daughter, the light of my eyes, I want nothing more for you than happiness. I want you to make sure that your life is a comfortable one."

Dalia finally replied, "Mother, I understand this is difficult for you—it is for me too. But I also know in my heart that Nasser will be back." Looking at her mother with defiant eyes, she added, "I'm not taking these rings off of my finger."

Mrs. Kenawy sighed. "I know you loved him, but it is time to move on." She paused for a moment. "I am your mother—you are the world to me. You can trust me."

She could see that Dalia was not buying it. "Is it because you gave him what he wanted?"

Dalia's eyes became fiery. "What did he want?"

"What every man wants," said her mother cavalierly. "But we can take care of that. No one would ever know. There's a clinic that can fix you. We can make you whole again."

Dalia was in shock. "How dare you make that assumption! Nasser respected and loved me. He never had that expectation!" She looked squarely into her mother's eyes. "But if he had wanted to have me, I would have given him everything!"

Mrs. Kenawy stood up, furious at her daughter's insolence. She lowered her voice, so as not to be heard by the other patrons, and said, "*Ya fagra!*"

Though her mother had called her a slut, Dalia held her ground. "No man but Nasser will ever have me."

That was when Dalia's younger brother, Seif, waltzed up to the table—late, as always, and never chastised. Dalia detested the double standard—boys always got away with murder, especially ones like Seif, who played the sociopolitical game like a master. A rising star in the military, he was untouchable, his upward trajectory all but assured.

Seif dutifully pecked his mother's cheek. "Where are you going, Mother? Let's sit, no?" He gallantly pulled back her chair. Mrs. Kenawy sat, red-faced, without a word. Seif noticed the tension in his sister's face. "What did I miss?"

"Nothing," she replied, brooding. Then something occurred to Dalia that gave her solace. *This is how* he *must have felt—like an alien from his own parent.*

Suddenly, and quite unexpectedly, she felt a hand squeeze hers as if someone were sitting next to her. Nasser's presence bloomed in Dalia's heart, as strong as ever.

2008: TIKRIT

SHARIF LOVED to watch Nasser tinker—in his element, methodical, precise, and focused. There were no cares, no distractions; just a pile of electronics looking to be tamed, decoded, and reconstructed. Their only light in this dim cellar was the headlamp on Nasser's head—fading by the minute as the remaining volts drained from its ancient battery. They had no spare.

"Pliers," said Nasser, his voice steady and calm like a surgeon. Sharif handed him a pair of needle-nose pliers, which Nasser used to loosen the connectors affixed to a circuit board. He was taking apart an iridium satellite phone intercepted from an unlucky marine they'd managed to ambush in the Triangle of Death near Al-Hillah. Even more urgent than appropriating his weapons had been confiscating the American's instruments of communication. That was the explicit mandate from their field commanders—especially now that they had an engineer like Nasser on the scene, someone who could hack and modify electronics to their advantage.

"Toothpick," he said.

Sharif had it ready, and he even knew what came next. "Here's the glue."

"Perfect." Nasser nodded his approval, which made Sharif melt.

"We make a good team," he ventured. Nasser smiled in reply. Sharif glowed.

He'd never known a man like this. There was nothing about Nasser that Sharif didn't admire, especially here in a war zone, where he seemed to have a superhuman ability to maintain his composure. All the fighters worshipped Nasser's brilliance at cracking the enemy's surveillance tactics, managing always to stay one step ahead of them. You definitely wanted this guy on your team. That was why Sharif made a point of staying within Nasser's orbit at all times. In a place where a drone strike could come out of nowhere and kill him in an instant, Sharif fed off Nasser's calm. *If Allah's will for me is to die here, then let my last breath be with him at my side.*

The best part of it was that they'd been given an explicit order to stick together from the Teacher himself. After Sharif had been released from prison, he'd received a message from Roken through an intermediary: *Find the professor's son, and bring him to the front lines in Iraq. Keep eyes on him at all times; do not leave his side.*

Locating Nasser had been the easy part, as had enlisting him to the cause. Sharif had anticipated some resistance from Nasser, but he seemed more than ready to leave his life, family, and friends. It was the overland trek to the battlefield in Iraq that proved the most challenging. They'd crossed the Sinai to a distant outpost, where they were to be met by guides. The designated rendezvous was a remote beach on the Gulf of Aqaba, halfway between Taba and Nuweiba, on the shore across from the Salah El-Din Castle on Pharaoh's Island—a smaller fort compared to the famous structure in Cairo, both named after the Muslim legend of the Crusades.

As instructed, they'd arrived at midnight on the new moon, which made it pitch black. Yet, as their eyes adjusted to the starlight, they noticed a camouflaged cavern in the rocky embankment. Several figures emerged carrying a wooden boat, which they used to cross the narrow strait. They were met on the Jordanian side by an escort with camels. Posing as Bedouins, they crossed the desert and entered Iraq through the unguarded frontier south of Trebil. The grueling journey of more than a thousand kilometers was enshrouded in silence, accompanied only by the soft, rhythmic crunch of footsteps on sand as they traveled by night and rested during the scorching daylight under tent flaps with rationed food and limited water—and it took the better part of a month.

For someone coming from a life of relative privilege, Nasser seemed unperturbed by the ordeal—accepting and even taking solace in the austerity. He performed his prayers with devotion, took time for scriptural study, wrote daily in his journal, and never complained.

Once they arrived in Iraq, however, Sharif noticed a shift in Nasser's mood. The first disappointment was not receiving a personal welcome from the Teacher, whom they had yet to see. Roken was always on the move—his whereabouts on any given day were a mystery to all but his most trusted lieutenants, who were tasked with relaying orders to operatives in the field, each team deliberately siloed from the others, again as a security matter. So, there was none of the camaraderie that Nasser and Sharif had felt in prison. They were on their own, scavenging for food, in constant danger, unsure of whom to trust, where to sleep.

It was highly stressful. They used disposable burner phones for communication, changing them once a week or so. But Nasser, with his knowledge of all things electronic, from software to geolocation code, was able to hack the phones to render them untraceable. That's when everyone realized how useful he could be. Their tactics changed overnight. Rather than inflicting mayhem in random opportunistic strikes, they gathered intel patiently through electronic surveillance, then attacked high-value targets.

Then, a month later, there was second turn in Nasser's demeanor. It happened after they'd been summoned to Tikrit at the northern tip of the Sunni Triangle—the most explosive area of the conflict. Nowhere was there greater tension between Sunni and Shia Muslims than in this volatile part of Iraq, a country where Shia were the majority, as in Iran. The rest of the Middle East—Turkey, Jordan, Syria, Saudi Arabia, and Egypt—was majority Sunni. Sectarian violence had surged in Iraq because Saddam had been of the minority Sunni sect. So had his loyalists, who'd gone underground after his fall. In the power vacuum that followed, angry Shias took to the streets, and the country devolved into an all-out civil war. The Sunni Triangle was the epicenter of the fight. That was why Nasser and Sharif had to be on high alert as they ventured north.

They were instructed to travel at night along the river, avoiding the main road at all costs and people wherever possible. When an encounter was unavoidable, Sharif would do the talking, having mastered a passable Iraqi accent. They had a close call one night, after a driver asked them for help getting his truck out of a ditch. When Sharif fumbled to make an excuse, the driver saw right through the ruse.

"Iskandrani?" he inquired. Not only had he known they were Egyptians, he'd pinpointed them as being from Alexandria. Sharif went into a sudden panic; Nasser kept his cool and smiled. The driver grinned. He, too, was Sunni—a supporter of their insurgency. After they helped to liberate his pickup from the muddy trench, the driver offered them a ride and delivered them to their destination—a forlorn slum on the northern outskirts of Tikrit.

Waiting for the driver to leave and scanning the area for any signs of surveillance, they followed instructions to head down the alley adjacent to the bombed-out hospital. Crossing an open sewer, they made a diagonal through the overgrown field that had once been a football pitch and spotted their destination: a small, unassuming cinder-block home with a blue-tiled roof—the safe house. They'd made it!

Exchanging a smile with Nasser, who was as excited as he was to see the Teacher, Sharif knocked on the door. One knock, pause, two quick knocks—and again: one, pause, one, two.

Nothing. Just as Sharif was about to repeat the knock code, the door swung open to reveal a jihadist sentry with a thick beard and a Kalashnikov. He squinted into the darkness. "Were you followed?" They shook their heads. "Inside," he whispered. "Quickly."

The sentry led them down a dark corridor where light was coming from an open door along the way. Sharif paused to glance into the room and felt his spine chill. He saw a metal box sitting on a workbench labeled:

Danger!!
Radioactive Waste

There was Hebrew writing below it that he didn't understand.

"This way," hissed the sentry impatiently. "No time to waste."

Sharif caught up, wondering if Nasser had also noticed the disturbing box. At the end of the hall, they came to a room where a large man, surrounded by bodyguards, was seated in an armchair. It was Abu Gabel, a Syrian, who was to be their handler.

No Roken. Sharif could see that Nasser shared his disappointment. They'd been in Iraq for nearly eight months, and not one meeting with the Teacher, the one who had led them to join this fight. There was something in Nasser's eyes—a flicker of unresolved curiosity. Nasser had mentioned once that he needed to ask Roken how he knew about the bullet, a mystery tied to his father. When would he get the chance? Questions lingered in the air, heavy and unspoken.

"Welcome, heroes, welcome," said Abu Gabel, gesturing for them to sit on a bench facing his chair. Turning first to Nasser, he said, "Brother Nasser, tales of your ability to deal with the enemy's electronics are becoming legendary."

Before Nasser could even nod, Abu Gabel frowned at him, saying, "But your refusal to carry out certain orders is unacceptable."

"I am not here to kill Iraqi civilians," Nasser stated calmly. "Only the American invaders who are here without cause."

"That's not how our jihad works," snapped Abu Gabel, his temper rising. "Innocents must die at times for the glory of Allah, who greets each of them in Paradise as martyrs. The goal is mayhem. That's the way to shake those infidels who have grips on power. The Teacher has used this tactic for decades—even in Egypt. The Palm Sunday attack, Sinai bombings, Luxor train massacre . . ."

Nasser did a double take. "Luxor train? What train? What year?"

"Train 63 in 1986," said Abu Gabel.

"*Train 63?*" Nasser's body tensed suddenly.

"Enough," came a voice from the shadows. Everyone fell silent as Roken stepped into the light from a darkened corner where he'd been observing the conversation. He walked up to Nasser and faced him squarely. "Asymmetrical warfare is never easy. We make difficult choices, using all means at our disposal."

"The goal is mayhem," repeated Abu Gabel, which brought a rebuke from Roken.

"Quiet!" He frowned before turning back to Nasser. "The Prophet Mohammed, peace and blessings be upon him, won battles against larger enemies, and we—"

No sooner had he uttered those words than the neighborhood was shaken by an explosion, followed by automatic gunfire. The sentry came rushing down the hall.

"Teacher," he shouted, "we are under attack!"

"Down the tunnel," shouted Abu Gabel. "Quick!"

He pushed aside his chair, revealing a trapdoor. Guards immediately helped Roken climb down the ladder to a subterranean escape tunnel, while Abu Gabel darted to retrieve something from the nearby room. Sharif saw it was the metal box labeled "radioactive."

Is Nasser seeing this? he wondered.

"Close the hatch after you come," Abu Gabel said to them,

disappearing into the escape tunnel as the gunfire got louder and closer.

"You go first," Nasser said to Sharif, looking out for his safety, as he'd done all along. Sharif descended into the blackness, which was putrid—clearly connected to the sewer.

He made sure that Nasser was with him before following the others, who were distant by now. Rats scurried at their feet as they scrambled to catch up. Sharif slipped on a puddle and fell. Nasser helped him to his feet. Finally, they reached the opening, where the escape tunnel emerged around the corner on the neighboring street. Sharif strained to see where the others had gone in the darkness. "There!" He pointed.

"No," said Nasser. "We're taking a different path."

That's when the second change began. Nasser would no longer be taking orders from anybody.

Several days later, they were back in their own safe house on the outskirts of Baghdad—a location no one else knew about. Sharif observed how Nasser's entire body language began to change— his eyes turning murderous, like a panther about to eviscerate his prey. He would smash things at random in a sudden burst of rage, without any explanation. Sharif tried his best to understand why Nasser was behaving like this.

"Is this about the radioactive material?" he asked. "You think it's to make a dirty bomb?"

Nasser eyed him enigmatically.

"You saw it, right?"

Nasser nodded.

"The Teacher is planning something—"

"There is no more Teacher," Nasser declared. "I am planning to kill him."

"Understood," said Sharif, despite his shock.

Kill Roken? Sharif was not sure why, but his loyalty was to

Nasser now, so he nodded, saying, "Yes, we must stop the calamity."

"This has nothing to do with the dirty bomb," Nasser said. "It's about the Luxor train. My mother died on that train." That was the last Nasser ever spoke of it.

Plotting his revenge over the following weeks, Nasser paced like a caged animal. He didn't sleep, hardly ate. Not that there was much to eat. The safe house larder was nearly bare—a few cans of beans, some MRE rations stolen from the infidels. The water supply was, likewise, dangerously low. Sporadic bursts of gunfire came and went, sometimes alarmingly close. An explosion rocked the walls one night, startling Sharif from his already fitful sleep. He turned and saw Nasser's bunk, empty as always. Sharif rose and ventured into the study where he expected to see Nasser writing feverishly in his journal, which he often did late into the night—especially when he was upset.

The journal was open on the workbench, but Nasser was nowhere to be found. Sharif became anxious. Had Nasser left the safe house? He looked everywhere. Automatic gunfire echoed through the neighborhood. Sharif began to panic. *Where did he go?*

Yearning for answers, Sharif returned to the study. He hesitated before the open journal. *Dare I read it?* Sharif approached cautiously. Light from the full moon slanted through the ventilation duct. Large, angry words practically jumped off the page:

THE GOAL IS MAYHEM!

The sentence was repeated—again and again in feverish hypergraphia.

THE GOAL IS MAYHEM!
THE GOAL IS MAYHEM!
THE GOAL IS MAYHEM!

As he stared at the disturbing words, Sharif was grabbed from behind by Nasser, who shoved him against the wall with a hand at his throat. "If I catch you reading my journal again, I'll kill you."

Sharif gasped. This side of Nasser was terrifying. He watched in silence as Nasser angrily snapped up his journal, ripped out the offending page, and tore it to shreds.

THE LIBRARY OF OMAR
EL-MOHAMMEDI

APRIL 8, 2014 • 2:03 AM

THE FIRST THING Omar noticed was the missing page. A folio had been torn out—*did that have significance?* He saw the white space too, with the gale reference: El-Fayda El-Kabira, "the Big Flood." *Another throwaway? Is there a pattern to these gales?*

The diary entry began with two quotes this time, both of which Omar knew—and they offered a glimmer of hope.

> "We removed thy veil, and sharp is thy sight this Day!"
> "Everyone sees what you appear to be,
> few experience who you really are."

The first quote was from the Qur'an, 50:22. The second came from a European source, Niccolò Machiavelli. While many took umbrage at the philosophy espoused in *The Prince*, Nasser appeared to be expanding his references—or at least broadening his perspective.

December 11, 2007

I came to see that Roken was like the rest of the tyrants—another puppet master, steeped in the Consequentialism of Machiavelli: *the end justifies the means.* In

Roken's chess game, everyone was a pawn—me, my mother; we were all expendable.

The disaster of Train 63 was no accident. How could sheets of glass fly through the air, severing bodies like scimitars, in a simple derailment? It had been a bomb—an explosive planted on the tracks by Roken's minions.

And he was proud, like bin Laden, of his mayhem. But make no mistake: Roken will pay for the murder of my mother . . .

Omar's eyes widened in astonishment. He slammed his trembling palm on the desk, accidentally jostling the antique hourglass and the bullet beside it. The hourglass shattered on the floor, and the bullet rolled away, stopping near the edge of the room. Omar felt his heart thumping like a jackhammer as he stared at the glass shards and sand scattered across the ground.

Mayhem! Just like the train . . .

The door flew open, startling him even further. It was Houda.

"Father—what happened?"

Omar closed the journal quickly. "Nothing. An accident."

Train 63 was no accident. Nasser's haunting words repeated again and again in Omar's mind. *Was that true?* Houda noticed the glass, and her eyes then caught sight of the bullet. She paused, astonished to see it out in the open. Carefully, she bent down to pick it up.

"Don't move," she instructed. "I'll get the broom."

Omar watched as she placed the bullet back on the desk before leaving to fetch the broom. He sat frozen in his chair, his mind racing like a locomotive. The bullet was there, a silent witness to his anger and turmoil. He wanted to scream at Roken, to demand answers, to make him pay for the pain he had caused. But he held it in, the fury boiling just beneath the surface.

He waited impatiently for Houda to return with her broom and dustpan to clean the mess, gathering himself, collecting his calm. It was past 2 a.m., and she knew how much pain he must be feeling—she felt it too.

"Do you need anything else, Baba?" she asked sweetly. "Some tea?"

"Just privacy," he said, trying to remain calm.

Houda could tell that something was amiss but decided not to pry, withdrawing quietly from the study. Omar glanced at the bullet, his anger momentarily directed at the man it represented—Roken. The memories of that night flashed before him, but he pushed them away. He had to focus. No sooner had she shut the door than Omar rose and moved with his cane to the file cabinet where he kept his clippings and memorabilia. He located his file on Fatimah, rifled through it, and found the article from *Al-Ahram* newspaper, with its banner headline:

67 DEAD IN TRAIN DERAILMENT NEAR LUXOR
Driver of 63 Kably Fell Asleep at the Wheel

Omar reread the article with discernment. The details were scant—a vague mention of debris on the track. It slowly dawned on him that he'd been duped. *Debris?* It would have needed to be much more substantial—a major rockslide or a stalled truck—in order to derail a train.

So, why hadn't they described and reported it in greater detail?

Government authorities, as they often did, may have white-washed the incident to downplay the threat of domestic terrorism, which would have undermined their hold on power. It made Omar feel sick.

And the final line of Nasser's diary entry—that was what caused Omar the most consternation. "Roken will pay for the murder of my mother . . ."

Is this how my poor Nasser got himself killed?

PART V

EL-SHAMS EL-SAGHIRAH

El-Shams El-Saghirah ("the Little Sun")
appears in February,
lasting only three days.

It is so named because,
despite the showers,
there are nonetheless
glimmers of sunlight.

2009: MARIN

GOLDEN SUNRAYS DAPPLED the redwoods that lined the Panoramic Highway winding like a river through the enchanting Muir Woods. Yet the mood inside the Nissan LEAF was stormy.

"It still bugs me that you're coming to a cookout and not eating," Risa said, clearly annoyed with her husband—an increasingly common feeling for her these days.

"No one will notice," Youssef shot back tersely, equally annoyed with her.

Three years of marriage, and the fun was gone. That magical first kiss in these very woods seemed like the fiction of a forgotten fairy tale. *What happened to them?* Looking back, Risa could pinpoint the exact moment the tension began. It was when she'd joined the *Stanford Law Review* in the fall of 2008.

Risa had had the idea to apply to law school right after their wedding, and Youssef had been her biggest supporter. Her tenacity impressed him; when Risa committed herself to a goal, she was relentless. Mainlining espressos, Risa studied day and night for the LSAT, and it paid off.

"One seventy!" Risa opened the envelope in astonishment.

"That settles it," Youssef declared unequivocally. "You're applying to Stanford."

"You think?" she demurred. Stanford was a moon shot.

"They'd be lucky to have you!" Youssef insisted.

His vote of confidence proved prescient—another envelope was ripped open in shouts of elation. Then Risa, with her strong writing and editorial skills, was invited during her first year to join an even more elite subset—the *Stanford Law Review*, boasting such notable alumni as Supreme Court Justices Sandra Day O'Connor and William Rehnquist.

Risa felt giddy at the trajectory she was on and what it implied for her and Youssef's future. But that was when Youssef's enthusiasm about Stanford began to wane. As Risa spent more and more time at the *Law Review*, she came under the sway of an editor named Ori Bergman, an Israeli upperclassman with a passion for human rights law, particularly women's rights, which dovetailed with Risa's area of interest. They spent hours upon hours discussing injustices across the world, particularly in the Middle East, where, Ori would explain, patriarchal tyrants acted as if they were above the law, not beholden to any moral code other than their own grip on power.

Human Rights Watch had been documenting systemic abuses of civilians by extremist groups like ISI, including rape, murder, beheadings, and even crucifixions. But what really enraged Risa was the sex trafficking and enslavement of girls, some as young as twelve, that had exploded after the American invasion of Iraq. Ori planted the seed in Risa's mind that they should visit the region in person to collect firsthand testimonies of the atrocities—and this was where Youssef drew the line.

"Out of the question!" He came down strong. "The people involved in that are dangerous. They don't respond to 'nonviolent conflict resolution.' They're madmen. I've seen it with my own eyes. You're not going! End of story . . . I won't allow it."

Ori was an Ashkenazi Jew—a first-generation Israeli whose parents had emigrated from Eastern Europe—and yet he claimed a complete understanding of the Middle East, which elicited eye rolls from Youssef.

He's jealous—that's what this amounts to, Risa concluded. She was feeling boxed in. Ori's ideas excited her, and she was dying to visit the Middle East—Youssef had never once invited her to travel home with him, never opened that part of his life to her.

Aspects of who he was remained hidden to her—his relationship to his faith, for example. Here they were, driving to a daytime barbeque on Stinson Beach, where everyone would be eating and drinking and having a good time—except her husband.

"It just strikes me as rude," she remarked as Youssef wove the Nissan down the switchbacks toward the Pacific. "You always keep the Ramadan fast, even if it means standing out at a social event, but I hardly ever see you pray. And you drink sometimes, which goes against your religion."

"An occasional drink is not going to send me to hell," he retorted.

"What about this morning?" she continued like a litigator. "Isn't daytime sex haram during Ramadan?"

Youssef rolled his eyes. "You really want to go there?"

"You tell me, Youssef." She shrugged. "You seem to be randomly picking and choosing parts of your religion to fit your life." To Risa, it felt like watching a dance where only he knew the steps, leaving her on the outside.

Is this really the best way to approach a doctrine, a faith, a worldview?

"What's the big deal?" Youssef asked, glancing briefly at Risa. "It's the same as Judaism is for you. Traditions and rituals keep me connected to home, to my family. And religion gives me a framework for morality, a way of honoring each person's humanity."

"There must be nearly as many interpretations of Islam as there are Muslims," Youssef continued. "It's the same with any religion, isn't it? People spend their lives arguing what this passage or that one means. Even people who claim they're living the whole thing out to the letter, they're picking and choosing too. They just can't admit it to themselves. Anyway, you're the last person I expected to hear saying I'm doing religion wrong."

Youssef parked the car on Seadrift Road in front of an elegant Charles Moore–designed beach house, which faced the lagoon where osprey dove for mullet and several teens were paddleboarding. Risa reached into the back seat and hefted the bowl of potato salad she had made, flavoring it with cumin, saffron, and nigella to give it an Egyptian flair. But Youssef wasn't budging.

"I plan to keep my fast," he declared. "And no one will even care."

He was right. The Palo Alto crowd was way too absorbed in catching up and comparing plans for the semester. Someone pressed a plastic cup of lemonade into Risa's hand. The salty air was fragrant with charcoal smoke and barbecue sauce. As greetings and conversations swept them into different parts of the yard, Risa kept an eye on Youssef.

It hadn't been worth getting bent out of shape over, Risa concluded, watching Youssef chat happily with her law school cohort and their various partners. She could see him nodding thoughtfully with this one or telling a story with that one, laughing and debating by turns. As impossible as he could be, Risa still marveled at his social ease—that Youssef was able, half a world away from home, to converse with everyone and enjoy himself so naturally. Nobody even noticed that Youssef wasn't eating. *He was right.*

Then Ori arrived, looking tan, trim, and stylish in his designer sunglasses.

Even before greeting Risa, Ori made a beeline for Youssef to say "*Alsalam ealaykum, akhi*" in passable Arabic—*peace to you, my brother.* He took Youssef's hand. "First day of your fast, yes?"

Youssef smiled. "Twenty-eight to go."

"I hope you stay until sundown." Ori flashed his teeth. "I brought falafel that will make your mouth water. My grandmother's recipe."

They made falafel in Europe back then? Youssef smiled to himself, amused.

To him, the quintessential falafel was an Egyptian creation, perfected in Alexandria with its unique use of fava beans and fresh herbs. That was why it was hard to find a good falafel in America. Falafel, with its many delicious variations in the Arabic world, was deeply rooted in Arabic culture. How a recipe from Europe had woven itself into the falafel conversation was puzzling to him; it was odd, even ironic, to hear an Israeli lay claim to a dish so deeply grounded in Arabic culture.

They were quiet in the car on the way home. Youssef was looking forward to breaking his fast with a warm bowl of matzo ball soup they'd made earlier. There was more—*holishkes* and brisket—prepared and waiting in the fridge. Youssef loved these American Jewish dishes Risa had introduced him to. But a black sedan was waiting for them outside their home as they pulled up. A federal agent approached Youssef, flashing his badge.

"Youssef Almasry?" he asked. "Please come with us." There were more feds in the car.

Risa stepped forward in sudden panic. "Where are you taking him?" she demanded.

"This is not an arrest," he assured Risa. "We just need to ask your husband some questions."

But it was hardly comforting. As a soon-to-be-lawyer, Risa knew all too well of the sweeping authority granted to law enforcement agencies by the USA Patriot Act, which, among other things, allowed for the indefinite detention of noncitizens. Though Youssef had his green card, he had yet to apply for his citizenship—a detail Risa knew made a difference.

"It will be fine." Youssef tried to put her at ease. "Warm up the soup."

Risa watched in dismay as Youssef got into the sedan, which disappeared down the street.

Youssef had tried to remain cool for Risa's sake, but his heart was pounding as he sat in the back seat of the sedan, flanked by the two dark-suited agents. One of the men had graying sandy hair and a lantern jaw; the other, a gingery buzz cut and an Irish snub nose. Neither said a word until they drove to the underground parking of an undisclosed location, where they ushered Youssef into an interrogation room. The room was stark and sterile, with a narrow window casting a thin strip of natural light that barely reached the cold concrete walls. A large two-way mirror dominated one side, reflecting the harsh glow from overhead fluorescent lights, intensifying the sense of surveillance and scrutiny.

"When did you last see Nasser El-Mohammedi?" was the first question.

"I—" Youssef stammered. "I haven't seen him in a very long time."

"So, why did you write him this email?" said the ginger-haired man as he pulled a thick file seemingly out of nowhere and began reading from a printout. "My dearest of friends. We miss you. I miss you." His voice was robotic, but Youssef recognized the words. "I would drop everything and get on a plane to see you—"

He'd never sent that email—Youssef hadn't even known *where* to send it.

Youssef's drafts folder was full of emails he'd written Nasser and never sent because so many of the prior ones had bounced back. *They have access to my unsent drafts folder?* Youssef glanced at his two interrogators in alarm but tried not to show it. *What's so surprising about that?* thought the software engineer. He knew how easy it was to create keyword-searching crawlers designed to scan the ones and zeros that made up the mountains of data stored on server farms across the Midwest. The Department of Homeland Security had a multibillion-dollar budget, along with carte blanche access afforded to them by the USA Patriot Act. Of course they'd be able to peruse folders buried within his Google account. But it was still unnerving—an unsent email bringing the United States government to his door.

Even more troubling was the fact that US intelligence had deemed Nasser to be a *person of interest*—stoking Youssef's worst fears about what his old friend may be up to.

"Let's talk about Adam Mekawy," said the other man. "How long have you known him?"

Youssef realized this investigation was comprehensive. His eyes drifted toward the wall mirror. *Who's watching me?* he wondered.

~

It was Matt—along with several other intelligence analysts.

Nasser El-Mohammedi had become a top priority for the Agency ever since they'd received that first encrypted message from him—*I can see you too.*

He'd identified himself as *Anas Almasry*, following the *mujahideen* formula for their *noms de guerre*—the first name was always one of the Prophet Mohammed's companions, and the last name told you where the *mujahid* was from. Anas, in this case, referred to Anas ibn Malik, one of the major narrators of the Hadith, the supplement to the Qur'an.

In order to establish trust, AA had been hacking electronics to feed Matt and his team advanced warnings of planned attacks by Roken, such as the recently averted bombing of Al-Arba'een, a historic Sunni mosque in Tikrit.

It had taken no time for Matt and his team to crack AA's true identity—clearly a crackerjack electronics engineer who'd crossed paths with Roken. CIA analysts guessed it had been behind bars in El-Hadra. By cross-referencing Egyptian prison and university records for engineering programs, they concluded it must be Nasser. But what sent shock waves through Matt was this: Nasser wasn't just a name in a file; he was deeply enmeshed in Matt's life. His best friend was married into Matt's wife's family, creating a web of complications that no amount of intelligence could have prepared him for. Now they were doing their due diligence by investigating every aspect of Nasser's past, which included interviewing his friends and associates.

"Tell us about Dalia Kenawy," the interrogator asked Youssef on the other side of the two-way mirror. "You went to the same university? How close were you? Nasser, Adam, and Dalia . . . ?"

"Very close," Youssef sighed. "Nasser called us the 'Alexandria Four.'"

Youssef gazed again at the mirror, appearing to stare directly at Matt. His eyes seemed to be saying, *Who are you?*

Matt had stopped asking himself that question.

He'd changed, certainly, since West Point. But the situation had called for it; the stakes were stratospheric. Matt had no compunction whatsoever that he'd ordered the detention and interrogation of the husband of his wife's cousin. He needed to know everything about AA, who was clever as a fox and twice as mercurial. AA had imagination and understood the reach of US technology, and now he was helping them with random tips. *But why? What is his agenda?*

There was one question that haunted Matt and kept him up at night: *Can Nasser be trusted?*

2010-11: ALEXANDRIA

THE SILENCE on the streets of Cleopatra Hammamat was like an indrawn breath, tense and hot, gathering power to speak a word or to throw a punch—who could tell? As far as Dalia could see, up and down the crowded streets of this middle-class seaside neighborhood, the crowd was poised, watchful, hoisting their homemade banners reading, "*Kulina Khalid Saeed*"—*we are all Khalid Saeed*. Many held placards displaying before-and-after photographs of his face. Before: a young Egyptian, twenty-eight years old, in a white T-shirt and gray hoodie, his dark hair slicked back from his smooth-skinned, clear-eyed face. He looked friendly and smart, with inquisitive eyes, his full lips pulled back in a faint smile. After: his ruined face was hardly a face at all. His eyebrows were uneven above eyes that stared at nothing; his teeth were broken, his jaw dislocated, his lower lip split all the way to the point of his chin. What separated *before* from *after* had been the intervention of two plainclothes policemen who'd stalked an internet café in the neighborhood where Dalia now stood—Cleopatra Hammamat, where Egypt's last pharaoh once relaxed in the soothing Mediterranean. And where, two thousand years later, Egyptian policemen, on some vague hashish-related pretext, kicked an innocent man to death and then kept kicking.

This had been the final straw for Dalia and so many others,

who stood now in both dignity and indignation, flooding this place that celebrated the female pharaoh who'd ruled over a golden age and held her own against the juggernauting patriarchy. Now, these protesters held above their heads the likeness of the one they'd lost. And his face became the faces of all the ones who had been beaten or murdered or who had vanished over the years. Dalia's mind, naturally, went to Nasser—not a day went by that she didn't think of him.

"*Ya shahid, ya shahid*," voices chanted all around her. *Oh martyr, martyr.* In grief and fury, they called on Khalid Saeed as if to wake him from the dead, as if waking would save them. As if he could return with the power to face down not only the two plain-clothes police officers who'd murdered him, but corrupt officials everywhere.

The music of the chant carried Dalia along, but when she opened her mouth to join it, something else came out, "*Yaskut yaskut Hosni Mubarak!*" she found herself shouting. *Down, down with Hosni Mubarak!* These were dangerous words, words Dalia would never have dreamt of saying, much less shout on a crowded street. Where within herself had she found them? And what inside of her had known that the crowd would take up her cry, repeat, and magnify it? Hundreds of voices around her, in front and behind as far as she could see, chanted, "Yaskut yaskut Hosni Mubarak," until it felt as if all of Alexandria reverberated with their challenge.

They were deviating from the plan. Since young Saeed's death nearly three weeks ago, Dalia had worked tirelessly with other online activists to organize today's silent stand. Nonviolence was the key to which they'd all agreed. Dalia even went through an online training course in "Kingian Nonviolence"—a resistance and protest modality that had been implemented powerfully in the West by Martin Luther King. King had taken inspiration from Mahatma Gandhi in the East, where Indians had used nonvio-lence to bring down an empire. Dalia and her fellow organizers knew that fighting hate with hate would get them nowhere—and Omar had been a big part of her thinking. He loaned her his copy of *The Leaders Manual: A Structured Guide and Introduction to Kingian Nonviolence*, which had been published in 1995 by Bernard LaFayette and David Jehnsen, longtime civil rights activists and organizers who'd worked closely with Dr. King. One of Omar's students at the university had found a way to receive certification in these techniques online, and Dalia jumped at the opportunity. Discipline was mission critical—along with level-headedness and calm.

We have to keep the focus on the Khalid Saeed case, they all agreed. *We cannot let it get political.* But now, as the defiant chanting swelled around her, Dalia realized she'd succumbed to the pent-up passions she'd been quashing for years—*I'm no Gandhi. I can't be passive.* All the anger, the anguish, the injustice, the pain—it had to be expressed.

Today, they will see and hear us!

Could things change? Dalia wanted to believe so. She *had* to believe so—for the sake of her country. She had to put it all on the line. Then Dalia heard the sound of glass breaking, and a wave of jostling suddenly swept through the crowd. She thought, with dread, *This could turn violent.*

It did.

Six months later, on New Year's Day, Dalia awoke to a massacre—a bomb had been detonated during a midnight prayer service at the Coptic Church of Saint Mark and Pope Peter in Sidi Beshr, killing more than twenty people and injuring nearly a hundred.

Dalia scrambled to her desk and opened her laptop to connect to the online forum where she and other organizers shared news. Rumors were flying, theories proliferating from every side. The attack was initially reported as a car bomb, then as a suicide bombing; some said an Islamic extremist group was responsible, others whispered that the Mubarak government itself had carried out the attack to sow strife between Christians and Muslims—*divide and conquer*, classic stratagem of the oppressor.

There were voices within Egypt that cried, *Christian crusaders don't belong here*. But as Omar had told Dalia countless times, Egypt's Christianity dated back to the first century of the Common Era, some five hundred years before the founding of Islam. Both religions were vital to the national culture, he would say, and yet neither was as old as the nation itself.

Staring at the devastating images of the bombing, bits of blood and flesh splattered against the centuries-old tile, Dalia felt a seizing in her heart, a feeling of helplessness, of desperation.

I need to see Omar. As she parked the car, Dalia heard the voices of men shouting and noticed two police cars. A crowd had formed as neighbors and passersby stopped to find out the cause of the commotion, hoping to ogle at the dangerous criminals who were being apprehended inside the dwelling.

The shouting gave way to the stomping of boots, and out of the apartment building and onto the tree-lined sidewalk came not a dangerous criminal but Professor Omar El-Mohammedi, limping with dignity toward the police cars, while four large policemen loomed over him.

Neighbors began to shout, "What are you doing? Where are you taking the professor?"

"Stay back!" a police officer warned. A fifth policeman approached one neighbor and shoved him roughly back inside the building.

That was all Dalia could take. She wanted to be professional, to let restraint be her strength, but not if it meant watching the cops manhandle her friend.

Pushing her way toward the officer, she shouted to get his attention, "Hey! *Fe ayah ya hadrat alzabat?*" The muscle-bound policeman swiped at her, clearly thinking a woman Dalia's size would easily be swept away, but Dalia planted her feet and used her low center of gravity to her advantage, a technique she'd learned in her nonviolence certification. She'd learned so much since that altercation when the corrupt policeman Abbas Abbas had shoved her aside in the Mansours' apartment, forcing Nasser to intervene—which had landed him in prison.

"Hey!" she shouted again. "Why are you arresting this man?"

The officer turned his full attention to her with a snarl, but Omar called out from the back of the police van, "It's all right, Dalia. Don't worry. They say they just want to ask me about Nasser." Before they drove off, Omar called out, "Don't call Houda. There's no need to trouble her about this." Then the policemen slammed the door on him and pulled away.

Dalia took a deep breath to calm her nerves. The professor hadn't wanted her to call Houda because she was pregnant—the soon-to-be grandfather wanted to avoid worrying his daughter unnecessarily. But now Dalia felt her stomach churning. A Coptic church had just been attacked, and now the police wanted to question Omar about Nasser?

After a whirl of dark thoughts, her mind went back to a day at their human rights office, when Nasser had said, "The Copts are more Egyptian than the Arabic language. We would not be who we are without them." She couldn't believe the man who had said those things would have anything to do with an attack on a church.

Yet Dalia had to admit that Nasser had done a lot of things she would never have believed him capable of.

When she followed Omar to the police station, it became very clear that they would not allow her to meet him. After her repeated requests were dismissed, Dalia decided to ask her father for help, knowing that he, unlike her mom, was more empathetic toward Omar.

When she dialed his number, he picked up right way, firing questions like bullets before she could speak. "Are you all right? Didn't your mother tell you to stay at home, to stay out of all this trouble? It's not right, my daughter, what you're doing. It's dangerous."

Dalia waited and said, "Father, I need your help. I'm begging you."

Her father began to panic. "Why, what happened? Where are you?"

"The professor was just taken from his house, and I came to the police station, but—"

Her father sighed. "Omar, again." There was a pause. "Omar is a good man, but Nasser ruined his family and your—" He stopped himself, not wanting to add to her suffering. "Give me thirty minutes. I'll call you back."

But he wasn't able to get anywhere. "No answers, I'm afraid. Nothing I can do for him."

Dalia felt defeated. She called Houda to tell her what had happened and embellished it with a lie. "Baba said that they'll keep him for a day or two. Nothing to be worried about. I promise." In truth, her father hadn't said this at all, but Houda was still crying helplessly despite Dalia's best efforts to console her.

When they hung up, Dalia also felt like she wanted to cry. She certainly did not want to go home. So, she told her mother she was staying with friends and drove herself back to Omar's place. Knowing where he kept his spare emergency key, Dalia let herself in and walked into Nasser's old bedroom. She let herself collapse in exhaustion on his bed. Smelling him still on the pillow, it happened again. She felt a squeeze on her hand.

Then she drifted off, clutching the pillow as though it was the last thread connecting her to a world that felt increasingly out of reach.

By January 25, Dalia was ready for the "Day of Rage" that had been planned by protesters across Egypt and, indeed, throughout the entire Arab world. Tunisia's president, Ben Ali, who had been in power for more than two decades, had just stepped down under the pressure of the people, and the whole region was stirring with the pulse of revolution. Omar had been in detention for over three weeks, and the weight of his absence was another thread in the fabric of Dalia's resolve. Dalia prayed for a strong turnout, for crowds that would stop traffic on every street across the land. In Alexandria, they didn't have a central focal point to march toward, like Cairo's Tahrir Square. Here, the resistance needed to be everywhere.

Dalia made it to Ramel Station, where she gazed up at the graceful, pale marble face of the Al-Qaeed Ibrahim Mosque, with its almost impossibly tall minaret pointing like a finger into the hazy winter sky. To her left, beyond the classical façade of the women's hospital, lay the Corniche, and beyond that sparkled the blue Mediterranean.

In front of the mosque lay a small open square, and Dalia was grateful to see that a modest crowd had already gathered. A few wore *abayas* or galabeyas, but most demonstrators were in track-suits or jeans and sweaters. Some were Dalia's age or older, a few even white-haired, but most were young.

As the mosque's clock struck ten, a chant arose from among them: "Bread! Freedom! Social justice!" Dalia joined in, descending the mosque's steps to take her place among the protestors, who swayed together to the rhythm of the chanting, their faces turned up to catch the sun. Before long, they moved out to the north, weaving through cars stopped at traffic lights on Mahattat Al-Raml Square.

By the time they regrouped in front of the hospital, Dalia was sure the numbers had swelled, and as they turned onto the Corniche, their dozens joined hundreds marching westward there. Dalia's heart beat hard with the thrill of it; she dedicated her rage to the unjust detention of Omar El-Mohammedi. The sea wind was brisk and briny on their faces as they raised their voices in a chant of peace: "*Selmia, selmia, selmia.*" It was a statement of their intentions, a plea for police restraint, and a reminder of the limits they had imposed upon themselves. "Remember, don't damage any private property," Dalia reminded those around her. She knew the peaceful nature of the protests would make Omar proud, and she wished he could have been here to see the number of Alexandrians who had come out to demand their rights. Omar's absence left Dalia feeling helpless, a helplessness mirrored by Houda's heartbreak. Despite being in her final month of pregnancy, Houda had gone to the police station every day, pleading for his release. But for Dalia, the revolution felt like the way she could fight.

After a long and tiring day, Dalia's heart was full of wonder, joy, apprehension, and exhaustion. She returned to Omar's place where she'd been staying, and when she entered the apartment, she noticed that Omar's office light was on. Had he returned? She rushed forward, and they met each other in the hall.

"Dalia! Isn't it wonderful?" he cried, not saying a word about his detention. "The people are freeing themselves. Mubarak will step down any day now, but we can't make him into the devil. We must have compassion. He loves our country, as we all do. So, we will build together, bringing everyone to the table; there are no enemies. It will take time, but this is the only path to sustainable justice."

"Inshallah," Dalia responded.

"And you have been at the heart of things here in Alexandria, my daughter. I am so proud of you. I want you to know that tomorrow I am going to Tahrir Square."

"You're going to Cairo?" Dalia was shocked that he wanted to go into the epicenter of the revolution. It was folly for a man of his age, especially given that his daughter was about to give birth. "Why go to Cairo when you can be of help right here?" She tried to dissuade him.

"Nasser," he said simply. His voice was clear and sure. "This revolution is what I raised him for. He will be there. He has to be there."

Dalia gasped at the truth of his words. Omar was right, of course. And she knew in that moment that she'd be going too.

But if the swelling numbers in Alexandria were any indication, there would be immense crowds turning out in Cairo. How could someone find a single man among a hundred thousand—especially a man who did not want to be found?

2011: CAIRO

"Maybe we should give Mubarak a chance," one of the young men said, referring to Egypt's longtime president. He had a round pockmarked face and wore a blue baseball cap that shielded his eyes. "He's stated publicly that he plans to step down after this term. Surely the world will hold him to that. Surely the Americans will."

With a snort of disgust, a knife-thin young man in an orange Adidas windbreaker held out an empty canister that had recently held tear gas. He turned it so that they could read the lettering stamped on its side: *Made in USA*. "Here's the American response for you," he sneered.

Omar and some friends sat with a group of young demonstrators in Tahrir Square, sharing simple sandwiches of *gabna beyda*, the local white cheese, and fresh tomatoes in *aish baladi*, Egypt's everyday rustic flatbread.

"That's not exactly fair," Omar pointed out. "That tear gas canister doesn't represent what ordinary Americans are saying about our revolution." His voice was drowned out by a tall, handsome young man with a port-wine stain along his cheek. "Ordinary Americans are powerless, just like we are, even though they still get to vote!"

"How can the American government still support Mubarak

after all these years?" demanded another, his voice full of anguish. "You know, just this morning my friend was telling me that, starting with Reagan, every American president has called Mubarak a friend. Bush—both Bushes called him a friend. Clinton. And even Obama. What does that say about the American leaders?"

Omar's old friend Magdi Abdelkader leaned into the circle so that his soft voice could be heard. "It's not in the way we think of our personal friends," he said, his gray curls bobbing with his emphatic speech. "In foreign affairs, friendship is entirely a matter of pragmatism. As long as Mubarak supports American policies in the Middle East, American presidents will call him a friend, no matter what injustices he commits here at home."

Magdi and Omar had gone to graduate school together, and now Magdi was a librarian of Islamic art and architecture at the American University in Cairo. He was as excited as Omar to see young people throwing themselves into political activism.

The tall young man with the stained cheek spoke up again. "I can't sign off on that model of 'friendship.'" He drew his long, tapered fingers tightly together. "America is supposed to stand for freedom. But by supporting Mubarak, they stand in the way of *our* freedom. They stand in the way of the freedom of all Egyptians."

Omar suggested, "America's leaders feel that they must choose the lesser of the two evils presented to them. Maybe they are thinking that a dictator is better than a fundamentalist theocratic state." He glanced around the square, reminiscing about the endless talks he had had with his son about politics, freedom, social responsibility. If Nasser were here—if he was, as Omar hoped, one of the revolution's architects—Omar prayed that he was seeing beyond false binaries of black and white.

A young woman, her fresh face emerging from a tightly wrapped hijab, asked fiercely, "How can they claim to support the will of the people if they want to choose the leader they think is right for us?" She shook her head, reached up, and touched her scarf. "I wouldn't support any religious state that took away our freedom. But that's the whole point of democracy. If I help elect a religious party, and they turn out to govern in a way I don't like, then I can also help elect their opposition the next time."

Magdi's daughter Miriam, once Houda's playmate and now studying medicine, agreed. "America is supporting a dictator who is oppressing all of us. Don't they know we dream the same dreams as Americans? Can't they—"

From across the circle, Dalia burst out, "Who *cares* about America? This is *our* country, and we shouldn't think about what the Americans are saying or doing. We shouldn't give anyone that kind of power over us. Mubarak's regime has kept us hesitating for years with their talk of conspiracy, their talk of evil forces just waiting for a chance to hurt Egypt. But guess what—"

Before she could finish her thought, distant screams and the clatter of gunfire shattered the square's peaceful fellowship. Everyone froze, heads up, listening. All was still for a moment, and then the din burst out again, closer now. And the meal was suddenly over. Someone helped Omar to his feet; all of them were on their feet and shouting.

"They're attacking!" someone screamed. But as Miriam attempted to guide her father and Omar into a nearby tobacconist shop for safety, the professor stopped in his tracks—his attention trained on an alley between two of the buildings edging Tahrir Square. For just a moment, standing there, Omar saw him.

Was it a mirage? Was Omar simply seeing what his mind's eye so desperately yearned to see? No, surely that was him—his son. A face etched into his consciousness.

Breaking free from his friends, Omar moved as fast as he could toward the alley, but by the time he got there on his unsteady old legs, there was no one there he recognized. Later, he would let himself dream, let the recollection play out differently. In one fantasy of the moment, he had run into that alley and fallen into the steady, welcoming arms of his beloved son. But now, as he stood uncertainly at the edge of a mass of bodies darting to and fro in panic, Nasser was nowhere to be seen, and Omar had lost track of his companions too. From the alley's shade, kind voices beckoned, "Here! Here, ya *hag*! Take cover!" He didn't take any of their outstretched hands, though. He kept walking, searching for that beloved face, and didn't turn around until a surge of people fleeing the square nearly swept him off his feet. Turning, he thought he glimpsed Nasser again—for an instant, in profile.

Then Omar lost him again, but he wouldn't give up. He made directly for the spot where he had seen him, weaving in and out of the crowd. Even in their panic, most people still made way for an old man leaning on a cane. In the sea of chaotic bodies, it should have been impossible, but Omar could have sworn he caught one more glimpse of him, some fifteen meters away, raising his arms and shouting encouragement to his fellow demonstrators. Behind him loomed a camel, its rider raising a sword. One moment, Omar was screaming, trying to warn his son of the danger behind him, willing everyone out of the way of this assault. And the next—

Omar was still screaming, only now his scream was silent. Somehow all the breath seemed to be gone from his body. He struggled to regain it, wondering why instead of looking across the crowd at his beautiful boy, now Omar, wounded, was looking up at a concerned stranger's face, and beyond that at the towering backs of dozens of heads, and beyond that at the sky.

As his breath returned, across his puzzlement washed a searing crimson pain, wave after wave. It felt as if his heart had somehow moved into his left shoulder, and it was beating harder than it should, cramping, choking on the blood it pumped. Now Omar was able to scream again—and scream he did. Between screams, he gulped air. He felt faint and his vision swam; he thought he saw Nasser bending over him—and then the world went dark.

❧

"Shh, it's okay, you're going to be all right," Omar heard. He struggled to open his eyes, to hear the voice. The world came into focus. Omar couldn't have been unconscious for more than a second or two. His throat was still rough with screaming; he could still feel the alley's cobblestones under his back. The face, voice, and hands tending him lovingly were Dalia's.

"Where's—" Omar croaked. "Did you see—"

Miriam was there too, pulling a scarf out of nowhere and tying it tightly around Omar's arm. Whether this lessened his pain or increased it he couldn't say for sure, but it changed its quality somehow. Omar blinked and took in his surroundings.

In keeping with its Protestant ethos, the Kasr El Dobara Church's large worship area was spartan. Stained glass windows brought in light and punctuated the tall space's plainness— compared with Coptic churches or mosques, Kasr El Dobara's overriding aesthetic principle was simplicity. The open space was bustling now, though, with cots and blankets and volunteer medical staff. In one corner, two women handed out free bottled water.

No one asked who was Muslim or Christian, revolutionary or pro-Mubarak. They asked only who was tired, who was thirsty, and who was hurt. In her final year of medical studies, Miriam was more than qualified for her shift splinting broken bones, removing bullets, stitching lacerations, flushing tear gas out of eyes, and doing triage to determine who needed an ambulance to a real hospital and who just needed rest, water, and first aid. Today, Omar was a patient, hardly capable of any awareness beyond his own damaged body.

Dalia held his hand reassuringly as Miriam bustled away to gather supplies. When she returned, she untied the scarf from Omar's shoulder and cut away his shirt, then cleaned the wound with gauze and antiseptic.

"The good news," she said as she finished, "is that this isn't nearly as bad as it looked. And not nearly as bad as I'll bet it feels right now. Does it hurt very much?"

Omar managed a weak nod, feeling a little foolish despite his relief at such a good prognosis. His shoulder was still throbbing in time with his heartbeat, a pain sharper than any he'd felt since his leg was wounded in Sinai decades ago.

Miriam gave Dalia some instructions, and Dalia set off in search of painkillers. Turning back to Omar, Miriam continued, "It looks like you have a pretty deep graze from a rubber bullet on your upper arm. That's a messy, painful wound, but it should heal completely. The bad news is I'm going to have to stitch you up. Are you ready?"

Omar agreed, and Miriam got to work expertly. Soon his shoulder was numb. He turned his head away from her stitching and looked across the room. A very young man in turquoise hospital scrubs caught Omar's eye. He was crouching beside a cot on which sat a woman whose eyes were wide in terror. He spoke with her gently, coaxing her to show him a hand she had wrapped in cloth and held tightly in her other. Tears trickled from her eyes, but slowly she relaxed and let him clean and bandage her wound. Rays of afternoon light filtering through the stained glass cast the image of a dove surrounded by blue across the back of the medic's shirt as he worked.

Later, when Omar woke up from a depthless, dreamless sleep, he found Dalia napping on the floor beside his cot, using her hand as a pillow. No more light came in through the windows; Omar had no idea what time it was. When she opened her eyes and saw he was awake, Dalia asked quietly, "How is your arm?"

"It's pulsing with love for the people of Egypt, my daughter," Omar said. "I think I'm prouder of this injury than I am of my leg." In truth, his entire arm was throbbing. But he was grateful to be here, in the thick of everything, making a stand for Egypt's future.

From the next bed, a young man with his arm in a sling called out, "Hey! Look who's awake. Share my supper, walidi." He held out a thick sandwich, and Omar's stomach rumbled. "I'm Samah," he added. He couldn't have been much older than twenty.

As Omar bit into the sandwich and savored its rich, spicy ful, the young man turned to the pair of friends who were keeping him company. "When is the nurse coming back?" asked one, a thickset kid with a one-week beard just starting to cover his round baby face. "It's time to get you home. Everything is going to be better now!"

Samah's other friend, a tall young man with a long horsey face, slapped his back and agreed. "Politics isn't really for me, anyway. I can't wait until things return to normal."

"No way!" Samah protested. "We can't stop now! We're just getting started!"

The kids at the next bed began arguing about who Egypt's new leader should be. One liked the Nobel laureate diplomat Mohamed ElBaradei; another rejected him on the grounds that he'd lived most of his life outside Egypt and worked only for international organizations. "And here we go," Dalia remarked. "This one is going to support this leader, and that one will support someone else. I just hope we'll honor the process."

The history professor in Omar couldn't let the conversation at the nearby bed go any further without intervening. "My children," he said to get the young men's attention. "This is the start of our journey, not its end. Now, more than ever, it's time to nurture our revolution—this child we have birthed. This is the time we all come together. Bring everyone with us, the policeman who might have thought differently than us, our brothers in the army, the Islamists who might have other dreams of power, the businessmen who might have played the old game, our Coptic brothers and sisters, every Egyptian everywhere. We need to build together and not destroy."

"It's time now for democracy," Samah insisted. "The old ways can't be accepted anymore, all those corrupt ways—"

"*Righteousness, democracy.*" Omar sighed with exhaustion and then continued, "Lofty words are not the way forward. Don't point the finger, don't threaten. Come together, work together. This is a long journey, and all of us are trying to find our way forward." Exhaustion was overtaking him again; Omar sank back on his thin pillow.

"Don't worry, professor," Dalia said, squeezing his hand. "We will look forward and not backward." Her cool, dry hand on his forehead was the last thing Omar was aware of before he drifted off.

Then Dalia's phone buzzed with a text that made her leap up in excitement.

"What is it?" said Miriam, on her way to help some new arrivals.

"I got a message from Tarek!" Dalia exclaimed. "Houda delivered a baby girl named Fatimah!"

"We must tell Omar." Miriam moved to wake him up. "He's a grandfather!"

"Not now." Dalia stopped her. "Let him sleep. What beautiful news he'll have when he opens his eyes."

Standing in the nighttime desert, Omar found himself alone and far from home. And yet he wasn't. A hundred thousand stars burned in the firmament above, and although his eyes did not see it, his son was right there with him. In fact, Nasser was everywhere.

In the logic of his dream, Omar knew the only way to "see" was to shut his eyes and cover them with his hands, which he did, pressing the heels of his palms against his closed eyes until bright spots of color bloomed under his lids, like the fireworks of the revolution.

And suddenly Nasser was there, so close that Omar could feel his breath against his neck. "Don't open your eyes, Baba. Don't look for me."

Omar kept his hands where they were, trying hard to remain calm lest he upset the miracle that was unfolding. "Come back to us, my son," Omar pleaded, not wanting it to end.

"I can't," his voice came—quieter now. Feeling him drifting away, Omar panicked, pulling back his hands and blinking to open his lids. No one was there—just the vast and empty desert with a lonely wind sweeping sand across the starlit dunes. The changeless desert stretched to infinity in every direction. And there were no footprints in the sand, not even Omar's own.

In the distance, a Bedouin fire flickered, and for a moment, Omar imagined he saw his son, silhouetted against its orange glow. *No*, he thought, *that's not him. Nasser is behind me.*

Then, as Omar turned, he beheld a vast, soaring pyramid rising up from the desert sand.

At its peak sat an eye. Watching him. Always watching.

A faint whisper reached him, carried on the desert wind. *When the three become the multitude, they become unstoppable . . . .* These unbidden words swam into Omar's mind and made his heart leap.

Omar looked around, searching the vast desert for his son. The Bedouin fire flickered and faded, the endless dunes blurred, and the towering pyramid dissolved into nothingness. The dreamscape crumbled, replaced by flickering light and muffled sounds around him.

"He is here," Omar whispered to himself, the echo of the words lingering.

Nasser is part of our peaceful revolution.

2011: MOUNT LEBANON

MATT HADN'T SLEPT in days—and here he was, about to jump out of a helicopter. The reason for his insomnia was a harrowing message they'd recently received from AA:

ROKEN HAS SPENT PLUTONIUM RODS FROM ISRAEL

This was a six-alarm fire for American national security. But was it true? Many at the CIA still questioned whether Nasser, who'd certainly been responsible for some American casualties in Iraq, was a reliable source. They needed more information.

"Six minutes to drop," squawked the pilot of the Sikorsky SH-60 Seahawk, which had taken off just before sunrise from the USS *Harry S. Truman*, deployed off the island of Cyprus. Cruising at 180 knots just fifty feet above the brilliant turquoise water, the helicopter rocketed past a formation of pelicans diving for sardines.

As a young Eagle Scout, Matt would have marveled at nature's magnificence, but present-day Matt wasn't interested in the scenery. Lost in thought, he clutched a stiletto, which he clicked open, then closed by slamming the blade against the chopper's metal hull. Open, close, open. They'd seized the knife from an arrested militant. It was a war trophy. Open, close, open . . .

"You good, sir?" asked Bailey, a barrel-chested Navy SEAL seated across from Matt.

Matt flashed a thumbs-up, then immediately thought, *Am I lying to myself?*

On the one hand, his life was soaring beyond anything he could have imagined. He was serving his country at the highest level, not only using his engineering skills to save countless lives but now taking on an operational role in the field—leading missions, making critical decisions, and serving directly on the front lines. Matt had played his cards to perfection—and it was thrilling to be a part of this sea change. Electronic intelligence gathering had been a game changer for the CIA, Mossad, and numerous spy agencies around the world. The technology allowed them to create comprehensive digital files on millions of people without their knowledge—cataloguing their likes, dislikes, vices, weaknesses, vulnerabilities—information that had revolutionized the traditional spy game. The best way to develop human assets was to know their secrets—know them better than they knew themselves.

On the other hand, Matt was now developing his own secrets —a growing addiction to the adrenaline of espionage. *Am I compromised? Is it affecting my judgment?*

It didn't matter on some level—the mission was flying ahead at warp speed; the stakes were astronomical; the mantra was *go, go, go.*

Given the explosive information they'd just received from AA, it was imperative to get confirmation from another source. That was the goal of this mission. They'd identified a potential asset by tracking the movements of his cell phone, which traveled routinely from his Haifa apartment to locations in the Syrian desert, South Lebanon, and parts of Iraq—a smuggler, no doubt. This man, who went by the name of Ismael, claimed to have valuable information to sell to the Americans; he'd proposed a rendezvous on a remote peak in the mountains of Lebanon.

Was it a trap?

They knew very little about this Ismael other than the fact

that he was sloppy. Most smugglers would have removed the SIM card from their phones when moving across frontiers, rendering their whereabouts untraceable. Ismael obviously didn't care, or, even worse, he was cavalier, which made him dangerous.

Matt addressed Bailey through his aviation headset. "You play poker, lieutenant?"

"Yessir." The Navy SEAL nodded.

"We might need a 'bad cop' bluff out there," Matt continued. "Watch for my signal."

"Affirmative, sir," responded Bailey.

"Two minutes," the pilot announced as they crossed the beach and began soaring in a rapid climb toward the hills to the east. Bailey and another SEAL, Mendoza, unfastened their safety belts and got ready for the jump. Within a minute, they'd ascended eight thousand feet to a remote peak in the Mount Lebanon range, where their source had set a pin locator. Hovering above a ledge, they threw down rappel lines.

"Go, go, go!" shouted the pilot as Bailey and Mendoza dropped down the rope, followed by Matt, who felt his heart thumping with the sudden rush of cortisol. He'd done a few practice jumps in his day, but this was real—this could be an ambush.

Matt landed hard, then followed Bailey's hand signals to take cover behind some rocks. Mendoza was already manning the perimeter with his M4A1 carbine. Bailey pulled out his binoculars and scanned the area for snipers. Matt glanced around. Their informant had picked the spot carefully for its isolation and security. He was likely observing them from higher ground.

They waited without moving. Hearing a sharp rapping in the nearby cedar grove, Matt spun with his automatic, then relaxed. It was a woodpecker, but Matt remained on high alert. Coastal clouds dissipated as the sun rose in the sky. A squirrel scampered across the clearing. There was a rustling in the nearby bushes. Matt wondered if it might be one of the striped hyenas that roamed this range.

Ten minutes later, a figure emerged from a cavern up the hill riding a mule, a Kalashnikov strung across his shoulder, his face covered by a *keffiyeh* headdress. The man rode down to the ledge where they were positioned but kept his distance, one hand on his gun. The SEALs flanking Matt at about ten yards' distance readied their carbines.

"Ismael?" Matt asked.

"Who has my money?"

Matt produced a satchel and tossed it to the man on the mule, who took his time counting out ten wads of hundred-dollar bills. Satisfied that the agreed-upon fifty thousand dollars were there, he addressed Matt. "I was approached some time ago to deliver a package to a secret location," he began.

"Spent plutonium rods cased in lead," Ismael continued without emotion. "I refused. It was dangerous. They offered five times my usual fee. I finally agreed."

"Why are you only telling us this now?" Matt asked, squinting at the rising sun that haloed the smuggler's headdress.

"They've asked for another delivery." He stared Matt in the eyes. "I can take the package to the same address again. Or I can deliver it to you—for the right price."

"Gimme a number," said Matt, narrowing his eyes.

"One million," answered the smuggler. "In Bitcoin."

Matt made a series of mental calculations. "When's the drop?"

"One month."

Matt glanced at his SEAL escorts. He blinked twice at Bailey, who picked up the cue.

"Permission to speak, sir," Bailey called out.

"Go," Matt replied.

"We do not have the authority to make a deal of this magnitude, sir," said Bailey.

Matt nodded. *Good boy.* Matt glanced at the smuggler, set his pistol on the ground with deliberation, and asked, "Can I approach you?"

Ismael looked at him suspiciously. "Hands in the air. No tricks!" He pointed his Kalashnikov.

Matt raised his arms and walked slowly toward the mule. "I've been given a secret discretionary fund," he whispered when he was close to Ismael. "One million is no problem. I can give you five, in fact. But I'll need a lot more than just the fuel rods from you." Matt looked back at his SEAL team, making it appear like he had something highly confidential to disclose.

"What do you need?" Ismael leaned in, lowering his rifle.

Quick as a panther, Matt pulled the stiletto from his sleeve and drove it up into Ismael's jugular. Then, in a smooth continuation of moves, he jammed the blade into the rump of the mule, which squealed in agony and stumbled. With a quick shove, Matt pushed both of them off the ledge.

Man and mule went plummeting into the abyss, crashing violently into the rocks below. The mission was simple: confirm and kill. Matt, once the engineer behind the scenes, had proven equally brilliant in the field. Years around the CIA and this war had worn down his measured approach, making him ruthlessly efficient. He felt nothing.

Satisfied and strangely calm, Matt turned toward the Navy SEALs. "A guy like that will pimp his own mother. No one can learn that we know about this. I know the ones who'll help when the time comes—this one was a dead end, just a messenger. And we're certain who sent him. We need to find the other end of this line—Roken."

"Understood, sir," said Bailey. "I think you made the right call."

Mendoza looked down at the ravine. "You want us to recover the cash, sir?"

"No need," said Matt. "Let's get the fuck out of here."

Bailey pulled out his radio. "Three Kings to Raptor—ready for evac."

"Roger that," cracked the voice in his headset. "Count fifteen to evac."

Matt stood silently for a moment, watching the horizon. *The ones who'll help when the time comes*—he knew exactly who: Nasser El-Mohammedi.

Two thoughts ran through Matt's head. First, his instincts had been right about AA—*Nasser could be trusted.*

Second, Matt wasn't going home anytime soon, which meant he'd likely miss his wedding anniversary.

THE LIBRARY OF OMAR
EL-MOHAMMEDI

APRIL 8, 2014 • 4:15 A.M.

Feb 11, 2011

> One begets two—creating light and darkness . . .
> Two begets three.
> And when the three become the multitude . . .

OMAR FROZE, his breath catching. He had heard those words before. No—not heard. *Dreamt.*

The memory came rushing back. Three years ago, lying injured in Tahrir Square, he had heard the whisper in a dream:

When the three become the multitude, they become unstoppable.

Now, here they were, written in Nasser's journal—but not exactly the same. Nasser's words were poetic, drawn from the *Dao De Jing.*

Was it a coincidence, or had Nasser somehow shared the same vision? Omar marveled at the symmetry of it all. He felt a glimmer of hope as he read the added gale notation in the white space:

> The Little Sun shows us that,
> even in torrent and turmoil,

the light can still prevail . . .

The phone rang. Omar answered.

"I'm here," said Matt.

"Here?" Omar was confused.

"Outside your door," said the American. "We've run out of time."

Omar fumbled for his cane and went into the foyer to admit the visitor. As he opened the door, Houda emerged from her room, her expression wary.

Matt started to greet her—"Alsalam ealaykum"—his accent unmistakably foreign. Houda raised an eyebrow, taken aback by the unexpected sound of the greeting.

But Omar quickly interrupted. "Houda, go back to bed. Stay with your daughter," he said, his voice firm but calm.

She looked at him for a moment, searching his face for answers, then gave a slight nod and retreated quietly to her room without a word. It was the day they buried her brother, and the sadness, combined with all the strangeness of it—including this foreigner—was overwhelming.

Omar turned back to Matt and led him into the library. As they entered, Matt's gaze fell on something across the room. His eyes narrowed, a mix of curiosity and something darker settling on his face.

"What's this?" Matt asked, his tone laced with an edge. Omar followed his gaze to the desk, where the bullet lay glinting under the dim light. The air felt heavier, as though the room itself were holding its breath, thick with words left unsaid.

Omar took a deep breath, his gaze fixed on the bullet. "That," he said, "is from a different time. During the 1973 war against Israel, after our early successes, my unit was cornered in the Sinai desert. One night, when all seemed lost, Roken appeared, fighting like a man possessed—one man saving our unit from out of nowhere."

He paused, his voice steady but heavy with memory. "When I was hit, Roken dragged me to safety. This bullet"—he gestured toward the desk—"was lodged in my leg. He stayed until the medics removed it."

Omar's tone darkened. "He called it 'the American bullet.' During that war, brand-new American weapons poured into the battlefield, replenishing Israel's arsenal. Fresh steel against us while we fought to reclaim Egypt's land—not to conquer, but to liberate."

Matt's eyes narrowed, taken aback. "Roken was there in the battle with you? We thought he was in a reserve unit and didn't see actual combat." He had grown tired of this blame on America, the country he loved and served. He'd heard it before, but true or not, now wasn't the time to agree, argue, or deflect.

"Yes. He saved my life and our entire unit," Omar said quietly.

After a moment, the professor spoke again, his voice measured. "Roken is Egyptian to the core, but Al-Nakba left its mark on him. His mother's family fled Palestine, losing everything. That scar shaped him."

His tone deepened further. "And then there was Bahr Al-Baqar. April 8, 1970. An Israeli bombing struck the Bahr Al-Baqar Primary School. Roken's niece was there. Maha, only eight years old, was killed that day along with forty-five other children."

Omar's voice softened. "She was a child with a bright smile, full of life. They found her clutching her schoolbook. She never let it go, even in the end."

He sighed. "It wasn't just his family's past—it was his present, his blood, his grief. That loss shattered him."

Matt interrupted, "So, that's what drove him? Losing her? It was a war. These things happen. Not everyone turns terrorist." Matt knew the CIA had once flirted with Roken when he visited America, unaware of all his motivations. His arrest in Egypt brought that to light.

Omar held his gaze for a long moment, his expression unyielding. Matt shifted uncomfortably, but Omar continued as if the words hadn't been spoken. "He came to see Al-Nakba and Bahr Al-Baqar as only chapters—a piece of a longer history filled with pain, shame, and weakness. He sought strength and purpose in tradition, clinging to roots he believed could hold him steady, but much of it was rotten—religion at its worst, twisted by hate and defeat."

His voice lowered. "And then Roken became the man who killed my wife—Nasser's mother. The man who led my son astray, turning him against everything I tried to teach him."

Matt sat back, absorbing this. "Did Nasser know about all of this? About Roken's past, your connection?"

Omar shook his head slowly. "I don't know. I've been looking, but I can't be sure what Nasser knew or how much of it was twisted by Roken."

Matt's tone was flat, his focus shifting back to the task at hand. "I'm not sure how this helps us with the diary."

Omar sighed deeply. "I don't know, but . . ."

He turned to the page where the entry about the Egyptian revolution was written. "See?" he said, pointing—*the light can still prevail*. Beyond that was another line that made Omar melt.

Walidi Alaziz has the eyes to see this.

Nasser had used the phrase "my dear father."

"See?" the old man repeated with pride. "My sweet Nasser will show us the way."

Matt nodded again, his eyes were darting across the page, parsing each word for meaning as his mind churned through the clues, looking for answers. He hoped Omar's emotions weren't blinding him to the reality of what might lie within these pages.

When Omar had said, 'Look here,' it was as if he was clinging to a fragile spark, trying to hold on to hope under the weight of his emotions.

"We gotta crack this, professor." Matt took a seat next to him.

PART VI

AWA WA BARD EL-AGOOZA

Nawet Awa wa Bard El-Agooza
"Gale of the Howling Wind"
(and "Old Lady Feeling the Cold")
emerges in late March.

There is no rain,
but the frigid air is so bitter
she feels it in her bones.

And yet, as the final storm of the winter season,
there is reason for optimism:
spring is almost here.

2012: ALEXANDRIA AND CAIRO

"*ADRAB DAMGHAK FI ELAHT*," Houda told her husband
—*you can bang your head on the wall if you wish*—"but I am
going to be wearing the hijab from now on." Her face looked calm
and beautiful, framed by the light cream color of her head cover—
so different and so much softer, she felt, than the black hood of
the niqab, which Houda had now decided she no longer wished
to wear, much to the fury of Tarek. While a man of few words by
default, Tarek now found himself quite literally speechless—
ambushed by his own wife.

Houda's loyalty up to this point had been absolute; that was
why this was such a shock to his system. Tarek had come to know
love with Houda in ways he hadn't thought were possible—a
union of souls with utmost respect for the roles within the
marriage. He was in awe of her unique combination of vulnerability and strength, but he never expected that strength to be
turned against him.

"I am your husband," he finally managed in the calmest voice
he could muster. "I have the say on this."

But Houda held her ground. "I'm sorry, Tarek." She shook
her head.

"This is not your decision!" As his voice spiked to object,

Houda wouldn't have it. "Please keep your voice down." She stood firm. "The baby is sleeping."

This annoyed him even more, for they were not in their own home. They were at Omar's, where Houda had just put little Fatimah to sleep in Nasser's old bedroom for an afternoon nap. Houda had waited for a visit back to her childhood home to spring this news on him, and Tarek felt entirely manipulated by the situation. Houda took his hand to reassure him, but he pulled it away from her grasp. She looked into his troubled eyes.

"Tarek, you're my husband. You're a good man, and I want to be with you. Please understand me; the niqab or the hijab doesn't change that or who I am inside. It has nothing to do with me being a good woman or a good mother."

Tarek spoke in a softer voice. "Houda, you must take some time to rethink this. Speak to my sisters. Maybe you need to talk to—"

"No," she said. "I'm done with others telling me how to be a Muslim woman."

Tarek eyed the eclectic artwork from Omar's collection that surrounded them—Persian miniatures, Christian relics, a Grecian urn, an Indian deity. To Tarek, this felt foreign. To Houda, it was home—a private museum of inclusion, celebrating differing antiquities of the world without prejudice or bias.

Yet it was this very leniency that Houda now realized she'd rebelled against by embracing the niqab—taking a stance that was entirely distinct from the strongly held positions of her father. But the niqab, too, had been its own trap. Houda now wanted a middle ground—somewhere between the rigidity of Tarek's views and the tolerance of her Baba.

As if on cue, Omar opened the front door, returning home from a walk. He lit up upon seeing them. "Where is my beautiful granddaughter?" he asked.

"Sleeping," said Houda. "Shall we have some tea?"

Tarek was in no mood for such pleasantries. He had half a mind to lay into his father-in-law for his liberal views. *Surely it was Omar who'd put his wife up to this nonsense. Or was it that crazy Dalia?* It was fruitless to discuss Islam with any of these people. Omar quoted from the Qur'an at times, but usually it was from books that no one else knew. And Dalia ranted incessantly about how the Muslim Brotherhood was hijacking the revolution. It was exhausting.

"I'm going home," he said suddenly. "I'll come back tomorrow. We'll discuss this then, ya Houda. Yalla as-salamu alaykum." He stormed angrily toward the door, avoiding Omar.

The professor seemed confused. "What happened, my daughter?"

"Can't you see?" She smiled. He was getting less alert these days.

Omar searched her eyes, which made her smile even more. *I'm more than my eyes now, Baba*, she told him mentally. And that's when he noticed. "Ya Allah, oh God!"

"Yes, Baba." She took a step back so he could take her in. "I am going to wear the hijab from now on." Omar understood finally why Tarek had been so angry.

"Don't worry, ya Baba," she assured him. "Tarek is a good man. He just needs to cool down, and we'll be fine. It will work. Trust me."

Omar smiled. "Inshallah—all will be well."

Would all be well? The worries never stopped for Dalia.

Mubarak had been deposed, finally, and Egypt now had its first democratically elected president in Mohammed Morsi—an engineer, no less—who'd studied in the West at USC. Morsi was a member of the Muslim Brotherhood, however, and they'd issued a temporary constitutional decree granting him unlimited powers. Some in the press were already labeling it an Islamist coup—and this wave was not restricted to Egypt. Throughout the Middle East, Islamists of all shades were trying to fill the political and power gaps that had arisen following the Arab Spring, proving the West's worst fears.

"Is this what you wanted?" Dalia's mother had called to nag. "Is this what you fought for when you wouldn't listen and blindly demanded change? You wanted these Muslim Brotherhood maniacs? What does your professor think now?"

Dalia didn't know. Many Egyptians had serious questions about the future of Egypt. But in what could be taken as a positive sign, the Muslim Brotherhood had invited prominent voices of the revolution for a meeting. That was where Dalia was headed. Feeling the need for a wingman, she drove to Kafr Abdu to pick up Omar, who'd graciously agreed to come along. The speaker they'd be seeing was named El-Nasah, one of the most important and prominent players within the Muslim Brotherhood. Omar was curious, certainly, to hear what he had to say, but the professor had his doubts about whether it would be a true dialogue or an exercise in propaganda. Dalia wasn't sure herself that this meeting would make any real difference. But it was a pretty big deal that Omar had agreed to come because the meeting was to be held in Cairo, a two-hundred-kilometer drive from Alexandria. Both of them knew it was important for Iskandrania to show up in order to demonstrate to Egyptians that this was not just about *Al-Qahirah*—Cairo. All of Egypt needed a voice.

Omar was ready with his cane as Dalia pulled up at the curb outside his apartment. Guilty about being late, Dalia leapt out to help him into the car. Returning to the wheel, she checked that his seat belt was fastened, then pulled into the road. "AC is good, ya professor?" she asked.

"Very good," he replied.

"The seat adjusted well? I have water for the road. Anything else you need? A sandwich?"

Omar laughed. "I'm not that old, my daughter. I bathed, ate, even went to the bathroom."

Dalia smiled, glad that Omar still had his sense of humor. But as they pulled past the mosque, her expression soured. The sign was still hanging there from the election: "Vote for Constitutional Reform. Voting YES is a religious duty."

"I still can't believe how they did that," she seethed. "Using religion to get people to vote their way."

Omar smiled and said, "Relax, ya Dalia, we all need clear heads."

"You know their history," she replied warily, still amazed that a small but vocal minority of zealots had swept the elections. It had been a lesson in the importance of good organization and having a clear, concise message.

"Yes." Omar nodded. "We keep struggling with these brotherhoods who think they're forces for good, returning religion to its core values. And time and again, they fail. But we must have sympathy toward them. They are still our brothers and sisters."

Dalia was astonished—this tolerance was impressive, even for Omar.

About halfway to Cairo, Dalia slowed down the car. "We are very close to the rest house, professor—you want to stop?"

"Yes, and maybe we can grab something to eat," he replied.

Dalia shook her head. "No, no."

Omar laughed and exclaimed, "No?"

Dalia had a different plan for lunch. "You remember Am Khalil, that wonderful little place near Tahrir Square where we used to eat during the protests? Very traditional and simple sandwiches. I really want us to go there and eat together again." Dalia was feeling nostalgic for their revolutionary days—what could have been, what almost was.

Omar smiled. "Mashy, of course, my daughter, we can do this. I'll be really hungry by then, and traffic will be heavy, so let's get going."

Dalia smiled and pressed on the accelerator.

One hour later, they greeted Am Khalil at his small establishment. The sandwiches tasted even better than last year, especially *el-batengan*—fried eggplant. It was a short walk from there to the meeting, and they made it just in time. El-Nasah sat at a table on the stage, facing the crowd, which was not quite as big as Dalia had hoped. *Where is everybody?*

Most had probably stayed at home, not as optimistic as Dalia, knowing there would be a lot of empty promises. In fact, his talk droned on and on—touting all the new government's aspirations and planned reforms. His claims and high words for democracy were loud, but they all felt meaningless to Omar. *Is this all fruitless?* As Dalia went to the microphone to address El-Nasah, she was surprised to see that Omar had risen from his chair as well to join her.

"Professor, by all means." She ceded her place to him.

Omar had the whitest hair in the room. He spoke softly into the microphone, but with authority and a clear sense of purpose. "You are still learning; we are all still learning." All eyes were upon him. *Age still commands some respect*, Omar thought, though he didn't expect the Brotherhood leaders on this panel to know who he was.

So, he was surprised when El-Nasah adjusted his seat, looked at him squarely, and asked, "What are we learning, Professor Omar?"

El-Nasah's authority forced the room into complete silence, and all eyes turned back to Omar for his response.

"We are learning about the revolution. We are learning about this process and the disappointment so many felt upon your election. We are learning about democracy, how to come together and negotiate power. We are learning how we can bring with us the many people still reeling from the loss of the last regime—their privilege, their feeling of service to this country. You might not agree with them, but these people feel threatened, and they are our people too. And they still control so much that you might not see or understand."

"But we are, we do—" El-Nasah sounded irritated.

Omar spoke on as if he hadn't heard him. "The silenced majority must learn to move forward in peace and dignity, even when they feel disoriented and doubt how you ended up in power, and—"

"You can't question the election's legitimacy!" It was El-Nasah's turn to interrupt.

Omar continued, undeterred. "Rulers can have the best intentions but still do bad things. We all need to learn. This is bigger than you; it is bigger than all of us unless we work together. No one minority group can carry Egypt forward alone, even after winning an election, unless they engage all of us. I studied history all my life, and it takes more than you—"

"Abu Nasser," El-Nasah said—addressing Omar as the father of Nasser.

"Don't you dare!" Dalia stood up suddenly and shouted, pointing angrily at the stage. "How dare you mention Nasser? You have no right!" She knew exactly what he was insinuating—that Nasser would have understood what the Muslim Brotherhood, what the Islamists, were trying to do. The implications, the unspoken words, cut her like a knife.

El-Nasah's face hardened, his jaw tightening as his eyes narrowed at Dalia. He wasn't used to having his authority questioned, especially by a young woman. Two men beside him began to rise, but he gestured sharply for them to sit down, his fingers stiff and tense. Omar turned and took Dalia's pointing arm, pushing it gently away from El-Nasah. "Let's go, my daughter. We have a long way ahead of us back to Alexandria." Omar glanced once more at the room before leaving, the weight of what had been said lingering in the air.

Everyone watched as the esteemed educator shuffled out of the chamber. No sooner were he and Dalia gone from the room than voices rose up again and assaulted the silence—protesting, arguing, and bellowing toward the stage.

2012: SOUTHERN TURKEY

THEY TURNED off Highway D400 and onto one of the countless farm roads winding through vineyards and fields of barley and wheat that patchworked the Turkey–Syria border. The driver, Asil, gunned the engine so that the jeep practically flew across the rutted gravel surface. Behind them lay the small Syrian town of Hawar Kilis; ahead, the Turkish village of Elbeyli. They raced along fields, lush with late-spring crops, the stillness broken only by the rumble of the jeep and the weight of what might lie ahead.

"How much farther?" Matt asked from the back seat where he sat with Lieutenant Bailey. Mendoza was riding shotgun, carbine in his lap.

"Twenty minutes," said Asil. Matt was trying to appear calm, but his mind was in turmoil. He was missing another family event —his daughter Claire's birthday—Stephanie would be furious. He hadn't told her yet and had no idea how he would explain this. But when he had gotten the message from AA, accepting Matt's invitation to meet, this had to come first.

"You married, lieutenant?" he asked Bailey.

"Affirmative, sir," Bailey responded without affect.

"How often d'you talk to your wife?"

"Twice a week without fail, sir. Only way to make this job work for her."

"I hear you." Matt looked out the window.

"Shall we go through our safety plan one more time, sir?" Bailey asked as Mendoza kept his hawk eyes focused on the terrain.

"Nah," said Matt. "I got it."

For a year now, AA's true motives remained an enigma. On the one hand, the intel they'd received from him had already saved many lives. He'd even given them a tip that had helped to stop a major operation in Europe. If AA was as well connected as they imagined, he could be the asset of their dreams. But there were also plenty of attacks he didn't warn them about. Half the team thought AA was just playing them.

That's why Matt had asked for this face-to-face meeting—the chance to look Nasser in the eyes. He prided himself on his ability to sense what people were thinking. They needed more information about Roken and his plans. But was Matt getting blinded by his own hubris? This wasn't a $250 Texas hold 'em pot at the Firstie Club. This was life and death. A mistake could spell catastrophe.

"Soon," said the driver. "Very soon."

On the horizon, Matt could see a small bunch of weathered, whitewashed stone buildings jutting up from the barley. He felt adrenaline begin rushing through his system.

"He made a smart choice in rendezvous points," Bailey observed. "They've been watching our approach from their high ground for miles and can see we have no backup. Even if we called in reinforcements from Turkey, he could quickly cross the Syrian border."

As Asil pulled the car up alongside the single two-story building, Mendoza asked Matt, "Can you confirm the abort code, sir?"

"*Quagmire*," responded Matt.

From inside the parked vehicle, Matt studied their surroundings. He wasn't certain whether it was a large enough settlement to qualify as a village. A couple of old Turkish-made jeeps and a dust-covered Citroën sat between the buildings, but none of them looked like they'd brought anyone here recently. An old woman napped in a chair beside the hut at the far edge of the settlement. She was the only soul in sight. Matt looked around the broken-down, deserted buildings for snipers, signals, watchers of any kind, but he couldn't see anything that didn't seem to belong to the place.

Bailey, meanwhile, was talking on his secure headset to the comm tower on the USS *Harry S. Truman*, which had eyes on them via the US satellite in geostationary orbit over the Middle East. Even at twenty-three thousand miles overhead, its instruments were sensitive enough to read a license plate; its infrared sensors could detect bodies through the walls.

"It appears to be empty," Bailey reported.

What does that mean? Is AA nearby—waiting for us to arrive first?

"Let's check it out," Matt said, disengaging the safety on his sidearm. All three got out of the car and moved toward the two-story building's open door. Asil took up a position flush against the building's front wall. "Make it quick," he hissed.

Matt followed close behind Bailey as he entered the building and scanned the open room that composed the first floor, essentially a small foyer. The door at the far end was pale wood, carved with intricate geometric designs surrounding a phrase in Arabic. Bailey opened that door, and they found themselves in a large open-plan area. Ahead of them, chairs clustered around a dining table; to the right, an old couch sagged under the glare from three big windows. Working systematically, they double-checked for people hiding in the kitchen, the small bathroom, and the two bedrooms with their sparse furnishings.

When they had confirmed that all the closets were empty and all the windows were closed, Bailey announced into the comm, "All clear."

Matt said, "Keep your eyes open. I guess he'll show up now."

Bailey stood with his back against the kitchen wall so that he could cover the entrance; Matt took up a position near the couch, keeping his eye on those three big windows.

But when AA appeared, it was from the back bedroom—the one with nothing in it but a bed and an empty closet. Matt had cleared that room himself. *Where the heck did he come from?*

Bailey commanded in a full voice, "Hands where I can see them!" He and Mendoza both trained their weapons on AA, who only laughed.

"If I wanted to kill you, you would already be dead, Lieutenant Bailey," AA said—and Matt's poker mind raced.

He knows the name and rank of my SEAL escort? How? He has that level of surveillance on us?

It was deeply concerning.

AA fixed Matt with his big, dark, almost feminine eyes. "Shall we chat?" His accent was soft and musical—similar to Youssef's, Matt noted. AA took a seat at the dining table casually, as if they were sitting down to break bread. Matt joined him, indicating to the SEALs to lower their weapons.

Nasser's gaze held steady. Matt took a breath, then leaned in closer. "I know you've been involved in killing American soldiers. Just recently, we believe you killed nine Americans in the museum—"

"Yes," Nasser interrupted, his voice sharp. "It was a trap. The first time, mercenaries killed five unarmed Iraqi guards—men with families—while they stole artifacts, stole history, for money. Your soldiers stood outside, watching as if nothing was happening." He leaned forward, his voice a low hiss. "So, I set a trap the next time, with your soldiers outside again, and they deserved their fate after they raised their guns first. This was justice—or are we terrorists because we fought back? How many Iraqis are you going to kill for that? Are you going to demolish their families' and friends' homes, lock up the men in a new Abu Ghraib, but this time, no one will know? What other insanity will you do next?"

A tense silence followed before Bailey, who had been standing watch, raised his weapon, his gaze locked on Nasser. "Permission to eliminate the target, sir?"

Matt didn't break eye contact with Nasser. "No. Stand down." His voice was firm, a subtle warning.

Bailey kept his weapon trained on Nasser, his gaze unyielding, but Nasser ignored him entirely.

Nasser kept his focus on Matt, unwavering. "I don't kill innocent Americans. I target those who torture, kill, or play conqueror in a country they have no business attacking. I see your media, I hear your news—your democracy hasn't handed down any real punishment for the killing of all these innocent people here." His voice dropped, calm and cold. "I know your father was a history professor. Mine is, too, as I'm sure you know. I hope you've read history, learned from it, and understood its lessons."

Matt felt a surge of tension as he thought of his late father and the lessons they had never had the chance to discuss. But he held himself in check. He took a moment to calm down, letting the silence settle before reminding himself: *One thing at a time. Mission first.*

Matt took a breath, then said, "The information you gave us about the plutonium turned out to be true."

Nasser nodded, unfazed. "They are not playing games. The first time they received the material, it wasn't usable." Nasser paused. "We've just learned they've obtained what they need to make it work. Roken wants to make a political statement using technology from the West by building a dirty bomb with plutonium from Dimona, the Israeli reactor constructed by the French."

"Roken doesn't have an engineer to make his bomb operational," Nasser explained, adding, "That would have been me. So, there's time. But not much."

"We need to terminate him," said Matt.

"We have that in common," Nasser agreed. "So, this is what I propose: I can continue to pass on the information we obtain about Roken's plans. We'll exchange encrypted messages in this chat room"—Nasser showed it to Matt on his phone—"using the same cipher. In return, I expect you to feed me any intel you receive about Roken's whereabouts." He looked Matt in the eye. "Do we have a deal?"

Matt nodded. Nasser was pleased.

Hours later, when he was back aboard the USS *Harry S. Truman*, Matt took a very deep breath and dialed his wife.

"Where the fuck are you?" came a female voice.

Matt steadied himself. Then he just came out and said it. "Off the coast of Lebanon."

"Lebanon! *Lebanon?*" Stephanie was apoplectic. "You told me you were in Phoenix."

"I lied," admitted Matt.

"Jesus Christ, Matt," Stephanie fumed. "How long have you been lying to me?"

Matt sighed. "How long?" she repeated.

"It's part of the job, Steph."

"Answer my goddamn question, Matt."

"Our entire marriage."

She was devastated. Neither of them spoke.

Duty means doing the right thing, no matter what.

Those were his father's words—words his mother had passed down to him. For a moment, he remembered how he had looked at those words just before flinging his mortarboard high into the air at his West Point graduation. It felt like a different lifetime.

"Stephanie . . ."

More silence.

Matt felt like an idiot. In his moment of weakness, he'd just made the situation a hell of a lot worse. He still couldn't tell her what he was doing, which made it unbearable. Now she knew he was in danger—and that was it. No details, nothing on which to hang a sliver of hope. She couldn't even ask, *When are you coming home?*

At this point, it felt like never.

"Steph . . ."
The line went dead.

2013: QUEENS

THE BAGEL from Youssef's favorite spot on the Lower East Side was as chewy and delicious as it had ever been, but he was having trouble enjoying it all the same. The neighborhood seemed bustling and vibrant, much more prosperous now than the first time he'd visited. When he'd bought breakfast here that Tuesday morning twelve years ago, he couldn't have known the horror that would unfold that day—the day the world had fallen apart.

But he and Risa had been together.

I just need a little time on my own. A little time to sort out how I feel. Her words from three months ago were still echoing in Youssef's ears. He hadn't believed them then, and he couldn't believe them now. Half of his torn and ragged heart couldn't imagine life apart from her, and the other half was furious with the knowledge that she was closer than ever to Ori Bergman.

Youssef remembered a time when it had been him and Risa against the world. After she finished law school, they had decided to start a family. Months passed without success, however. After making the rounds from one doctor to the next, eventually they lost momentum, and Risa buried herself in work. She teamed up with Ori Bergman, and their professional relationship only grew stronger. Youssef couldn't stand the way Ori's voice softened when he spoke to her, or how his eyes lingered on her longer than they should. There was a familiarity there that wasn't earned—something that made Youssef want to cross the room and shove Ori against a wall. Before, Youssef had felt Ori was trying to lay claim to spaces that defined his culture. But this time, it was something much more personal.

Risa played it off, as if nothing was amiss, but Youssef was certain she knew. She prided herself on the direct, practical advocacy they were doing in human rights law. She didn't mind burrowing in and imposing her vision, however disconnected that vision was from history or the nuanced experiences of the people she was supposed to be helping.

Maybe she and Youssef had reached a stalemate that had less to do with the baby each claimed to want than with the differences between them that they'd always managed to tamp down.

It was July now, and Youssef was feeling another kind of longing. He needed time to regain his bearings. He wanted to go home—to Misr. So, here he was in New York, on his way to spend the summer in Alexandria. The longing weighed on him like a heavy anchor, pulling him back to where he belonged.

Youssef took the R train toward Adam's place. It would have been quicker to take the 4 uptown and transfer, but he needed a moment to collect himself. Still, by midmorning he was knocking on his old friend's door. He knew Adam was doing well and had moved again since he'd visited last, but he still hadn't expected the new place to be quite so big, its lawn to be quite so landscaped, the street's trees to be so majestic. Youssef also hadn't expected the round of full-throated barking that his knock produced from within. When he heard it, he double-checked—was he at the right house?

He was. Through the door, Youssef heard Adam's unmistakable voice calling, "Butkus! Chill! Quiet, boy!" Then the door opened, and there he stood, a few pounds heavier but with the same grin, his hand gripping a bullmastiff by the collar.

"Come in, come in!" Adam sang out, throwing his other arm wide to hug Youssef. "You should have stayed here with us," he added as Youssef took off his shoes and placed them on the rack inside the door. "We have plenty of bedrooms. Come in," Adam beckoned. "I'll make you some tea in the fifty."

Both of them laughed at the familiar expression from home. "In the fifty" rhymed with the Egyptian expression for making very dark and concentrated tea, and they always added it in when they were feeling playful.

"We'll have some time before Jummah prayers, and after that, I'll take you to some real lunch—someone from Alexandria who makes real *hawawshi* here in New York," Adam said. The beloved Egyptian street food was like a meat-stuffed flatbread baked to crispy perfection. "I love this town, ya man," Adam added with an easy laugh, a sound that spoke of someone fully at home in this city, with his family, and in this moment.

Adam's kitchen looked like something from a magazine. Opposite the six-burner industrial gas stove, a mix of iron-framed windows and patio doors looked out onto a neatly trimmed back lawn edged in herbs and flowers. Suspended over the enormous concrete island was a rack that held a dozen copper pots and pans just above head height.

Adam settled Youssef at the large pedestal table by the window, then strode over to the kettle that was steaming on the stove and began pouring hot water into oversize mugs.

"Would you like some mint with it?" he asked.

"Always," Youssef answered.

Adam cut fragrant sprigs from a potted plant on the table, then finished preparing the tea. Youssef's mind tried to reconcile this prosperous American Adam with the young man he'd once known. Adham was unrecognizable. *How much have we grown apart?* Youssef wondered. How had he built this life with Valería? Youssef had been sure Adam would have asked her to convert to Islam, but a milagro here and a sacred heart there in the house made it clear she was as Catholic as ever. *Can friendships survive when people change so much? Once,* Adam had been the one to keep them all on the straight and narrow, reminding them that this thing and that were haram; now it seemed he had run away from everything, forgotten everyone. Youssef felt jealous in ways he didn't dare to admit. While life seemed to be soaring for Adam, Youssef, despite his privilege, was starting to feel like a failure.

Youssef watched as his friend fiddled for a moment with an iPod in a dock, then the iconic Lebanese singer Fairouz's voice flooded the kitchen, singing, "Shore of Alexandria." Nostalgia squeezed Youssef's heart like a lemon. "What a song!" he laughed, his voice catching a little in his throat. Adam smiled.

They listened together for a few moments, not talking, and then Youssef's nostalgia, combined with the conversation he had just overheard, made him think of the one whose name they'd stopped speaking. "Do you still think about Nasser? Wonder what happened?"

His pointed words found their mark. Keeping his gaze on Youssef, Adam put his tea down with slow, deliberate care. His voice was quiet but intense. "Think of Nasser, you say? I don't need to." He closed his eyes and turned his face away. "Nasser lives with me, ya Youssef. He never leaves me. He is the brother I turn to when I am happy and when I need help. He lives inside me." Adam clutched at his heart. "I don't need to defend Nasser to this world, I don't need to justify him, and I don't need to keep fighting a fight that he would tell me is not mine."

Both of them held their tongues as Fairouz's voice filled the silence. *The pain carried away by the wind*, she sang, *in the sunset, far into the sea of Alexandria.*

When the song ended, Adam shook his head as if clearing away a lingering thought, then smiled at Youssef warmly. "Yalla," he said, turning toward the door. "Let's go and pray Jummah and then get the hawawshi lunch. We'll go pick up Gibrail from his day camp. You won't believe how grown up he is!"

~

After an uneventful flight from JFK, Youssef landed in Cairo and found the city gripped by fresh protests and growing political unrest under the rule of the Muslim Brotherhood. The mood in Tahrir Square was strangely festive: no rubber bullets, no tear gas.

Egyptian flags and face paint were as much in evidence as signs denouncing Mohammed Morsi and other leaders as traitors to democracy. Observing a placard of President Barack Obama crossed out with a heavy red X, Youssef found he wasn't certain what this image meant about its bearer's stance on Egyptian politics. Had he been away from home for too long? Would the man gripping the placard have any clearer understanding than Youssef did of the relationship between opposing Obama and deposing Morsi?

It was a puzzle that perturbed Youssef and many others. Despite claims to the contrary, the Muslim Brotherhood had showed little interest in sharing power with Egypt's more liberal groups or in relaxing its grip on power. People were outraged; the military was getting restless.

Youssef had dropped his bags at a hotel in Heliopolis and ventured out, encountering this demonstrator who was ready to blame the Muslim Brotherhood's disastrous mishandling of power on America. Before Youssef could strike up a conversation with the man, currents within the crowd swept him and the anti-Obama placard away. Then Youssef saw a sign that read, "America, stop supporting terrorists! Stop supporting the Muslim Brotherhood." This sentiment was more cogent, but nonetheless too simplistic. America had always been the devil, an easy target to vilify, no matter the setting or situation. But Youssef was happy to see the Egyptian people once again demanding change. He, too, felt swept up in a mood of patriotic optimism.

Along the square's edge, living room furniture was set up. People lounged, chatted, and drank tea as if they were at home. A young man called out to Youssef, offering him a glass, and Youssef sat down with his group. The young man introduced himself as Tamer.

"I was in the square two years ago, and now I've been here for three days," he announced. "Morsi has got to go. The whole Muslim Brotherhood has got to go. The direction they took was not what we were dreaming of when we threw Mubarak out."

"Morsi was elected democratically." Youssef tried to introduce some nuance into the conversation. "If he's deposed, won't it be a blow to Egyptian democracy?"

"We could have a referendum to remove him," Tamer suggested. "That would clear our path forward."

"I hope you're right," Youssef said.

"Where are you from?" Tamer then asked with a gentle, curious smile. Dalia had loved this about the Revolution two years ago, the way people in the square had asked questions and gotten to know one another. Youssef had been half a world away then; it nearly brought tears to his eyes to get to live it now.

"Alexandria," he said, "but I've been living in the US for some time now."

"Wow," said Tamer. "What do you do there?"

"Software engineering," Youssef said.

Tamer's eyes shone dreamily. "You must have such a life in America," he said. "I'd like to go soon. My uncle lives there. And, also, a girl I met online." He blushed a little, went on shyly, "She lives in Cleveland, but she's originally from Jordan. We've been chatting a lot; we've gotten pretty close." He sipped his tea; his eyes came back from a faraway dream to the here and now.

Youssef smiled. "I hope things work out."

"Inshallah," Tamer agreed.

Youssef made his way out of the crowd in Tahrir, but he wasn't quite done. He wanted to experience the opposing viewpoint by seeing what was happening at the pro-Morsi demonstrations, which were concurrently underway outside the Rabaa al-Adawiya Mosque. Knowing it was an opportunity he likely wouldn't get again, Youssef flagged down a taxi.

As they drove east, away from the river, Youssef leaned his cheek against the window and looked out at dusty, sand-colored Cairo—so familiar, but so different from the terrain he'd left behind in California. The streets were crowded with people going about their daily business. Youssef wondered whether these people also wished they could go and celebrate or protest. What did they think of the direction the country had taken these past two years? The Muslim Brotherhood had proved incompetent—

mistake had piled upon mistake, with disastrous economic policies. But was the Brotherhood entirely to blame?

The first thing Youssef saw when he stepped out of the cab at Rabaa al-Adawiya was a burning American flag. Pro-Morsi demonstrators carried signs that read, "America is at war with Islam," "Legitimacy Is Ours," "Allah Is With Us," and "*El-Shar'iyya, El-Shar'iyya*"—*legitimacy, legitimacy*. Youssef could see their point.

"America is against us," a younger man put in, and heads nodded in agreement.

"Why would Americans support deposing Morsi?" Youssef asked. "I mean, if you look at it, the Americans—and, sorry to say, even the Israelis—have been happy with the tough way he's dealt with Hamas. He seemed pretty eager to please them. So, why?"

"Why anything?" the young man asked. "It's politics. It's just politics. They're at war with Islam; they want us out."

Again, heads nodded, and then another young man changed the subject. "I'm starving," he said. "Let's go for *koshari*. Who's with me?"

At the mention of koshari, Youssef's mouth began to water. Egypt's national dish was next to impossible to find in Berkeley. He imagined a steaming plate of rice, lentils, and macaroni in spicy, vinegary tomato sauce, garnished with chickpeas and a heap of crispy fried onions on top. His stomach rumbled; he hadn't eaten since breakfast. "I'll go," he said. "I've been missing koshari for the longest time."

"What do you mean?" asked the young man who'd said America was at war with Islam.

"I've been living overseas for a few years now," Youssef said. "In America," he added a bit shyly. "It's been a while since I had any koshari."

"Ahlan beek," the young man said, welcoming them. He extended his hand. "I'm Hazem, and I know the best koshari man in Cairo. Come on, he's not far." Several other young men were hungry too, and they all headed off down a side street in a companionable bunch.

"How do you like America?" Hazem asked Youssef, suddenly curious. Now that they weren't arguing politics, his whole demeanor had changed—he was friendly and interested.

"I love it there," Youssef said. "It's my second home."

"I just finished my degree at Cairo University," Hazem said. "Architecture. I'd like to get my master's at the University of Denver. Have you ever been to Colorado?"

"Not yet," Youssef admitted.

Hazem went on, "They have a wonderful program. I'd love to go and learn. The hardest part will be getting a visa, but inshallah . . ."

"Inshallah," Youssef echoed.

Back in Alexandria, Youssef spent some time with Dalia and Omar. Everyone was concerned about Egypt's future. Things were so tense that they hardly even saw Houda anymore because of Tarek's affiliation with the Muslim Brotherhood. It broke Omar's heart, but he understood. A woman must be loyal to her husband.

Youssef's family tried to get his mind off politics by inviting him to spend time at their villa at Marina, west of Alexandria. It was nice to relax and go for beach walks with his older sister, Iman —it took seeing Iman in person to realize how much he had missed her. But there were ways in which she still drove him crazy, and one of them soon reared its head.

A few days into his stay, Iman asked him to put on a nice shirt for dinner—she was inviting a friend. The "friend" turned out to be a recently widowed woman, Yara—a biologist educated at the American University in Cairo, whose English was fluent. Youssef shook his head in disbelief. *A setup?* He was still married!

Yara was pleasant enough. Youssef found out over dinner that she'd lost her husband four years ago to cancer and had a six-year-old boy. She was sophisticated, even attractive—but Youssef was not ready to give up on Risa, no matter what Iman and the rest of his family felt about her.

After dinner, Youssef let his sister have it. "Are you crazy? What do you think you're doing?"

"You should be more open, little brother."

"I'm married!"

"It will never last, Youssef," said Iman. "We're all surprised it went this far—a Jew from America? It doesn't matter how modern you think you are."

Youssef was seething inside, but he decided there was no point in arguing with her. He grabbed a set of keys and headed for the door.

"Where are you going?"

"Wael's place."

Iman raised an eyebrow. "Things can get pretty crazy over there."

Youssef left. It was so annoying when she acted condescendingly.

Wael was an old high school friend from a very rich family. He hosted parties at their beach house practically every night—as wild as anything in the West. Drinks, pot, music.

Youssef felt like cutting loose, so he grabbed a beer and found a girl to talk to. Once she learned he lived in America, she tried using her English, but it was strongly accented, nothing like Yara's. Youssef didn't care. This girl was hot, with long dark hair, dark eyes, and a full body. A couple of drinks later, they were upstairs in one of the many bedrooms.

Afterward, Youssef felt a wave of self-loathing. This was the first time he had kissed another woman since meeting Risa, let alone been with one. And yet, in his mind, the thought of Risa with Ori cut deeper than his own betrayal. *Did she let him kiss her? Did Ori want more?*

Lying half-naked and smoking a joint, the girl tried to make small talk, but Youssef's mind was elsewhere. He checked his iPhone hoping for a message from Risa. Instead, the screen lit up with breaking news from Cairo: the security forces had raided the Muslim Brotherhood demonstrations, with reports of violence.

He put down his phone in disbelief. He looked at the girl lying next to him and thought of his best friend in America and felt guilty. Even if they had been fighting, Youssef knew that Adam would never have cheated on Valería.

Youssef pulled on his clothes. "Where're you going?" asked the girl.

"Home," said Youssef. To his surprise, he realized that he meant America.

2013: ALEXANDRIA

"ALHAMDULILLAH ALA KOL SHIAA" —*praise be to God for everything.* Shahinaz sighed, and Houda felt her pain, mirroring her own anguish. The recent political upheaval—the overthrow of the Muslim Brotherhood with the support of most Egyptians— had swept up many of the guilty, but others were caught in the chaos. Among them was Houda's husband, Tarek, now behind bars.

"Everyone's making us feel like devils," Shahinaz said, her voice breaking. "They don't even see us as Egyptians anymore— just some foreign tribe. They blame us for everything—because my family is connected to the Muslim Brotherhood. The bad economy, the revolution's lost hopes—everything falls on us."

Houda placed a comforting hand on her shoulder and murmured, *"Bokra kolo hay adi." Tomorrow, it will pass.*

Tears welled up in Shahinaz's eyes. "I'm still an Egyptian. I didn't cause this—I've done nothing wrong."

"I know, ya Shahinaz," Houda said gently. "We're all tired and upset."

At least Houda would soon return to her father's home—a place where she could feel grounded. With her husband's recent imprisonment, she felt an undeniable pull toward the safety of her childhood home and the wisdom of her Baba, Professor Omar El-

Mohammedi. It was where she belonged—for herself and for Fatimah. As they spoke, Dalia was already on her way with the car to help Houda pack up her belongings and move.

The country was now finding a new path, and no one knew where it would lead. Houda, who was still trying to figure out her place in all of this, gazed at her beautiful daughter, Fatimah, sleeping peacefully in her rocker with not a care in the world. *I was like that once*, thought Houda. *We all were.* The outside world was in upheaval, its future unclear. Yet there, in her rocker, Fatimah lay in blissful serenity, her being filled with curiosity, wonder, innocence, and joy.

"You must be worried sick about your husband," said Shahinaz, interrupting Houda's thoughts.

"Tarek is an upstanding man," Houda said with quiet conviction. "He did nothing wrong. They'll release him—I'm sure of it."

"Inshallah," said Shahinaz, looking skyward. Then, trying to lighten the mood, she said, "You know what I heard yesterday?"

"What?"

"Someone blamed the Muslim Brotherhood for the Egyptian football team not making it to the World Cup."

Houda laughed. "We have to blame someone, right?" She thought of her brother and Adham—how many times they'd shouted at the television when the Egyptian national team players missed easy shots on goal. "It's the curse of the damn Brotherhood." She pictured Adham yelling and shaking his fist at the screen while Nasser gave him a look, as if he'd lost his mind. Houda giggled so hard, she had to cover her mouth.

Then came a knock at the door.

"That must be Dalia," said Houda, standing up. Shahinaz hastily put her niqab back on, covering her face, as Houda opened the door.

Adham stood on the other side, his hand tightening on the doorframe. He'd prepared himself for this moment, but Houda's laughter stole away his words. The girl he once knew was now a striking woman, even beneath her hijab. He blinked, grounding himself in the present. He loved his wife, but Houda had always lingered in a quiet corner of his heart—a shadow that time couldn't erase.

For her part, Houda felt a strange lightness. Adham had come all the way from America in her hour of need, and for an instant, she felt an urge to hug him—not as the man she loved, but for the echoes of Nasser she saw in him.

The thought of those younger days—of Nasser and Adham in her father's apartment—brought a warm smile to her face as she said, "So, Adham—the funny man is at a loss for words. But what are you doing here?"

"I came back suddenly," he explained. "My mother is not well."

"I'm sorry, ya Adham," Houda said, her tone gentle. "I'll go and visit soon. I didn't know."

"It's okay," Adham replied, a small smile tugging at his lips. "Let's get you home to the professor. Dalia roped me into helping you move," he explained. "We couldn't find parking, so she's waiting below. Didn't you get the text?"

Shahinaz stared at this stranger, noticing the warmth and friendly chatter between them. *Who is this man?*

Adham stopped in his tracks, noticing Shahinaz looking at him in alarm from the slit in her niqab with her iridescent eyes. Momentarily flustered, Adham turned back to the task at hand. "Do you have anything ready to go? I can take several trips."

"Start with this." Houda indicated a suitcase near the door. "But it's quite heavy. Shall I ask the doorman for help?"

"I need the workout," Adham joked.

Shahinaz, meanwhile, was becoming increasingly uncomfortable. She disappeared into the baby's room as Adham picked up the bag and carried it out of the apartment.

Houda walked down the hall to Fatimah's bedroom, where Shahinaz was gathering up the last of her toys. "Don't worry about those," said Houda. "I'll take just the blanket. It's her favorite." The blanket was draped across Fatimah as she slept. She looked so peaceful; Houda wished she didn't have to disturb her.

There was another knock on the front door, forceful and insistent. *That can't be Adham. It's too soon, isn't it?* Leaving Shahinaz with Fatimah, Houda went to open it and beheld two women in niqabs—Tarek's sisters, Azziza and Affifa, who lived with their parents on the floor below. Houda had never gotten along with them, and even now, seeing just their eyes, she knew there was trouble. Tarek was a solid husband but his sisters' disapproving glances and whispered judgments were a constant nuisance. It always felt like having watchdogs in her life.

"As-salamu alaykum," she greeted them politely.

"Who was that man I just saw leaving your place?" Azziza demanded.

"Adham. He's like my brother, and he's coming to help me—"

"He is *not* your brother." Azziza was incensed. "He is a stranger to you and not allowed in this apartment. That is *eyyeb*—you should know better!"

"Adham is no stranger!" Houda felt herself heating up, but she tried to stay calm. "He is a close friend of my family, coming to help at the request of my father."

"Your home is here," said Affifa.

"I already told you that I'm moving in with my Baba until Tarek comes out of jail," Houda explained as patiently as she could.

Affifa snorted, "These are not the manners of a good wife or a respectable woman."

Houda sighed without answering.

"This is not right," Affifa continued. "You stay here with us. If you're feeling alone or scared in Tarek's apartment, then you can move downstairs with us, as Mother has said."

Azziza nodded. "You have no right to take my niece from her family."

"We'll come back and visit you," Houda offered. "I'm just going across town to my father's place—"

"Your father!" Affifa was livid. "It's people like him who have caused all of our suffering. You all stood aside when the police came for my brother and others in the Brotherhood. Blood is on your father's hands! On yours too."

"*Ahtrmey nafesk*, ya Affifa," Houda said coldly—*have some respect*. "My father had nothing to do with what happened to Tarek, or with anyone in the Muslim Brotherhood."

"Go, if you must." Azziza was getting furious. "But you are not taking my mother's granddaughter. Fatimah stays with us!" She went marching toward the bedroom, but Shahinaz was there with a sleepy-eyed Fatimah in her arms. Fatimah blinked sweetly as she arose from her slumber and looked around to get her bearings. With both Azziza and Houda closing in on her, the girl naturally chose her mother, extending both arms for a hug.

Shahinaz looked forcefully toward Azziza as she handed the baby to Houda. "There's no need for this, ya Azziza. It is her child."

Affifa barged up to them. "Look what you have brought upon us! *Nas malhash asel.*" *People with no roots, no class, no respect.*

"I've told all of you my decision," Houda said, her tone firm. "Please, let's not go over that again, and let's not make a scene. I'm leaving with my baby."

Azziza tried to restrain Houda as Affifa wrestled her for control of the child, who started to scream in confusion. Houda's body tensed with rage, "Let go! Are you crazy?"

Adham suddenly appeared. "What's going on here?"

Houda rushed over to him. "Adham! Take Fatimah downstairs to Dalia." She handed him the child, now sobbing, and pushed them out into the apartment stairwell.

Affifa followed, screaming for help, "*Alahkona ya nas! They're trying to kidnap our child!*" Neighbors spilled out of the apartments below as Adham made his way down the stairs. Affifa and Azziza punched and kicked Adham from behind as Houda struggled to pull them away. It was utter chaos. "Yalla, yalla! Let's go," Houda yelled.

"What about your bags?" asked Adham, fighting his way through the increasing crowd of neighbors trying to block their escape.

"I don't care about them," Houda replied in growing panic. "Let them keep it all."

Houda's heart pounded. *Would they even make it out?*

Just then, Shahinaz appeared at the top of the stairwell. In a voice that was deep and commanding, unlike anything that had ever come out of her mouth, she shouted down to quell the mushrooming riot, *"Bintaha be Elsharia we Elkanoon."* She pointed at Houda. "That is the child's mother. The child belongs to her! This is Islamic law and every law; respect the words of Allah and his Prophet."

With everyone staring up at Shahinaz, Houda and Adham seized the moment to escape with Fatimah into the street. They ran toward Dalia waiting in the car, not stopping until the voices still arguing outside could no longer be heard. "Get in," Adham said, his voice low but firm, as he ushered Houda into the back seat and scanned the street for any signs of pursuit.

The car door slammed shut as Houda cradled Fatimah tightly. Adham slid into the front seat of Dalia's compact black Skoda, the car warm from the lingering heat of the day. Then, pausing to catch their breath, Houda and Adham stared at each other in shock. What had just happened was utterly surreal.

"Yalla, Dalia. Go," Houda urged. "Tarek's crazy family might show up any second to cause even more trouble."

Dalia shot them a look but didn't hesitate, shifting the car into gear and maneuvering quickly through the narrow streets. Her jaw tightened as she accelerated, weaving through the heavy traffic.

Adham shook his head, glancing out the rear window as they turned a corner. "That was insane. They actually tried to stop you from leaving—and take Fatimah?"

From the driver's seat, Dalia's sharp voice cut through the tense silence. "Who do they think they are?" Her knuckles whitened as she gripped the steering wheel. "I swear, I'll sue them. I'll drag them through every court in the city."

Adham let out a low chuckle, shaking his head. "Still the same Dalia. Always ready for a fight."

Houda's lips twitched into a smile, and before she could stop herself, a laugh escaped, easing the tension. "I know, right? She hasn't changed one bit."

Houda leaned forward slightly, catching Dalia's gaze in the mirror, but her eyes flicked to Adham when he quietly asked, "Are you okay?"

"Alhamdulillah," Houda replied with a smile. Fatimah whimpered in her lap, clutching her blanket tightly. Houda kissed her daughter's head, whispering, "It's okay, *habibti*. We're safe now."

They pulled up outside Omar's building. Adham was the first to step out, holding the door for Houda as she carefully climbed out, Fatimah still nestled in her arms. He grabbed a small bag from the trunk, his movements deliberate but calm.

Dalia used Houda's keys to open the apartment door, letting them inside. The quiet of the space was immediate, a stark contrast to the chaos they had just escaped. Houda adjusted Fatimah on her hip as the child, still clutching her blanket, glanced around sleepily. The calm of the apartment enveloped them.

"Where's the professor?" Adham asked. His eyes swept the room, pausing on the sofa in the living room. The familiarity of the space tugged at him—echoes of laughter and shared moments with Nasser lingered, blending with the present.

"He's out right now," Houda replied. "But this is home."

Adham placed the bag near the entryway and turned toward Dalia and Houda, his hands slipping into his pockets. He hesitated, then spoke quietly. "I have to leave for the US tomorrow—I'm only here for three days—but I'll be back soon."

Dalia stepped forward and gave him a quick, firm hug. The tension of old arguments still hung in the air between them. "Ya Adham, I miss your laugh," she said, her voice unusually tender.

Adham extended his hand to Houda. A hug would have been too much. His grip lingered for a moment longer than necessary. "Take care, ya Houda," he said. "If you or the professor need anything—anything at all—don't hesitate. Nasser akhoia—he'll always be my brother. You're family."

Houda's expression softened as she replied, "Travel safely. *Rabana ma'ak*, ya Adham."

Adham nodded once more, then turned and walked into the dimming light of the evening.

～

Later that evening, it felt like another world. Happy and relieved to be home, Houda asked Omar to watch Fatimah so she could do her evening prayers. Delighted in his new role as a grandfather, Omar led Fatimah into Nasser's old room, which they had turned into a cozy nursery. He sat on the floor with her and played peekaboo, covering his face to make it vanish behind his hands, then reappearing suddenly with a big smile. Fatimah squealed with delight. Omar did it again. Fatimah giggled. Again. A guffaw. She couldn't get enough of it, and neither could Omar.

Who is having more fun? Houda wondered, watching them silently from the doorway, having finished her prayers. Her heart was filled with love.

Peekaboo! Cackle. *Peekaboo!* Snicker . . .

The baby's eyes were starting to droop, however. "Time for bed, ya Baba," said Houda gently, crossing to pick up her daughter, who yawned. Houda carried Fatimah over to Nasser's bed, which had been decorated with a monkey, a camel, and other stuffed animals. She tucked her in and sat next to her. Omar dimmed the lights and watched as Houda began to sing an Arabic lullaby she loved:

> *Nami nami ya saghyrea* • Sleep, sleep, baby
> *Yalla aghfy 'al hasira* • Take a nap on the mat

Omar smiled, cocooned by the warmth of the room, as Houda's soothing lullaby wove a gentle barrier against the chill of the howling wind outside.

> *Bokra baba gahy* • Tomorrow your father will come

308

Gaib shames medwieah • Bringing the sunlight
Bokra ghalo gahy • Tomorrow your uncle will come
Gahazlek be aionah shall • Making a shawl with his eyes
Ya defiek shatwieah • To keep you warm in winter's chill

Omar exchanged a smile with Houda; they were both thinking of Nasser, of course. Little Fatimah was fast asleep as Houda sang the final line: *Tomorrow the sun will come, will make us warm with big love and bring all those who are gone.*

2014: SINAI DESERT

WHAT DRAGGED her back to consciousness was the screaming pain in her head. Her temples throbbed; her tongue was like cotton in her mouth. *Is this dehydration? Low blood sugar?* She tried to remember the last thing she'd eaten. Yeast, sugar, smoke. Yes. *Mutabek*, delicate and hot, from the little bakery Ori had taken her to in Jerusalem's crowded Souk Khan Al-Zeit. When had that been? She couldn't say. Risa's eyelids were grainy and raw. When she opened them, they clung together gummily. The world was a searing orange. She squeezed her eyes shut again, turned her head, fluttered them back open. A dim flicker—what was burning her eyes was only the low, guttering flame of a lantern, but it was enough to flood her once again with pain. Risa tried to raise her hand to her head, check herself for wounds, but she found that she couldn't. Her hands were tied.

Risa closed her eyes again and tried to wriggle free of her bonds, but she only managed to make the tough plastic of the zip ties bite more cruelly into her wrists and ankles. The surface she lay on was chilled and hard; the air smelled cool and mineral-like despite the suffocating heat that surrounded her now, as it had been ever since she'd stepped off the plane. Her body felt bruised all over.

Through the rustle of her own thrashing came a whisper, its hush echoing a little against the rocks. "Risa! Risa, are you okay?"

Risa forced her eyes open, holding her face away from the lamp. Two shadowy forms to her left resolved themselves into Ori and their driver, Hamdan. They, too, were bound and lying on the stone floor.

"Ori!" she whispered urgently. "Where are we?" The scattered pieces of her memory were beginning to reshape themselves.

"We'll be okay," he began.

Does he really believe it?

Risa tried to get her bearings. "Last thing I remember was those men making us get out of the car."

"I think they hit us or drugged us," Ori said. "My head is killing me." He felt guilty, more than anything—it was he who'd steered them to take on this mission, investigating war crimes by ISIS militants. While certainly dangerous, Ori had checked with his contacts within the Israeli Mossad, and they'd assured him that they'd be watching. The refugee camp they had been heading to was supposed to be out of the main conflict zones and was well monitored by Israeli security with a safe passage from Israel.

They'd flown into Jerusalem, where Ori was determined to show Risa around the ancient and holy land. They had a private security team—cleared by the Mossad—to meet and escort them to the refugee camp for their interviews. The security team knew how to avoid any wrong turns into Hezbollah checkpoints or any other emerging threats. But somehow the plan had backfired. It happened so quickly—the ambush, being forced out of the car. Now the security guards were long gone. *Killed? Or was that the weak link? Were they double-crossed?* Ori cursed himself for getting them into this mess.

"Don't panic," Ori said. "Israeli security knows how to deal with situations like this. We'll be out of here before long." Risa was not sure who he was trying to reassure, her or himself.

"I hope you're right," murmured their driver, Hamdan, a Palestinian, who'd been conditioned to feel expendable. Ori was feeling the opposite, or hoping it, anyway. There was no way they'd harm an American human rights lawyer and an Israeli one. *Will they?* Surely all the kidnappers were after was just ransom.

Despite his forced optimism, Risa could see that Ori's face was grimacing in lines of anxiety and pain. Hamdan didn't look any better. Miserable, the three of them lapsed into silence.

The whole situation was surreal, utterly removed from anything Risa had ever experienced.

"What's that sound?" she asked, hearing what seemed to be snorting.

"Horses," mumbled Hamdan. And her nostrils confirmed it —that unmistakable scent.

All her senses were on high alert. *Horses?* Was this a barn? What had she gotten herself into?

Risa replayed the sequence in her mind. She'd been drawn in by the human rights work and her desire to help—or so she'd told herself. But self-denial was harder to sustain when bound by zip ties in a dark basement. Hadn't she done this, in the end, to prove a point? Wasn't this just one more shot in her yearslong argument with Youssef?

Everything came back to Youssef in the end, even now, even this. How many times had Risa accused him of armchair activism, of passivity, of mere whining? She'd just had to show him what engagement with a cause was supposed to look like, hadn't she? *Maybe,* she thought with absurd, astonishing solipsism, *this whole situation is just karma.*

Risa could feel guilt suffusing her, all the way to her fingertips. Fourteen years with Youssef, and he'd never taken her to Egypt, not even once. And now, here she was in the Middle East for the first time with Ori, driving Youssef wild with jealousy—Ori, the friend she admired; Ori who, let's face it, wanted Risa in a way Risa would never want him.

But at least Ori was living in the present, working toward a vision of the future—that was the justification Risa had been making to herself. Human rights work had become everything to her, and it didn't seem to be sitting well with Youssef, whose only vision of their own future had been the baby—the baby who had never materialized, the baby they should have conceived but somehow never did. And as long as there was no baby, it seemed Youssef was stuck, riveted to his memories of the places, experiences, and people who made up his past. *What good can possibly come from obsessing about the past?*

Had Risa been too hard on Youssef? On nights when she struggled to fall asleep alone, she thought so. And also when she caught Ori looking at her in a way she'd only ever looked at Youssef. She still loved him—that was clear to her. Especially now, tied up and not knowing whether she'd live to see another day. Risa took momentary comfort in imagining being back in their Berkeley apartment, lying in the warm and safe embrace of Youssef's powerful arms—and she almost had to laugh at herself. *Look who's stuck in the past now.*

We'd have secrets, you and me. Even from her . . .

The haunting words were playing out in Matt's mind, over and over, like a broken record—that Faustian bargain he'd made with Senator Pete Bradford on his wedding night to join "the Company" as part of an elite subset of spies working with cutting-edge digital surveillance. It had felt like an opportunity that could not be refused. Matt could never have known that just one year later, four weaponized airplanes would change the world forever, making his job among the most vital positions within the intelligence services. Matt's top-secret position had given him direct access to the top brass. But it had come at a price. The ice was so thin with Stephanie that Matt could feel it cracking with every deceptive word he spoke to her—his credibility entirely evaporated. And when he'd received the early morning text from Uncle Pete ("Meet at the corner of Jefferson and Third, SW corner, 0900 hours"), Matt felt dread. *What now?*

He'd shown up ten minutes early and was waiting dutifully. Swallows circled the First Ladies Water Garden, where an eastern bluebird preened itself in the eight-petaled fountain, but Matt hardly noticed the birds. His eyes were glazed. The teen version of Matt, who'd won a merit badge as an Eagle Scout for ornithology, was nowhere to be found.

The stretch limo pulled up at nine sharp, and Matt climbed in. As Matt settled into the plush leather seat, the cool, dimly lit interior felt oddly claustrophobic, amplifying his sense of expectation and worry about what was to come. Senator Braford got right to the point. "This is strictly off the record." He looked Matt in the eye. "I will deny ever having this conversation. Do you understand?"

"Yessir," responded Matt, feeling an odd combination of anxiety and excitement.

"What you do with the information I'm about to give you is entirely up to you. You're on your own."

"Understood, sir," Matt assured him.

"Someone in our family is in trouble in the Middle East—Stephanie's cousin, Risa," Senator Bradford began, his voice tinged with raw vulnerability. "She's like a daughter to me, though I never approved of her marriage to that Muslim Egyptian." He paused before regaining his professional composure. "She's been kidnapped by Islamic militants. We think they may be associated with Roken."

Holy shit! Matt took a breath. Everyone had been concerned when Risa had gone on that human rights mission.

"Your asset might have intel," the senator suggested. In his role as chairman of the Senate Intelligence Committee, he'd asked for a briefing and learned of Matt's connection to AA. What the briefing hadn't revealed was that AA—Nasser El-Mohammedi—was the closest friend of Youssef, the very Egyptian Muslim Senator Bradford disdained.

I'm going, thought Matt without hesitation, even though he'd just promised Stephanie that there would be no more clandestine missions. But this was *Risa*, her favorite cousin.

"You're aware of Reg 38?" The senator gazed outside through the tinted windows.

Matt nodded. Regulation 38 in the Covert Ops Manual

mandated recusal in cases of direct family ties. Uncle Pete turned back to lock eyes with Matt. "Do not fly commercial."

The senator did not need to spell it out. The situation was binary. Success would cement Matt's hero status in the Bradford family. Failure would end his career.

~

"We're human," said Father Greg. "Yet we also possess indwelling divinity. That's the lesson of Jesus." Gazing at Matt with great compassion, he added, "You're doing your best, Matt. Give yourself some credit."

"Thank you, Father," said Matt. He loved his pastor, though it was still odd to call him *Father* given that he was barely thirty— just a few years younger than Matt—which made him so relatable. Most of the priests Matt had known in his churchgoing life had been twice that age. He admired that Greg had made the choice to enter the priesthood at a time when many were fleeing the Church, which seemed to be under assault from all sides. For Matt, his life choices had always been about duty and honor. Those were his guiding principles.

Where are those principles now?

His inner turmoil had caused Matt to reach out to the pastor of the church he attended on the rare Sundays in DC. Father Greg was more than happy to drop everything to meet Matt and hear his confession—yet even *this* was a ruse. Matt rushed over to St. Dominic after meeting with the senator, but it had nothing to do with confessing his sins. That was the smokescreen.

"I've taken up enough of your time, Father," said Matt, standing in the pews at the back of St. Dominic. He reached for his phone, which appeared to be dead, but it was actually just shut down, the SIM card removed.

"Shoot," said Matt in feigned frustration. "I'm out of juice. Mind if I use your phone, Father? I need to check on something."

"No problem, Matt," said the priest, handing over his iPhone —a device Matt knew was unlikely to be monitored. There was a time when Catholic priests *had*, in fact, been under surveillance in a top-secret program to ferret out potential confessions from guilty Mafia dons—the brainchild of J. Edgar Hoover who, himself, ran the FBI like a mob boss. But that was another era, a different technology, a different religion.

Now, American intelligence was entirely focused on the world's fastest-growing faith: Islam. Using backdoor access built clandestinely into satellites and cell phone towers, the NSA was secretly recording, transcribing, and analyzing every conversation by every imam in America. And no one had the bandwidth to pay attention to the electronic footprints of a parish priest, which was why Matt had sought out Father Greg and asked for his phone.

Opening Safari, Matt navigated to the obscure chat room for soccer lovers that Nasser had identified, where he typed a quick message using the cipher from the Bible they'd agreed on. After deleting his browsing history and closing the app, he handed the phone back to the priest.

Forgive me, Father . . .

～

Nasser, Sharif, and a small band of followers had moved away from the battle zones of Iraq to the small fishing village of El-Arish on the northern coast of the Sinai Peninsula, where they'd tracked Roken. He was believed to be hiding underground in the desert, like many others, since the Egyptian revolution. Sharif, a master of old-fashioned human intelligence gathering, had just heard a whisper on the streets of a possible location where Roken was stashing his dirty bomb.

He watched as Nasser carefully coded a new message using numbers in the corners of his journal. Sharif wasn't entirely sure why Nasser was choosing to communicate this way instead of using the online chat room he'd proposed to the American CIA operative. All Sharif knew was what Nasser had told him: *only my father, Omar, will be able to decipher the hidden message.*

Nasser had made it clear that he wanted Omar to know the

full story, the whole truth of what had happened to him. This was the only way he could ensure that would happen. Nasser knew his life was in God's hands . . . but his story—that could be immortalized in these pages he was writing specifically for his father. "There is no other way," he reminded Sharif.

"Should we check the chat in case they've sent something about Roken?" Sharif asked.

"Be my guest." Nasser handed Sharif his phone, remembering how he had taught Sharif to use the biblical cipher for communication in the chat room, needing this backup in case something happened to him. Nasser trusted Sharif more than anyone in the world now.

There was, in fact, a message, which Sharif decoded using the Bible passage. Nasser stared at it in shock:

THE WIFE OF YOUR FRIEND YOUSSEF
BELIEVED CAPTIVE BY ROKEN
NEED CONFIRMATION ASAP
ARRIVING SHORTLY.

"We need to find her," said Nasser gravely.

"I'll ask around," said Sharif, grabbing a stack of cash from the lockbox.

It didn't take long. Sharif had gained the trust of a group of Bedouins who had their ears to the sand. By the time he returned to the safe house, the hours of night felt numbered. Nasser had already assembled three of his foot soldiers who were loading provisions into an inconspicuous-looking Lada Niva—a rugged Russian jeep.

"You're not going to believe this," Sharif blurted breathlessly. "It's the cave we saw on our way to Iraq."

As the jeep crossed moonlit sand dunes that stretched for miles in every direction, Nasser typed the coordinates of the cave into the chat room for Matt.

~

"Gulf of Aqaba—south of Taba, north of Nuweiba, closer to the shores across from the Salah El-Din Castle." Matt called out the location he'd been sent as a coded message by Nasser. "Yessir," said Mendoza from behind the wheel of an unmarked SUV while Bailey sat between them. All weapons were out of view. This was not an official mission; they needed to keep a low profile.

"Avoid the main roads," Matt said, rubbing his bleary eyes. He'd taken two Ambien pills to ensure that he slept on the plane, a privately chartered Falcon 7 that made a pit stop in the Azores to refuel. He'd paid in cash. No one asked questions. Senator Bradford had advised him years ago to establish an identity that no one knew about—for moments like these. And he had: Helmut Wagner, a Dutch petroleum engineer.

Sharm El-Sheikh International Airport, at the tip of the peninsula, was where Matt went through customs with the forged passport, and Bailey and Mendoza met him in the SUV. The small terminal was nearly silent, with only the faint hum of air-conditioning and the soft swish of an old worker cleaning. Outside, the cool night air hinted at the approaching predawn hours.

As they settled into the SUV, Matt kept the details of the rescue mission to himself, claiming it was strictly "need-to-know."

Matt was all in—on his way to a Medal of Honor or a court-martial. Or both.

~

Desperate scuffling and thrashing nearby interrupted Risa's thoughts. The whisper of Hamdan's trouser legs against one another and the slap of his bare forearms against the ground echoed like applause among the cave's rocky surfaces. "Keep quiet," Ori hissed. "What are you doing?"

"I'm almost . . ." Hamdan grunted softly, and a moment later he held up his hands, free, a small switchblade catching the lantern light. "I always keep it hidden in my sleeve," he whispered.

"I guess they didn't think the driver was worth searching." He got to work on the zip tie that secured his feet, then turned to Ori's bonds.

"What's the plan here?" Risa whispered. "Once we can move —what then?"

Hamdan opened his mouth to answer, then held up his hands and turned his head to listen. From somewhere outside came the dull *whump* of something soft and heavy hitting the ground. Then came a confusion of shouting and gunfire, nearby but muffled, as if in another room.

"Hurry, hurry," Ori urged unnecessarily as Hamdan sawed the plastic at his ankles.

From two or three yards away now came the metallic *thunk* of a dead bolt opening.

Beams sliced through the darkness directly through Risa's still-throbbing skull as a door was pushed open a crack. Hamdan sprang to his feet, and Risa felt Ori go to work on her ankles with the knife. The light from the hall was dazzling. Silhouetted against its brilliance, Risa could make out the figure of a man who seemed somehow too slim for the massive machine gun he wielded.

"Yalla, yalla!" the man urged them, and stumbling, her hands still bound, Risa got to her feet. The man was behind them now, herding them toward the door, Hamdan in the lead.

Risa's legs were like jelly. How long had she lain on that floor? She stumbled past a heavy wooden door, scarred and ancient, into what seemed to be the wide mouth of a cave. Not a warehouse, as Risa had imagined. The fighting she'd heard was over, or else it had paused; everything was quiet.

This area, so much brighter than the room from which they had emerged, was itself in heavy shadow. Outside the cave, the pale light of early morning brushed over an open stretch of desert, softening the rugged outlines of tall, rocky crags. Sand, muted in the dim light, covered the cave's floor in uneven drifts and patches; it soaked up the blood that dripped from three bodies that lay horribly still, face down, in awkward postures. Another larger man was being held at gunpoint.

Dawn was rising outside.

Against the sunlight at the cave's mouth, two men in checkered black-and-white keffiyehs stood guarding the entrance. Ori stumbled on the cave's uneven floor, and though stiff and unsteady herself, Risa put her bound hands to his back to steady him. As the man with the enormous gun turned to face them now, Risa saw that his features were somehow familiar. How could that be? Where did she know him from? His big eyes were liquid and black, his cheekbones elegantly carved, his lips full and purple. A question flickered between his dark brows as he gazed at Risa.

It can't be, Risa thought—but she'd never been more certain. All of Youssef's photographs, all of his stories, were here and now. The past became flesh, and it stared at her.

"You will be safe, Risa," he said in perfect English. "But you must return home to your husband. Tell Youssef it was Nasser, and please convey my deepest love to him."

Risa nearly gasped. It was him—it was Nasser!

He handed a set of keys to Hamdan. "Take our car. Drive to the police station in town; don't trust anyone, don't stop." He handed Risa a burner phone. "Good luck."

Risa was at a loss for words. She wasn't ready to leave. This was monumental.

"You will be safe," Nasser reassured her again with quiet calmness, escorting them outside toward the waiting jeep. "It's time to go."

Risa kept her eyes locked on Nasser as Ori pushed her anxiously into the back seat of the Russian jeep. Nasser's energy reminded her so much of Youssef—how he moved slowly, making sure she felt taken care of at all times. *Convey my deepest love to him.* It was a mantra that Risa would repeat to herself again and again on the long journey back. She was going home. Home to Youssef.

∿

Sharif watched Nasser waving to the departing jeep as it kicked up a wake of sand, which shimmered faintly in the light of the approaching dawn. He was proud to be a part of Nasser's team. It had been years now since they'd split off from Roken to form their own cell, which was growing in numbers. Nasser was brilliant; his knowledge of history knew no bounds. And he had even more charisma than Roken, which was why Sharif had taken the liberty of referring to Nasser as "the Teacher" now.

As Nasser scanned the horizon and above to make sure no one was on to them, he noticed an approaching blip in the early morning sky and quickly returned to the cave, whose entrance was camouflaged. Walking up to a scowling Abu Gabel, who was being guarded at gunpoint by his men, Nasser asked, "Where's Roken?"

"Fuck you," snarled Abu Gabel.

"I can hurt you." Nasser narrowed his eyes.

"Really, college boy?" Abu Gabel laughed. "I'm petrified."

Sharif spotted pliers and a saw on a nearby workbench. "Let me do it, Teacher."

Nasser glanced at him. *Are you sure?*

"Five minutes." He was eager to prove his mettle. "That's all I need."

Nasser nodded. As Sharif grabbed the tools and signaled to the bodyguards to drag Abu Gabel past the horse stalls into the back room of the cave, the Syrian went white. Soon there were screams as loud as gunshots.

Four minutes and fifteen seconds later, Sharif emerged with blood-spattered clothes.

"You cut his fingers?" asked Nasser.

"That's not all I cut," responded Sharif. "Roken is hiding in plain sight, behind the mosque on the main road in Taba."

Nasser had already saddled one of the horses. "I'm going."

"I'll come with you, Teacher," offered Sharif.

"No, you stay here," said Nasser. "Wait for the Americans."

That was when Sharif noticed a movement in the corner of

his eye—one of the fallen guards lurched up from the floor, dagger in hand, and lunged toward Nasser.

"Look out!" screamed Sharif, rushing to intercept the wounded guard, who spun, redirecting his attack. The dagger intended for Nasser went deep into Sharif's sternum. Before Nasser could react, the guard's head exploded as one of his followers shot him.

Time slowed and seemed to stop; as Sharif and Nasser stared at one another, Sharif recalled the prayer he'd whispered to himself when they'd first joined the jihad: *If Allah's will for me is to die here, then let my last breath be with him at my side.*

"I love you, brother," he croaked as he looked into Nasser's devastated face. "Go," insisted Sharif. "Avenge your mother." Nasser looked around in mounting panic. "The Americans will be here soon," Sharif assured him. "Along with the Egyptian forces as well. You must go."

"Stay with him," Nasser ordered the guards. "Stop the bleeding. Tell the Americans about Roken's location."

Then he leapt on the horse and galloped away.

Having completed his Fajr prayers, Roken, beardless now, sipped a cup of tea, gazing from his balcony at the sunlit casinos and resort hotels that rose like towers from the desert sands of Taba—the "Red Sea Riviera" tourist destination on Egypt's border crossing with Israel. Because of its position at the northern tip of the Gulf of Aqaba, the town had been seized, reclaimed, occupied, and fortified for centuries by the Ottomans, British, and Israelis until finally being returned to Egypt in the wake of the peace process following the 1973 war. It made perfect sense that so many powers had fought to control Taba, which was both strategically placed and also stunning, especially in the light of dawn.

Soon this will be a wasteland, Roken thought with conviction and psychopathic calm.

As a beautiful woman with long dark hair came for the tea tray, Roken went back inside to his study.

～

"We've got company," said Bailey, glancing up through the dusty windshield at what appeared to be a drone. "Did you call for backup, sir?"

He hadn't. Not officially, anyway. But given the distrust of AA among his CIA colleagues, Matt had told his superior about the chat room they were using to exchange messages. They'd obviously monitored this latest exchange and decided to send a drone. It meant Matt's success or failure would be seen on live TV.

～

The wall monitors in the CIA operations center displayed Matt's movements when, suddenly, a voice crackled through the feed: "We've got a rider on horseback—out in the middle of nowhere. Definitely unusual."

The main screen switched to an aerial angle of the lone rider galloping across the desert. The vast expanse of sand stretched endlessly, the jagged rock formations casting long shadows in the early light. The horizon blazed with hues of amber and crimson, the colors spilling across the landscape like molten gold. The rider's solitary figure seemed impossibly small against the immensity of the awakening desert, his path etched faintly in the windswept dunes. Pete Bradford couldn't help but think, *This is a David Lean film.*

It was hardly a moment for sentimentality. Another operator chimed in: "We've still got eyes on the SUV. It's still moving."

"Good," said the ops chief. "Stay with the horse on Drone Four. Drone Two, track Matt and the SUV. All other drones, scan the area for any additional movement."

The rider continued toward the outskirts of Taba, his movements displayed prominently on the main screen, while the SUV trundled along the coastline on another. The multiple feeds provided the ops team with a comprehensive view of the unfolding events.

~

"This is it?" Matt asked in disappointment, climbing out of the SUV.

"Yep," responded Mendoza, who'd disguised himself in a keffiyeh.

It was a desolate strip of beach under rocky cliffs—nothing around for miles. Matt felt deflated. Had his instincts been wrong? Had Nasser double-crossed him?

Matt took a deep breath, praying silently for guidance, and that's when it hit him: the smell. Mixed in with the briny air of the Gulf of Aqaba was the faint odor of manure. Matt noticed horse droppings in the distance, then he saw the tracks. Following them backward like the Eagle Scout he once was, Matt quickly spotted the cave in the cliff. He signaled silently to his SEAL team.

Moments later, they were flanking its camouflaged entrance. Bailey covered the doorway with his carbine while Mendoza threw in a stun grenade, shouting, "Fire in the hole!" Matt covered his ears as it exploded, then they raced inside.

There were seven bodies lying prone from the stun grenade. But no Nasser. And no Roken. A slumped man, a little away from the other downed men, with his back to the wall and barely alive, signaled to Matt, who came over to hear what he wanted to say.

"Main road, Taba, behind the mosque," Sharif whispered, his voice weak and strained. "That's where you'll find Roken." Trembling, he forced out the crucial information, knowing it would be his last act.

"Gimme the keys," Matt called out. "Stay here and search the place."

Mendoza threw him the SUV keys, exchanging a brief glance

with Bailey. Neither said a word—this wasn't the kind of mission where they could argue.

Matt bolted to the vehicle. He floored it, following the horse tracks along the beach, where the first rays of sunlight danced on the waves.

~

Peter Bradford watched the drone tracking the horse and rider as they moved swiftly along a dirt road on the outskirts of Taba. A small group of people, having finished their prayer, emerged from a small mosque. Circling to the back, the rider trotted toward a small home nestled in the hill.

"Pursuit vehicle approaching," said an intel officer monitoring a second feed from the geostationary satellite, which revealed the SUV roaring past the mosque.

Pete Bradford turned back to the drone feed, which showed the rider dismounting and rushing into the structure with his automatic weapon.

"Switch to infrared," ordered the ops chief.

The video feed was now able to see through the walls of the modest abode, revealing several glowing figures scrambling inside and a sudden muzzle flash.

~

Upon hearing the gunfire, Roken emerged from his study to behold a murderous Nasser, standing over his fallen bodyguards.

"I had so much respect for you once," Nasser said with derision. "Now I see you are just like all the hypocrites—you preach mayhem, corrupting everything to suit your own ends, corrupting Islam, and corrupting even justice."

Roken smirked at first. Gesturing toward the dead bodies, his expression quickly darkened. He pointed angrily at Nasser, eyes blazing. "Justice should be killing you and your father. You are the real traitors to our people. Men like you weaken us from within."

Nasser's eyes narrowed, anger flaring at the mention of his father. Then, in a voice as cold as steel, he said, "Then my justice is revenge. For the murder of all the innocents, including my mother—" He raised his machine gun, aiming it squarely at Roken.

Just as Roken dropped to his knees, smiling bitterly and lowering his head to await execution, Matt burst onto the scene. In that moment of distraction, Roken managed to pull a hidden pistol from his cloak, shooting Nasser in the chest. Spinning, shocked, Nasser squeezed his own trigger, spraying bullets.

"Freeze!" Matt shouted at Roken. But there was no need. The Teacher was dead.

Matt rushed toward Nasser, who clutched his bleeding chest and croaked, "The bomb—they'll use it now that Roken is dead . . ."

Nasser groaned in agony, trying to roll over, which only increased the bleeding.

"What are you doing?" Matt hissed. "Save your strength."

"In my shirt . . ." Nasser faltered. Matt saw what appeared to be a hidden chamber in the back of Nasser's shirt. Nestled inside, Matt found it—the journal.

"Give it to my father. He needs to know my story," Nasser whispered. "He will know how to decode it. No one else."

Then his eyes froze. Glassy and lifeless. Holding the journal, Matt felt the gravity of Nasser's legacy pressing into his palm, a bridge between past secrets and urgent futures.

Matt whispered the prayer for the dead that he'd learned in Arabic: *"Allahumma aghfir lahu warhamhu."* Forgive him and have mercy on him. Matt's own hands trembled as he murmured the prayer.

THE LIBRARY OF OMAR
EL-MOHAMMEDI

March 27, 2014

La Elaha Ela Allah . . .
O Allah, I am your slave,
the son of your slave . . .

THERE IS ONLY ONE GOD. This was the last page of the journal. Omar felt a lump in his throat. Nasser had begun this final entry with a prayer for the departed, along with the *dua* for grief and sorrow.

"He knew he was going to die," Omar whispered.

"It was a dangerous mission." Matt nodded, pressing closer.

The grandfather clock ticked in a corner of the study, a ceaseless reminder of the pressure they were under, just shy of dawn, to solve this riddle. Matt was going out on a limb on this. Most of his intelligence colleagues suspected that he'd been played, that Nasser could not be trusted. *Once a jihadist, always a jihadist.*

Even if he'd left them a clue, where was it? Nasser's journal had stymied the world's foremost cryptographers. Arabic scholars had come back with flummoxed shrugs. Matt's only remaining hope was Omar, an ailing professor well past his prime. The stakes went well beyond Matt's reputation and career. A mistake could trigger Armageddon.

"See anything?" asked Matt, trying to keep his cool.

Omar's attention turned to the gale reference in the white space, where he noticed something curious:

The city shutters itself tightly in the face of El-Khamaseen . . .

"*El-Khamaseen* is not a gale," Omar declared unequivocally. "It's a sandstorm."

Matt listened intently as the professor elaborated, "The other added references were all gales: Washing the Dates, the Broom, Qasim, the Big Flood, Little Sun, Gale of the Howling Wind. Gales—all of them. Not this one. Nasser knew this."

What can it mean? Matt wondered.

Omar remembered having a conversation with Nasser about El-Khamaseen being different from the other gales, but he couldn't recall the context. Nasser had been a teenager at the time, of that Omar was certain, but his mind was unable to reconstruct anything beyond that.

Omar continued reading the journal:

The arrival of Easter made me nostalgic. I missed my friend group, the Alexandria Four . . .

That's when it suddenly clicked. Omar leapt up and crossed the room toward his bookshelf with the zeal of someone half his age—no need whatsoever for his cane. Matt rushed up beside

Omar as the elder scanned his precious volumes until he came upon a set of four books—*The Alexandria Quartet*, by Lawrence Durrell.

As Omar pulled down the first book, *Justine*, he journeyed back two decades in his mind, remembering the scene as if it were yesterday—the day they'd discussed El-Khamaseen.

Young Nasser had been diligently reading the novel in English, and he'd paused to discuss a certain passage with his father on a page he had bookmarked. Omar gasped. The bookmark was still there! He flipped to part three to reread Durrell's words:

That second spring, the Khamaseen was worse than I have ever known it before or since. Before sunrise the skies of the desert turned brown as buckram, and then slowly darkened, swelling like a bruise and at last releasing the outlines of cloud, giant octaves of ochre which massed up from the delta like the draft of ashes under a volcano. The city has shuttered itself tightly as if against a gale.

"Baba, how can El-Khamaseen be a gale when it has no rain?" young Nasser had asked curiously.

Omar smiled. "Where does the author characterize it as a gale?"

Nasser responded with confidence, "He states so in the final sentence."

"Does he?" Omar prodded. "What's the name for the grammatical phrase *as if*?"

Nasser racked his brain. "A conjunction?"

"And what is its function?"

"To make a comparison." Nasser figured it out. "He is likening El-Khamaseen to a gale because the torrent of sand is equivalent to a rainstorm, forcing us to shutter our windows."

Good boy, Omar thought.

The conversation had occurred right here—in this very room. The memory was so vibrant it brought tears to the professor's eyes. If only he could travel back in time and hug him again—allow him to be a boy, rather than a pupil. *Ya Nasser, my son, my poor son . . .*

"You did it!" Matt practically jumped in excitement. "You cracked the code!" He grabbed Durrell's novel from the professor. "This is it! This is our cipher."

PART VII

EL-KHAMASEEN

El-Khamaseen ("the Fifty-Day Storm")
descends in spring with fury.

It's not a gale.
It's a sandstorm.
A storm that lasts for fifty days.

THE SEA AND THE DESERT

2014

"It's here," said Omar, glancing above. He pointed skyward with his cane and repeated, "It's here." Matt looked up. The sky was brown, not blue; palm fronds trembled in anticipation.

"El-Khamaseen," whispered Omar. Matt nodded.

They walked down one of the quiet streets of Kafr Abdu toward the unmarked SUV, where Bailey and Mendoza had been waiting in local civilian attire, like Matt wore. Omar had been asked to accompany him to the operations center; more secrets may be embedded in the journal, and time was of the essence.

They piled into the SUV, which weaved through the narrow alleys toward the main road. As they turned onto Abu Qir, the breeze was building, blowing sand in every direction. Mendoza engaged the wipers to brush it off the windshield.

Omar stared ahead at the dust and became deeply wistful.

The elder turned to Matt, seated next to him in the back, and asked, "You were there? When my son died, you were there?"

Matt nodded. They drove in silence for a moment. Then Matt felt compelled to say, "He was brave. I don't know if I would've had the guts to do what Nasser did. Your son was a hero." Omar's eyes welled up with tears.

The SUV drove through Mostafa Kamel to the lights of

Smouha Square, then turned past the old Alexandria Zoo, which brought another flood of memories for Omar.

The swelling wind whistled like an agonized ghost. Noisy wipers swished to and fro.

Noticing his ruminations, Matt wondered what the professor was thinking.

Mendoza pulled up to the fence surrounding the El-Nouzaha airfield, an old airport that was no longer used by commercial jets. An Egyptian army officer opened a side gate, allowing them direct access to the tarmac, where a helicopter was waiting. Everything was coordinated with the Egyptian security forces; it was apparently a joint effort.

The chopper rotors came to life, adding confusion to the eddies of swirling wind. Omar had to squint to keep sand from his eyes as they escorted him aboard. "Hurry!" shouted the pilot, worried about the rapidly escalating sandstorm. They hustled into their seats. Matt helped Omar with his safety belt and gave him a communication headset. "If you want to talk," he explained.

But Omar had no interest in conversation. As the bird soared up into the mayhem of wind and sand, Omar rocketed backward into a memory so vivid it felt like he was actually there.

It was early spring of 1986.

Fatimah shuttered the windows, making sure the latches were tightly fastened. This Khamaseen was strong. She checked first on Nasser, whose bedsheets were scattered—he was always restless. Fatimah lovingly tucked her boy back in. Then she went to the other bedroom, where five-year-old Houda slept soundly. Nothing ever bothered her.

Turning, she encountered Omar standing at the door with a somber expression. He noticed something missing on her finger.

"Where's your ring?" he asked.

"None of your business." She pushed past him.

"You can't go," he said.

"You can't stop me," she responded tersely. "I miss my family. And my children have a right to meet them."

"Out of the question!" His voice sharpened. "Your uncle is a terrorist."

"My father is an imam," she countered. "A man of God who leads a mosque."

Omar rolled his eyes. "A man of God who disowned you when you wouldn't bend to his will."

"That's rich—coming from *you*." She rolled her eyes right back at him.

Omar gazed at his wife wondering, *What happened to us?* "Come to bed," he said softly.

She stood her ground. "I'm sleeping here—with Houda."

Omar sighed. "Fine. We'll discuss this in the morning."

"No," Fatimah said with surprising conviction. "No more discussions, Mr. Liberal, with all your opinions about 'backward thinking' and 'saving me' from my own family. They're my flesh and blood. My heart was shaped by my father's Qur'an teachings and my mother's modesty and dedication. Yes, I chose to leave them—but now I am choosing to return." Her voice rising.

"Keep your voice down," shushed Omar. "You'll wake Houda."

Fatimah smiled mockingly. "Maybe she needs to wake up."

Omar hardly slept. The extra pillow over his head did nothing to muffle the wind battering the apartment from all sides. The storm raged outside and churned just as fiercely within.

When dawn arrived, it was even worse. Sand had seeped through cracks in the ancient walls, dusting every floor and surface. The sharp scent of dust pressed on his chest like a warning. He coughed as he stepped into the kitchen and froze.

Fatimah was gone.

A folded pamphlet on the table made his pulse spike: the train timetable. His hands trembled as he unfolded it, scanning the lines with growing dread. There were no direct trains to Luxor. She'd need to change in Cairo, which meant—

She was taking the 6 a.m. train to Cairo!

The thought struck like a slap. He glanced toward the children's rooms. Was it madness to take them into the storm? A good father would leave them at home where they would be safe. But what kind of father lets their mother walk away? He pressed his fingers against his temples, as if trying to stop the spiraling thoughts.

I can fix this. I can make her come back.

Nasser was awake first, his eyes gleaming with curiosity as he jumped out of bed. Houda asked, "Where's Mama?" Her voice wavered, barely above a whisper.

"We'll see her soon," Omar said, though the words felt like ash in his mouth.

Grabbing the car keys from the bowl, he hesitated for a moment, the weight of his decision pressing heavily on his chest.

As they left the apartment, Houda clutched her brother's hand tightly, her small fingers gripping his as if afraid to let go. Nasser glanced at her, noticing the tension. He called out, "Wait!" and darted back to Houda's room. Moments later, he returned, holding his sister's favorite doll in both hands. He placed it gently in her arms. Houda hugged the doll close, burying her face in its familiar softness.

Omar ushered his children into the car and drove.

The wind howled as they approached the Rest House, the halfway mark along the road to Cairo. Houda clutched her doll tightly, her small shoulders trembling as the first sobs broke free, rising above the roar of the storm.

"Baba, I need to go to the bathroom!" she wailed, gasping for air between words.

Omar's grip tightened on the wheel. He glanced at his watch, his stomach knotting. "We're almost there," he said, though he knew it wasn't true. Her crying pushed him to the edge.

When the dim outline of the Rest House emerged from the

haze, he gave in. "Fine. We'll stop," he said, sharper than he intended.

The car jerked to a halt, and Nasser bolted out before the engine stopped. "Look at me, Baba!" he shouted, spinning in gusts.

"Stay close!" Omar yelled, but the boy was already a blur.

He turned to Houda, who sat curled into the seat, her arms slackening around the doll as her wide eyes followed Nasser darting into the storm. "Nasser!" she called, her voice thin against the storm. "Come on," Omar urged, pulling her door open.

But she shook her head violently. "No!" she screamed. "I don't want to! I don't have to!"

Omar's head dropped for a moment, his hand bracing on the edge of the doorframe. He left Houda in the car and stumbled into the tumult to retrieve Nasser, his chest tightening with every step.

"Nasser!" he shouted. The boy's laughter came faintly. By the time Omar had grabbed him by the arm and dragged him back, his throat was raw, and the wind felt like it had scoured his skin.

When he climbed back into the car, Houda was still curled into her seat. Her sobs shuddered through the quiet space in the car.

Omar restarted the engine and pulled onto the road. The wind pummeled the car in relentless waves, muffling the engine but never drowning out Houda's cries. "Where's Mama?" she pleaded. "I want Mama!"

Minutes passed, each one dragging at Omar.

Houda hiccupped, her head drooping onto the doll's worn fabric. Her breath came in small, uneven puffs, leaving faint tear tracks on her flushed cheeks. Beside her, Nasser leaned closer. "It's okay, Houda," Nasser said, his voice wavering despite his brave front. He patted her arm, his small hand shaking. "We'll see Mama soon. I promise."

By the time they had reached Mahattat Misr, bedlam reigned, and the storm merged with the uproar. The station teemed with life—loud voices shouting over one another, the metallic screech of train brakes, and a chaotic symphony of noises rising and falling. In the square outside, the towering statue of Ramses II presided over the scene, his eternal gaze fixed on the frenetic energy below as if pondering the fate of his countrymen in this age of disorder. Even as the dusty air churned around them, the pulse of the place endured.

Omar parked haphazardly, finding no empty spots, and stumbled out of the car, clutching Houda tightly as Nasser rushed ahead.

"Mama!" Nasser called, his voice full of hope, cutting through the cacophony.

Omar felt numb, his body moving on momentum alone. The train to Luxor was already pulling away.

The sight of the train leaving the station hit him like a punch to the chest. For a moment, the din of the station faded into silence. The train to Fatimah's final destination was vanishing into the haze. Omar stood frozen, powerless to stop it—or her.

"Is Mama here?" Nasser asked, his voice barely audible.

Omar didn't answer.

~

When the news came, it was reported as a train accident, with many dead. Omar finally confirmed that Fatimah was among them.

In the quiet of the library, Omar sat at his desk, staring at the timetable lying there, its edges curling from the damp air. The same paper that had set everything in motion now mocked him with its uselessness.

If I hadn't stopped at the Rest House. If I'd pushed harder. If I'd listened. Maybe she'd still be here.

Fatimah had been stubborn, yes, but she had also been kind. Her world shouldn't have been something to correct or fix, but something to understand, appreciate, and shape together into a world they could both share. Yet Omar had always thought he knew better—better answers, better plans, a better way forward.

The apartment was silent without Fatimah's laugh—the lifeblood of the place, as every mother is.

The night of the lie, Houda had retreated to her room. She lay curled beneath her blanket, the doll tucked close as if it could shield her from the world.

Nasser stood in the doorway to the library, his small frame silhouetted against the faint glow from outside, his face etched with questions Omar couldn't bear to answer.

In the dim light, he knelt before them. His voice broke as he began. "Your mother . . . she died of a heart attack while visiting a friend," he said, the words slipping through his teeth, sharp and bitter. His chest burned, but he forced himself to continue. "We need to stick together now. We need to be strong."

Nasser's wide eyes searched his father's face. "How? What happened?"

Omar placed a hand on his son's shoulder, gripping tightly. "Be strong for your sister," he said. The boy's lip quivered, but he nodded.

Later, when the children had gone to bed, Omar returned to the library. He sank into the chair at his desk, the silence seeming to echo his thoughts, amplifying the weight of his lie. The apartment felt smaller now, as if the walls themselves were closing in.

He told himself it was to protect them.

Is it to protect them—or yourself?

The thought settled over him, heavy and unshakable.

Little Nasser, who worshipped his father in those days, did as he was told.

But secrets, like sandstorms, consumed everything in their path.

The guilt, the pain, the shame—it was all flooding back.

"Professor," Matt called through the headset, "we're landing."

Omar blinked, coming back to the present moment. *Where am I?*

The chopper swayed violently from side to side in hundred-mile-per-hour gusts as it descended toward the helipad on the USS *Harry S. Truman*. Omar's eyes widened in astonishment—he'd never seen a ship so enormous.

"Watch yourself, professor," said Matt, helping the elder onto the tarmac. They were escorted immediately to the ship's command and control center, an impressive room lined with supercomputers and wall-mounted screens. A dozen analysts and navy officers were busy tracking feeds from drones and geostationary satellites.

Matt had used the fifteen-minute flight to the carrier, twenty-four miles offshore in international waters, to begin transcribing Nasser's numeric code by using the book cipher.

"Show us what you have so far," demanded Admiral Delaney, the operations CO.

"Casting now," responded Matt, taking his place on the perimeter. As he broadcast the feed from his laptop, all eyes turned to the main monitor, which displayed the words:

BEWARE OF EL KHA . . .

Omar figured it out in an instant. "He ordered them to use the sandstorm to spread the radiation!"

"Who's this?" the admiral asked, looking at Omar.

Matt hesitated for a split second, searching for the right words. "That's Professor El-Mohammedi," he finally said. "The man who cracked the code. He knew Roken personally, the mastermind—and he's the antithesis of everything Roken represented."

As he said this, Matt glanced at Omar, offering a small nod. He reached out and briefly tapped Omar's arm, a quiet acknowledgment of the older man's resilience and the silent burden he carried.

"The winds of El-Khamaseen blow northeast," said Omar gravely, "from the Sahara Desert into North Africa, the Levant, and Palestine."

"God help us," said the admiral. "Do we have intel on the bomb's location?"

"On it, sir," responded Matt, applying the key he'd just learned. He flipped rapidly through the pages of Durrell's novel and jotted down words identified by the numbers in the corners of Nasser's journal.

COAST ROAD
SEVEN MILES SOUTH OF TABA

"Get me eyes!" said the admiral.

An officer used his joystick to aim a spy telescope in geostationary orbit above Egypt. Its mind-bending resolution was able to zoom in to a crumbling structure along the coast.

"That's an Ottoman garrison," offered Omar. "Late nineteenth century."

"Response time?" Admiral Delaney asked his team.

"A Tomahawk could strike it in four," said the operations officer, adding, "but there'd be no guarantee of radiation containment."

The admiral frowned and turned to the SEALs. "In this weather," reported Lieutenant Bailey, "we'd need at least forty-five minutes to safely deploy the Black Hawks, sir."

Admiral Delaney took a breath, weighing the risks.

Omar's heart was pounding. *Nasser, guide me*, he begged inwardly. *My son, my teacher. I need you . . . .* An answer came suddenly, and Omar blurted out, "The goal is mayhem. They will wait until the afternoon to have the biggest impact!"

Every eye in the room turned to Omar. The weight of their attention didn't disrupt his thoughts. He added, "The El-Khamaseen winds blow the strongest when the desert warms up —in the afternoon."

"You knew him well—this mastermind?" Admiral Delaney asked.

Omar hesitated. "Years ago. It's been a long time."

The admiral nodded and made his decision. "Send in the Black Hawks."

"Yes, sir," affirmed the ops chief to Bailey. "Go!"

Bailey saluted and made eye contact with Matt. "Joining us, sir?"

Instead of springing into action, Matt stopped himself and tried to tune in to inner guidance,

just like Omar had. He glanced up at the feed from the Situation Room, where Senator Bradley seemed to be locking eyes with him. And the answer came to him: *No. Family first.*

Matt had made a promise to Stephanie—no more dangerous missions.

He looked at Bailey. "I'll stick to deciphering." There were still many numbers to decode in the pages of Nasser's journal. Bailey nodded with tacit admiration. This was a big moment for an adrenaline junkie like Matt.

~

Moments later, Matt watched stoically from the bridge as the SEALs took off in a pair of Black Hawk helicopters, which rose precariously into the violent zephyrs of sand.

In his mind's eye, Matt pictured how the mission would unfold; the details he imagined were surprisingly accurate as confirmed later by the top-secret after action report.

Flying at a very low altitude from the Mediterranean to the Gulf of Aqaba, the Black Hawks glided across the Sinai under all radars, including the Israelis'. The world's most elite soldiers rappelled down ropes and surrounded the abandoned Ottoman garrison, where three of Roken's surviving jihadists were preparing to detonate their dirty bomb. They were overpowered within minutes.

Only two dozen people knew of the global disaster that had been so narrowly averted. Matt was one of them. Another, the only non-American, was Omar, who took a solemn oath of secrecy. As officers cheered in the ops center, Matt looked at Omar and finally understood the profound bond this man had with his son.

Matt was elated—and relieved—that his risk had paid off. By ignoring the naysayers and slipping the journal directly to Professor El-Mohammedi, as Nasser had intended, not only had Matt done his part to avert disaster, he'd saved a family too.

And family was everything.

Taking Omar's palm in both hands, Matt looked him in the eye. "Thank you," he said quietly.

Omar nodded, but his weary gaze drifted over the cheering officers, as if the jubilation belonged to a distant world. After a brief pause, his voice—broken yet firm—rose just above the clamor: "Don't mistake this for an American victory."

Matt blinked, a flicker of anger rising at Omar's words. But the emotion faded as quickly as it had come, replaced by a quiet, growing compassion. He opened his mouth, uncertain, before managing a hoarse reply, "Nasser helped us. He is a hero."

Omar regarded him for a moment, his expression softening. "You live in a land that speaks so often of ideals," he said quietly, his words meant for Matt alone. "I've always admired that hope. But ideals . . . they do not matter until they guide you not only in the silence, when no one is watching, but also in those harder moments when the right path is anything but easy."

Matt swallowed. The room's laughter and applause seemed to fade as his father's old saying echoed in his mind: *Duty means doing the right thing, no matter what. And patriotism means that America sets an example for the world to follow.* He wondered what Omar would say if he knew that America, for a brief moment, had considered making a bargain with Roken—just as it had with so many other strong men, those armed with guns, extremism, or both. The bargains, Matt thought, weren't made lightly. They were made out of necessity—or at least what was believed to be necessity—and, yes, at times they reeked of opportunism, and other times of desperation. In a chaotic world where strength often outweighed ideals, could there have been another choice? Omar's voice, resolute and grieving, carried a challenge that could not be dismissed.

"The lines are never as clear as we wish," Omar went on, his tone steady but tinged with sadness. "And where there is power, there's always a choice: lift others or crush them, step forward or retreat, heal or do harm."

Matt's throat tightened. He wanted to speak, offer something in return. But Omar's words left no space for easy answers. They demanded more.

Omar broke the stillness. "This is my people's battle," he said. "My son died fighting for his choice—not just to stand against those who destroy and twist faith into a weapon, but to resist the deeper wounds they exploit—the anguish of those left behind, burdened with pride, yet silenced by humiliation, their suffering unheard."

He didn't say more. He didn't have to. Neither spoke. The cheers ebbed and flowed behind them, a distant echo against the gravity of Omar's words.

Their eyes met. For a moment, Matt thought he saw Nasser's face in Omar's grief. But then another face flickered in his mind—not one from his childhood or old photos, but one he imagined: his father, older and wiser, shaped by the years Matt would never know. The resemblance between them—Omar and that imagined version of his father—was unbearable.

And then, sharp and unexpected, came the pang of envy—an envy Matt knew was wrong. Nasser was dead. He'd paid the ultimate price. And yet, the bond between father and son lingered, awakening the buried ache of Matt's father, Ambrozy.

Omar grieved for what had been lost; Matt wrestled with the absence of what had never been. They were haunted by the same struggle—to reconcile their ideals with the mistakes they had witnessed and the ones they had made. And together, they grappled with the same question: Why do we stray from our ideals? How do we find our way back?

OLD SHORES AND NEW LANDS

2014

"Baba," Houda repeated. Omar looked up to see her standing above him. He'd fallen fast asleep at his desk, holding the most precious note he'd ever received. It had come from the coded corners of Nasser's journal, a secret message that Matt had diligently deciphered from its final pages and delivered with reverence to the professor.

It began:

Dearest Walidi,

There is anger in these pages that I know must have hurt you, pent-up feelings I needed to express. But it's not where I wish to end. We have both made our mistakes, stumbled on paths we thought were right. Yet you are my father, you are my Teacher, and in the deepest corners of my heart, there is only love for you.

Omar was so overcome with emotion when he'd read those words—a message from his son he so desperately craved—that a wave of exhaustion swept over him. Now, he blinked a few times to get his bearings as Houda leaned down to kiss his cheek. Guests were coming for tea.

Houda helped him up with her strong, gentle arms, and Omar's heart was flooded with the warmth of memories. He thought of all the young people who had passed through his life—his son's friends, the countless students he had challenged to think and feel deeply. How many times had he pushed them to open their minds and their hearts, knowing that this was what mattered most, that they were the seeds of the future? How beautifully they'd grown, each with their own spark: thoughtful, capable, kindhearted. In them, he saw the promise of a world he had helped shape, and he felt a quiet pride in the part he had played.

Emerging from his study, Omar noticed that Houda had laid out a tea service and snacks for the arriving guests. She led him to his favorite chair, facing the window in the sitting room, where the afternoon sun flooded the room with light.

∽

Halfway across the world—in Alexandria, Virginia—Stephanie opened her front door to see her favorite cousin, Risa, holding hands with Youssef, who looked relaxed and happy.

"Come in, you two." Stephanie smiled. "Everyone's out back."

She led them to the yard, where friends and family had gathered for brunch: a homecoming celebration for Matt. And for Risa too—though only Matt knew the full extent of the dangers she'd faced. On explicit instructions from Senator Bradley, Matt had sworn Risa to secrecy. How information flowed in intelligence-gathering had to be kept under wraps to protect future operations.

"But Nasser gave me an explicit message for Youssef," Risa pleaded. "I have to tell him."

"No," Matt insisted. "I'm putting my foot down." She finally agreed, and he was relieved that he didn't need to remind her that sharing intelligence secrets was against the law. For Matt, handling matters like this had become second nature. Yet he was starting to question the life he was leading—a life of secrecy, where even those he loved were kept in the dark. He knew it was time for a change. Stepping away from the shadows, from the CIA, felt inevitable. He wanted to serve his country in a way that allowed him to be fully himself. Perhaps he'd embrace something different —something truer to the person he wanted to be.

As Matt contemplated his future outside the shadows, Risa, too, found herself at a crossroads, weighed down by the secret she was keeping from Youssef, yet driven by the love she felt for him. But things were looking up. Since each had returned independently from the sunlit sands of Egypt, they found themselves in a second honeymoon, a rekindling of what had once seemed lost. Risa resigned from Human Rights Watch, severing ties with Ori as if cutting old worn threads. Youssef, with a trembling voice, confessed that he had strayed in Egypt; tears fell like those of a repentant child, and she embraced him with the warmth of forgiveness. Little did he know that she had also walked the same Egyptian soil. Her encounter with Nasser had become a fulcrum in her life, shifting her perspective like the turning of a great wheel, and from its axis sprang a renewed love for Youssef.

Now, with Nasser gone, Youssef knew that life was too short for jealousy or regret. They could create a beautiful life together, child or not—adoption was possible, as were so many other ways of growing their family. All that mattered was the love he held for her, a love he chose to nurture every day going forward.

Youssef sniffed the humid, late-morning Virginia air and caught a whiff of what Matt was cooking up on the outdoor grill. "Smells like pork."

Matt winked devilishly.

"Perfect dish for Jews and Muslims," Youssef joked. "I can't wait!"

Risa smirked and gave him a playful slap. "Be good," she admonished.

"I'm always good." Youssef grinned, going over to greet Matt with a bear hug.

"Hey!" Matt smiled, surprised by the affection from his cousin-in-law—but liking it. "Good to see you, buddy. And don't worry, we've already got the beef and chicken ready inside."

~

In Kafr Abdu, the quiet sitting room was suddenly full of life. Dalia and Houda bustled in together, fussing over a tray of *ma'amoul*. Houda felt a renewed sense of purpose as she looked forward to Tarek's arrival; the changes she'd seen in him since his release gave her hope, and she knew he was ready to rebuild their life together. Soon he would move in with her and Omar, and their family apartment—a place of memories with Nasser and her mother—would become their new home. She embraced the responsibility of caring for her family—her growing daughter, her changing husband, and her father in his twilight years.

For Dalia, the legacy of her love for Nasser meant she would never marry another; her loyalty and devotion to him would endure beyond his death. She cherished the two rings she wore— the one from their engagement and the one from his mother—as symbols of their eternal bond. Though she would never be a mother, she knew she would always be a steadfast sister to Houda and a loving aunt to Houda's daughter. She would continue to dedicate herself to nonprofit work, striving to support families haunted by the mistakes of their sons and fathers.

Fatimah came darting in from the back of the house and threw her arms around one guest first, then another. It warmed Houda's heart to see her daughter so happy. And her joy only magnified when Adham walked in with his almost-teenaged Gibrail and Valería, who was holding their newborn. They'd had another son—and they'd named him Nasser.

Adham seemed to have settled down—he was still very much himself, but something had quieted within him. While he knew Nasser now lay at rest, he could never believe that Nasser had been a harbinger of terror or a peddler of doom, just as he was certain his brother hadn't been one either. Embracing the unknowable nature of his brother's disappearance with gentle grace, he would love them both forever.

Little Fatimah couldn't get enough of baby Nasser. She hovered close to Valería, giggling and reaching out to touch his tiny fingers. His first squeals sounded nervous, but soon they turned gleeful as she clapped and twirled happily nearby. When Valería moved to sit by Omar, Fatimah trailed after her, still giggling and watching the baby closely. Omar reached out to Valería, who carefully handed the baby to him. But Omar's arms had become weak as of late. He strained to lift the boy; then he felt Adham's hand under his arm, supporting him. Little Nasser was suddenly on his lap, with Fatimah sitting on the arm of his chair and Gibrail kneeling by his feet.

"Tell us a story, Professor Omar," they begged.

He studied baby Nasser's chubby little face, so different from his own son Nasser's, yet sweet all the same. Feebly, he jiggled the boy on his knee.

"I am going to tell you," he said carefully, "about another Nasser." Omar smiled into the little boy's wide lash-rimmed eyes. "A Nasser who was the best son, just like I know you will be." He put a gentle time-worn finger on little Nasser's nose.

"The other Nasser was destined for great things in life," he continued, his voice dreamy, his gaze drifting from the children out into the distance. "I will teach you the history I taught him, because you are our destiny now. Your turn will come before you know it. It will be you who will make the world a better place. You will bring glory to our beloved Misr and lead America with compassion and understanding; you will be the bridge . . ."

But here his voice trailed off; his head nodded, drooping onto his wrinkled neck.

"Why don't you go out and play now, my darlings?" Dalia whispered to the children, gently taking little Nasser from Omar's lap and handing him back to Valería. Everyone watched with great love and respect as the esteemed patriarch drifted off, his breathing softening into something lighter, as if surrendering to sleep—or something beyond.

Houda brought in a blanket and tucked it around Omar's shoulders.

"Walidi," she murmured, kissing his cheek; she found it wet with tears.

—The End—

ACKNOWLEDGMENTS

To every reader, thank you. Stories exist only when they are read, carried forward in thought, in conversation, in reflection. If this book has left its mark on you, I hope you'll share it—through your words, your voice, your perspective. Leave a review, pass it on, let the conversation continue. Every story finds its true shape in the minds of those who engage with it.

This book could not have come to life without the love, patience, and encouragement of those closest to me.

To my wife, for your unwavering belief in this journey, even in its most uncertain moments. Your wisdom, your insight, and your steady presence have shaped this book in ways that extend far beyond words.

To my daughter, whose smile reminds me why stories endure— why we tell them, why we listen, why they matter. In your laughter, in the lightness you bring, I found the will to keep going.

To my family and friends, for your faith in this vision. Your encouragement was a quiet force, a reminder that stories, like all things of meaning, are worth the effort.

To the editors, translators, collaborators—those who lent their craft to this work—you carried these words across languages, perspectives, and distances. Your dedication, often unseen, is felt in every page. For that, I am deeply grateful.